KEEPING HIS
SIREN

KIERSTEN FAY

KEEPING HIS SIREN
Published by Kiersten Fay
Copyright 2017 by Kiersten Fay.

www.kierstenfay.com
All rights reserved.

This book is a work of fiction. All of the characters, names, and events portrayed in this novel are creations of the author's imagination.

ISBN-10: 0-9975491-1-4
ISBN-13: 978-0-9975491-1-9

CHAPTER 1

What the hell am I doing here? Naia DeVoe asked herself. She wasn't a friggin' spy. And yet here she was, crossing the nearly deserted parking lot toward the building on the corner of Chester and Fifth. Ever Nights: the most popular nightclub in town. It didn't look like much now, but every evening, this place was hopping.

There were a few cars peppered throughout the lot. Most belonging to the staff, she assumed, or to those cut-and-paste individuals who practically lived at every bar, whose friends consisted mainly of servers, bartenders, and the women on stage with their faux smiles, gyrating hips, and eyes on their wallets. She knew those types all too well. Not because she shook her ass on stage, but because she worked as a part-time singer and waitress at Dante's Pit, otherwise known as The Pit, or more crudely referred to as *The Pussy Pit*.

Naia never liked to call it that.

She opened the door to Ever Nights and stepped into the darkened foyer where a bouncer was usually stationed during the bustling late-night hours. Right now there was no need. It was too early for rabble rousers.

In the lobby Naia marveled at the high-end decor. This place was like the Sistine Chapel of nightclubs, a touch of elegance lingering in every feature, from polished wood floors to the coffered ceilings and sparkling chandeliers throughout. There were several rooms allocated to the different shows that went on each night, a flavor for every taste.

She'd visited this establishment only a handful of times before, always looking for work, always rejected. The excuse? They either weren't hiring, or were only seeking experienced top-tier acts. Ever Nights was known for providing over-the-top performances, incorporating burlesque with other genres of entertainment such as acrobatics, theatrics, music and dance, which is why she so badly wanted to work here. A position at Ever Nights could slingshot her toward bigger and better things.

Of course, all she needed at this point was some quick cash. This time she had to get hired, if only for a couple of days. So much was riding on it.

She peeked into one of the main ballrooms, spotting several tables scattered throughout, some occupied, others set with white tablecloths and clean glasses awaiting purpose. A woman on stage was getting intimately acquainted with a pole. The only other employee whom she could see resided behind the bar, his back turned to her as he dried and put away glasses for the evening to come.

Before entering, Naia checked her reflection in a full-length mirror that hung in the lobby. The employees at Ever Nights were all attractive. She'd taken extra care with her appearance today. Her makeup was perfect, her curls just right. Her ombre-dyed hair merged from her natural chestnut to a brilliant jewel toned purple. The ends were tipped by a sultry sapphire; a homage to her stage name.

Her outfit was designed to entice. The tight purple and black crop top covered her chest while revealing her stomach and slim waist. Her black mini skirt hugged her hips. But the *piece de resistance* was the sleek, knee-high fuck-me boots that she had borrowed from her friend, Goldie, and was seriously considering confiscating for life—if she didn't think Goldie would straight up tackle her to the ground to retrieve them.

Completing the ensemble was her most prized possession: the vintage, floral-etched locket given to her by her mother. Pure silver. The only thing she owned of value. She rarely took it off.

After adding a last touch of lip gloss, she was ready to nail this interview. Well, if she even got an interview. *I have to.*

As she approached the bar, her heels clacked on the hard floor. The bartender faced her.

Stutter step.

Attractive was an understatement. This man was one step down from godlike. A full head of tousled brown hair framed a set of whiskey-iced eyes, so unbelievably iridescent they nearly glowed like a mocha-colored sun. She didn't normally like facial hair on a man, but his five o'clock shadow made him look rugged and dashing while the sport coat over a black T-shirt gave him an urban sophistication.

In short, everything about his appearance was lickworthy.

She smiled, hoping to charm him from the start. First impressions were everything, and he was an obstacle on her way to Cortez, the club's owner and her best chance at getting hired.

The bartender's quick perusal of her body was like a whip to her spine, forcing her to straighten to her full height and crank her chin higher.

"Hi," she said, realizing instantly how lame and unprofessional that sounded. She cleared her throat. "Hello. I'd like to speak with Cortez, if I may." She'd been instructed to ask directly for Cortez and deal with no one else. He'd see it as a ballzy move and a sign of initiative, according to Dante.

The bartender's brow arched and his lips quirked on one side as though he found her request rather amusing. She tried not to be insulted by that...or drawn in by the way it made his features all that more handsome.

Her chin went up another notch. "Is he available?"

"What is this regarding?" His voice. My god, his voice! How could a simple, rumbled sound tap directly into her knees? The weakness quickly traveled north, invading the rest of her body. If vocal cords could cause spontaneous orgasm she'd be ripe to put on a better show than the woman on stage.

She mentally shook away the ridiculous thought. What was wrong with her? She never reacted this strongly to anyone from the opposite sex.

Psyching herself out here, she decided. Dante had to be mad to have asked her to apply for a job at Ever Nights in order to spy on Cortez and his crew. She should have declined, but the money was too good to pass up, especially now.

"I was told to speak with Cortez," she said. "I believe my talents can benefit his establishment greatly." A true enough statement.

The hottie's eyes darted to the stage, where the woman had taken to spinning around the pole upside down at jet speeds while dressed in skimpy lingerie, then came back to her for another inquisitive body-scan...as if he found her lacking?

Turning his back to put away the glass he'd been

drying, he told her. "We're not hiring new *talent* at the moment."

"Not that kind of talent," she said, giving his back a derisive glare.

"Oh?" Over his shoulder, his gaze shot to her cleavage, indicating something more salacious had entered his thoughts. "We've got plenty of T and A too."

What an ass! She balked, instantly cured of her attraction to him. "Not that either! If you don't mind, I'd prefer to take it up with your boss." And because she wanted to belittle him the way he was belittling her, she added, "Not some unimpressive bar monkey."

He chuckled at that, and her traitorous knees responded, growing gelatinous once more. She locked them down tight. His laugh was *not* bedroom-sexy. It was grating!

He grabbed another glass out of a soapy sink, rinsed it off, and began drying.

She recognized his type: good looks, charm, the guy who never got rejected by anyone he wanted, whose off-the-chart arrogance only made him more attractive to those of the opposite sex. His type took advantage of that natural power...

She had the scars to prove it.

"I don't think anyone has ever dubbed me unimpressive." He cocked his head at her. "In fact, quite often the opposite."

She opened her mouth for a snappy retort, then reminded herself, if hired, she could be working next to this guy for the foreseeable future. Best to keep their interaction civil and her opinions to herself. Plus, he could roadblock her if she wasn't careful.

Softening her features, she worked a smile over her lips and shrugged. "Hey, some of my best friends are bar monkeys. A noble profession. Look, I know

Cortez is going to want to hire me." *I hope Cortez is going to want to hire me.* "He wants the best this town has to offer working for him, right?" She gestured to herself.

At first, he looked unconvinced. Then he went still and tilted his head, as though he was listening to something in the distance. All trace of humor gone, he examined her closely for a second, a crease forming between those intense amber eyes. Almost incredulously he glanced at the stage, then in turn at each patron before landing a narrowed gaze on her once more.

What in the world? She almost felt exposed. Like he somehow knew what she was. A spark of adrenaline shot through her and she had the very strong urge to bolt.

But no. He couldn't know. That was impossible. *Psyching myself out.*

Finally his expression relaxed, and once more his half grin took her aback. Rag still in hand, he laid his arm atop the bar, studying her like one might a textbook. "Boss man is a busy guy."

She saw it then. Fangs! Peeking from behind his grinning lips.

Vampire!

Very likely he was part of Cortez's inner circle. And she'd practically insulted him. *So bad at this.*

Think cute and flirty thoughts, Naia.

She flashed him a smile dipped in honey. "Would it be possible to set up an appointment to meet with him?"

He returned to drying glasses, his expression now shuttered. "He'll be available later tonight. Why don't you come back after-hours?"

She snorted. "This place doesn't *have* any after-hours. It's open twenty-four-seven."

"Except on holidays," he quipped.

She rolled her eyes.

"I'll schedule a meeting around one. How does that sound?"

One in the morning was like afternoon to vampires. "Sounds perfect." She pivoted around to leave before she said or did anything to screw this up.

"Wear something sexy," he called after her.

Tension stiffened her shoulders. She glared over her shoulder. "I told you, I'm not that kind of talent."

He only shrugged and then faced away from her. Before leaving, she stole an extra couple of seconds to appreciate his physique. There was a hint of titillating muscle under that sport coat, and a glimmer of powerful legs under his perfectly fitted slacks.

He glanced back at her as well. Then his lips formed a smile that was both arrogant and knowing. "Still unimpressed?"

Busted.

Whirling around, she hurried out to the parking lot.

The contrasting light of day seemed to crush her as she stepped out of the slightly darkened foyer, and for some reason, her heart was racing, her cheeks flushed. Had he been flirting with her?

She felt a ridiculously girly giggle threatening to rise.

Inner shake. She knew better than to allow a frivolous attraction mess with her judgment. Especially at a time like this. Too much was at stake.

She checked her watch. Eight in the morning. It was going to be a long day.

The trek to her apartment on the edge of town was brutal in her high-heeled boots. Eventually she took them off, walking the last stretch barefoot. She had a few hours till her mid-day shift at Dante's and could get in a quick nap beforehand.

Dropping her boots by the door, she passed the couch that doubled as her half-brother, Cole's, bed. He must still be at work. After they paid off their debt and saved up a little money, maybe they could finally get a place with two bedrooms.

That dream was a long way off.

In her room, she relaxed on her bed and closed her eyes. Visions of whiskey-colored irises invaded her mind. Her lids popped open. Why the hell would she be thinking of him right now? She mentally shook herself and once more closed her eyes.

A cocky smirk flashed. She groaned and sat up, rubbing her eyes till she saw stars. Then her mind called up the memory of his roughened voice. *Wear something sexy*, he'd practically ordered.

Prick.

So why was her body warming at the idea?

Irritated, she flopped back down, covered her face with a pillow, and bopped herself in the head. She wasn't going to nap any time soon.

She went to her closet and riffled through her clothes, most of which were second-hand bargain buys. Functional, faded, and stretched out. Which meant not sexy.

She was going to have to borrow another outfit from Goldie. She cringed at the thought. Already everything she wore was a Goldie exclusive. Everything but her undergarments, of course, because *ew*.

She hated asking for more favors, but if doing so would add to her chances of landing a position at Ever Nights she would kick her pride to the gutter and step on it three times over.

The walk to Dante's was even longer than her hike home from Ever Nights, but this time she had on a sensible pair of tennies while she carried her boots in a plastic tote looped around her shoulder.

She wasn't waitressing tonight. And though she only had one ten-minute time slot on stage, it was a much needed performance. She could feel her skin itching for it. Her vocal cords were throbbing to get to work; it had been too long since her last gig. She shivered, recalling another time she'd gone too long.

The parking lot of Dante's was barren. One unfamiliar car was parked in the stumble spot, the spot so close to the entrance no one, no matter how inebriated, could get lost on the way to their car. She glanced up at the three-story building. Paint was chipping off nearly every surface. The neon sign was so old, several portions were snuffed out so that it looked like it read: DAN E'S IT. A couple of the windows showed cracks, but the security bars kept B&Es to a minimum.

Compared to Ever Nights Dante's was a shithole. The dichotomy so much more stark now that she'd just come from the other establishment.

The cloying scent of ashtrays and booze billowed around her as she entered dust mite central. Sunrays sliced through shuttered windows, sparkling fragments of dust in the air. The sight alone made her feel like she needed to sneeze.

Her sneakers stuck to the surface of the floor as she passed the stage where Jayney was busy contorting herself for the amusement of their single patron. One surprisingly toned leg went over her head as she pivoted on the poll, her other foot sweeping the floor. She was practicing her new routine.

Naia waved at Cole behind the bar as she sidled around toward the dressing room. He grinned and jerked his chin in greeting. He had no idea where she'd been today, or where she would be going tonight. She hated keeping things from him, but Dante had been explicit in his instructions not to tell anyone—*anyone!*—what she was up to. And Dante was scary enough...that order was only lacking an *or else*. If she had any question about her task not being on the up and up, that clenched it.

In any case, she didn't want Cole involved. He was already in enough trouble. The Boyle twins were breathing down his neck.

And when the Boyle twins breathed, they breathed fire.

CHAPTER 2

Naia checked her reflection in the grungy back-stage mirror, waiting for her time slot. Five of the ten bulbs that lined the mirror were burned out, but the remaining light softly illuminated her skin. Ignoring the harsh crack down the middle of the glass, she applied one last layer of lip gloss and sat back, satisfied.

She practically vibrated with anticipation. It was the same before every performance, but it wasn't from nerves. Excitement surfed her bloodstream. She felt alive on stage. It was home to her; her voice stoking and guiding the mood of the audience lit her up like nothing else ever did.

Unlike the other ladies getting ready for their turn on stage, her clothes would remain on. Her talent was in singing, not stripping, though she'd been told she'd make bank doing both. Many of the girls teased that she was *wasting the goods*, and that she could *clean up*, but they never really pushed her to join the ranks. Truth be told, they didn't want the added competition. Goldie had told her once, "With that sick voice and rad bod, you'd put the rest of us out of commission."

Just then, Goldie stumbled into the dressing room on three-inch-high platforms that sparkled like diamonds with each step, even in this dim light—well, cubic zirconia.

Judging by the wads of bills sticking out of her bejeweled thong, the room must be packed now. As soon as the sun even hinted at setting, patrons began meandering in. Each night was the same. Naia could almost set her watch to it. It was as if men clocked out of work and beelined it to the nearest dive. Many of them wore wedding rings—or a telltale tan line around their ring fingers. Scum. If Naia had a partner waiting for her at home, she certainly wouldn't spend her time at a broken-down place like Dante's. But then, men were stupid.

Two vanities down, Tiffany applied a generous amount of mascara to her fake lashes. "Nice haul," she said to Goldie. "I hope you left some for the rest of us."

Goldie turned the money into a fan. "Ooh, suckers are just *begging* to hand over their cash tonight. Though they're awfully rowdy. One guy grabbed my ankle and wouldn't let go. Finally Landon noticed and came over to pry the guy off me. Bastard took his time, though."

Landon was one of the bouncers. Nice guy for the most part, but he definitely had his favorites. Naia and Goldie weren't among them. But then, they'd never given him any *favors*.

Naia said, "You should have kicked him in the balls with those bejeweled clodhoppers you're wearing."

"Who, the client or Landon?"

"Either. Both."

Goldie lifted her leg forty-five degrees and twirled her ankle. "And scuff these beautiful babies? Besides, I could see Dante's response now. Oh, wait, no I can't, because I'd be dead." Goldie plopped down in the seat next to Naia, counting her bills. "Maybe you could sing something soft to calm them down a bit, Sapphire."

Naia contemplated that, already coming up with a list of songs that would do the trick.

"Boss don't want 'em calm," Boomer scoffed from the doorway. Skeevy letch that he was, he always liked to linger there when the girls were changing. "Boss wants 'em good and loose. Especially their pockets."

Naia never liked to engage Boomer in conversation—or eye contact, for that matter, but sometimes she didn't have a choice. There was something about him that gave her the willies, which surprisingly had nothing to do with his grotesque potbelly, perpetually stained shirts, greasy hair, or the green tint to the few teeth his gums managed to cling to, though none of that worked in his favor. Without all that, the guy would still be a walking sleezeball. But she had to play nice if she wanted to remain on the evening schedule. Piss Boomer off and you might never work nights again. Some of the girls would cuddle up to him for the best time slots. *Ew. Gag. And ew again.*

"Hi Boomer, baby," Goldie beamed. She shared Naia's view of the man, but *a girl's gotta work.*

Naia forced an easy smile. "I can loosen them up all right. Just give me that mic and they'll be as loose as you want."

"Not too loose, honey. We don't want 'em falling asleep out there." He tossed something at her feet. "Why don't you wear these instead of that top you got on?"

Naia glanced at the old tattered pasties that could have been living in his pocket for the better part of a year.

Hold back the dry heave.

She turned her lips down into a pout. "You know that's Crystal's signature look. Wouldn't want the other girls to think I'm encroaching on their style. Could cause discontent among the staff."

Tiffany snatched them up and tossed them back at Boomer who managed to catch only one of them against his big belly while the other flopped to the ground. "Go on, you dirty old man." She said playfully. "Stop teasing our little Sapphire. And you know you're not supposed to be back here during work hours."

"The club never closes," he said. "All hours are work hours."

Tiffany countered, "Then it's a wonder you're always back here. You're going to have to start coughing up some dough for all the peep shows you get."

He chuckled and scratched his gut. Then with a lingering look at all of them he backed out of the door.

"What a dickhead," Goldie muttered when he was gone.

"He's just a horny old fart," Tiffany lightly defended.

"You wouldn't be saying that if you had to work the day shifts like me and Sapphire here usually do."

Tiffany shrugged haughtily. "Give him a little slap and tickle, and you might get better time slots."

Naia shuddered. "No thank you. I'd rather swan dive into concrete."

Goldie folded her cash over and secured it with a rubber band. "That's only because you don't rely on randy fellows throwing dollar bills at your crotch while you're taking off your clothes so that you can afford to buy the clothes that you'll later be taking off."

"True," she allowed. As a waitress, she worked for salary and tips. It wasn't much, but, in her book, it beat the alternative. And she got a cool fifty every night she got to sing. Bonus!

Double bonus, actually, considering, were it to come down to it, she would sing for free. Nobody needed to know that, however.

She was lucky. With the economy in the bucket, times were rough. Many would grapple to slip into Goldie's glinting plastic shoes for a night. And not just women. On Wednesdays, Dante hosted an all-male revue. He'd gotten the idea from an Ever Nights' flyer, though he would never admit that.

Most of the town's income came from entertainment facilities such as Dante's Pit. But it was Ever Nights that brought the crowds. Tourists flocked there since it was also a hotel.

"But I also don't get paid the big bucks like you and the other girls." Naia applied a final layer of powder to her face. "I get a flat fee per performance, and my money is strictly for food and shelter." *And paying off my brother's debt, she didn't add.* "New clothes are a luxury." Once more, she admired the borrowed boots climbing up her calves.

As if reminded, Goldie pointed to the boots "Scuff my shit, and I'm going to have to kill you before I snatch them off your cold, rotting corpse."

Naia lovingly petted the smooth leather. "Don't let her scare you, babies, you can stay with me as long as you like."

"Oh, god. You're getting attached. I knew this was going to happen. *Not a shoe person* my ass!"

Tiffany pointed out, "If you want a pair of your own, you could probably have Boomer add you to the roster tonight. That is if he's feeling generous. A little skin goes a long way, sugar." She winked. "A lot gets you everything."

Goldie moaned, "Ew, Tiff, really? I think I just

threw up in my mouth a little." She turned to Naia. "Don't listen to her. If I had a voice like yours, I might sing for my bread, too, rather than shaking my ass for it."

"You sure about that?" Tiffany reached out and snatched Goldie's cash, then hopped back and fanned herself with the pilfered loot.

Goldie leapt up and ripped the wad back from Tiffany's clutches. Shoving it in her purse, she chirped, "The key word was *might*. I do have expensive taste after all."

Tiffany laughed and turned back to her mirror.

Through the scratchy backstage speakers, Naia heard her introduction. "You just enjoyed the beautiful and talented Goldie," the announcer said, "and now for the girl with the golden voice, let's hear it for the sexy Sapphire!"

"Good luck," Tiffany called after her as she hurried to the stage.

"You're supposed to say *break a leg*," Goldie chided then added something else but Naia didn't catch it.

As the steady beat of music started, she pasted on a smile and sauntered to the microphone at the center of the stage. Typical, she was greeted by a barrage of hoots and hollers.

Some of the men in the crowd sidled up to the edge of the stage with dollars in hand, looking as though they thought she was another stripper. Most of the regulars knew her as filler entertainment, intermission while they refreshed their drinks and did a little gambling in the back rooms.

That didn't mean they could keep their eyes off her. She wondered if some of them ever realized how often their gazes strayed to her, many having to squint through latticework that walled off the gambling tables while the dealers claimed their winnings.

Were they ever curious why they just *had* to look at her while she sang?

Though her performance didn't call for her to disrobe, she had moves. Her routine was provocative. Yet a little pop of her hips and sway of her body wasn't the reason they found it difficult to tear their eyes away.

It was the siren in her blood. In her voice.

Several years ago, she learned she descended from an ancient line of sirens; the kind from mythology said to lure seafarers to their deaths. Everyone believed she had worked tirelessly to perfect her voice, but it was a talent she'd been born with. A natural ability. A natural curse.

No one but Cole knew what she was. She spotted him behind the bar serving drinks. She gave him a wave. Some of the other men thought it was for them and waved back.

She'd managed to get Cole this job a couple months ago, just after she'd been hired. Good thing too, because they would need all the money they could get if they were to pay down his gambling debts.

The Boyle twins, hard-ass bookies, had been circling him like sharks for the last month. It was either pay them off, or run for their lives. And without a decent amount of cash, neither option was feasible.

Cole responded with a double thumbs up accompanied by a funny face with his tongue sticking out to one side. She smiled, but it didn't trip her up in the least. She was used to his fun-loving, sometimes childish, personality. He almost seemed too innocent for a place like this, though she knew better. He was only a few years younger than her, and just as hardened.

She hated that he had to work here. However, he was having the time of his life. He got propositioned daily by many of the female patrons looking for a little *fun*—as well as some of the working girls—because he

was, according to what people told her, a hottie. *Blech.*
If she had to think about that too much, she'd give
herself a headache. To her, he was just her little brother; the kid who used to whine to their mother about
an ouchy on his finger or a tiny scrape on his knee.

Yet, at some point, when she wasn't paying attention, he'd gone and turned into a man. Since their
mother's disappearance ten years ago, she'd done her
best protecting him, raising him, and he'd done his
best keeping them both in the black with his talent at
counting cards. That is until his luck had run out six
months ago. A string of bad games had them fifteen
grand in the hole. He'd never lost so badly in his entire
life, even when he was wet behind the ears.

Part of her suspected those games had been rigged,
but you don't go around accusing gangsters of cheat-
ing unless you're prepared to get shot in the face for
your trouble.

When they decided he should step away from
gambling for a while, supporting them had fallen on
her shoulders.

Before this gig had come along, she would sing
outside busy establishments while Cole manned a bag
for donations. But as much as people loved to stand
around and enjoy her voice, getting money from them
was like pulling teeth. Everyone was hurting for funds
these days thanks to the human/vampire wars that
had ripped through the country over the last century.
The world couldn't seem to pick itself back up.

A lot of people believed the fighting wasn't over,
that some factions were still recruiting for the next assault. Naia wasn't even sure what they were fighting
over. Money? Power? Territory? *Guess what, bitches.
We all lost. Time to give it up.*

Her grandmother used to spin tales of a nation that
had been united by a strong government. Of opulence

and excess. If you wanted something, you just ordered it over the Internet and wham bam it was yours. Naia couldn't even imagine that kind of world.

Must have been nice.

The Internet still existed, but most people couldn't afford it, and from what she understood, it was mostly used for porn anyway.

On the same token, very rich people had cell phones, and could call other very rich people and talk about very rich things.

Dante's Pit had a general landline. It rarely ever rang.

In some parts of the world, she'd heard folks had gone as far as rejecting paper money all together, returning to the barter system. But no matter where you were, commodities were always preferred; jewelry, stones, precious metals.

When she had offered to pawn her mother's locket, Cole had vehemently objected.

Accelerating her tempo, she drowned out her thoughts and let her song carry her mind away. Her enthrallment tonight was just a light dusting over the room, drawing energy from those who were caught in her *snare*, as she liked to call it.

She often wondered if her ancestors ever hated what they'd been compelled to do. If Naia didn't sing, over time she would weaken, eventually growing ill. She'd been just a teen when her siren nature emerged. Her mother warned she could even die if she resisted the need too long.

But she hated having to suck energy from the unsuspecting. It made her feel like a leech. A freak. Unnatural.

Wrong.

At sixteen, she'd tried to go cold turkey. She could still remember the extreme exhaustion that dogged her. But she had persisted, hoping to change what she was, push past it. Be like everyone else.

But that turned out disastrous.

One terrible night, something dark had taken her over. She had awoken in the middle of the street that fronted their home, singing her lungs raw with no recollection of having left her bed in the dead of night. She'd decided later she must have sleepwalked.

Terrifying, yes, but that wasn't what still sent shivers through her bones to this very day.

Barefoot and frightened, she'd spotted several males from the neighborhood coming for her with lust in their eyes, some half-dressed. Some not dressed at all...

Horrified, she had sprinted back inside to her mother's room as deranged men started banging on the doors and windows. Without even packing, her mother had snuck them out the back.

They'd never returned.

Her mother warned her later that she could literally have driven men to insanity with her voice. She'd claimed that was what happened to sailors eons ago. Ships would pass by islands inhabited by Sirens who'd been trapped by the ocean, alone and mindless with starvation, never dying courtesy of their pureblood. They could not control their hunger, and the poor men, unable to resist the Siren's song, would hurl themselves into the ocean, drowning as they battled waves to reach that beautiful sound.

Mindless with starvation, she thought. Yup, that was what it had felt like. Ever since then, she strived never to get to that uncontrollable point again. If she felt as though she was getting close, she would amp up her wattage ever so slightly—like tonight.

However, lately it didn't seem to be enough. Last week, that same starved urge had unexpectedly come over her. This time it had jerked her awake at dawn, her vocal cords already hard at work.

Her instinct had been to run—what if the neighbors had heard? Cole was immune, but even still, he'd already left for work. There'd been no one to help her keep a lid on it. And the lid had been about to explode. If she let it, they'd have to move yet again, something neither of them could afford.

Dressed in nothing but her nightgown, hand slapped over her mouth, she had tripped through the living room on her way to the back door. Their building complex was nestled against woodland foothills— the whole reason why they'd rented the ground-floor apartment.

She'd raced into the surrounding woods, down the familiar path she and Cole had carved for just such an occasion. The plan was like a fire drill. She was to seek complete isolation in the foothills and let her voice free till the danger passed. Then, when she was more in control, she could feed freely without zombifying anyone. That was the theory. Except, in all their planning, Cole was meant to be there to help.

After what felt like half an hour of hiking the rocky hills, her vocal cords fighting every inch of the way, she finally unleashed her voice—

—and had immediately started to feed.

A hunter's tent, hidden in the darkness, was several yards from her. But she couldn't bottle it back up. It was too late to stop...

Two men had emerged wearing fatigues. They appeared dazed at first, but quickly focused on her as if she were their next prey, burgeoning madness in their eyes.

There was no churning ocean to stand bastion between them. A few terrifying seconds more and she would have discovered what happens when an ensnared male catches his Siren.

But before they reached her, they had turned on each other like wolves, grappling and clawing each other like savage dogs. Fighting for the sole right to claim her?

She hadn't stuck around to find out. Able to finally cage her voice, she'd slipped away, racing back down the mountain.

After slamming the apartment door closed and engaging the lock and chain, she had hunched by the back window, puffing out harsh breaths and watching for her doom to stalk out of the forest.

The two hunters didn't seem to have followed her. Perhaps they had killed each other. If so, their blood was on her hands.

That same morning, she had confessed everything to Cole.

He'd been a ball of positivity, reassuring her that he would protect her, that everything would be fine, that they just have to figure out how to keep it from happening again. Then he had instructed her to feed a little more than she had been. Even joking with her. *Don't forget, you're a growing mythical creature. Got to make sure you eat your veggies.* Though his voice had been teasing, she could tell he was worried more than he was letting on—

She gasped, her voice stuttering to a halt as she completely froze up on stage.

One of those hunters was sitting at the corner booth! And he was staring straight at her!

CHAPTER 3

Heartbeat thudding in her throat, she dropped the mic with a resounding thud, then turned on her heel and scurried off stage to the back room. Goldie took one look at her face and sat up straighter. "Jeeze, girl. You about to be sick or something?"

Tiffany glanced up from her vanity. "What happened? You look like I felt the day after a client shared a *whole* bottle of tequila with me. Worst morning ever. Best payday though."

"I'm fine," Naia blurted too quickly, then cracked open the side door and peeked into the main room. That corner booth was empty! *Oh, God! Where did he go?* Her gaze darted around, coming to land on Cole, who was clearly worried as he headed her way. As was Boomer, only he appeared pissed.

She stepped out of the dressing room to address Boomer first, but he cut her off.

"What the hell was that?" he hissed. "We don't pay you to choke on stage. Not unless there's something interesting in your mouth."

The wretch.

"Are you okay?" Cole asked her, glaring at Boomer

like he wanted to snap the man's neck.

"Get back to the bar, pretty boy," Boomer snapped. "There are customers waiting."

There actually weren't, but Naia waved Cole's concerns away, surreptitiously sweeping the room with her gaze. Neither of them could risk their jobs. "I'm alright. I'll talk to you later." Should she tell him what she'd seen? He'd want to run. What if she was mistaken? The lights could have obscured her vision. She didn't see that man anywhere now. Could she really have imagined him? It was likely her thoughts had conjured his visage. Like a ghost from her past.

"Come with me," Boomer demanded, gripping her by the elbow. "The boss wants a word with you."

"I didn't mess up that bad," she protested as he tugged her along. Was she about to get fired?

"He asked for you earlier, but I'm damn sure going to tell him what just happened, and you're off the schedule for the rest of the night."

"That's not fair. It was just a little hiccup. It won't happen again."

He paused, and scanned her body with lewd innuendo. "There's a free room downstairs if you want to persuade me to change my mind." The sublevel rooms were reserved for private shows—and whatever else clients arrange for.

Somehow not yacking at his proposition, she said, "Dante doesn't like to be kept waiting."

In Dante's office, a slighted Boomer proudly detailed Naia's fuck up, stating for good measure that she should be suspended, if not outright fired.

Dante glanced up from his computer screen displaying several live security feeds around the property. He rolled a listless gaze at Boomer. "Add Debbie to the roster tonight and make sure James stays on for the second shift. That will be all. Sapphire, have a seat."

Boomer frowned. "What should I do about her?"

Dark eyes turned threatening. Apparently, Boomer was dismissed. Getting the message, he left, closing the door behind him.

Naia settled into the hard metal chair across from Dante's desk. He was a big man, or rather vampire, as almost all the local business owners were, with wide-set shoulders and an I-can-kill-you-with-my-thumb aura. His dark, short hair matched perfectly with his nearly black irises, tanned skin, and dark tailored suit. Past his thinned lips, she knew there was a pair of razor-sharp fangs just waiting to sink into flesh.

High-class attire aside, he did not resemble a gentleman. He looked like something from an ancient time, better suited to a battlefield rather than a desk. She'd heard rumors that he was unnecessarily rough during feedings. She pitied the humans he tapped. Sealed in a room alone with him, he was terrifying.

As unnerved as he made her feel, she refused to telegraph it, using her confident exterior as a shield. "Boomer made it sound worse than it was. I..."

Dante waved his hand in the air. "That's not why I asked you here. Have you accomplished your task?"

Ah. He wanted a report. "I have an opportunity to meet with Cortez later this evening."

That pleased him, but the smile he flashed was more like the cat who got the canary—and would gleefully rip the ever loving shit out of it.

He stood and strolled to a sideboard, filling two glasses with a golden liquid from a decanter. He offered one to her. A little afraid to decline, she accepted the glass and took a small sip. A warmth that hinged on burning heated her esophagus as the liquor worked its way to her belly.

"I hear your brother is in a bit of a jam."

Discreetly, she cleared her throat. "What do you

mean?" Her uneasy feeling tripled. Had Cole been blabbing about their debt?

"Rumor has it the Boyle twins are looking for him. *Breaking of thumbs* was mentioned." He tsked. "Got yourselves in a bad way with that lot."

Dread tumbled like marbles and splashed into her stomach. The Boyle twins never made idle threats. She and Cole were running out of time. Together, they had only accumulated thirty-five hundred dollars. It wouldn't make a dent in their debt. Maybe if they handed it all over now, they could buy another week or two.

"Oh, chin up," Dante cooed. "Complete the job and there's five grand in it for you."

She nodded. That was more than she'd make in six months waitressing at The Pit. "I will. But once I'm hired at Ever Nights"—*if I'm hired*—"I'm still not sure what you want me to do."

He smirked. "All I need is some information. Day-to-day activities. Any unusual purchases or transactions. Keep your eyes peeled for anything out of the ordinary."

"What do you mean by out of the ordinary? Do you suspect they're engaging in illegal activity?" If so, would she be putting herself in danger?

He shrugged. "Not sure. But if they are, I want to know about it."

She'd do anything to keep Cole from harm. Surely she could snoop around without turning heads. Still she asked, "Why me?"

He leaned back, appearing as though he was choosing his words. "Of all my employees, you're the best fit for this particular task."

"How so?"

"Let's just say you're...unique."

She managed to keep her eyes from darting guiltily.

What did he mean by that? Could he know what she was? She decided to play dumb, feigning as though she was flattered by his words. "Unique? I don't know about that." *Smile, smile.*

He took a swig from his glass. She mirrored him.

"There's a certain...mystery about you. I think it will intrigue Cortez. He might even be drawn to you. If he is, use it to your advantage. I want to know if he's running things on the up and up, or rather, if he's *not*."

Realization hit. "You want a reason to report him to the VEA." The Vampire Enforcement Agency, like cops for vamps. The only authority their kind recognized.

"Keen girl. That's exactly it. It's not personal. It's business."

Then was Dante planning to take over the city? She suspected the Boyle twins were already working that angle, accumulating IOUs throughout town.

"If you suspect something, why wouldn't you just call the VEA and report him now? If he is doing something wrong, they'd find out, I'm sure."

"The VEA is busy. Without solid evidence, Ever Nights would be a low priority. And if they did follow the lead and came up empty, I could incur some major fines for wasting their time. No, I'd need a little sweetling such as yourself to—" he cocked his head "—discover something."

She blinked, trying not to narrow her eyes. "*Is* there something to discover?"

"No doubt in my mind, sugar. I have reason to believe he's abusing the humans in his care, tossing them at any vampire with enough change in his pocket, forcing women into prostitution for his own gains. Hell, he could even be the one bringing drugs into this town."

She'd heard about that. A new drug was floating around with an overdose rate that was off the charts. Goldie mentioned a good friend of hers had died from it a few months back.

She took another small sip of her drink. Swallowed hard. "This sounds dangerous."

"Only if you get caught," he said. "So don't."

She fretted her lip. Could she really add spy to her resume? "Make it ten thousand." Had she really just said that?

His eyelids slitted dangerously. She worried she was about to lose this opportunity. Or worse....

Then he barked out a laugh. "I can appreciate your position. Five thousand is very generous, but..." he teetered, "I can add two grand to the total...once you get me what I need."

Seven thousand dollars! With that she and Cole would be well on their way to paying off the debt.

"Deal," she said, even as a swath of apprehension wrapped her spine. "But what if he doesn't hire me?"

His gaze turned menacing. "Make sure that he does."

CHAPTER 4

For the second time today, Naia entered Ever Nights. The atmosphere had changed. That bartender had said to come after-hours. For normal people, that would be weird, but vampires were night-crawlers. Most of the business they did was by the cusp of the moon.

She tugged at the hem of her ridiculously short red dress with a V in the front that displayed her cleavage. Goldie had practically insisted she wear it tonight. Naia had told her she was going on a date. She hated lying to her friend, but couldn't see any other option when she had asked to borrow something, *ahem*, sexy.

Though it was late, the club was hopping, dance music blasting, burlesque in full swing with a trio of flexible ladies on stage doing an impressive acrobatic routine using black hanging fabric. Goodness, the muscle strength needed to move like that! No wonder this place was so popular. The entertainment was light years beyond The Pit.

Dante had to be losing money because of this place.

A smart business man would visit his competition, take notes, up his game. Dante wasn't dumb, so either he couldn't afford to provide better entertainment, or he didn't want to. That meant he was looking for an easier option, hence her infiltration. He wanted to crush this place to dust.

If Dante's accusations were correct, Cortez and anyone else complicit in his crimes deserved it. If she found something worth finding, she'd relay it without bias. But if Cortez was clean, she'd still have done her job, right? Dante couldn't fault her if there was nothing illegal going down here.

By the same token, he couldn't expect her to be *Naia The Super Spy*. You don't send in an amateur if you're looking for gold. Still, she'd do her best to get the job done. In the meantime, she could potentially be working alongside this town's elite talent! Making connections.

Win, win.

She glanced around in search of the bartender from earlier, but a different man was behind the bar now. She was oddly disappointed. She hoped he told Cortez to expect her like he'd said he would. By their flippant exchange, she had to wonder if he'd just been screwing with her. There had definitely been a teasing light to his eyes.

Just then she spotted the bartender in a side room with an open archway. He glided around a pool table holding a cue stick.

A few other big guys were with him. Two were smiling and drinking while a third lined up his shot.

She crossed toward them, avoiding the enamored crowd as the three women on stage wound their toned bodies up those drapes and then spun precariously to the ground in a gracefully coordinated display. Stunning.

The sharp crack of a ball being struck greeted her as she stepped over the threshold. A striped ball met the corner pocket with authority.

"Nice shot," she said.

All eyes turned to her, and she wondered if she wasn't welcome. She glanced at the bartender, willing him to recognize her from this morning. A weird kind of tension stole through his body.

"Christ," he muttered, taking his time scanning her body.

Well, at least she'd nailed the sexy part.

"Thanks," said the man who had just sunk his shot. "Can I buy you a drink?" He had a surfer's style, loose shorts, shaggy hair, and a boyish grin synonymous with lazy days on a beach. He reminded her a little of Cole. Except the look he was giving her was so not brotherly.

"Actually, I'm here on business." She slanted her gaze back to her acquaintance. Damn, he looked even more handsome than before, if that were possible. He'd changed into a black sweater that lovingly hugged each and every muscle in his torso. The sleeves were bunched above his elbows, displaying strong forearms lightly dusted with hair. His short haircut was somewhat messier than before, as though he'd been running his hands through it all day, but it looked good on him, and combined with that five o'clock shadow, it gave him an edge. Their eyes locked and she nearly groaned. She'd been hoping she'd imagined that whiskey iridescent hue.

"You said I could meet with Cortez," she reminded him lightly.

The other men seemed to go stiff. They glanced between her and the bartender. Was it unusual to try and get a meeting with the club's owner?

"I did. Stick around and have a drink. You can

have your meeting later. For now, I'll be doing the pre-interview."

"Pre-interview?" she asked, incredulous. "And you want me to *drink*?" She smelled bullshit.

"We *are* in a club, after all. If you can't handle your alcohol, then it's not the best place for you to be working, is it?"

The others went back to focusing on the game, but there was an underlying strain among them. She tried not to let it make her uneasy.

This time when the surfer shot, he scratched, and the cue ball found a home in a side pocket. The bartender was up next. He scanned for a clean shot.

"I wouldn't be drinking while I work," she pointed out.

The bartender replied, "You might. Patrons love to buy shots for our female employees. And the more drinks *they* buy, the more money we make." He lined up his shot: seven ball, corner pocket. Of course he sunk it. She'd lose respect for him if he'd missed such an elementary shot.

Years ago, while her mother had bartended, she and her brother would have nothing better to do than hover around the pool table. At first it had just been a game. Something to do to pass the time while they waited for their mother's shift to end. Then they'd discovered how to hustle, and what a team they'd made.

The bartender stood and gestured for a server. A petite blonde in pigtails and micro mini skirt bounced over. "You boys need another round?"

"Yes, luv, and whatever she wants." He gestured to her.

The waitress sent her an assessing look that held a hint of surprise and curiosity.

Naia didn't need to be getting tipsy on an interview, no matter what this bartender thought was appropriate. "Water would be fine."

Groans all around.

Surfer Guy said, "Don't be so stuffy." While the other two just shook their heads in derision. The bartender, leaning over the table with the cue resting on his left hand, raised a contentious brow at her. Apparently she was bombing this *pre-interview*.

"Fine." To appease them, she ordered a beer.

Peer pressure was a bitch.

"There's a girl," The bartender faced the table and swiftly landed his shot: Four ball, side pocket.

"And a water," she called after the waitress.

The bartender scowled, but said nothing, making his last shot and winning the game. "Rack 'em up," he said to the others. He approached her then, and she was suddenly acutely aware of his size. She had to tilt her head back to meet his gaze. His wide shoulders gave him a natural way of looming, even though he'd buffered several feet between them.

Even still, as if some sort of primitive instinct were warding her away, she nearly stepped back, but held her ground.

"What's your name?" he asked.

Briefly she wondered if she should provide her stage name or her real name. She decided on the latter. "Naia. Yours?"

"If all goes well for you, you can call me Boss Man. But for now, Sir will do."

"You want me to call you *sir*?" The arrogance!

The other men hid amused smiles behind their drinks. They were screwing with her, she decided. Perhaps there was no meeting later with Cortez. Either that or they were hazing her.

Maybe that was a good thing. Like coworkers hazing the newbie. You didn't haze a potential coworker if you didn't plan to hire them, right? Unless these guys were just dicks.

In any case, she had nothing better to do than play along while she waited to find out. *Seven grand*, she chanted in her head. But there was no way she was calling this guy *sir* in any kind of serious manner.

"Well, what can I call you if I beat your ass in pool? Would *chump* work for you?"

All four men swung surprised gazes at her. Surfer Boy eagerly handed over his stick. "I have to see this."

The other two backed up against the wall as if she'd thrown down a gauntlet.

With an amused expression, the bartending prick fanned his hand out toward the pool table. "Racked and ready, luv. Be my guest."

Oh, it was on. First break? Yes please.

Swiping the stick from Surfer, she sauntered to the table. The felt was practically new, and she had the urge to run her hand over the surface of it. Dante's pool tables were worn to the base and slightly lopsided, which made every shot a surprise, no matter how good the player.

Aiming the cue ball, she steadied her shot. The weight of the stick in her right hand was familiar, calling up memories of bygone days with Cole. Hustling and drinking and laughing. Not a care in the world.

God, she missed those lazy days.

However, while she'd been in it for fun; Cole had been in it for the money, hustling bigger and bigger fish. It was a wonder he hadn't gotten in trouble sooner. She'd called it quits when their shenanigans caused Cole to get his ass seriously kicked one night. Not that he hadn't had his share of ass-whoopings, but that night had been particularly bad.

Even Naia's easy smile and sex-pot voice hadn't been enough to cool the rage of a drunkard who'd just lost a pocket full of cash to them. What she and

Cole hadn't known was the man they'd hustled was a vampire. One who didn't like to lose. Outside the bar, he'd beaten Cole soundly as she'd watched in horror, helpless to help. Worse, someone had called their mother out to the alley for the last two meaty pummels to Cole's face before the vampire let him drop to the ground, unconscious.

To add insult, before walking away, the vampire tossed some bills onto Cole's unmoving body. It had taken a week before Cole could see out of his swollen right eye. Another month before he was back to hustling, but after that, she had lost her taste for it entirely, and from then on had only played for her own enjoyment.

The whole experience should have taught her not to mess around with those of the pointy-tooth variety. Yet here she was.

Seven grand.

Though she knew she should go easy, her pride demanded she wipe the floor with these guys. Put an end to this jock-fest ribbing, maybe earn a little respect right out of the gate.

Tightening her grip on the base of the stick, she rammed it forward, striking the cue ball hard. It rocketed into the triangle gathered at the other end of the table. Balls exploded in every direction, ricocheting off one another and the bumpers. Three of them found homes: the one, the four, and the nine. Two stripes and a solid.

The bartender's friends hooted with jubilance, claiming nearby stools as if settling in for a show.

She faced the head jerk with a cocky grin, wanting to see the surprise on his face as well. But that wasn't what she found. In its place was something else she couldn't decipher, something that had her body growing warmer under his intense gaze.

"I'll take solids," she chirped, then turned back to read the table.

The waitress arrived then, carrying a tray of drinks. She fluttered around the room, passing them out to everyone and finally setting Naia's beer and water down on a side table before making herself scarce.

Before the guys could jibe her, she took a hard pull from her beer. A couple sips would cool her nerves.

"Cheers," Surfer called and followed her lead. "Now kick his ass, girly."

She planned to do just that.

"Whose side are you on?" The bartender snapped.

"Hers," replied Surfer Boy with a *duh* hanging at the end of his tone. The other men shrugged and nodded their agreement.

"Bunch of turncoats."

She grinned at that. Maybe these guys weren't so bad after all.

A moment of assessing the table, and she had her game plan set. This would be a clean sweep. Her next two shots went in without a hitch: the two and the three.

The bartender decided now was the time to question her. "So you were pretty adamant earlier that Cortez would want to hire you. Well, what is it you do?"

Straightening, she leaned on her cue stick. "I'm a singer."

He waited as if there should be more.

"And I have waitress experience. But singing is really what I love."

He glanced out into the main room where those talented women were flying around the stage in a wide circle while twining their fabrics together.

Naia swallowed, feeling suddenly inadequate.

"It might not be as exciting as Cirque du Soleil over there, but I'm good." Better than good. While she pulled strength from a crowd, she could feed it right back to them, energizing them as well, lighting them up with excitement and passion. It was a marvel to see, according to Cole.

"Hm," was all the bartender said.

Did he think she was just talking herself up? Well, it didn't matter. All that mattered was getting face time with Cortez. Dante had assured her once Cortez met with her, he would want to hire her. How Dante was so sure, she didn't know, but she had to assume he knew what he was talking about. Why else choose her for this covert mission?

All serious now, she lined up her next shot.

From behind her, the bartender asked, "When did you learn to play?"

The girl who used to hustle spoke, "Oh, I only learned recently. Pretty sure I'm still riding beginner's luck."

He snorted. She glanced back at him. Nearly gasped. His eyes were fixed on her backside. While hustling a group of men, she'd often purposely bend a little too far for effect. Redirecting a little blood away from the brain tended to handicap men. But this time hadn't been intentional, and flames entered her cheeks. It didn't help that she'd never played pool in such a short dress.

She quickly shook it off. *Look all you like.* It could only help her win. "You don't believe me?"

"I'd sooner believe the sky was purple."

"I've seen that happen you know. Usually at sunset." She re-focused on the table and made her shot. The six ball bounced off the ten and then slowed, hovering just on the edge of the pocket she'd been aiming for. A breath later, it fell in like a co-ed who'd had one tequila shot too many.

Dang that was close. *Head in the game, Naia*. Her next shot was on the mark. She wanted to gloat, but the bartender just stood there, raking his gaze over her body as if he didn't care he was getting smoked. His lids were heavy and his gaze was on her in a way that made her feel stripped. It was unnerving. It was intriguing. She tried to ignore it, figuring he was just attempting to throw her off her game, but every time she glanced his way, his penetrating eyes were lapping her up.

Men had looked at her in a similar fashion, but not quite like this. While other men's eyes might be filled with lust, his burned with something more.

Usually she could shrug off such intense attention, but her body seemed to be responding on a primal level. Her skin became over sensitized, prickling as though being caressed wherever his gaze landed. Thankfully the somewhat thick fabric of her dress hid her puckered nipples. She couldn't help imagine what he might do were she alone with him...

Thoughts like that were dangerous. Draw too much interest from a vampire and you're likely to wind up down a few pints with a ghastly neck wound. Not exactly her idea of a good time, even if he was hot as hell with a voice that stoked a slow furnace within her.

Goldie had admitted to dating a few vampires. Once, with a dreamy look, she'd admitted to Naia the experience was like nothing she could explain, following up with a shiver and a sigh.

And why had that thought popped into her head?

"Tell me how long you've *really* been playing," he said, interrupting her mind's descent into the gutter.

"Very well," she said. "The truth is I've been playing my whole life." Until recently. Lately all she had time for was work.

"Clearly. You haven't missed a shot yet."

"Getting worried, *Sir*?" She made her tone mocking.

His friends chuckled.

"Not at all, Naia." Her name on his tongue shouldn't sound so good. "In fact, I'm thoroughly enjoying my beating." He pointedly scanned her body again. Again warmth bloomed in her, and again she regretted her dress choice. She should have donned something more professional rather than following the bartender's dictate. She still wasn't sure if he was messing with her for his own amusement. But another glance at his expression said he might actually be into her.

It was disconcerting what a simple look was doing to her. Was this merely a chemical attraction or was he working some of his vampire mojo on her? Rumor had it they could hypnotize anyone into doing anything they wanted. She shuddered.

It wouldn't be a major leap to think a certain type of vampire might abuse that kind of power.

She suddenly worried she was in way over her head with this lot.

With that in mind, she checked the clock on the wall. More than thirty minutes had passed since she'd arrived. "When might I be able to meet with Cortez?"

The three men in the corner all seemed to get very thirsty in that moment, and they found the surrounding walls quite interesting. By their reactions, she was willing to bet Cortez wasn't even coming.

"Getting tired of my company already, luv?" the bartender said. "Got another interview after this? Or perhaps a date is waiting on you? I know I said to dress sexy,"—he gestured to her outfit—"but this is ridiculous."

"Is something wrong with my outfit?" Damn it, she told Goldie it was overkill, but the second her friend had heard *date*, she'd been gung ho.

He blinked at her. "*Wrong?*" He stepped into her personal space, his face coming inches from her ear so that only she could hear. "You look out-of-this-world mouthwateringly delicious." Before she realized what he intended, he brought her hand to his mouth and kissed her knuckles.

She sucked in a breath, her heart speeding up. She knew he could hear it.

Yanking her hand away, she cursed the flush creeping into her cheeks. "You're just trying to make me miss my last shot." She only needed to sink the eight ball to win.

"Perhaps." He shrugged, his lips twisting into a crooked grin. "It's only fair since it took you a mere second to floor me with this stunning dress."

Needing a moment, and some distance, she turned to take another swig from her beer. *Head in the game.*

As if he knew his words were getting to her, continued. "I thought you were beautiful before, but I was wrong. You're positively gorgeous." She glanced back at him. His gaze was eating her up. "And that blush you're building up is making you even more so. Does your man not compliment you enough?"

"I don't have a man," she blurted, instantly regretting her words.

The other three men sat silently, their eyes volleying between her and the bartender. Curiosity lit their expressions. They almost appeared surprised by this interaction.

The bartender cocked a brow. "No man? But you must have many admirers."

"Sure," she said flippantly. *If you count salivating*

pervs as admirers. If she had a dollar every time a guy tried to pinch her ass while she delivered their drinks, she'd be able to afford a better apartment.

"I assume you have a date later, though?"

"That's really none of your business."

"I wouldn't want your meeting with the boss to intrude on your busy social life."

"Is this a fishing expedition or an interview? If you must know, I do have a date." *With a bed.* She was beat. Today seemed to have gone on for ages. "But it can wait till after my meeting with Cortez, though I'm starting to doubt there even is a meeting. Admit it, Cortez isn't even here, is he?"

"Oh, he's here," Surfer Boy gave a hearty laugh. "And he's getting his ass handed to him."

One of his buddies punted him in the chest.

Naia got a sinking feeling then. She faced the bartender suspiciously. His expression was shuddered.

At that same moment, the pigtailed waitress entered. "Hey Cortez, do you need anything else before I clock out for the night?"

Naia's lips parted on a breath. *No.* Her eyes snapped to his...to *Cortez.*

To the waitress, he said, "We're fine, Cindy. Have a good night."

Cindy nodded and then scurried out of sight. It took Naia what seemed like an eternity to regain her composure. "You're Cortez?"

At length he nodded, then winked.

If she didn't need this job, she might have slapped him.

CHAPTER 5

Before, she'd been turned on by his flirtatious banter. Now she just felt foolish. He'd been playing games with her. Making jokes and secretly laughing at her with his buddies.

Humiliation burned in her gut. Dante had been wrong. So wrong. Setting her stick on the table, she spun on her heel to leave.

He blocked her path. "Leave now and forfeit the game." She had yet to sink the eight ball, but winning no longer mattered.

She sidled around him. "I don't appreciate being made a fool of."

He halted her with a hand on her elbow. "That wasn't my intention."

She pulled out of his grip and kept walking.

He was right behind her. "I merely wanted to see how you would act around me, not knowing who I was."

She stopped. "Why?"

"You provide a rare experience for me."

Because she was the only dummy in this town who wouldn't know him on sight? Come on. Sure he was a big deal, but it wasn't like his face was plastered all over the place. "Your friends sure did get a good laugh at my expense."

He shook his head. "They were more amused by

my behavior."

"Because you tricked me." In her haste, she knocked into a guy, spilling a bit of his drink. "Oh, I'm so sorry," she called, but kept going.

Cortez kept pace. "Because I'm not often so taken by a female."

That made her stop. Taken? Could he really find her attractive? She studied his expression for falsities, but found none. Though, clearly he was a good liar.

"Stay and have a drink with me."

She *had* intended to land an interview. Well, here he was. She fretted her bottom lip. His gaze followed the movement, and something intense flashed behind his eyes. The ice in her veins flashed red-hot. How did he do that?

He grinned as though he sensed her reaction to him. Drinks with a hotter-than-sin wealthy club owner who possibly found her attractive? Or a chilly walk home at two in the morning? Cole hated when she went out alone this late at night. This town was filled with predators, not only the vampiric kind.

Still, she felt out of her league here. Super spy she was not. Face to face, she hadn't even sighted her mark. How could she gather intel on supposed illegal activity without getting caught? She glanced at the exit. She could leave now and end this charade. Tell Dante he'd picked the wrong girl for this task.

But that seven grand? Cole was depending on her. If anything happened to him, she didn't know what she would do.

"Perhaps a wager would encourage you to stay," he hedged.

Why would he want her to stay? Hadn't she endured enough embarrassment? Now she understood the strange looks his buddies had given her when she'd first shown up. They must think she was an idiot for not knowing who this man was. Not to mention....

Did he say wager?

"What kind of wager?"

"First have a drink with me." He gestured to an empty table at the edge of the room. "Come sit and talk with me."

She eyed him hesitantly.

"You wanted a meeting with me, didn't you?" He spread his arms out invitingly. "Are you hungry? I'll have our chef make something special."

Still mentally debating, she allowed him to direct her to the table. He even pulled her chair out for her before taking the seat directly opposite her.

Feeling eyes on her, she scanned her surroundings. Peppered through the crowd, several employees gazed at her with open curiosity. On the other side of the room, a waitress was paused in the middle of filling a water glass. Not paying attention to her task, the water began to spill over. The two men sitting at the table let out a sound to alert her to her blunder. The waitress jumped and hastily sopped up the mess with napkins.

Finished with their routine, the entertainers on stage were taking their bows. Naia caught one of them elbowing the others to direct their attention toward Naia and Cortez.

His buddies from the pool room were peeking around the wide arched threshold.

What in the world was going on?

Cortez called a waitress over and requested a menu. Apparently Ever Nights boasted a full three course menu. Dante's only offered basic tavern grub, and she would warn anyone away from the chicken wings. *Blech.*

As she scanned the menu, her tummy growled. The last thing she'd eaten was some pilfered chips from

Dante's kitchen. "You're paying?" she asked Cortez.

He responded with a single nod.

Naia glanced up at the waitress. "Then I'll have the lobster, darling."

The waitress reclaimed the menu and hurried off without a word.

"You have expensive taste," Cortez observed, but he didn't sound put out.

Oh, the irony. "Not really. I've never had lobster, but you deserved that and more for your little trick."

"Maybe I do." There was an ease to his smile that managed to settle her nerves somewhat.

"Your employees are gawking."

"They are not used to me chasing after women."

She supposed women just naturally fell at his feet. If she was smart, she'd be doing the same. "So what would you like to know. I can give you my work history."

"Is Naia your real name or a stage name?"

"Real. On stage, I go by Sapphire."

"Are you a dancer as well?"

"Uh, if you mean with clothes *on*, then yes. Otherwise no."

"So yours is a clean show."

She lifted one shoulder. "I'd say my dancing is provocative, but not X-rated."

"If you're not a dancer why not just go by your regular name. It's beautiful enough. And it suits you better, I think."

"Thanks. The girls told me a stage name would give me an added level of anonymity." They'd emphasized that stalking is a problem in their line of business.

"Girls?"

She nearly bit her tongue. "Yeah, some friends of mine who work over at, uh, one of the other clubs."

"Oh? Which club?"

Damn. She decided to stick to the truth as much as possible during his inquiry. "Dante's Pit." There was nothing wrong with knowing people who worked there, she told herself.

"Couldn't your friends have gotten you a job there?"

Double damn. She had to tread carefully here. It would be easy to ferret out a lie. He knew her stage name. Her real name. All he'd need was to do a little research to find out her previous, or rather, continued employment. "I've worked there," she admitted. "Waitressing and singing."

He assessed her for a moment. "Do you still work there?"

Triple damn! She resisted a guilty squirm that wanted to snake through her body. "Kind of. But I don't want to." That at least was one hundred percent true. "Unless I want to start a career in stripping, I'm not making enough to cover my bills." *Debts*, she mentally amended.

"So you think you'll make more if you work here?"

"I know you pay even your lowliest employees better than anyone around."

Her lobster arrived then. Big, red, alien looking thing. Though they were only miles from the coast, and seafood was a staple in this area, she'd never had the opportunity to dine on lobster. Too pricey. Curiosity had her digging in.

With an elbow on the table and his chin perched on his palm, Cortez watched as she took the first bite. She chewed, and chewed. The texture was not what she expected. Almost rubbery, but not quite, and not in a bad way. The flavor was somewhat sweeter than she'd anticipated, salty and buttery and distinctly its own, but nothing marvelous. Why did people rave about this?

When she finally swallowed, she muttered, "Huh."

"Not what you expected?" he asked, mirroring her thoughts.

"The girls at the club prattle on and on whenever a date buys them lobster. I thought it would be like crack."

Almost as if he couldn't help himself, he barked out a laugh. "It could be more of a status thing for them."

"How silly."

"Silly? How so?"

"I don't know. I guess I never understood all that status stuff. If it's not the best, why pretend it is just because it costs more?"

"Perceived value, I suppose."

"See, that's a silly notion. You could mark two identical items different prices, and people would automatically assume the higher priced item is better."

"True. But how else should they determine value? Price is often equated to quality. In markets where people are not completely sure of how to assess quality, price is often used as a qualifier. And it's human nature to want what others covet. It's why since as far back as history allows, women have covered themselves in shiny rocks and metals to attract the best mate, because they believe the rocks add to their beauty and therefore their perceived value. Same goes for some men and luxury sports cars. Isn't that why you ordered the lobster in the first place?"

"I ordered it to ding your wallet as payback."

"Then you'll have to do better than that."

"And I don't adorn myself in jewels to attract a mate."

"Likely because you can't afford it. I see you wear silver around your neck."

She fingered the locket, and huffed. "This has sentimental value. I suppose you drive a luxury sports car?" She took another bite of her lobster, determined to enjoy it.

By way of answer, he said with a grin, "I'm not looking for a mate."

The way he stared at her now told her what he might be looking for. Her heart rate ratcheted because all that intense, unbroken attention was directed her way. Perhaps Cortez flirted this strongly with all his potential employees, to see how they'd handle themselves in a real-world scenario. A waitress in this town had to be glib of tongue and quick on their feet to handle some of the miscreants that popped into town to harass the locals. She decided she would ace this interview no matter what Cortez had to throw at her.

When the waiters came by to check on them—they were very attentive to their boss—Cortez ordered another round of drinks and then a second main dish, toasted sesame ginger salmon, stating that Naia might enjoy it more. Then he continued with the questions. "Do you live around here?"

She nodded. "I live near the hills."

"You can't have been in town for very long."

She cocked her head. "Why do you say that?"

"I'm sure I would have noticed you before now."

Flirting again? "Well, you're not as observant as you think. We-uh-I've been here for a few years now." At the last second, some protective part of her decided it was best not to mention Cole in any way. If she wasn't careful, things could go south for her in a bad way, and he was in enough trouble. But Cortez noticed her cover-up.

"We? You mean the man who's waiting on you

even now?"

"No one is waiting on me. I have all night."

Again he scanned her dress, this time dubious, clearly not believing her.

"Why haven't you applied here sooner?"

"I did. A couple of times. I don't have a phone, so I had to keep checking back, but I was told there weren't any openings. You have such stellar acts on your roster. I guess a simple singer didn't measure up. But I'm good. I can promise you that. Your clientele will love me."

He leaned back in his chair. "Who did you speak with?"

"Huh?"

"Which one of my employees did you speak with when you came looking for a job?"

"I, uh." She glanced around as if their faces would pop out at her. "Not sure I remember exactly. A woman with long dark hair the first time. A guy the second. Why?"

"Just wondering who I need to punish for not sending you straight to me."

She stiffened, then caught the teasing light in his eyes and returned a smile. "In that case, I *really* don't remember. If I'm going to work here, the last thing I need is to start off by throwing my peers under the bus, handsome though that bus may be."

Something inscrutable flashed behind his eyes. Oddly, some of his humor faded. Did he not like compliments?

The salmon arrived then, and with her first bite, she groaned. "My god, this is incredible!"

His chest puffed up a bit and that pleasing grin was back. "I'm glad you like it. It's one of my favorites."

She glanced up at him, incredulous. "You *eat*? I mean, like, people food? Not people food, I mean *human* food. You actually do eat people food, though don't you...." She huffed at her stammering and fought a blush.

He chuckled. "I enjoy human food, but I couldn't live on the stuff."

How interesting. She'd never seen Dante so much as snack on a chip.

Around another mouthful, she muttered, "This is *so good*," And she wasn't even putting on airs. An explosion of flavor invaded her mouth with each bite. Before she knew it, she was scraping the plate for more.

"My god, doesn't your man feed you?"

She flushed and set her utensils down. She was supposed to be impressing this man, not scarfing down food like a starved mammal. "I guess I didn't realize how hungry I was. Give my compliments to the chef."

"Would you like to tell him yourself?"

Meet the chef? "I'd love to. But I wouldn't want to bother him while he's working."

Cortez shook his head. "He loves it. To be honest, he can get a little grumpy when he's not flattered enough." He snapped his fingers for the waitress and had her retrieve the chef, Victor.

She expected a pudgy middle-aged man with a gut and an apron. Well, he had on an apron, along with full chef garb, sans hat. And he was drop dead gorgeous! Tall, with wild dark hair, the shoulders of a linebacker, and a jaw so chiseled it could slice bread. She wondered if even the cleaning crew looked like cover models.

"Da." He said to Cortez with a distinctly Russian accent.

Cortez gestured to her. "This is Naia...." He was looking for her to provide a last name.

"DeVoe," she said without thinking. She realized too late it was a mistake to give her full name. *So bad at this.* Burying her irritation with herself, she shook Victor's hand. "I wanted to tell you how much I enjoyed the salmon. Honestly, it was the best thing I've ever eaten. Better than the lobster. Uh, though that was good, too," she added hastily, not wanting to insult him.

"Lobster is shit," he said. "They used to feed it to prisoners long ago. A peasant dish. You have good taste." He smiled, and a set of fangs poked out from behind his lips.

A vampire chef? Huh.

It would be just her luck if Cortez only hired vampires.

"You want dessert?" Victor continued. "I make you something off menu."

"Oh, I couldn't," she rubbed her stomach. "I'm stuffed."

He waved away her statement. "I make you something." Then he stalked back to the kitchen before she could utter another protest.

"I think you made his night," Cortez told her. "He'll be high on his own importance for weeks."

"Your chef is a vampire." She had inadvertently leaned forward as if she were revealing a secret.

He mirrored her. "You caught that did you?"

Their faces mere inches apart, a strange spike of adrenaline burrowed through her. She caught a whiff of his cologne, and it seemed to go straight to her head. It was a faint scent, musky and enticing. Not cloying like some men who often smelled as if they'd bathed in rat piss. No, Cortez smelled...perfect.

She just managed to stop herself from inhaling deeply and giving herself away. With effort, she sat back in her seat. Cortez did the same, seeming to go through a similar struggle.

The music and chatter from the other guests filled in around them as if the volume had been turned up, even though nothing outside of their little bubble had changed. She cleared her throat, mentally acknowledging the moment. Something was going on. Maybe it was just in her head, or maybe he was feeling it as well. This whole interview was unorthodox.

She tried to find her footing. "I'd be happy to audition for you."

His eyes lit with a kind of humor that bordered on mischievous. Had she said something funny?

"Perhaps something can be arranged." He stood and held out his hand. "Come."

"Where are we going?"

"I want to give you a tour."

Tour. That was a good sign, right? "But the dessert?"

"Someone will bring it to us."

She slipped her hand in his and allowed him to guide her around to the back of the room toward a set of elevators. As he pressed the up button, she glanced down at their clasped hands with fascination. His hand nearly swallowed hers, making her fingers look dainty in his grip.

The doors slid open and he pulled her inside, pressing the button for the top floor. As the doors closed, she detangled herself from him, feeling the space constrict around them. She wasn't normally claustrophobic. It was him. His presence was almost too much in the tiny compartment. As if both needed the extra distance, they moved to opposite sides of the elevator, facing each other.

The look he gave her now was almost carnal. Like he was starved and she was the only meal in sight. It was unnerving. It was exhilarating. Receiving such unwavering attention from a vampire should not send forbidden tremors through her spine. Her heart began a slow drum. Her breaths began to shallow. The effect must have been causing her chest to noticeably rise and fall because he lustfully glanced down at her breasts, then back into her eyes, smiling when he realized he'd been caught.

"You are exquisite."

"Thank you," she breathed. My god, he was making her feel as if she were the sexiest woman in the world.

Ding. The doors parted. She practically dove out. He followed her, albeit, more slowly.

They were in another hallway, and there were doors lining either side.

"This way." Cortez started down the hall, not taking her hand this time. Relief and disappointment took turns kicking her in the gut. But when they got to a dim stairwell, he once more held out his hand to her. She glanced up cautiously. Where in the world was he taking her?

Maybe it was the stark switch from being surrounded by a crowd to the sensation of complete isolation with this engrossing man, or the sporadic strobe of the cold, blue-tinged halogen bulbs that lit the stairwell, but she was suddenly hesitant.

"It's safe," he said as if he sensed her wariness. "You are safe with me."

Her mind split into two camps. One vying to believe him one-hundred percent, recklessly willing to follow him through hot coals just to experience more of the delicious way he was making her feel. The other wondered if, to her at least, he wasn't the most dangerous man alive.

Battling her uncertainty, she took his hand and up they went.

CHAPTER 6

A beautiful sea of twinkling stars above greeted her as cool ocean air rolling in from the coast fanned across her face.

They were on the roof. She marveled at a three-sixty view of the darkened city. Ever Nights was the tallest building in the city, so for miles there was nothing to obstruct her view. To the west, she caught the moon glancing off the Pacific, like liquid white-gold on black. What must it look like in the day? Sunsets had to be breathtaking.

Half of the roof was set up like a mini retreat, complete with a pool, hot tub, sidebar, and a seating nook under a trellis of wisteria. The other half looked like a greenhouse. The scent of different herbs and sweet fragrances mixed in the air.

They were completely alone.

Now that the initial awe had worn off, she faced Cortez, suddenly aware that he'd been watching her, not saying a word, as she had taken everything in.

This couldn't be a normal interview. In fact, it felt very much like a date. But that couldn't be right. She had to be imagining things. Except the look he was giving her—had been giving her the whole night—said she might be on the money.

He strolled to the bar. "Would you like a drink?"

"I think I'm confused. Is this an interview or a date?"

He pulled out two flutes and a bottle of Champagne, cracking it open. After filling each glass he passed one to her. "Which would you prefer?"

Her mouth briefly popped open. She squashed her surprise behind her glass, taking a quick sip. Wow! This Champagne was delicious. The garbage she'd had before must have been squeezed through the ass of a donkey.

She took a bigger sip and tried to get her bearings. "Is this how you welcome all your new employees?" She was suddenly racked with inexplicable jealousy over all the beautiful women she'd seen below. But why should she be? She'd only just met this man.

"I don't date people I work with," came his simple reply.

Her brain took a pause. Surely that meant that they wouldn't be dating. "You just feed them unbelievable meals and ply them with Champagne?"

He turned wry. "Not quite. I'm sure you could tell by the reaction of some of my employees earlier, there haven't been many to garner such treatment."

"Why me then?"

His smile was elusive. "You fascinate me."

You fascinate me too. But he shouldn't. There was a danger in this dance. She couldn't get too tangled up in his game. And that was surely what it was. She wasn't an idiot, her features were pleasing, she might even go as far to say above average, but not by much and there certainly wasn't anything *fascinating* about her...aside from her siren lineage, which no one could know about. Was that what he was sensing? Was he drawn to that part of her? Her voice had never had any effect on vampires, thank the Lord! She could run from a human. She could even...kill a human...

She shivered. *Block that out.*

...but against a vampire? She had no chance at all. Point. Set. Match.

He sidestepped the bar and came to stand in front of her. His forefinger hooked under her chin, and he lifted her gaze to his. Tawny eyes bore into hers. "Tell me what you're thinking."

Once again she wondered if he was mesmerizing her, but she didn't feel compelled to answer. She could refuse.

She decided not to. "I fear you're playing a game with me."

His big hand came up to cup her cheek. "I don't play games with people."

Her heart rate was slowly rising, his nearness filleting reason. A mysterious crackle of energy seemed to pass between them. Just as her eyes dipped to his lips, his tongue darted out to wet them. She swallowed, and worked to get more air into her lungs. *He's going to kiss me.* Her pulse was banging in her ears now, blood rushing to her brain, fogging her thoughts.

His head dipped, and warm lips molded over hers. She was helpless not to kiss him back, leaning into him. Her heart thundered now. Every vamp in a five block radius could probably hear it.

When his tongue delved, testing, she welcomed him into her mouth. Fire roared through her blood, burning away what little resistance she had left. Giving into him completely, her hand came around his nape to hold him close as she deepened the kiss. His arms hooked her waist, drawing their bodies together. Her heels practically left the ground, her tiptoes barely touching, but she only wanted him to hold her tighter.

She'd been kissed before, but never like this. Never in a way that was so frighteningly consuming, so deliciously decadent. Never in a way that made her mind grow dim and her body spark like a live-wire. Never in a way that made her want to groan into this man's mouth with primal triumph.

He let out a guttural sound as though he were on the exact same page, and the sound bounced around her every nerve like a pinball, lighting her up.

A small gasp to their right had her eyes flying open. Breaths heavy, she pulled back to see one of the waitresses holding a plate: Victor's special dessert.

Cortez shot the poor woman a look of such malice, Naia wasn't sure she shouldn't worry for her safety. "Apologies, I-I'll just leave this here." She hastened to set the dish down on a nearby table and then tripped over herself to get back inside.

Too late. The spell was broken. Naia was appalled at her lack of self-control. Untangling herself from Cortez's arms, she took several steps back while her lungs continued to battle for the proper level of oxygen. God, she was out of her element. She was here to get a job and scrounge up some information for Dante, not to seduce the boss. Or rather, *get* seduced.

Cortez still appeared perturbed by the interruption, but wisely gave her space, though he studied her expression closely. She must look half in shock. Or half in lust. She couldn't decide.

"I think we should go back." She didn't wait for him to agree. She beelined it to the door and started down the stairs, her heels clanging on the metal. She still had her Champagne glass in her left hand. How she'd managed to hold on to it, she couldn't say, but she did notice some of the liquid had spilled over the edge onto her clutching fingers.

At the elevator, she triple pressed the button.

"Will your man be upset by what just happened?" he asked, sidling up beside her.

She was about to snap again that she didn't have a man, but wondered if that was wise. Could she salvage her mission if he thought she was taken? "Wouldn't you?"

His jaw clenched. "If you were mine, I'd be murderous." At her slight intake of breath, he added. "Any man who attempted to take you from me would be risking death."

"You can't be serious!"

"I said *if* you were mine. You're not...yet."

She gaped at him, speechless, as the elevator doors parted. He stepped inside and held the doors for her. For several moments, she couldn't quite get her legs to obey. Stiffly, she made it inside and then was once more entombed with the man who was both terrifying her and amazing her with his every unpredictable action. What would he do next?

"Stay the night with me."

Stunned, she said, "You don't waste any time, do you?"

That half-smile returned to his features, blasting the butterflies in her stomach into a frenzy. "When I see something I want, I go after it."

And he wanted her? She liked the idea way too much. "You don't date employees, but you sleep with them?"

He frowned. "No."

"So then if I stayed with you, I'd be ruining my chances at a job." They landed on the first floor, and she exited the elevator.

"What if I told you I have no intention of hiring you anyway?"

Her heart sank, but she didn't let it show. "Then

I'd say I'm wasting my time here. And as you pointed out, I have better things to do." His lips thinned at the double-entendre. Let him think she had someone waiting on her. Served him right for pulling that rug out from under her. Seven grand went poof in her mind, gone from her future with not so much as a snap of the finger. Her dream job with it. She realized then that there was no way she and Cole could gather the money in time. They were going to have to run.

She was already mentally packing when Cortez said. "What about that wager?"

"Huh?"

"I proposed a wager earlier. You seemed interested."

"And what would that be?"

"Another game of pool. If you win, I'll give you a job."

The whole reason she'd sought him out! She faced him, steeling herself for the catch. "And if *you* win?" She almost didn't need to ask.

"You'll blow off your date and stay the night with me instead."

She bit her lip, seeing that money land back in her future. The hustler in her bellied up, while logic danced like a prizefighter ready to box. Cortez was good at billiards. As good as her, if not better. Playing him was a risk. If she agreed to this ridiculous wager and she lost, he'd expect her to pay up. She'd have to stay the night with him. As in *with* him with him? It wasn't like he was asking for a pajama party and Parcheesi. He wanted her body at his disposal. And would that really be a hardship? Part of her knew a night with him would be mind-blowing. She was using all her willpower not to picture it.

A successful club owner such as he could have his pick, of both vein and body. Literally. Toss his room key into the crowd and women would be throwing elbows to get to it. So why was he so focused on her?

"I suppose it's my blood you're after."

He shook his head. "I have plenty of donors ready and willing. Biting is off the table if you'd prefer."

"I would." Had she just said that? Was she seriously considering this?

And why not? It was practically a win/win scenario?

She was smart enough to admit to herself she wanted him too. That small taste on the roof had parts of her brain still fogged with lust.

Now that she thought about it, her mission had nothing to do with her landing a job, per say. Sure, as an employee, she could snoop around, but as a lover, what sort of doors might open to her?

Of course, that was only if she *lost*. If she wiped the floor with him again, would he keep his word and hire her? She glanced back at the shiny stage, imagining herself up there singing her favorite tunes, Cole's debt paid, no more worries for either of them.

She studied Cortez, and her thoughts turned to those talented lips, those hard muscles...at *her* disposal.

It seemed no matter how she viewed the situation, she was looking at a win/win.

Grinning up at him, she said blithely, "I'll break."

CHAPTER 7

"I'll go ahead and assume you've played nine ball," he said, racking the table.

She dusted the top of her cue stick with chalk. "Of course." Only nine balls were used in nine ball, hence the name, numbered in order from one to nine. Aside from the break, the balls must be pocketed in numerical order, or the cue ball must at least contact the lowest-numbered ball first, after which any numbered ball could be legally scored, meaning the one ball could be struck and then the nine by either the one or the cue ball, and if sunk, the game is won. It was a fast-paced game with fewer balls in play. Is that why he'd chosen it? Eager for his prize?

Not if she had anything to say about it.

The pool room had been abandoned. She didn't know where his friends had gone, or if they would return. A new waitress was attending them now, only sparing Naia a cursory glance of curiosity before dropping off their drinks. Knowing she no longer had to bother with an interview, Naia had ordered her favorite drink: Hurricane. It was sweet and strong, and synonymous to its name, too many of them and you'd wake in the morning thinking you'd been hit by a storm.

Cortez ordered a whiskey sour. He sipped as she inspected his prowess at racking. Not a ball out of place.

"Are you ready for this?" she taunted. "In a few moments, you're about to welcome a new employee into the fold."

Grinning devilishly, he said, "Or you'll welcome me into yours."

She turned away to hide her flush. Bastard. "Not going to happen." She chalked her cue stick, planted her stance, and aimed for the apex of the triangle. Inhaling a deep breath, she raised her elbow, drew the stick back and then plowed forward through the cue ball.

Crack.

The sound rang out like gunfire, balls smashing around like chaotic bumper cars. And though her break was impressive, it was exceedingly unlucky. No balls were pocketed. Damn. She may have already lost this game before it had begun.

Cortez strolled up to the table. "I thought you were going to provide me with a challenge."

She glared at him and then turned to nurse her drink.

He had a straight shot at the start, and the one ball bit the dust. The two ball quickly followed, then the three. He was going to sweep the table. Her heart sank when he lined up the four. He was going for a bank to sink the nine. Game over. But then something interesting happened. The cue ball knocked the four into the pocket no problem, but then came to rest just inside the corner, behind the nine and flanked by several others. The five ball was at the complete opposite end of the table, near the adjacent corner. He had to go for the five, but couldn't hit the nine first. If he hit the nine or didn't manage to sink five, it was her turn.

She sat up in her chair, curious how he was going to get out of this.

Before plotting his move, he sent her a cocky smirk. He raised his cue stick at a forty-five degree, aiming the tip just below the cue ball's center point. A trick shot? He was going to jump the nine.

You have got to be kidding me.

The cue ball sailed over the nine, rolled along the bank, and then kissed the five. The five took its time edging to the pocket and then dove in.

"Impressive." The hustler was being hustled. Naia drew a long swig from her glass.

To his credit, Cortez didn't gloat. He just focused on the next ball in line. The six was back at the opposite end, taunting him with its position, guarded heavily by the eight ball. Naia saw what she would do: bank the cue off the railing, tap the six, driving it into the eight at just the right angle to send it to a side pocket. Legal but risky.

Cortez was lining up a different shot entirely. By his angle, she wondered if he was playing a safety, planning to forfeit his turn but leave her in a position where her only shot would be impossible to make.

Yet he seemed to be aiming straight for the eight ball. The only way to make his shot that way would be to—

He struck the cue ball. As it traveled down the table, it spun like a ballerina on speed, curving the line, skirting the eight ball, and smacking the six into the corner pocket.

Naia remained remarkably calm. "You've got some skill."

"Thank you," he said, devising his next shot. This one was straightforward. A wham bam thank you ma'am. *Just what he plans to do with me.*

Time for something drastic.

Bringing her drink with her, she hopped off her seat and sidled up to the table across from him, near where he'd have to aim so that she'd be in his line of sight. *Time for a little handicapping.* She leaned forward with her elbows on the pool table, pretending to gauge the shot with him, but really, she was giving him a bullseye view of her cleavage.

He grinned. "Resorting to diversion tactics? Displaying my prize is only going to make me focus harder on winning it."

"Can't blame a girl for trying." She stood, discouraged, but not showing it.

"Please, try all you like. I appreciate the effort."

You asked for it. As he drew back on his cue stick, she sipped from her drink, tilting it a touch too much. Liquid ran down her front. She moaned, "Oh, I've got myself all wet."

His gaze snapped to her dampened breasts just as he made contact with the cue ball. It struck its mark, but was a fraction off. The seven ball was caught like a ping pong, bouncing back and forth within the edge of the pocket. It didn't go in.

Her grin was Grinch-worthy.

He stood, glowering at her. "Dirty trick."

Still smiling, she plucked a napkin off the table and dabbed her chest. She'll have to get the dress dry-cleaned before returning it to Goldie, but it was worth it.

Better still, she was left with a perfect shot. "All's fair," she chirped, lining up her shot, and sinking the seven. Her set up was a dream. A straight shot for the eight.

Cortez took a seat directly behind her, and suddenly she could think of nothing but how short the hem of her dress was and his eyes on her ass. She glanced back. Yup. He was staring right at it.

She quirked an indignant brow.

He took a long leisurely pull from his whiskey, his penetrating gaze never straying from her backside.

She cleared her throat.

"Feel free to take your time," he said. "I've got the best seat in the house and the view is impeccable."

She rolled her eyes. Determined to ignore him, she focused on the eight ball. She only needed to kiss it for it to go in, except the position of the cue ball meant she'd have to lean quite far over the table...

She faced Cortez. "Would you mind moving."

"Why?"

"You're obscuring my shot."

He indicated the space between them. "You have plenty of room. And I'm just sitting here, quiet as a mouse." His expression was pure mischief.

"You're distracting me on purpose."

"All's fair."

She piped her lip and blew a strand of hair out of her face. "Fine. Look all you want, because you're never going to get to touch." To add insult, she hiked up her skirt an inch, turned, and eyed the seven ball like it was a bullseye on his crotch.

As she bent, she let out a husky sound.

She tapped the cue ball with just the right pressure to knock the eight in, but her act of rebellion backfired. Now she was really damp, and it had nothing to do with spilled drinks.

When she turned back to Cortez in triumph, she was floored by his heated expression.

"I think you want to stay the night with me, even if you do win."

"Hm. A one night stand with you or land a nice cushy job? The scales aren't balanced in your favor, are they? You'd really have to step up your game."

He stood, and in one, step invaded her personal space. His big, callused, ninja palm gripped her backside and jerked her against him. Forced off balance, she planted her hand on his toned shoulder for leverage.

"Ah-ah, the rules are clear." She sounded too breathy. Her traitorous body soaked up his heat like a thirsty sponge.

He buried his face in the crook of her neck and inhaled deeply. The furious beat of her heart made her light headed as his mouth trailed along her jaw at a mind-numbingly slow pace, coming to feather along her lips. All she could do was breathe, wait, want. But he pulled away and released her.

"You're right, I'll work on my game."

She was left speechless, breathless, aroused, and... longing.

"You should take your last shot."

Woodenly, she faced table and struggled to restart her brain.

Nine ball. Right. Last shot.

Her line of aim was perfect. Her follow through was off. The cue ball trailed the nine into the pocket.

She scratched.

She lost.

CHAPTER 8

Cortez's suite was more like an apartment. A very lavish apartment. He wasn't hurting for funds, that was for sure. It had an open layout, three bedrooms that she could see, probably more, and there was an office slash study with an impressive desk and bookshelves filled to the brim. One entire wall was made up of floor to ceiling windows that carried out into the living room, through which she luxuriated in a magnificent view of the city.

A soft breeze drew her attention to a set of French doors that led to a balcony decorated with lush exotic plants.

Playing her hunch, she said, "Your decorator did a lovely job."

"She's the best," he replied from behind the bar where he was mixing her another hurricane. She wasn't feeling *too* buzzed yet, only the sting of defeat.

When he came around and handed her the drink, she was reminded of their first meeting. "You're the owner of the club, so why were you bartending yesterday?"

"You think I should remain up here? Surveying all

that I command?"

She sipped her drink, waiting for his answer.

"The work is simple and mindless. I enjoy it on occasion."

"But there were hardly any people to serve."

"That's why I was there." At her curious look, he added, "I'm needed elsewhere during the rush. During the day, I clean or take inventory so I know what to stock. And it gives me time to invent new drinks to add to the menu. I enjoy that."

"You invent drinks? Cole...uh...cool." Cole liked to experiment as well. "Can you make me something you created?"

"Sure." His eyes lit on the glass in her hand. "You like sweet drinks, so I'll make you a gyrator. It's similar to a hurricane with its alcohol content, except I use a different juice for the sweet, and add mint, cinnamon and a touch of lime." He'd returned to the bar and started mixing. It was a pleasure to watch his nimble fingers at work, deftly pouring from an array of bottles. The mint and cinnamon seemed an odd choice in combination with everything else, but she didn't comment. Finally he squeezed in a wedge of lime and began shaking everything together before dumping it out into a large glass. Final touch was a tiny straw to sip from. He slid the concoction toward her and waited expectantly.

His expression was so earnest, like he was actually interested in her opinion.

Taking a long sip, she let the liquid swish in her mouth before swallowing it. "Delicious!"

He dipped his head in thanks. "It's going on the menu next week."

"You can't even taste the alcohol." After taking another sip, she pointed to the glass and laughingly said, "This is dangerous. Are you trying to get me drunk?"

"I'm trying to get you to like me."

She smiled, "I do like you. You're nothing like what I expected."

"What did you expect?"

Another Dante, maybe even crueler, more frightening. "I don't know," she settled on.

Holding her gaze, he approached with obvious intent. Was he expecting to get started already?

"Um..."

He ran his thumb along her jawline with a tenderness that shocked her. "Join me for a dip in the hot tub?"

"Huh?"

"It's a beautiful night." He shrugged out of his shirt, revealing an expertly cut upper body packed with toned muscle and beautifully tanned skin.

"Uh..." She was riveted, unable to look away, and, apparently, unable to form a proper sentence.

When he started undoing his belt, she finally tore her gaze away, turning her back.

"You are modest," he observed. The thud of his belt hitting the carpet made her jump. Then she heard him walking away, out onto the balcony. At the sound of sloshing water she followed him outside. His arms were spread out along the lip of the hot tub, his expression teasing. She wondered if he was even wearing underwear, but didn't see a pair lying around.

"I...um, don't have a bathing suit," she said.

One challenging eyebrow rose. "Neither do I."

Okay, he was definitely naked in there. She shivered at the thought. He mistook that as her being cold.

"It's much warmer in here. A lot less lonely too."

She bit her lower lip. His eyes zeroed in on the action, going hooded. When he spoke, his tone was guttural. "I'll turn my back if you need to preserve your modesty...for the time being."

It wasn't her modesty that needed saving. Hell, she was surprised she had any left after changing in front of the girls at Dante's—along with Boomer and, on occasion, some of the other lecherous bouncers.

No, modesty wasn't the issue. It was the choice she was about to make.

If she went in there with him now, she'd basically be telling him yes to the rest of the night. Their wager had brought her up here, but she could still change her mind, take her ass back to Dante's and continue her life without knowing the power of this man's magnificent body, who was now staring at her as if he wanted to eat her up, and it had nothing to do with his vampiric nature.

He'd told her he wouldn't bite her, and she believed him. Why? She couldn't put her finger on it, but this man did not seem like the type that needed to lie to get what he wanted. And he wanted *her*.

Oh, oh, how she wanted him too.

As he gazed at her with a desire that she felt deep in her bones, she reached up and undid the clasp at her nape that held up the top half of her dress. The fabric slipped down her chest, falling to her waist and baring her breasts.

His brows shot up. Apparently he hadn't been expecting that.

He cleared his throat. "Getting impatient for you in here."

She shimmied out of the skirt, leaving her panties on, and allowed him to drink her in. His gaze was intense, carnivorous, consuming. Seeing him look at her the way he was now could lead to a serious addiction. And if she didn't get in there soon, there was a good chance he was coming out to get her.

She piled her dress next to his clothes before sauntering to the tub. The water was a pleasant temperature, churning from the jets. "Mm. This is nice."

"I'm resisting the urge to snatch you up and plant you on my lap," he told her in a roughened tone.

She grinned coyly and then eased across the tub to slip into his lap, her legs to one side. Again her actions seemed to surprise him. "There," she said brightly. "Better?"

"Much." His arms came around her as though it were the most natural thing in the world, yet she inadvertently stiffened. *Definitely naked*, she mentally confirmed, turning red. He'd adjusted himself so that he wasn't poking her awkwardly, but he was still hard as granite underneath her.

"Look," he said softly, pressing his lips to her shoulder and inhaling lightly. "I know we had a bet and all, but I'm not about to make you do anything you're uncomfortable with."

As though he couldn't help it, his hands slowly caressed up and down her sides. She swallowed at the titillating sensation combined with the warm flowing jets.

He placed another soft kiss on her shoulder. "I'm a patient man. I don't have to touch you." He continued even as his left hand trailed around her stomach and yanked her around so that she was sitting with her back to his front. "I don't have to kiss you," he said, trailing his lips along her nape. Her eyes closed as her head lulled to give him better access. "We can just sit and talk. It's your choice. I'm enjoying your company immensely." All the while, his lips trailed a hot path along the crook of her neck.

"I think if you stop now, I'd have to kill you."

He chuckled, low and deep, clutching her closer. "Are you going to let me do wicked things to you?" he rasped in her ear, then he sucked on her pulse point.

Not with fangs, just his lips and tongue, and it was bliss.

He ran his nose along her neck. "You smell divine."

"You said no biting, right?" she figured it might be a good idea to remind him.

"You've no need to worry. I don't bite on the first date."

As if there was going to be a second. Yet she couldn't bring herself to care. She rolled her hips along his crotch.

He growled against her skin. "You need me to take care of you tonight, don't you?" His hands moved to her hips, fingers playing with the lining of her panties.

"Cortez," she whispered, her heart pounding erratically, her thoughts scattered, her body on fire. She'd never been pushed to lust so fast. "You're driving me crazy."

A humorous sound rumbled out of him. "Baby, I haven't even started."

CHAPTER 9

Thick fingers breached the hem of her panties, sliding toward third base. He growled when he found her slick. "So hot and swollen. I bet you taste as good as you feel."

She let out a half gasp, half whimper, rolling her hips.

"Are you going to come for me so soon?" he asked in a dark voice. "Ride my hand. Show me how you like it. What you need."

His naughty words and wicked touch were making her mindless, heedless. Her brain gracefully bowed out while her body surrendered, doing exactly as he commanded. Her head lolled back to rest on his shoulder while her hips rocked into his embrace. The friction was delicious.

As her body toiled for release, the arm that had been locked around her torso loosened, and he reached up to knead her breast.

Her body was on the verge of release. He turned his face into the crook over her neck. "As soon as you've come I'm going to rip these panties off of you and have you on my cock."

His words tipped her over the edge. An orgasm exploded through her body, "Yes!" she screamed. "Oh, God!" Her hips worked furiously as a wave of pleasure blasted through her. Throwing her arms around his neck behind her, her back arched slightly, jutting her breasts above the waterline for him to see.

Another growl escaped him. "Woman, you've had me hard as stone all night, and yet, somehow, I grow harder still."

She felt a tug on her hip, and her panties became scraps, discarded to drift freely in the water. With her still on his lap facing away from him, his big hands gripped her waist, and he lifted her over his dick.

Post-orgasm fog still impeded her brain, but as soon as she felt him prodding her entrance, adrenaline cleared that right up.

Oh, God, am I really going to do this? She'd been swept up to his suite so fast, and then into the hot tub. Had she thought this through? Was she really about to have sex with a vampire? A *stranger* at that—A mindboggling sexy stranger. But his kind bit during sex! Or so she'd been told. Using their fangs during the throws. Could he really restrain himself? Did she care?

"Your heart is pounding so fast, luv. Don't tell me you're having second thoughts? My poor dick couldn't take it." As if to prove how hard he was, his hips jerked up and the tip prodded her.

Lust fired anew. He lowered her onto his shaft. The invasion was slow, as though he was testing her fit, not wanting to hurt her with his size. He was a big guy, and her body had to make room for him, but she was dying here.

"I can take more, Cortez."

Groaning, he let her sink down on her own. They both let out sounds of relief. Yet she still felt a tinge of discomfort, her body stretching to accommodate him. It was sublime pleasure kissed by pain.

She wasn't exactly a virgin, but neither was she experienced. Of all the men she'd been with, Cortez was by far the most well-endowed. Never had she felt so full.

He pulled her back flush against his chest, his lips brushing her nape as his hips bucked.

"Oh, God!" Red-hot pleasure dissipated any pain, and ecstasy spiked her brain.

He thrust again, and she moaned low in her throat.

Tone roughened, he rasped, "You feel so damn good. Need to..." His hips jumped, drilling his cock deeper.

Her head fell back on a long moan.

As if he were unable to hold back any more, his hips went to work, rocking in and out of her with the power of a steam train, his cock pistoning harder, faster, deeper. Her breasts bobbed in the water, her moans broken between gasps. The pleasure was immense, almost too much. She only wanted more.

He buried his face in her neck and snarled. The danger of his fangs no longer frightened her. It oddly heightened her pleasure. As if to taunt him, she rolled her head to the side, displaying her tender flesh. Was she mad? All the while he drove into her with fierce measured thrusts.

"Oh, sweet girl, you tempt me so. Testing me?" His hips paused briefly. She cried out in protest, making him chuckle. "I'm going to have to..." One hard thrust sent sparks of bliss through her nerves. "Punish you for that."

Punish? "Don't stop!" she heard herself moan.

In a blur he adjusted their position so that she was bent over the edge of the hot tub with him behind her.

His hips resumed their delicious, punishing assault....

And then his hot palm came down hard on her backside in a kind of slap, though he held onto her flesh, fingers digging into her cheek. The sound that came from her was unrecognizable. Her lungs worked between her mindless moans, screams, and shrieks of pleasure. This wasn't just casual sex. This was a thorough fucking that would forever overshadow all that came before or after.

She glanced over her shoulder, marveling at the way his muscles toiled, all animal grace and power.

Again his flattened palm came down on her ass. Her body arched, as if begging for more. Why did that feel so good?

He reached out and wrapped her hair in his fist, his hips still working like a piston topped off with high-octane, and pulled her to stand with him in the middle of the tub, bringing her head around for a searing kiss. As his tongue tangled with hers, he slammed into her harder and harder.

"Oh, God! She moaned into his mouth. "Oh, yes! Don't stop. Harder! Faster! Fuck me!" She was like another creature, on the verge of her second orgasm, screaming into the night and not caring if anyone heard.

As she blurted out rash words, he growled and groaned and snarled against her flesh like an animal, his body ramming into hers with so much strength it was a wonder she could take it. Yet she only wanted more. She wanted to feel him long after they were through. She wanted to feel him for eternity.

He let her drop back down to grip the edge of the tub and then all she could do was hold on as his power increased, his tempo maddening.

He bellowed to the sky as his release took hold. She screamed with pure, undiluted ecstasy, the power of it splitting her every nerve. As they rode the wave together, her fingers dug into the edge of the tub so hard her knuckles turned white.

Finally he slowed, still languidly thrusting. His big body curled over her, his front to her spine, his arms coming around her torso. Slowly, as they both worked to regulate their breathing, he turned them so that he was once more seated with her on his lap. Eyelids growing heavy, she rested her head on his shoulder while he stroked her back.

They sat like that for several moments, catching their breaths and rebooting. When they finally emerged from the hot tub, her body still tingled.

He handed her a towel from a small compartment hidden under a bench before wrapping one around himself. Then, without a word, he went inside.

She stood for a moment unsure of what she was supposed to do. Should she get dressed? She glanced at where her clothes had been carelessly tossed to the ground and cursed. Some water must have splashed during the throws. Her borrowed dress was dangerously near a puddle.

Snatching it up, she inspected it for chlorine stains. Thank goodness. It had escaped harm. To be safe, she should probably rinse off before slipping it on.

Towel tucked under her armpits, she headed inside. Embarrassment was creeping in. Just before leaving the deck completely, she glanced around to see if there were other balconies nearby. In the dark, she didn't see any peeping toms, but that didn't mean someone hadn't just gotten one heck of a raw, X-rated show.

Inside, she didn't see Cortez, but she could hear his muffled voice. She called out, "Do you mind if I use your shower?"

"Go ahead."

She poked her head around a corner. He stood at the kitchen counter, a phone pressed to his ear.

She was still reeling from the most mind-blowing orgasm of her life, and he just had to make a phone call? She supposed what happened between them was nothing out of the ordinary for him. He probably experienced sex like that on a nightly basis. More than likely he had countless orgies in that tub. She glanced back at that still churning water, seeing it differently now. A cornucopia of DNA. Yuck.

When he hung up the phone and started toward her with a very pleased look in his face, she couldn't help but snap, "I suppose that hot tub has seen a lot of action."

He paused at her tone, eyeing her. Then his lips quirked. "You think I bring women up here every night?"

She pursed her lips, miffed that he had practically read her mind. "It's none of my business."

"You're right, it's not."

She blinked. He was still gazing at her with amusement. He thought her sudden indignation was funny. She schooled her features and turned toward the bathroom, closing herself in.

Everything within was arranged just so, with the shampoo next to his conditioner linked up perfectly, fresh soap on a small ledge, newly opened, and an electric waterproof razor on another. Hmm. Thinking back to the feel of him, she realized he must manscape down below. And wasn't that just super considerate of the guy. Though she hadn't gotten a good look at the area to know for sure. And now she'd missed her opportunity. Bummer.

When she finished washing, she quickly dried and then slipped into her dress. Her ruined panties were still out surfing tiny waves from the hot tub jets.

Towel drying her hair, she entered the living room. Cortez stepped out of his bedroom at the same time. He, too, seemed to have come from a shower. Unlike her, he was naked but for the terry cloth around his waist.

Unabashedly she took in the sight of him, fighting a sigh; toned defined pecs stacked on top of six-pack abs with a V at his hips pointing to his...

Her nipples beaded under the fabric of her dress as if preparing for round two.

He was gazing at her as well, but with a quizzical expression. "Why are you dressed?"

She blinked. "I figured we were done here."

"According to our wager, I get you for the whole night."

"Seriously?" She gave him a sardonic look. "Most men would be passed out by now."

"I'm not most men."

"You really think you can top what we just did?" She gave a disbelieving snort.

A confident grin was all he gave in answer.

She almost dared him to prove it—*another go? Yes please*—but she thought she shouldn't seem so eager. "I don't know." She glanced at the door as if debating.

He frowned. "Do you think you can leave now and salvage your date?"

"What?"

With a menacing look he stepped toward her, gripped the collar of her dress and then tore the fabric down the middle, exposing her breasts. "Try explaining *that* to him."

"You fucker!" she yelled, covering herself. "This dress didn't belong to me!" The skirt part was still intact. Maybe a skilled seamstress could save it. *Goldie is going to kill me.* And why was that her first thought instead of how frightened she should be of Cortez right now?

He was undaunted by her glare. "You can call me all the horrible names you want while I'm making you come yet again."

"I will, you asshole!" Wait, what?

He hoisted her over his shoulder and bolted for the bedroom, tossing her lightly onto his bed. She scrambled over to the edge as if to get away, but he tugged her by the ankle, drawing her back towards him. Then he finished destroying her dress, ripping the skirt in two. Once more completely nude in front of him, he gazed at her most feminine feature with something like hunger in his eyes. She gasped, lust battling her alarm.

"You like my games?"

"No," she denied instantly, though the evidence to the contrary was blatant.

"You want to punish *me* now?" he asked slyly. "What would my mistress have me do?"

Okay, things were taking a turn. And she was absolutely loving it! Panting, she hissed, "I think you need to make me come with your tongue."

He grinned wickedly, and then fell on her with ravage intent. The first scalding lick had her crying out. This was insane. This was depraved. This was.... so fucking good!

She cried out once more when he sucked her clit between his soft lips. Her nails dug into the sheets, her body writhing as an orgasm slammed home. And still he didn't stop, sucking and licking and laving her, relentlessly feasting. Amazingly, a second orgasm was teed up when he pulled away.

No!!!

"Someone's at the door," he said casually, seconds before a knock sounded.

Her head shot up. "What?" Pushing him away, she

scrambled back. "You didn't invite a friend did you?" Her expression had to be horrified because he put his hands up in a calming gesture.

"Of course not. I don't share. But I do have a surprise for you."

Desperately she wrapped herself in the comforter. He frowned at that, but didn't say anything. With the towel still around his waist, he went to answer the door. While he was gone, she marveled at her own behavior. He seemed to have the power to turn her into a wanton creature.

She gazed down sadly at the tattered dress. Done for. Briefly she calculated the hours of waitressing it would take to cover the cost. Then she heard the door close and he returned alone, pushing a cart of...dessert toppings? So that's what his phone call was about.

She gulped and met his exultant gaze.

"Get ready to be devoured."

CHAPTER 10

The next morning, the sounds of the shower running in the other room roused her.

Naia stretched under the covers and cracked her eyes open. She'd stayed the night. Not that she could have left if she'd wanted to. After the devilish things he'd done to her, she'd fallen into a practically comatose state. The man had been a machine.

She wondered if she should sneak in there with him and surprise him with a morning quickie.

A grin spread across her lips at remembering everything they'd done to each other last night. Chocolate syrup would never look the same again. And somehow she knew the next time she saw whipped cream, she would shiver with laden desire. He'd been insatiable. He'd been carnal. He'd been—

AN ASSHOLE! her mind shouted.

At some point he'd set her purse on the bedside table—next to which sat an incriminating wad of cash that hadn't been there last night. She fingered through it, counting. Three hundred dollars! He couldn't seriously have intended that for her, could he?

As if she were an escort he was paying off?

Her lip quivered. Something like jagged ball bearings dropped into her stomach. Her nightly romp now held a new perspective. What only seconds ago had been a fond memory of unhampered passion and pleasure was now dark and dirty. *A job.*

Had Dante been right? Was this how Cortez lured girls into prostitution? By screwing them boneless and turning them into mindless carnal creatures? A couple more nights like this, and she could see herself growing addicted. The way he'd made her feel had been like nothing she'd ever experienced. It had been so good. Too good.

But if all he wanted was a working girl, why bother playing hide the salami with her when he could just as easily utilize his vampire ability of compulsion? Why make her feel like she was unique? Wanted?

Special?

You think I bring women up here every night? he'd said. In hindsight, his words were less of a denial and more of an evasion.

She traded her self-reproach and disappointment for one singular objective. *Have to get out of here.*

She shoved the covers away, slinked off the bed, and then padded naked toward what she thought was a closet, stepping over her ruined dress on the way. After the story she had to tell, hopefully Goldie would forgive her. It wasn't her fault some prick had rend it in two. What she'd ignorantly mistaken for drugged passion was, instead, a calloused attempt to keep her here. And it had worked.

The closet was huge. Inside were rows of men's shirts and pants. Shoes lined the wall. In a hurry, she yanked a white button-down off a hanger and slipped it on. The pants were several sizes too big, and the belts were no help. Their little holes didn't travel far enough up the swath of leather to fit snuggly around her waist. The shirt she wore hung to her knees. It could work as a shirt-dress if she could just find...

Ah, perfect. There was a vanity belt attached to Goldie's ravaged outfit that was still intact. Snatching the fabric off the ground, she ripped away the excess and then fastened the swathe around her waist.

The outfit would never make a magazine cover, but it would have to do. Her panties were still deep sea diving as far as she knew. She'd go without.

After stabbing her feet into her high-heeled boots and grabbing her purse—disregarding her *payment* altogether—she raced for the door. Just as she turned to mutter, "See you never, you unbelievable ass," the showered turned off.

"Did you say something?" His voice filtered through the apartment.

Damn. She forgot vampires had crazy good hearing. Adrenaline hammered her into action. She shut the door behind her and walked swiftly toward the elevator, heart pounding. She half expected him to come waltzing out buck-naked to confront her, but at the first press of the button, the metallic doors glided open, saving her from a long wait.

In the lobby, something delicious invaded her nostrils. It smelled like toasted bread and warm syrup. Her stomach clenched and grumbled as if to scream GIVE IT TO ME NOW! She couldn't remember the last time she'd had warmed syrup poured over hot buttered—

She mentally shook herself and made a beeline for the door. Her heels clacked on the floor, the sound echoing in the nearly empty club, drawing attention.

A curious head poked around the corner. It was Surfer Guy from last night. He smiled with recognition, "Hey!" Then he seemed to take in her unusual outfit before seeing something in her expression that wiped away his friendly grin. "Everything okay?"

"Tell your boss he's a dick," she snapped as she passed without slowing.

Outside, morning light didn't greet her; it *assaulted* her. Accused her. Underneath the *chirp, chirp, chirp* of birds alerting the world to dawn, there was a note of disapproval in the air.

Her heels now made a duller yet no less severe sound on the parking lot asphalt. It was a condemnatory beat. She'd heard the term walk of shame, but this was ridiculous. At least it was so early in the morning not a lot of people were out and about. She might make it home without anyone even noticing. Ironically, her outfit screamed street walker. Ugh.

She'd made it several blocks before a car slowed to a crawl next to her. Inward groan.

She glanced over to tell the guy to fuck off, but her words were cut off when the passenger side window rolled down and it was Cortez who stared back at her. His hair was still damp from his shower and he wore a dark T-shirt that displayed his tightly muscled arms. Arms that had held her close while his body took her to the moon.

She faced forward, anger increasing her pace, even though there was no point in trying to speed-walk away from a running vehicle.

"If I'd known you had somewhere to be, I would have waited to take a shower so I could see you off."

"Fuck you."

Much like Surfer Guy, his brows arched at her choice words. "You're livid." His tone was irritatingly even. Of course she was livid. Why wouldn't she be?

He cocked his head to study her as though trying to decipher the reason behind her anger. She wanted to slap that confused look right off his face. He muttered something to the driver. Before the car even stopped, he was stepping out. When he gripped her elbow to halt her furious steps, she ripped her arm away.

"Don't touch me!"

He pulled back in surprise, but kept pace behind her. "What has spurred this displeasure?"

"Are you kidding me?"

"Naia," he warned as if *she* were getting on *his* nerves. "Stop and tell me what's wrong."

She didn't stop, but his chagrin had her mouth running away with itself. "Oh, I don't know, Cortez. Maybe it was the wad of cash by my purse and the fact that I didn't realize I should have negotiated a price beforehand!"

He went quiet for a second. "Is it the money that's angered you? Was it not enough?"

She choked out a sound of disbelief.

"I thought you would be appreciative."

What did he think? That she'd be delighted with being paid for sex? That just because she'd wanted a job meant that she'd do anything for a paycheck? *You'd gone there in the first place with the promise of money*, her traitorous mind reminded. *To infiltrate his club and then later betray him for a tidy windfall.* Yet Cortez's smaller sum seemed so much more...wrong. And if she was going to sell her body, she'd be worth a helluva lot more than a measly three hundred!

Letting out a noise of frustration, he gripped her by the shoulders and whirled her around to face him. "I'm no good at guessing games, Naia. I've never needed to be. Tell me what has angered you?"

"How do you not get it!" she snapped, facing him. He halted as well. "You won't give me a job, but you'll try to turn me into a prostitute? I have never been more disgusted, or insulted, in my life!" Then, as if she'd been touched by madness, her palm whipped out and cracked him hard across the cheek. His surprise mirrored her own. Only once in her life had she struck another in anger. Everything about the action was repugnant.

Too late she realized she'd just hit a vampire in the face. And not just any vampire, a clan leader and possible crime lord! These could be the last words she ever uttered.

Her already fast-beating heart went into overdrive.

Yet his mighty shoulders seemed to lose some of their tension. "That's what you thought the money was for?"

She blinked at his incredulous tone. "Well, yeah. What else would it be for?"

"I wanted to reimburse you for the dress I ruined. I see now how you could come to the wrong conclusion."

All the fight left her. Shifting her weight, she battled the sudden wave of embarrassment. "Oh." Humiliation and regret teamed up to drag her gaze downward. Her hand came up to shade her eyes. "Oh, God. I'm sorry. I just assumed...."

"This misunderstanding is as much my fault as it is yours. I should have realized what you might think if you woke up alone next to a stack of cash. Come. You must be uncomfortable in that outfit." He opened the car door for her.

After a moment of hesitation, she maneuvered her butt onto the backseat and then tucked her legs in after her so she didn't inadvertently flash him. His shadow of a grin told her he knew the reason for her awkward entrance, but said nothing as he scooted in next to her and closed the door.

She expected the driver to flip-a-bitch, but the car lurched forward instead. A few decisive turns suggested they weren't headed back to the club at all. "Where are we going?"

"I'm taking you home. That's where you were going, wasn't it?"

It was, but...

Without any direction, the driver turned right and then made the first left, heading south...toward her apartment. She sent Cortez a curious look.

He sighed, and then admitted, "I may have had Donovan follow you home yesterday."

"What!? Why would you...?" Did he suspect her of nefarious intentions? She *had* nefarious intentions, but she thought she was a better actress than that.

She glanced up at the driver she guessed was named Donovan. Stone faced, he offered a clipped wave in the mirror. She had no doubt the only teeth he'd display was in a fang-filled sneer rather than any form of a smile. In fact, this entire trip his expression hadn't changed, and he hadn't spoken a word. His dangerous aura just now registered. If Cortez asked him to break someone's bones, he might merely inquire, "How many?" never losing that hard expression.

Anxiety heated her blood, yet she shivered.

Cortez misunderstood and ordered Donovan to blast the heat. That actually settled some of her nerves. He was treating her with kindness. If he knew she was a double agent, surely he'd be less concerned about her comfort.

Still, she asked Cortez, "Where else did *Donovan* follow me?" If he'd seen her walk to Dante's, she might still be in trouble. Although, she'd already admitted to having worked there, so maybe all she had to do was stick to her story about wanting a better job. That would be easy since it was true. So far it didn't seem like Cortez suspected Dante of wanting to take him down, or of employing her as a spy.

They pulled up to her apartment—straight to her

friggin' door! How had she not noticed being followed?

Her front door looked like home base right about now. A few small steps and she could finally relax.

With a relieved sigh, she thanked Cortez and apologized for the misunderstanding. So eager to end her poorly executed stint as a spy, she wasn't even going to ask for the money for the dress. He could keep it. She'd pay Goldie back some other way. Meanwhile she'd have to let Dante know that she wasn't cut out for this type of work. He'd have to find someone else. Besides, there was no way Cortez would hire her now. Not only had she basically accused him of trying to turn her into a streetwalker, she'd physically assaulted him to boot. Not to mention, as a rule he didn't hire anyone he slept with.

Worst of all, he probably never wanted to see her again.

So when he followed her to the door, she glanced back at him in surprise. "What are you doing?"

"Coming inside," he replied as though it should have been obvious. "The least you can do is invite me in for some tea or coffee." For effect, he theatrically rubbed his cheek.

She cringed. "Sorry about that."

"No worries. If someone tried to pay me for sex I'd be...well, flattered to be honest." He smiled so wide she had to laugh.

She worked her key into the lock, jiggling it the way she always had to before it clicked open. By the time she realized what her dismal apartment looked like compared to his top-floor suite, he was striding through her living room. *Today's humiliation will never end.*

"You live with someone," he announced, though it looked as though Cole had folded and put away his blankets, so the couch just looked like a couch.

"How did you know?" The question was unnecessary. He probably caught Cole's lingering scent.

Moments later, Cortez confirmed that. "I can smell him. Is it the man you were meant to meet up with last night?"

"I wasn't meeting anyone," she said. "And besides, my personal life is just that. Personal. I don't appreciate you sending your driver to follow me yesterday." Was that something he did with all his employees? Perhaps he was just really paranoid. Hell, he should be.

As if to prove her point, he glanced around like there were secrets hidden in the cracks of her walls. Then he shrugged as if her complaint were immaterial. "Is this your room?" He pointed to a closed door to the left. Without waiting for her answer, he barged through it.

"Hey!" She rushed after him.

Her room consisted of a bed with no frame, two cast-off, mismatched dressers, and a couple posters of her favorite singers. Other than that, it was pretty bare. She tried not to blush at that. Not everyone could live like a sultan at the top of a tower.

"Snoop much?" she chided.

"You like Kenny Raymond?" he inquired lightly, glancing at the poster of the singer sitting on a stool with his trademark acoustic guitar.

"No, I hate his music," she joked sardonically.

Cortez shot her a crooked smile. "I've piqued your ire again."

"I don't typically bring guys home for a tour of my ratty apartment."

"I suppose the man you live with wouldn't like me here."

He wouldn't, but not for the reasons Cortez was thinking. She crossed her arms in answer.

His expression only grew mischievous as he strolled toward her at a slow, predatory pace. Some latent instinct to run had her dropping her arms as if readying to do just that, but she was caught in his gaze like a cobra to its tamer. And suddenly it was like he had command over every nerve in her body. Her heart revved as though in answer to his carnivorous gaze. Her nipples puckered behind the thin fabric of her shirt as if mutinously angling to draw his attention lower.

It worked, and his expression grew intense, hungry.

Breaths coming faster now, she tried to tamp down her response, but even as she did, a soft thrumming fired in her loins.

Reaching her, his hands lightly clasped her hips, and she allowed him to maneuver her against the wall before he kicked the door closed with a decisive thud.

She met his heavy-lidded gaze. A nervous lump in her throat made her audibly swallow. He followed the movement along her throat with the backs of his fingers, his eyes now rapped to where her pulse beat strongest. She shivered, goosebumps sprouting over her increasingly sensitive skin.

More to distract herself than a need for an explanation, she asked, "Why did you have me followed?"

"Because I was curious about you," he muttered, still eyeing her throat. But then his warm, whiskey eyes met hers. "And, if you couldn't tell, I'm attracted to you." His right hand slipped to the small of her back, his body now deliciously flush against hers.

She let out a shaky laugh. "Oh, really? I didn't get that. You should try being more obvious—" Her sarcastic words died in her throat as his lips claimed hers in a sizzling kiss that had her heart seizing and her body throbbing.

His strong hand traveled southward, reminding her that she still had no panties, making it too easy for him to breach the tail of her shirt and grab her backside. But she didn't mind one bit.

She sighed into his mouth, turning her head to deepen the kiss. His tongue delved to lick the seam of her lips and she shuddered with an almost violent need. It blasted through her like a bullet through warm butter.

More.

Just when she hooked her arms around his neck to draw him closer, she heard the front door open and close.

Eyes flashing open, she broke the kiss in alarm. Did Cortez's driver decide he'd rather not wait for him out in the car? She didn't know how she felt about having *one* unmanageable vampire under her roof, let alone two.

Cortez pulled back and snapped, "Who's that?" his tone dropping a shade darker. He was suddenly all rigid muscle, tense and suspicious as if she'd managed to lure him into a trap...or he was about to take out his purported competition.

Her blood pressure spiked. What time was it? Eight in the morning? Nine? Cole's shift had ended at least an hour ago. In fact, she was surprised he wasn't home already.

"Shit!" she whispered, then went into panic mode. "You have to hide."

Cortez arched a dubious brow. "Are you serious?"

"Yes. Please. The closet!"

Letting go of her, he crossed his arms, indicating without words that was not an option. Briefly she debated trying to shove his massive, supernaturally strong form toward her closet, but quickly crossed that off as a pointless pursuit. Unless he allowed it, he wouldn't budge.

"Fine. Just, uh, stay in here, then. Okay?"

Turning away from his deepening frown, she gripped the door handle.

"Is he your husband?"

She whirled around, appalled by the very notion. "Ew! NO! Gross!"

Surprised by her emphatic response, he blinked, losing some of the tension in his jaw.

"Just please do me a favor and stay here," she repeated.

He gave a curt nod, but didn't look happy.

CHAPTER 11

"Morning," Cole said brightly as he looted the refrigerator. Behind her, she discreetly closed her bedroom door with a soft click—*nothing to see here*—and then crossed toward the kitchen. Though he'd worked a double, he seemed wired, which wasn't unusual coming off the night shift. Another hour or two and he'd be passed out like the dead.

She just hoped Cortez would be willing to stay hidden that long. He didn't seem like the patient type, and she seriously doubted she'd be able to convince him to sneak out her bedroom window like they were two teens trying not to get caught by her parents.

Seconds later, any hope of a clean getaway was dashed.

Cole snapped upright, all tense, and glared at something over her right shoulder. His features twisted into an expression she'd never before seen him use. He looked wary yet ready to fight.

She didn't have to turn around to know Cortez had unabashedly emerged from her room. Pivoting, she shot him a you-are-dead glare and hoped he could taste her disapproval in the air.

Yet Cortez seemed oddly...upbeat? "Ah, you are siblings." The way he said it held no mark of doubt.

She and Cole shared a look. No one ever guessed that they were related. They looked nothing alike, a result of differing fathers, and maybe something more with regard to her siren lineage. Whereas her skin was pale, his was tan. Her hair was dark, long, and ruler-straight, his was blond and cropped short. Her frame was small yet curvy, Cole was packed with tight muscles. Aside from the color of their eyes, piercing blue, they could not look more unalike if one of them was a different species entirely.

Which, technically, she was.

But that didn't stop them from loving each other like full-blood relations, and being fiercely protective of the another. Which was why Cole's first question wasn't *Who is this man you've brought home, dear sis?*

He met her gaze head on and asked, "Did you pick up that butterscotch I wanted?"

She smiled and shook her head. "No, they were out." It was their secret code to let the other know all was well...or if she'd said yes, danger, danger, we need to bounce because all hell was about to break loose. They'd invented the codeword as children and used it when they were misbehaving and wanted to hide whatever deed they were engaging in from their mother. Then later when they were hustling and one of them thought their situation might get too heated. Everyone who knew them thought they just weirdly loved butterscotch. It was a great cipher that no one had ever decoded.

No one until Cortez.

He shifted his weight. "Did you just ask her if I was a threat?"

Her jaw dropped. Cole's narrowed eyes slanted at her in betrayal. "You told him about *butterscotch*?"

"No! Of course not. " she hissed. "But you just confirmed it."

How had Cortez deciphered their code, in only seconds? Had he jumped to that conclusion because it was the first question out of Cole's mouth instead of the obvious: *Why is this strange man exiting your room at ten in the morning? While you're dressed like that, I might add.*

She realized with a blush how damning her outfit was.

"You dummy," she said. "It was the first thing out of your mouth. Of course he's going to figure it out." She turned on Cortez next. "And you, you ass, were supposed to stay in the room."

"And miss out on this enchanting meeting? I'm Cortez by the way." He held out his hand to Cole.

Cole eyed him with suspicion and palpable aggression. She had never brought a strange man home before. Cole must be reeling. But to his credit, and with an encouraging nod from her—the last thing she needed was for Cortez to take insult—he stepped forward and shook Cortez's hand, offering his name in return.

A hard glance at her from Cole said they were going to talk about this later in private. She expected nothing less. Any guy she dated had to meet his approval or he'd do everything in his power to run him off. And if that didn't work, he'd been known to utilize seedier tactics, such as getting the guy drunk to see if he could push other women on him...a test of loyalty. Which pissed her off to no end—not a lot of guys passed his tests.

By the way he was eyeing Cortez, Cole was already organizing a plan of action. When they were alone, she'd tell him he needn't bother. Cortez wasn't the long term relationship type. In fact, she didn't really understand why he'd bothered chasing after her at all. Most guys would chalk up her leaving as the perfect end to a one night stand. Yet here he was, invading her space and introducing himself to her brother.

Her musings were interrupted when she noticed the men were still clasping hands...hard. Cole's arm bulged as though displaying his strength through his grip. Cortez wore a pleasant smile, just a slight curling to his lips, though there was something strangely menacing about it as they silently glared at one another. Cole didn't realize he was engaged in a standoff with a powerful vampire, and since her uninformed brother wasn't suffering from a crushed hand, Cortez was holding himself in check.

She cleared her throat. "Uh, Cortez was just leaving." She placed her hands on their forearms to snap them out of their mini tournament. At her touch, their arms drop.

"*We* were just leaving," Cortez corrected, glancing at her as if daring her to protest. "We just stopped by to gather some of Naia clothes. She'll be staying with me for the time being."

"Who the hell is this guy?" Cole spoke directly to her, growing angry now. "What is he talking about?"

She was still struggling to pick her jaw up off the floor. He wanted her to stay with him? For how long?

"Would you excuse us," her brother said to Cortez, employing a lot more civility than she knew he was feeling at the moment. "I need to speak with my sister alone."

Cortez inclined his head. "Of course, take your time. Naia, I'll just pick out a few items for you, shall I?" He turned and headed back into her room, not waiting for her response.

"What the hell is going on?" Cole snapped the

moment he thought Cortez was out of earshot. "Who is this asshole?"

"He's the owner of Ever Nights and a vampire, so he can probably hear every word you're saying." *Hint, hint. Shut up, baby bro.*

Cole's brows shot up. "You're involved with a vampire?" His tone was so sharp, she almost flinched. Not only were vampires impulsive, volatile, and animalistic to the point of being dangerous, but they were completely immune to her siren powers, same as Cole. In theory, that was a good thing, but if any of them figured out what she could do, it wasn't a far stretch to assume they'd want to use her to their benefit.

Dante hadn't figured it out yet, but patrons always spent more money on the nights she sang. In theory, if she really cranked up her powers, she could have humans eating dog shit out of her hands...that is, if she could control it. As of yet, all she'd ever accomplished was turning them into mindless ravaging beasts with nothing but rutting on their minds. Which was why it was so important for her to sing on a regular basis, so she didn't get to that dangerous point.

Had Cortez figured out what she was? She didn't think so. She hadn't so much as spoken in a sing-song voice in front of him. And considering he didn't even intend to give her a job, there could be only one other reason he'd want her to come stay with him, and it wasn't for her intellectual conversation.

She tried to muster up some indignation over that, but she could still feel his heated kiss on her lips, and her body sang with thwarted desire. Secretly, she was disappointed that Cole's arrival had interrupted them. It seemed she already craved what Cortez's had to offer.

"My god, what happened to your finger?" She reached for Cole's left hand. He yanked it away, and tried to conceal the splint behind his back.

"It's fine. I slipped...and bashed my pinky in a cupboard."

"You *slipped*?" she said dubiously. "*And then* bashed it in a cupboard?"

"I mean a door. I smashed it in a door...after I slipped." He screwed up his face, knowing she wasn't buying it. Cole had always been an atrocious liar. With a resigned sigh, he admitted, "The twins paid a visit."

Her voice lowered to just above a whisper. "They did that to you?"

He shrugged as if it wasn't a big deal, though the clenching of his jaw said he was putting on a brave face for her. She'd heard the horror stories. The twins started with fingers, then moved on to larger limbs... then started cutting things off.

She hugged him so tight it was a surprise he didn't complain. With her face next to his ear, she lowered her voice to a level only he would hear. "I've got a plan. I can't tell you what it is, but trust me. I'm going to fix this. Don't worry. But just in case, pack a bag and be ready to jet at any moment."

He nodded and hugged her back. "I really fucked up this time, didn't I, sis?"

CHAPTER 12

That seven grand was back on the table!

Though it was insane for Cortez to invite her to stay with him after only knowing her a day, and she was seriously contemplating his motives, she wasn't about to balk at her good fortune. He was essentially giving a stranger an all-access pass into his life without even batting an eyelash. Was she better at seducing a man's heart and mind than she'd thought, or was he just a sucker?

Still, he must have been surprised when she smiled up at him sweetly and chirped, "I'm ready." But if he was, he didn't show it. Maybe he was just used to everyone falling over themselves to do his bidding. Evident by the way Donovan had carried her suitcase to the car without having been asked while stifling any comment he might have had about its shabby, thrift-store appearance. It was filled with most of the clothes she owned. So, essentially, it was light enough for a large bird to carry away.

One last time, Cole protested her "plan" in angry whispers even though he didn't exactly know what it was. She cringed at the notions that must be swimming around in his head. The words *sugar daddy* and *mistress* came to mind. And he kept slanting threatening glances at Cortez, like at any moment he might produce a knife to slit the man's throat on principle.

Cortez noticed of course, and when they thought she wasn't looking, the two seemed to be having a silent conversation with their eyes. Although she wasn't fluent in glare, she imagined it went something like Cole: *Hurt her and I'll kill you. Cortez: You could try.*

A softer glance at her said Cole was filled with shame. Not towards her, but directed at himself. It wasn't difficult to understand why. He thought because of *his* debt, she'd had to sell herself to the highest bidder. She reminded herself she couldn't tell him the truth. Not yet. Dante had made it clear if she gave anyone the details of her mission, including her brother, the money was forfeit. There'd been a darker threat mingled in there somewhere that she didn't want to think about.

As Cortez waited for her by the door, she did the only thing she could to dispel Cole's worry. She lied, informing him that she was getting a job at Ever Nights and it was very magnanimous of Cortez to offer all his employees free room and board while they trained. Cole looked dubious, but did seem to lose some of his tension. Cortez, who'd heard the whole thing, hadn't corrected her. He let the lie go. For that she was grateful...

But perhaps she could coerce him into offering her a job. Then it wouldn't be so much of a lie. Right?

In the backseat of the sedan, Cortez rested his chin on his hand, his elbow on the armrest and his fingers curled over his lips as he studied her with a laser focus. The knowing glint in his gaze made her want to squirm, but if he'd suspected her of any deception, he'd have said or done something by now, killed her maybe, and probably Cole too. Though he had a reputation for being a decent boss, cross any vampire and you were bound to meet the grave. She was dancing on the edge. She had a brief moment of doubt over her undercover abilities, but it was too late to back out now. Cole was counting on her.

Donovan pulled up to the club's front entrance. Cortez unfolded his big form onto the sidewalk and then held out his hand to help her out of the car. With her short, makeshift outfit, she managed to accidentally flash on the way out.

The guttural sound that rumbled up from the base of his lungs had her lower parts clenching.

Blushing deeply, she feigned aloofness. "So, what happens now?"

His tone was still roughened. "As much as I'd like to keep you dressed like this for me, I suppose you will need some appropriate clothes. I saw what you packed and it wasn't enough to last the week."

A week? Was that how long he planned to keep her? Would it be enough time to get what she needed for Dante?

"But first, you must be hungry," he went on. Victor should still be serving breakfast. If not, I'll have him make you something special. Would you like to change into your own clothes before you meet everyone?"

"Yes, and a shower would be nice. I could have taken one at my place, but you swept me out of there so fast."

His grin was playful. "I didn't want to give your brother the chance to figure out a way to get rid of me."

She blinked up at him, stunned because that was probably exactly what Cole was doing.

"He had that look about him," Cortez promptly

explained. "He's protective of you, that was clear." There was admiration and approval in his tone.

Back in his room, she quickly showered in the guest bathroom and then dressed in a pair of her favorite, if not holey, jeans and a floral patterned blouse that had seen better days.

In a slow manner, he appraised her, but didn't comment on the state of her clothes so she wasn't sure if he found them modern chic or gauche. The jeans might be frayed in places, but they still hugged her ass like paint to finely molded plaster. She was proud of her figure. To show him, she turned and wiggled her hips.

He hissed in a breath. "Stunning creature."

He was across the room in moments, scooping her up over his shoulder. She squeaked with surprise. Another few strides and they were in his bedroom, and she bounced with a giggle as he tossed her lightly on the mattress. He followed her down, his mouth covering her lips while his hands affixed to her backside. She laughed through his kisses, his passion heady, drugging. Then from behind, he slipped his fingers between the apex of her thighs and a sledgehammer of desire killed her mirth, replacing it with unadulterated lust.

Breakfast forgotten, she rolled him to his back and straddled him, slipping her blouse off. He reached to unhook her bra and then his hot hands cupped her breasts, kneading. With her still astride him, he leaned up to suck one taut peak into this mouth. Her head fell back on a moan, his tongue teasing her into a dizzy, needy state.

She tugged his shirt up. He broke away and shrugged it off. Glorious muscle danced and rippled under her fingertips.

With blinding speed, he flipped her to her back,

yanked her jeans and panties off, his own jeans followed, then covered her naked flesh with his. They groaned in unison as he slipped inside her.

"This is how I should have woken you up," he rumbled next to her ear. Then he began to move with almost feline grace, his body rocking into hers with the most delicious friction.

On a husky growl, he kissed her, his tongue delving out in time with his thrusts. Her body shuddered with pleasure, her nails digging grooves into his back. Breaking the kiss, he groaned as his tempo increased, making her gasp. Sparks of ecstasy flashed behind her eyes.

My god the way he moves! Each thrust pulled a cry from her. The sound only seemed to encourage him. Supine muscles danced under his flesh. Bolts of pleasure crashed over her, her blood burning with an overdose of bliss. The room fell away, the bed fell away, and suddenly there was only the two of them. Him and her. A universe unto themselves where passion was their sun, pleasure their moon, and everything else in between writhed to the beat of nirvana.

He seemed as lost as her, focused solely on his carnal invasion.

Hands on her hips, he yanked her down on his cock while at the same time thrusting into her. A sublime scream rippled from her. His hips found a wild rhythm, blissfully slamming home.

As if unable to hold it back, he snarled, burying his face in her neck, though he didn't bite her. At the moment, she wouldn't complain if he did—later she'd admonish herself for that passing thought—the carnal, rich sound tipped her over the edge, and she screamed her orgasm to the ceiling.

Riding the edge of his own release, his pace increased, his dick hammering her so hard her breasts bounced to the rhythm. Another orgasm shot through her. Once more, she screamed, her back arching as pleasure whipped her. He muttered something incoherent before letting out a rough, guttural sound, his body shuddering from the strength of his release.

When the excitement ebbed, his weight came down on her, and he cradled her in his. His hot breaths fanned out over her skin. Then he rolled them so that she was half on top of him and held her to his chest so that her head was just under his chin. Her upper body shifted along with the heavy rise and fall of his chest. Sighing, her fingers painted a path over his sculpted flesh. In response his muscles contracted pleasantly.

"You definitely should have woken me up like that this morning," she teased.

"Noted," he replied, all seriousness. "We must get moving if you're going to catch breakfast."

"Strangely, I'm suddenly only hungry for one thing, and it isn't food." To punctuate her words, she playfully nipped his flesh.

His head lifted so he could gaze down at her. A grin stretched his lips. "Do not tempt me. I'm seriously debating locking you in here with me for the rest of the day."

That sounded like a decent plan. Her stomach growled, and his grin slipped slightly.

"Up, you temptress. You and I both have things to do today."

We have things to do?

She knew he wasn't talking about her inevitable snooping, but as he extracted himself from under her to sit on the edge of the bed and stab his legs into his pants, reality splashed her with a heavy dose of guilt. She *did* have things to do, deceitful things that had nothing to do with laughing and joking and making love all day. Her mission had taken an unlikely turn.

She hadn't expected to attract the attention of Cortez in such a salacious way. Hadn't meant to, but here she was. Worse, she *liked* him. Maybe a little too much for having only known him a day. Mind-exploding sex had expedited her attraction. She'd never had a casual fling before, and she feared her heart wasn't ready for one now.

Box it up, Naia. Can't go getting attached. She was going to have to steel her heart if she was going to emerge from this unscathed.

"Aside from breakfast, what is it you think I have to do today?" she asked. If he discovered what her real purpose here was, would he believe it had been her plan all along to seduce him, merely to get close? Would he see it as the worst kind of betrayal?

I know I would.

In answer, he only gave a grin. That simple curl to his lips sent a zap to her chest, and another wave of guilt surfaced. A wild thought followed. She could confess and try to salvage...whatever this was between them. But what if he took it badly? What if he never wanted to see her again? As it was, she was only guaranteed a week with him. If she confessed now, she'd have lost Cortez *and* the money. With Cole's dire situation, she couldn't risk it.

Her fascination with Cortez would fade, she told herself, just as his interest in her was bound to. She didn't believe for a second that he didn't have other women up here on the regular. A man with his appetite for sex would need to.

Suppressing a sigh, she watched him walk into his closet wearing only his jeans, those gorgeous muscles like living steel under lickable flesh. When he was no longer in sight, she slammed back onto the mattress and rubbed her hands down her face. *How am I going to get through this?*

CHAPTER 13

After her second shower of the day, she dressed once more, and Cortez brought her down to the employee lounge. It was set up like a small restaurant with booths along one wall and tables scattered throughout. A buffet of breakfast foods lined one wall next to a set of swinging double doors, beyond which she could hear pots and pans banging and food sizzling over heat.

The scent of syrup and bacon and other delicious treats invaded her tummy, making it growl.

Despite the late morning hour, there were still a few stragglers filling their bellies. At her and Cortez's entrance, everyone paused what they were doing to glance at them. Just like the previous night, their curious stares were mostly on her. Again she felt like an exhibit on display.

"Everyone, this is Naia. She'll be staying with me for the time being." Then, too fast for her to remember, he listed off his employee's names, and in turn they waved at her. The only one that stuck was the Surfer Guy's: Ryder.

He was sitting at a booth with a slender red-head,

a mug of dark liquid in his hand and a nearly empty plate of eggs in front of his companion. After the introductions, Ryder offered Naia a jovial thumbs up. "I gave him your message, word for word," he said proudly. She had no doubt he'd done it with that same exuberant grin on his face, too.

"Thanks," she replied sarcastically, then muttered to Cortez. "Sorry about that."

His only response was a wry twist to his lips. Then he addressed a beautiful, petite female in the corner booth sitting with two others who were equally attractive. "Kenzi, after Naia eats she'll need new clothing. Take her wherever she wants to go, but have her back before five."

Five? Did he think it was going to take all day to shop for clothing? With the paltry tip money still in her purse from her last shift at Dante's, it would be a miracle if it took more than an hour, and that was if she was picky. Normally she would put most of her tips into the grocery budget for her and Cole, but unless Cortez was going to make her pay for breakfast, it seemed she'd have a little extra to spend.

Kenzi smiled brightly at Cortez.

As if she'd asked a question, Cortez lifted a negligent hand. "Fine. Take the Mercedes. You know where to find the keys."

Kenzi squealed with delight.

Naia cleared her throat. "I don't need an escort. And it will probably only take me an hour or two to pick up some outfits. Maybe a new pair of shoes." She could drop off Goldie's boots on the way, and explain about the unexpected death of her dress. *Totally not my fault!*

"You should get more than that," Cortez suggested. "Kenzi will help. She knows what I like and has access to my expense account."

The fact that burning jealousy was the first wave of emotion told her in some basic, primal way, she was already way too attached to the enigmatic man next to her. Later she'd try to figure out how that could possibly have had happened so quickly.

Once the spike of irrational, seething, envy-filled hatred toward Kenzi abated, she registered the second part of his statement. His expense account? *He* was paying for her clothes?

Her riotous emotions played a game of tug-of-war. Sure she could use a couple extra outfits, but how was his buying them any different than a stack of cash on the nightstand? To be fair, she'd misunderstood the reasoning for that cash. Still, this was more than just replacing a single dress. He was sending her out with a personal shopper and a six-hour time frame. How much was he expecting her to buy? Part of her rationalized that it was too much for her to accept while the other, destitute part got on her knees to beg, *please. It's just some new clothes. Please, please, please.*

A couple of the other employee's mouths dropped, apparently working it out too. She got the impression that Cortez's generous offer was not normal. Nor was his introducing strange women during breakfast.

Done dropping jaws, Cortez turned to leave.

"Wait a second," she said, shaking her head.

Before the door closed behind him, he waved at her with the back of his hand, "Have fun." Then he was gone and she was alone in a room full of strangers still staring at her like she'd just planted a flag in the ground and declared *this shall now be mine.*

Her gaze landed on Kenzi's kind smile.

"We eat buffet style," Kenzi said, pointing to the table packed with breakfast foods. "Grab a plate and come sit." She patted the space next to her.

If her tummy wasn't gnawing for that sweet syrupy

scent, she might have run after Cortez to refuse his offer, but a moment alone with his employees so soon was too much to pass up. If there was anyone who knew if something untoward was going on around here, it would be one of them. She had better make nice, quick.

After packing a plate with a couple slices of French toast and syrup and, oh, yes, butter, she sidled in next to Kenzi.

"Hi, I'm Kenzi." There was an upbeat, bubbly quality to Kenzi that showed in every aspect of her character, from her bright hazel eyes, to her engaging smile, and pleasant voice. It made Naia feel instantly welcome.

"Naia," she said, offering her name in return. She noticed a couple people at the other table still slanting glances at her. "I have to ask. Is my presence here unusual?"

The question caused Kenzi to glance around as well, catching the curious gazes of others. Then she smiled at Naia. "I guess you are a bit of a surprise. We haven't seen the boss man take a liking to someone so quickly. They want to know what your secret is. You have no idea how many women...and men....have tried to bag that man. I heard you even got invited to the roof."

"Is that weird?"

"Weird? No. A miracle...?" At Naia's expression, she explained, "Except when there's a special request to use that space, it's practically his private sanctuary."

Naia didn't know what to say. The place was off limits to employees but she was dragged up there on day one? More evidence that he'd never hire her? Why was Cortez giving her this special treatment? A queasy feeling had her pushing her plate away. Since she'd met him, he'd made her feel like a princess swept up in her very own fairytale...but fairytales were nothing but the fanciful musings of the lonely and broken hearted. They never came true. Something else was going on here. The question was what.

After breakfast, Kenzi led her to a neatly kept office. The nameplate read *Cortez*. This was his office.

Kenzi crossed to a key cabinet, but found it locked. "Damn, I forgot. I have to go sign out the Mercedes so I can get the key. Be right back."

When she was gone, Naia jumped into action, checking a nearby filing cabinet first. There were mostly employee dossiers. She checked a few, but found them to be standard, and replaced them exactly as they were. Next, she took the seat behind his desk to snoop through his drawers. The top one held office supplies: pens, pencils, paper clips, a stapler. All very normal. The second drawer was slightly larger and held three binders. She pulled one out and flipped through it, finding a lineup of shows scheduled six months out and a roster of potential stand-ins. The second binder seemed to be his personal itinerary. Everything for the next week had been crossed out. The third binder was an employee schedule with notes for requested time off.

In a third drawer, she found a list of vendors along with pricing, quantities, and delivery dates that didn't mean much to her, but she scanned it closer for any evidence of drug smuggling or something equally abhorrent. As if he'd be careless enough to mark in big red letters: Illegal Sex Trafficking Enterprise, Thursdays at Five.

The sounds of someone approaching had her stuffing the binders back in place and closing the doors. She had just extracted herself from behind the desk when Kenzi waltzed in.

"Ready for some fun?" She crossed to unlock the

key cabinet and then claim the key labeled Mercedes, Red. There was more than one Mercedes listed.

Kenzi led her to an underground parking lot toward a cherry red convertible with the top down. Kenzi's excitement was palpable as she slid into the driver's seat. A twist of the key, and the engine purred to life.

Slipping into the passenger seat, Naia just managed to lock her seatbelt in place as the car lurched out of the parking space. The tires squealed before the engine punched them forward. Kenzi let out a whoop as she jetted up a wide ramp. Daylight blinded Naia for a moment before her eyes adjusted. They were already pulling onto the road. She noticed her nails were digging into her seat's armrest.

Kenzi laughed, slowing the car to a reasonable speed. "Sorry. I couldn't resist. This baby has some serious kick. So, tell me about yourself, Naia, and how you managed to snag the attention of the most eligible bachelor in all the land."

Naia was still trying to get her heart rate back to normal. "I was just looking for a job." She caught the sight of Ever Nights in the side mirror, shrinking into the distance as they sped away.

Kenzi gave her a pitying look. "A job, huh? Too bad. What were you looking to do?"

"Sing. Why too bad?"

"Because Cortez doesn't hire anyone he's, uh, dated. Though I don't suppose that's the right word for it. At least not where he's concerned. So you're a singer. What do you sing?"

"A mix of things. Pop mostly. You're saying he won't ever hire me now that we've...started seeing each other?" He'd said as much, though Naia was still holding on to a shred of hope.

"Sorry," Kenzi replied as if she were apologizing

for a taking the last dinner roll instead of delivering a devastating blow. Naia hadn't been counting on a job merely for financial purposes, though that would have been a bonus. She *needed* to sing. Already she was feeling the itch, like a tickle in her throat. At least her energy wasn't waning. Yet. There was time for her to figure something out while she was undercover. Maybe she could slip away and grab a shift at Dante's.

"He doesn't date anyone that works for him either," Kenzi went on. "I don't know why. I think he's been burned once too many. Or maybe he doesn't want to be seen as playing favorites. A lot of girls go after guys like him to climb the ladder, you know. Or for notoriety. Or money." It was barely perceptible, but there was a tinge of something in her voice. A question? An accusation?

"I can imagine," Naia said. She wasn't about to try and convince Kenzi of her innocence on those matters. It wasn't like she'd *intended* to finagle herself into Cortez's bed. In fact, now that she thought about it, the situation she'd gotten herself into would likely work against her. With everyone's attention on the new girl who'd managed to beguile the boss, her task would be that much harder. But the fact remained, she was using him.

"So how do you like working at Ever Nights?" she asked Kenzi, partly to change the subject, partly to gather information.

"It's great." The statement rang of truth. "I coordinate most of the dances. Burlesque," she clarified. "I'm on salary, so the tips are icing, and everything's fair, split equally among the performers and stagehands, so there's no animosity like some other places."

Naia had seen so many fights over cash on stage that hadn't been fully collected before the next act started. Girls on their knees scrambling for change.

"Plus we get full control over what we do. Some girls bare it all while others just perform beautiful dances. There's no obligation to service the fanged clients, but the pay is so tempting, so most of us do."

Naia blinked. *Service?*

"Plus, *yowza*! Am I right? You ever been on the dinner menu?" She faux fanned herself. "It's not exactly a chore, is it? It'll make a girl crack a marble, if you know what I mean."

She didn't, but she thought she might want to.

Kenzi pulled onto a highway with a wicked grin. "Now, hold onto your seat." The car went turbo and momentarily sucked the oxygen out of Naia's lungs. It took her a couple of breaths to get used to the frantic airflow, but when she did, she let out a jubilant laugh. Kenzi's smile turned devilish and she switched to another gear.

As they flew down the highway at what had to be dangerous speeds, Kenzi's words inspired images of Cortez taking her neck with his succulent mouth as he did sinful things to her body. She was still mulling the idea over twenty minutes later when they pulled up to *La Parfait*, a top of the line boutique. The place had valet parking for crying out loud!

"Surely there's a less expensive place we could go."

Kenzi handed the keys to an attendant. "Of course there is, but why on Earth would we go anywhere else. Everything we need is right here. Come, let's get high on shopping."

CHAPTER 14

Kenzi was getting high; Naia was getting ill.

While Kenzi combed through clothing racks in search of her next fix, Naia was mentally tallying the cost of everything she'd piled in their personal dressing room. The room was comfortably sized, lined with mirrors, soft lighting, and a mix of floral scents that were probably pumped in like a drug, lulling clients into a relaxed state of consumerism. There was also a small seating area with a luxurious cabriole sofa.

They'd been handed flutes of Champagne while they'd settled in. An attendant had already asked her twice if she needed a refill. When Kenzi returned with yet another armful of overpriced clothing, she took the attendant up on that offer, jostling her empty glass for emphasis.

From her stack, Kenzi pulled out a blue sheath dress and held it up to her own body, twisting to admire it in the mirror. "Have you found anything you like?"

Naia glanced at her much smaller selection. Two blouses, a pair of form hugging jeans, and one replacement dress, intended for Goldie, all of which cost more than three months' rent.

Kenzi gazed at her choices in mock horror. "Is that all you're getting?"

Naia shrugged. "These prices are too much."

"Blasphemy!" Kenzi went back to rifling through her stash, yanking free a deep maroon wrap dress. "Try this on."

Naia sighed, doing as requested. They'd been here three hours already, and no matter what protest she might come out with, Kenzi's fun would not be denied.

Once the dress was on, Kenzi was at the ready with a pair of flesh colored heels and a sparkling diamond-studded necklace that Naia hoped was costume jewelry. She peeked at the price tag and her stomach did a flip. Not costume jewelry!

She went to take it off, but Kenzi pulled her in front of a mirror, and they both gaped.

"That's the one." At Naia's look, she clarified, "That's the dress you'll wear tonight."

Apparently Cortez had something planned later. He'd called her *brand new cell phone*, which he'd had couriered over, to let her know he had a surprise in store. He wouldn't say what, just that he was taking her somewhere. Then he'd told her Cole had received a similar phone, and the number was programmed into hers.

After hanging up in a daze, she'd tried the number to verify. Cole answered with a brusque, "I hope you know what you're doing with this guy." It seemed a strange vampire dropping off a cellphone so he could "keep in touch with his sister" had been somewhat alarming to her baby brother.

She didn't admit to Cole that she might very well be in over her head. New clothes and now a personal cell? That seemed a little much for a quick fling. Or maybe Cortez was just so wealthy that the extravagance didn't even register.

Then Cole lectured her about guys, gifts, and expectations. He finished with, "I just don't want to see you get hurt."

She wasn't the one with a broken finger. She could manage a little heartache if it saved Cole from more run-ins with the twins. All he'd managed was to set her resolve. Then he finished with a muttered, "They say he can read minds."

"Who says?"

"Goldie. A few of the others have heard it suggested as well."

"That's ridiculous." If he could read minds, he would have kicked her out of his club the day they met. Instead, he'd invited her back, seduced her, and screwed her ever-loving brains out.

"I don't know if it's true or not," Cole continued. "Just please be careful."

"I will." Reading minds? *Right. And I can harness the power of unicorn farts.*

His interaction with Kenzi at breakfast suddenly cut into her thoughts. Kenzi hadn't said a word, but Cortez had known what she'd wanted. That could be attributed to working closely together for many years. Naia often knew what Cole was thinking before he spoke his thoughts aloud. It inevitably happened when people got close to one another.

As she put the phone away, Kenzi hollered for the attendant. "Wrap it all up and put it in the car." She indicated the dress Naia still wore. "And ring this up, too. She'll be wearing it out."

With that, a small army descended on the dressing room, packing up their purchases and cashing them out in a matter of minutes. Naia almost fainted at the total, though most of the damage was done by Kenzi.

She nearly sighed in relief when it was over and they were tucked back in the convertible. Until Kenzi slammed the gearshift into drive and exclaimed, "Now to the salon!"

That was when the real torture began by a team of beauticians lead by a flamboyant man named Javier with a Spanish accent who probably went through more lipstick and hair products than all the ladies at Dante's combined. According to him, she needed a cut and color, because her "ends were split" and her look "needed updating." (His hair was swept up in an exaggerated style from a bygone era.) He snippily informed her that her nails were "wrecked" and she clearly "gnawed on them constantly." (His nails were black, long, and sharpened like daggers.) Oh, and her unibrow—she did NOT have a unibrow—required "mowing." He gleefully tweezed her like a sadist until the pain made her want to *slap a bitch*.

The pedicure was nice, until the pedicurist decided the pads of her feet needed a heavy duty scrubbing, and then it was death by tickle.

By the time they were finished with her, she was exhausted. Conversely, Kenzi, who'd undergone the same treatment, seemed relaxed. Amazing.

"Wasn't that wonderful," she sighed.

Yeah, if by wonderful she meant emotionally scarring.

Javier swept into the room. "You are like shiny new pennies, no? My little chicklings, I give birth to you and send you off into the world. Go now, fly free. Break the hearts, yeah?"

Kenzi and Javier air-kissed each other's cheeks. "You're the best, Javier," Kenzi said.

"I know this." He gave a theatrical wave of his hand. "When are you going to send my boyfriend to me? Tell him I give him special massage." He winked.

"You know Cortez doesn't swing that way."

"He would when I get done with him. Once you go Spanish, your other preferences vanish."

Naia laughed at that. Now that he wasn't having her tortured, she could actually find his colorful personality endearing. She wasn't at all surprised that he had a crush on Cortez. The man was sex on a stick, after all.

An understatement, she found twenty minutes later when Kenzi pulled up to the small fenced-off airstrip just outside of town. Several yards away, Cortez stood under the spinning blades of a black helicopter, the rushing air barely disturbing his dark tailored suit, but brushed through his hair like a lover's caress. So regal and confident, he looked in all regards like the world would do well to bow down at his feet.

The second she stepped from the vehicle, his enigmatic amber eyes lit on her. Arms that had been folded stiffly around the wide expanse of his chest deflated to his sides. Yet tension made his posture rigid. Her heart jumped with excitement at seeing him. *Stupid heart.*

Though she knew she was imagining it, their time apart seemed like years rather than hours; their pending reunion sizzling with something unnamed. Starting toward them, his ardent eyes took in her formfitting dress and brown wavy locks enhanced by golden highlights.

Smiling, she spun, giving him a three-sixty view. His gaze consumed her like the sun ate through darkness, thoroughly and without compromise. She swallowed, losing her breath under his avid stare.

She didn't even realize she was moving toward him till they met halfway. At the way he was drinking her in, she figured he would have swept her up for a heated kiss, at the very least, draw her close, but he did neither.

Instead, he reached out to balance the weight of the dazzling necklace on his fingers—the one she'd forgotten to remove! To Kenzi, he said, "Diamonds. I assume I'm now bankrupt?"

Naia gasped in horror. "Oh, no! I forgot to take this off before leaving the store." Clumsily, her fingers fumbled with the clasp. "It's not real though, right? Surely it's glass or cubic zirconia." Wishful thinking— the price tag suggested otherwise.

As she slid the piece off, Kenzi replied, "*La Parfait* doesn't deal in cheap knockoffs. And stop teasing her, Cortez. It was like pulling teeth to get her to buy anything at all."

Cortez's brow arched as he studied her anew.

"I only needed a couple of things," she said, feeling weird for defending her *lack* of spending his money. She held the necklace out to Kenzi. "Here. Return it."

Ignoring her, Kenzi went on. "I had to pretend the large pile of clothing I'd gathered was for me!"

Naia's jaw dropped, her hand still cupping the necklace. "All that was for me!? You're insane. There had to be more than thirty outfits there. I'm only going to be here for a week!"

Cortez chimed in. "A week, huh? Is that all I'm allotted? Better make the best of it then." He jerked his head at the helicopter. "Kenzi, fit what you can in the storage compartment."

While Naia stood speechless and stunned, Kenzi pulled out select bags and boxes of clothing, transferring them to the copter. Cortez took the too-expensive necklace from her grip, stepped behind her, and fastened it once more around her neck. Then he leaned in to whisper in her ear. "These few hours apart, I'd convinced myself I'd fabricated your beauty. Yet here you are, proving me wrong."

His tone was decadent and rich, sin and chocolate,

and the compliment pleased her more than it should. She couldn't prevent a tiny smile, even as their implied transport wrapped a thread of terror around her lungs. "We're not flying in that, are we?"

He hooked his arms around her like she'd wanted him to do in the first place, but now it seemed more like he was doing it to prevent her from bolting, which she had to admit was a real possibility.

"Have you ever been in a helicopter?"

She shook her head, though, as it seemed, that was about to change. "Is it necessary? Can't we drive to wherever we're going?"

"I want to get there before the sun sets."

She glanced at the sun, well into its evening dive. How far did they have to travel that he worried about the losing the light? When she asked, he just smiled and told her it was a surprise, then he guided her into the helicopter, bags of clothes, *her clothes*, apparently loaded.

Glancing at Kenzi out the window, Naia placed her hand on the window in a silent plea for help. Kenzi merely waved goodbye before driving off, the tires kicking up a plume of dust that was quickly carried away by the helicopter's manufactured air current.

"Your heart is racing." Cortez grabbed her by the hand.

She abandoned the window to gaze at him, knowing her eyes had to be as wide as saucers.

"Don't worry. You are perfectly safe." He claimed that with total confidence, even as he'd had to yell it over the ruckus made by the metal beast that had them trapped. "Mendez is the best pilot within twenty miles!" When that didn't seem to ease her, he added, "I've got you."

The beast lurched heavenward. A caustic squeal escaped her, and her heart hammered even harder.

After a moment of unnatural elevation that made her head swim, she realized she was digging her nails into Cortez's hand.

He made no complaint.

With effort, she eased her death-grip. Then she glanced out the window, watching with amazement as the earth glided away. It was frightening, but also beautiful, with all the treetops fanning out like a choppy green sea, the roads splitting off like the workings of a spider's web, the cars, growing more distant and appearing more like ants than two-ton vehicles. When the first sign of clouds dashed past her window, her terror had waned, morphing into gaping awe.

The whole time, Cortez watched her with a pleased expression, as though enjoying her reactions. She tried to tamp down her building excitement—where was he taking her?—but when she saw the edge of the ocean, she practically bounced in her seat with restlessness, unable to tear her gaze away. Though they lived but miles from the water, she'd only ever seen it from a distance, and never from this high up.

As that great wide expanse grew even closer, she gave Cortez a quizzical look. Was he taking her somewhere that overlooked the Pacific? He responded with a clandestine smile, giving nothing away.

Finally, when they were practically over the ocean, the view more than she could process, they began their descent. Terror returned as she watched the earth careening back at them, unable to look away lest her inattention caused them to crash—an irrational notion, but undeniable all the same.

The landing was much softer than she'd anticipated. At the sound of the blades above slowing, she let out a long, relieved breath. Then an electrified thrill skittered through her—the ocean was just yards away! She wanted to race for that sandy beach to see if it was as soft as it looked. Would the water be warm or cool?

"You've never been to see the ocean," Cortez guessed.

Was it that obvious?

"Vacations are a luxury," she said by way of explanation, practically yanking off her seatbelt. He wasted no time in shoving the door open and helping her out. But instead of leading her to the ocean, they headed in the opposite direction.

When she tugged on his arm, he said, "We have a little way to drive yet. Ten minutes at most."

Glancing back at the ocean, forlorn, she wanted to protest, but Cortez hustled her into the back of a stretch SUV. Inside was like a compact club complete with neon-blue lighting that lit up a fully stocked bar that took up the entire length of the interior's left side.

At her look, he said, "Ostentatious, I know. It was all I could get on short notice."

"You think I'm balking?"

He chuckled. "No, I think you're thinking it's too much."

She was, but she didn't satisfy him with her confirmation, though he could probably read it on her face.

"Just wait till you see what's next," he muttered under his breath.

Opposite the bar was a soft, cushioned bench that wrapped smoothly along the back of the vehicle, allowing for six or more people to sit comfortably. The whole area was partitioned off from the driver, who apparently already knew where they were going since Cortez hadn't offered directions.

Once they were settled, they headed onto a long stretch of road with the impressive sea to their left. Sandy beaches taunted her. "Can't we stop for a minute? Just so I can put my feet in?"

He handed her a flute of Champagne, which she took out of politeness, but she didn't intend to drink. "I promise you'll have plenty of time to experience the ocean where we're going."

"And where is that?"

A secretive grin played around his lips. He didn't respond.

Compared to the flight, the drive was reasonably short, but just as frustrating. Seeing the ocean, and not being able to touch it was driving her nuts. So close, and yet so far.

Finally, when the anticipation seemed all but too much, they pulled up to a marina where several large boats were docked. "Which one is yours?"

His eyes lit with amusement at her assumption, and he pointed to a particularly exotic looking, three tiered yacht that towered above the rest.

She chuckled. "Of course."

CHAPTER 15

The illustrious yacht gleamed brighter than a thousand diamond necklaces could ever aspire to, and in comparison she felt common and inferior, even in her posh new digs. The luxury-steeped interior was a world—no, a universe—away from anything she'd ever known.

She was an imposter in this affluent realm reserved for society's elite. At any moment, she expected to be quietly shoulder-tapped and asked to leave.

She squashed the self-mutilating thought, determined to enjoy this impromptu outing. When would she ever be aboard another yacht?

Probably never.

The salon boasted tall clear windows that offered a panoramic view. The sun was still above the horizon, but the tone of the sky was already deepening.

She turned to Cortez with a smile. "Look at that, we made it before sunset."

"And we only risked your having a heart attack."

She waved that away. "Only a little one. Soooo worth it!"

The grin he gave her caused her heart to flutter.

Knowing he could hear it, she looked away.

Along the dock, several deckhands were untying the boat. Another flourish of excitement bombarded her. They were actually going to set sail! Her first-ever sea voyage.

A worrying thought had her stepping back from the windows. "What if I get seasick?"

"It's not as common as you might think. And we have seasickness medication if you need it."

She allowed that to ease her, and her good mood returned full force.

A stewardess entered, greeting them with a pleasing smile. "Hello, I'm Emily, and I'll be attending you throughout our journey. Let me know if there's anything you need. Can I get you something to drink before we shove off?"

Cortez answered. "We'll take dinner and drinks on the upper deck."

"Yes, sir." Emily scurried off to fulfill the order.

On the topmost deck all Naia could do was stare, agog. A three-sixty view of the surrounding ocean and land rendered her speechless. With the sun slipping toward the horizon, soft orange gilded along the ocean's surface. At the center of the deck was a charming table dressed in fine white linens and decorated by a large arrangement of roses in a bulbous crystal vase. The table was accented by coral colored shells which matched the napkins, tied neatly by gold ribbons. Several pale candles within glass spheres had been lit in anticipation of their arrival.

Not for the first time, Naia felt overwhelmed, her throat going dry. This whole day had been too much all at once. The gifts, the chopper, the boat? It was like she'd been dropped into a divergent dimension. How was she supposed to act? What was she supposed to say? What did he expect?

When the stewardess returned with a selection of wine and top shelf liquor, she accepted a glass of white wine and took a long pull, mulling over this drastic change in her life.

Cortez selected a vodka with lime wedges and mint. "I'm unsure of your reaction to all this," he declared without preamble. "You seem pensive all of a sudden." He sipped his drink and claimed a seat on the bench that stretched around the outer rim of the deck, using the railing as an armrest.

Here was the evidence that Cortez couldn't read minds, not that she ever believed he could. The notion was ridiculous. But if he could, he wouldn't be curious about how she was feeling. She waited for the stewardess to leave before responding. "What do you want from me?"

He blinked as though the question threw him. He glanced at the pristine table set as if for a banquet then slid his gaze over the sea. Almost to himself, he muttered, "I guess this is all a bit much to take in, isn't it?" Louder he admitted, "I only want your company."

"Hew-hockey."

"Pardon?"

"We both know you want a lot more than that."

His expression remained stony, but he didn't deny the implication.

"I'm not complaining," she told him. "It's just, I'm curious. Why me?"

Something fleeting passed over his face, but the expression was too swift to decipher. "Why not you?"

"Do you know what I thought the first night we met?"

"I really don't," he said leaning forward to rest his elbows on his knees, his tone was layered with meaning.

His words tripped her up for a second, and a

strange thought fluttered to the forefront. She shook it away. "I remember thinking if you tossed your room keys into the crowd at Ever Nights you'd have the world's largest all-female wrestling match on your hands. I'm talking nails out, hair pulling, teeth-meets-flesh brawl."

His lips twitched.

"You can't deny the crook of your finger would have women lining up."

"Your point?"

"Well, you're here with *me*..." She left the *duh* off the end of her statement.

"You think I should want someone else?"

Her mind screamed in instant rejection of the notion, but she answered honestly. "I think you're slumming."

He leaned back and turned his head to watch the sun, going quiet for so long she thought she'd ruined the evening he'd so meticulously planned.

Finally he faced her, pinning her with his gaze. "You know what I thought when we first met?"

She shook her head, swallowed, heart in throat.

"I thought *finally*."

Her jaw dropped. His gaze overflowed with all that was packed in that simple word, declarations that practically thickened the air around them. Somehow he'd manage to say everything and nothing at all.

Finally? *Finally?* What did that even mean?

As he lifted his hand to crook a finger at her, his lips curling with a teasing twist, she realized she was damn well going to find out.

CHAPTER 16

After dinner, they watched the sun sweep gold and orange hues over the ocean as though weaving a liquid banner to the heavens. The colors danced, seemingly chaotic, yet with the most beautiful coordination. So touched by the display, Naia had to choke back tears brought on by the ethereal scene.

Or maybe she was still overwhelmed by the man at her side.

Sometime during dinner, the boat had set off. Behind them, the land was now fading to a dim silhouette peppered by building lights and streetlamps that were still visible from this distance. As the sun made its crescendo past the horizon, Cortez silently pulled her into his lap, wrapping one arm around her waist while he held his drink in the other. Together they gazed out at the sea. He seemed so at ease with their closeness. So content. She was getting there.

Throughout her meal, she had fretted over his earlier statement. *Finally.* She couldn't figure it out, having already dismissed her initial assumption: that he'd finally met the woman of his dreams?

As if.

Though she'd probably never be rolling in dough like Cortez, she was generally happy with her life, liked herself as a person, and tried to be as honest as one could reasonably be these days—current assignment excluded. But most of all, she wasn't stupid! Love at first sight was a fabricated myth, invented by story tellers and romantics.

But what else could he have meant by that laden word? If he was slumming, as she'd accused, he was playing the cruelest joke of all. Messing with her heart. Setting her up to be crushed.

But if he wasn't....?

A ringing erupted from her purse. Oh that's right, she had a cell phone now. And the only person who would be calling it was...

She jumped up and scrambled for her phone. "Cole?" Her voice was a little high-pitched from anxiety. Was he in trouble?

"Naia? Hi, how are you doing?" Cole replied cooly.

"I'm fine," she answered hastily. "Is something wrong?"

"No. I'm about to head into work and I just wanted to check in."

Translation: he was checking up on her. She didn't blame him. Relief made her release a tenuous breath. Giving Cortez an I'm-going-to-take-this-in-private gesture, she climbed down to the lower deck and made her way to the railing at the front of the ship.

Secret mission aside, she and Cole were always one-hundred percent honest with each other— current assignment excluded—so she didn't think twice about opening up to him. "You won't believe where I am!"

"Well I hope it's more interesting than behind the bar at the Pussy Pit."

She scowled. "You know I hate when you call it that."

"I know. Why do you think I do it?"

"You're such an ass." She hissed. "Well, prepare to be sick with envy, mister crude-face, because I am sailing the ocean blue...on a friggin' yacht! And I tried caviar for the first time! Which is disgusting by the way." Cortez had laughed after her eyes had bulged and she'd asked if it had gone rotten. When he told her it was fresh, premium stuff, she couldn't help thinking *rich people were nuts to eat this crud!* The guy who popularized fish eggs as a delicacy was either a marketing genius or the greatest prankster of all time. Probably laughed his ass off all the way to his grave.

There was a moment of silence on the other end of the line. "Are you with *that guy*?" Cole asked evenly.

"His name's Cortez."

"Should I be worried?" His tone was soft now. Concerned.

She bit her lip. "No." *Probably.*

"Why did that sound like a question?"

She tried again with more conviction. "You have nothing to worry about."

"Let me talk to him."

It was her turn to be silent now. No way in hell was she letting the two of them chat.

"Naia, *I want to talk to him.*"

"Why?"

Before she received an answer, movement caught her eye. Cortez was suddenly next to her, holding out his palm for the phone. A little stunned that she hadn't heard his approach, she passed it over before even realizing what she was doing.

Phone to his ear, free hand in his pocket, he was all business. "Hello Cole, this is Cortez." There was also a level of amusement that seemed to ripple off him.

Cole was saying something on the other end, but she couldn't make it out.

"I promise to take very good care of her," Cortez replied, smirking at her.

Naia rolled her eyes.

There was another pause, and then Cortez blinked wide. At her questioning look, he covered the receiver to mouth, "He's threatening me."

Humiliation and horror flooded her. "Give me the phone," she demanded, reaching for it.

Cortez dodged her attempt. "That's very graphic," he countered to Cole. "The whole foot? Or just the tip?"

"Cole!" she yelled, still grappling for the phone. "Stop it, right now!"

"Well, you could try," Cortez said, as though responding to another barrage of threats. To avoid her grasping clutches, he turned away and headed back up to the top deck, the receiver glued to his ear while he commented, "Uh-huh. Oh really?"

She followed close behind, but he continued to elude her desperate reach.

"While that sounds like fun, let me assure you, your sister is in good hands. She is the most precious of treasures. I will let nothing happen to her."

She abandoned her caper at his touching words. Cole seemed to have been rendered silent as well, giving Cortez the opportunity for a brisk, "Have yourself a good night," before hanging up and shocking the hell out of her by remarking, "I like him."

She let out a clipped laughed, still reeling at his words. *Precious treasure?* Surely he said that for Cole's benefit.

Grabbing her by the hand, Cortez guided her back to the bench where they had been seated earlier. She stared at their intertwining fingers, the heat of his palm seeping into hers. She was suddenly breathless.

He took a seat, facing her as she stood before him in a daze. Their positions had him looking up at her while she gazed down, but there was a challenge on his end. Like he was daring her to take the lead.

Mentally shaking away her nerves, she eased onto his lap, knees on either side of him. The action caused her dress to inch high up her thighs, but she didn't care. It put them closer, which at the moment was imperative. Her arms circled his neck; his strong hands folded her waist, the delicious warmth of his palms now penetrating the fabric of her dress.

Emboldened, she dipped her head. Their lips met, soft at first, just a feather touch before turning harder, and then desperate, crushing, the shackles of lust slicing free. Nothing mattered but getting as close to him as possible. Kissing him harder.

His palms slipped over the contours of her sides, trailing a hot path that she could feel through the fabric of her dress. His hands found their way under the hem. He growled when he found her pantyless. She hadn't been permitted to try any on in the store, so what she'd bought was still packed away. His expression turned carnal as he cupped her sex. Her hips rocked as if to tease his grip, her body already primed. A thick finger penetrated, pulling a gasp from her. Her head fell back as he played her, giving her exactly what she needed. Arms wrapped around him, she held on as her body rolled to ease him in and out of her, the friction building. He added another finger, and she moaned.

"You are breathtaking," he muttered. "Come for me."

She was close. Her body undulated against him, on the verge of euphoria. Her brain tapped out as her hips worked feverously, seeking more friction. "Cortez, I...oh, God, so good."

Sparks dotted her vision as she came. Delirious and panting, she slumped over him.

The sound of a zipper had her coming back into her body, desperate for more. Widening her legs, she eased down on his engorged cock. He pumped his hips, making her moan. He gripped her hips, doing it again.

"Yes," she cried. The pleasure was sharp, agonizing, addictive. As he fed his cock into her, she lowered herself, drawing him deeper. The pressure was exquisite. They settled on a slow, but delirious rhythm. She met his gaze as their bodies toiled.

With a hand at the back of her neck, he lowered her forehead to his, their breaths mingling as he drove into her. She felt him swell within her, and arched her back to ride him harder. Hands still on her hips, he helped guide her up and down, both of them groaning with each thrash of her hips.

"Fuck," he muttered. "I can't hold out. *Ugn!*" As his seed spilled, she cried out to the sky, pure heaven ripping through her.

After a few more drinks, he declared he hadn't had enough and took her with his mouth, driving her once more to orgasm. Then they stared at the stars in companionable silence before he led her to their stateroom and she returned the favor.

In her mind, this night was magical, a fantasy made real.

Then she woke up to a heartbreaking sight.

CHAPTER 17

Cortez wasn't next to her in the bed where he'd been when she'd fallen asleep, though it was still dark out. She checked the clock. It was well past midnight. She called out for him, a bit disoriented. There was no reply. At first she thought she'd had too much Champagne, then realized it was the boat rocking, not her brain.

Easing out of bed, she found one of his shirts and slipped it on. It covered her adequately. Then she peeked into the small, but softly-lit hallway. No sign of the crew. Most of them must be asleep but for those needed to guide the ship.

She padded toward the stairs that led to the salon, which was lit only by the moon, as was the figure on the deck she spied through the panoramic windows. She squinted to see better. A shirtless Cortez with his arms around Emily, the stewardess. His fangs were in her neck and she was moaning as though she was loving every second.

The unexpected sight made Naia gasp out loud.

Cortez lifted his whiskey eyes, meeting her gaze. Unable to look away, she watched as he nuzzled the woman's flesh, his fangs seated. Her stomach and heart took turns flipping around, making her nauseous and dizzy and desperate for an escape.

Pushing past the shock, she turned and raced back down the stairs to their compartment. There she paced, anxiety and adrenaline going to war.

He needed to feed, she reasoned. He's a vampire. That's what they did. He wasn't getting nourishment from her. She'd taken that off the table, so of course he had to go elsewhere. It didn't mean anything. It shouldn't mean anything.

So why was she so staggered?

Moments later, he entered the room, eyeing her warily as if expecting her wrath. She wanted to give him so much wrath.

Not my place. Not my right.

Breathe in. Breathe out. "Good snack?" she inquired, her tone light but with an underlying bitchy quality that she hadn't meant to weave in.

"Did it bother you to see? I'd hoped to do it while you slept."

"It's fine." She said. "Totally fine. I didn't mean to intrude." What was the correct response here? Was she supposed to be angry? Hurt? Or glad that he'd fed so that he didn't inadvertently bite her when they made love. Her feelings were mixed. And she was battling a primal urge to go back up there and throw Emily overboard.

"Tell me what's going through your mind," he said. "I need to know."

"It's fine. Totally fine."

"You said that. Somehow I don't believe it."

She plopped down on the edge of the mattress. "I'm not sure what I'm feeling. I never expected to... I mean, I've never seen that happening before. It's always been done behind closed doors at Dante's. But then there it was. Right in my face. And it was *you*. And we've only known each other a couple days, so it shouldn't be a big deal. But I...well...I'm rambling." She took in a heavy breath, let it out slowly. "I should have realized you'd be feeding while we're together. I have no right to be upset."

"So it did upset you?"

She shrugged.

He sat next to her. "Out of respect for your wishes, I must feed from others while we're together. But I would much rather take from you, should you allow it."

"I..." Could she let him feed from her? Somehow she knew him taking her blood would be outrageously intimate, more so than sex alone, and could even spur a connection that she might not be able to fathom. Already she could see herself falling for him without that arcane link. Even if she'd only be with him for a week, she'd need to actively shield her heart, which had no business getting involved in this caper. After he was through with her and they separated, she'd need to be able to walk away intact. A clean break. Giving him her blood could only bring them closer....

But the thought of him drinking from Emily again, or any of the other crew, cut something dark and possessive through her. Could she give him a taste of her essence while remaining detached? "I...I have to think about it."

He nodded. "If it's not something you can condone, I completely understand. I don't want you to feel pressured."

He meant it, she realized. Feeding for him was a way of life. A non-issue. Equated to her own dependence on food.

Only, *her* food didn't moan in ecstasy when she took a bite.

CHAPTER 18

In a brief instant she knew she was dreaming, then the notion slipped away like a puff of steam cooling in the air. She was a misty rain on a warm summer's day, lethargically riding the wind, basking in the ebb and flow of an air current and letting it rock her like a mother to her child.

A mountain came into view several hundred yards below.

The moment her logical mind registered her unnatural flight, she began to descend. She fought the Earth's pull, but it was as if an invisible tether took hold, yanking and tugging with jerky effort. It was like a strange, ghostly tug of war. One moment she thought she gained altitude, only to slip lower in the sky.

She gave up and prepared for a rough landing. Instead, the tether eased up, drawing her in slowly as if her acquiescence cooled its fervor.

Soon she hovered just feet above a rough gravelly road. A good distance ahead, the surface of the road transformed to a smooth inky black, as though pavers had given up halfway through and left the job incomplete.

Movement ahead drew her attention. On the glittering asphalt, she spotted the dark figure of a man walking away. She recognized the breadth of those shoulders, the confidence in that gait.

She called his name, but Cortez kept going, his pace leisurely. She started down the path at a brisk pace, hurrying to catch him, but somehow he seemed to gain distance. She increased her speed. The space between them stretched and for a moment her task seemed impossible. She called for him again, but an ornery gust drew her words away.

She doubled her efforts. Closing the distance was taking all her concentration, but inch by inch, she gained ground. Why would he not stop? Could he not hear her? It was imperative that she reach him soon, for if she didn't...well, something terrible was about to happen, she could feel it in her bones. And there was something she needed to tell him before it was too late, though she couldn't quite remember what that was.

Like a rubber band snapping, the distance between them evaporated. As she was ready to plant her hand on his shoulder, he whirled around to face her so fast, it startled her. Then she got her first good look at him and stepped back in terror. Gazing up at a face twisted with rage, she realized she'd been chasing Dante, not Cortez.

But that couldn't be. She'd been so sure it had been Cortez.

Abruptly Dante's features rippled and morphed, and Cortez was staring down at her, mouth curled at the edges, tight and unkind.

Yet Dante wasn't gone. Like a shadowed apparition, he stepped out from behind Cortez, that same cold smirk in place.

She glanced at the man she'd put her trust in.

"Cortez?" Her muttered plea echoed as though off the jagged face of a cavern wall before growing heavy and falling to the ground.

Cortez didn't respond, only broadened that hated smile, displaying his sharp fangs.

Icy betrayal chilled her heart, freezing it in her chest. She knew without knowing that they meant her harm. If she didn't get away, they'd—

With a slathering roar, Dante grabbed her by the throat. She struggled to scream, but her voice was sucked back into her lungs as if by a black hole opening up in the pit of her stomach.

Somehow she managed to turn away from the two men. They clamored and clawed at her, trying to trap her. The ground beneath her softened and muddied, grit turning slick and watery. She began to sink, first to her ankles, then her knees, and finally past her waist and up to her neck. She couldn't breathe. Her vision dimmed. Black sludge inched its way up her straining chin, over her lips, stealing her vision and cresting her forehead. Was she about to die? Black emptiness all around. She was stuck, unable to move, losing air. Suffocating.

With all her might she thrashed, but a thousand tentacles leashed her limbs, staying her struggles, dragging her down, down, down to a dark bottomless pit.

Suddenly the world tilted on its axis.

With a jarring gasp, she awoke, clutching the mattress as if to keep herself from tumbling off. The nightmare drifting at the edge of her subconscious and the slow rocking of the ship registered.

She drew in a long breath and let it out slowly, the dream-induced adrenaline gradually evaporating.

Once again she found herself alone in bed. Shrugging off the last clinging unease of her nightmare, she swung her feet over the edge of the mattress and padded to the bathroom, contemplating the dream. It wasn't all that difficult to decipher. She was under a lot of pressure, was projecting her fears onto Cortez. Who she really feared was Dante—and the twins; Dante, because she had no idea of his true intentions in sending her to spy on Cortez, or what he'll do if she comes back empty-handed. The twins, for obvious reasons. Cole was her life. Her blood. They had a couple weeks to pay up, or they'd have to jet.

At this point full payment seemed unlikely. That seven grand wouldn't be enough, though it might buy them time. That is, if she ever got it. Not only did Cortez appear to be a nice enough fellow—a sexy, drop-dead-gorgeous fellow—but even if he was up to something nefarious at his club, it would be a miracle for her to discover what it was here on this boat. Dante probably hadn't expected him to take such a liking to her. To spirit her away from the club, inadvertently keeping her from doing her job. Dante would expect her to be at Ever Nights even now, snooping for clues like a trained bloodhound.

Would Dante understand her restrictions? Give her more time? Or send another in her place? Goodbye seven grand.

Or maybe not. She had the attention of the most important man at Ever Nights. If she was charming enough, maybe he would let down his guard and confide in her.

Her stomach twisted painfully at her conniving thoughts. She wasn't made for this kind of devious work. But for Cole, she would do what she must.

In the bathroom, a small package rested on the counter, topped by a folded note that read *this is all you should need to wear today. ~Cortez.*

In the box was an olive green woven bikini and black sheer wrap. The bikini bottoms were little more than a patch of fabric and some string. She smiled. He was going to lose his shit when he saw her in this. After a quick shower, she put it on and examined herself in the mirror. The wrap was small, but managed to give her a semblance of modesty. Still, the outfit was sexy as hell. Quickly she ran her fingers through her hair and let it fall to one side, damp with a slight curl.

Satisfied with her appearance, she exited the room. On her way through the ship, she passed Emily, who was all smiles and bright greetings, as though she hadn't practically been wrapped around Cortez like creeping vine the night before.

At Naia's scowl, the woman frowned, seemingly confused, but said nothing.

Putting the woman from her mind, Naia sauntered out to the lower deck where a table was set for breakfast. At its center there was a coffee thermos, milk on ice, and orange juice, along with some delicious looking pastries.

Several yards away from where the boat was docked there was a sandy beach sandwiched between a crystalline surf and a jungle-like forest that crept up a low sloping mountain. Farther down the coastline, she saw what looked like a bungalow on stilts over the ocean attached to a boardwalk that stretched like a long leash as though to keep the building from drifting away. With the morning light glinting off the ocean, the scene was picturesque.

Cortez stood at the end of the deck facing away from her, arms braced on the ship's railing as he peered out over calm waves that licked the pearly sand. He wore only tropical grey and black board shorts, his naked back packed with tight muscles that moved with feline grace.

Her body instantly reacted, her skin tightening with want, but she stood motionless. Awkward. After what she'd witnessed last night, she wasn't sure how to act now. After she'd fallen back to sleep, had he returned to Emily for another bite to eat?

As if finally sensing her, he turned and then stunned her by flashing a movie-star smile. "So odd... I'm not used to how quiet you are. It's refreshing."

"Huh?"

"And my god, you look..." As he slowly took in her appearance, his eyes darkened with desire. "...gorgeous."

Every nerve ending in her body fired as though he'd caressed each one in turn. Emboldened by his hungry gaze, she pivoted for him, untying and tossing away her wrap as she did.

He sucked in a breath. "I owe Kenzi a *serious* thank you."

"She may need a raise," Naia agreed with a nod.

"I was going to let you have breakfast first, but now I can't resist." He crossed the deck, his imposing form closing in, his glittering eyes spelling out dark promises. Reaching her, he took her mouth with his firm lips. The kiss was hot and hard and carnal. Too soon he pulled away, and she didn't recognize the twinkle in his eyes till it was too late.

"Wait, No!"

He hefted her over his shoulder and raced across the deck, spring-boarding off the railing and flinging them both into the ocean. She was suddenly engulfed by cool, salty water. Bubbles tickled their way along her flesh, seeking an escape from the dense liquid. Kicking her feet, she breached the surface, both shocked and amused by his playful behavior.

He roared with laughter at her expression.

"You ass!" she splashed him and he ducked from the spray, laughing even harder.

Then he dove, swimming toward her. She giggle/

screamed, trying to swim away, but he caught her ankle and lightly tugged to halt her progress. Her head whipped around, trying to find him under the surface. He easily circled her as she helplessly bobbed and...

"Ow!"

Did he just...?

When he surfaced right next to her, she smacked his chest. "You pinched me!"

He chuckled and hooked his arm around her waist, drawing her close. "You sure that wasn't a fish? They like to nip on succulent treats."

She pursed her lips, going for a censuring expression, but her smile broke through.

"Don't worry I will protect you from those sleazy lecherous ocean dwellers," he said, acting as though he were glancing around.

"Ow!" Another pinch to her rear.

"Uh, oh! They've broken through my defenses!"

"Ow! Stop it!" She laughed and wrapped her legs around her attacker.

"Ah, ha! A little goose and you cling to me like a barnacle. Note taken."

"You'd better knock it off."

"Or what?"

"Or this barnacle might have to defend herself."

"Oh? And what are you going to do about it?"

She dipped her head and nipped the flesh at his shoulder in warning.

His tone roughened. "I think I might like your retaliation."

"Ow!" She attempted to climb him to get away from his pinching fingers, but he didn't stop till she was in hysterics.

With her head tossed back on a laugh, she caught several of the deckhands and stewardesses casting curious glances over the side of the ship, incredulous. She instantly grew self-conscious, tempering her mirth. Cortez sensed the change in her and cut a glare up at the crew. Heads vanished like gophers in a hole.

"Are the women you date always such a spectacle?"

Wry grin. "You won't have to worry about it for long."

Because she wouldn't be with him much longer?

"Let's get some food in you and then I'll show you around the island, hmm?"

"Oh! We're on an island?" She studied the land and beach once more, only now noticing how it curved drastically, disappearing behind itself. How cool! How exotic. She'd never been to an island before.

And yet....

It might have been subconscious, but she suddenly felt the natural isolation of the place.

"I bought it a few years back."

She gaped. "Shut up!"

"Pardon?"

"You own your own island?"

Curt nod.

"That is baller!"

"Thanks?"

Excitement permeated over her body. "How big is it?"

He gave another crooked grin. "Big enough."

"Can we go on the beach? Can we hike up the hill? Can we go over there?" she pointed toward the bungalow over the ocean.

"We can stay there one night if you like."

One night? "How long are we staying?"

"As long as you like."

She bit her lip. This could turn out to be the perfect place to weasel information out of him. She stifled a cringe and pushed down a surge of guilt. He'd brought her to paradise, and she was planning to thank him with a backstabbing.

He cocked his head at her strained expression. "Everything alright?"

She forced a smile. "Just hungry I think."

"Then let's get you fed."

Breakfast was practically an affair. Stewardesses' paraded plates past, offering everything from quail eggs to buttered toast.

Cortez didn't join in on the meal...because he was still full from last night?

When Emily made a final pass, Naia stiffened, avoiding eye contact. Cortez must have noticed, because as soon as she left, he informed her he'd wiped Emily's memories of last night. He'd said it as though he might inform her he'd changed a light bulb. "She'll have no memory of our encounter."

"Um. Okay." So Naia's glare this morning would have meant nothing to the woman.

"I figured that would please you."

It does! Immensely. "Why would you think that?" She wasn't his girlfriend. She was a fling. He owed her nothing.

"It has been my experience that human women are just as territorial as vampires."

She shrugged and glanced down at her food. "You think I see you as mine?" She feigned a laugh. "So soon?"

At length, he repeated in a droll voice, "It has been my experience that human women are just as territorial as vampires." After a moment, he added, "But I *will* need to feed from time to time." There were layers to the statement: would she prefer him to go elsewhere during their time together, or would she be willing to provide for him?

She gulped, her meal growing heavy in her stomach. He'd posed the question last night in so many words, but she hadn't given a definitive answer. She'd figured by morning she'd be over her flash of jealousy, but still the thought of him drinking Emily maddened her like she never expected. "I-I could maybe, you know, try it?" That couldn't have sounded more uncertain. She tried again. "Yes. We can give it a shot."

His grin was all wolf, his tone dipping. "I could make you crave it."

Lord almighty, she believed him.

CHAPTER 19

The island was a marvel, a jewel, a paradise for her and her sexier-than-life-itself vampire lover.

After stepping from the boardwalk, Naia sprinted for the beach, feeling the sand in her toes and the surf on her legs for the very first time. It pushed against her shins, racing for shore, and pulled on her calves as it receded. Like a lung taking liquid breaths. Amazing!

For the next few minutes, Cortez watched patiently as she delighted in the waves, a little smile playing on his lips, but he didn't join her, content to let her frolic and splash and dive and play with each marvelous wave. There were no words for the sensation of the frothy bubbles on her skin, the sand in her toes, and the warm, salty sea, like a living beast forever restless, always toiling.

When she finally did return to him, she was high from her experience. She ticked off a list of objectives. "First things first, it's imperative that we make a sand castle." She and Cole had always dreamed of doing so. Being so close to the ocean, yet never seeing it, had worn on them. "We need to go surfing. And snorkel! Do you have diving equipment? Oh, I want to fish!"

Cortez's lips turned up in a half-grin. "Plenty of time for all that."

Oh really? He must plan to stay here more than a day or two.

While he showed her the bungalow, a small, cozy one-room hut with a canopy bed, the yacht's crew unloaded their luggage. Then together they all hiked inland to a larger, more modern home, filled with all the amenities you could ever want. The kitchen was a masterpiece of innovation, the living room was one step down from a movie theatre, the bathrooms were ripped straight from a spa, and the bedroom, well, that was the only thing that seemed to have been downplayed. The master offered a bed, a dresser, some closet space and not much else. Their things were already being put away by the crew.

While he continued the tour, she couldn't help but contemplate the weird looks she continued to receive from the crew. Why did all his employees look at her like they would a six-headed moose?

When Cortez took her out back to show her a large heated pool, she asked, "Why do all of your employees look at me so funny? Like I have an extra nose or something." Like a freak, she didn't add.

"They wonder about you," he admitted. "That's all."

"What do you mean?" She needed more than that. Were they suspicious? Was her undercover act even more transparent than she'd initially suspected?

"I brought you here to get away from all that. We won't have any distractions here."

No distractions? He could focus all his attention on the *undercover agent*. She was playing a dangerous game with two vampires, a pair of homicidal twins, and her brother's life. A little unwanted attention from some of Cortez's acquaintances was just icing on a very unappetizing cake.

Thinking of her brother made her want to check on him. "Do you mind if I make a call?"

"Not at all. I'll go inside and double check our stocks."

When he was gone, she retrieved her phone from her purse and selected Cole's number.

There was a few seconds of fumbling, then Cole came on the line. "I'll never get used to this thing. Everyone is laughing at me now because I had it on vibrate and your call made me jump like a chick that just spotted a mouse."

Naia laughed. "So you're at work?"

"Yeah, I was called in a bit early. Tiffany and one of the bouncers didn't show up, so Boomer's scrambling to fill spots. Too bad you're not here. You might have landed your first all-night gig." Tiffany was one of The Pit's main dancers, performing several times a night.

"Is she sick?"

"Not sure. Anyway, how are you?"

Excitement rolled out of her. "Cole, I'm on a freaking private island. I repeat, a *private* island."

Cole went silent for a moment. "I don't like you being alone with this guy."

"I know. But he's really nice, I promise." She lowered her voice. "And this could be our ticket to getting the twins off your back." She wouldn't dare explain more. "You just have to trust me."

"This whole situation sucks. I don't want this for you."

"It's not like this is a hardship, Cole."

"Ugh! Say no more!"

She laughed. "Get back to work, you lazy ass."

"When will you be home?"

"I'm not sure. A few days, I think."

"Hm. I have the apartment all to myself," he

mused.

Oh the trouble he was plotting. "No ragers. And no hookers."

Snort. "A good sister would let me invite hookers over for a rager whenever I wanted."

"I guess I'm a terrible sister, then."

"The worst. If you want to stop me, I guess you'll just have to come home then, won't you?"

She laughed. "Just stay safe, Cole."

"You too," he said solemnly. "You too."

Hanging up, she gazed out over the sea. The sun was low in the sky, hinting at setting behind the horizon. The day had gone so quickly. Sparkles danced on the ocean as saltwater perfumed the air. Clouds were sparse, suggesting a clear night ahead, and the yacht was...being untied from the dock!?

Its engines roared to life, deckhands, like little ants from this distance, swiftly undoing the last of the ropes before hopping back onto the boat.

"What are they doing?" She watched in horror as the yacht drifted out toward the ocean. "What are you doing!" she yelled, her tone slightly shrill, but she was too far up the hill for them to hear. She didn't need an answer anyway. They were leaving!

Rushing inside, she hollered for Cortez.

After a frantic moment, he burst into the room, looking tense and ready to hurt whatever it was that offended her. "What's wrong?"

"The boat. They're leaving us." *We'll be stranded!* the siren in her screeched in horror.

He heaved out a breath, his shoulders relaxing. "Yes. I told them to go."

She stilled, her mind scrambling for calm. "Oh. Oh.....okay. Um. Why?"

"So we could be alone."

"Alone?" A siren. Alone. On an island. Wasn't that

every siren's nightmare?

As if sensing her unease, he assured her, "I can call them back whenever I like."

Relief sang through her. She tried not to let her sigh sound too mitigated.

"You didn't change your mind, did you?"

She cocked her head. "Change my mind?"

"About me feeding from you."

"Oh." Heat skated into her cheeks. He thought her distress was from the prospect of giving him her blood. She was nervous about it, sure, but now that she'd decided to go through with it, she was oddly eager. Couldn't stop imagining it.

He didn't know her fear stemmed from something more primitive. Something she didn't even fully understand. To a true siren, isolation was akin to torture. Being a half-blood, with no humans to draw energy from, given enough time, she could die.

But that was an extreme scenario. Very unlikely. Surely he wouldn't keep her here for any disastrous length of time, and a couple days alone with Cortez was all too tempting. In fact, it sounded like a dream.

One she definitely planned to experience.

CHAPTER 20

Naia glanced around the elegant, yet understated room, hardly believing her current circumstances. She was on a private island, sharing time with an enigmatic, gloriously handsome vampire who should frighten her. Instead he warmed her blood like melting chocolate over an open flame. A simple look from him had her blushing, which normally was a rarity considering she worked at a seedy club where catcalls were practically a form of currency. A simple touch from him had her skin heating up, her body willing to burn for him. A simple kiss nearly drove her out of her mind. She couldn't get enough. No, he didn't frighten her. He excited her.

Conversely, when they weren't making love, he behaved more gentlemanly than she ever expected from a man like him, making sure she was comfortable and fed and content. If one was doomed to be stranded on a deserted island, it might as well be this one. The ocean was a crystalline feast for the eyes, the fine sandy beach was like stepping through powdered silk. The estate was a state-of-the-art, automated, nerd-paradise with a remote for just about everything from the window shades, accent lighting, and surround sound music in whichever room one desired. And the kitchens—count them, two! One on the first level, and one on the third—were stocked with enough goods for a doomsday scenario.

She changed into one of the dresses Kenzi (his assistant of sorts) had purchased for her, a sexy stretchy number that wrapped her torso like it was to be worn by her. The bottom flowed freely, allowing a side slit to reveal her right leg as she headed down to the cozy den where he now sat, a drink in his hand and a glass of wine waiting for her on the sidebar.

Cortez watched her intensely as she crossed to pick up her glass. She thrilled at the thought that he might jump her on the spot. She could tell he wanted to, but he restrained himself.

She suspected just barely.

The room was dimly lit, giving the ambiance of something that resembled warm candlelight. A sofa and coffee table took up the middle of the room. Cortez sat in one of the two armchairs, looking regal and edible at the same time. Soft music fluttered through unseen speakers, and a set of French doors were opened, allowing in the exquisite ocean breeze. The sun had dipped behind that watery expanse, leaving behind only traces of its dying light, not yet night, but no longer day. "This place is beautiful," she sighed.

"I think so too." He was still watching her, seemingly content in doing so.

The silence suddenly made her feel a little awkward. She was alone with a man she'd known for all of two days. A man she'd been hired to spy on, or rather, on his business, an assignment she still wasn't sure how she felt about. Especially considering the wild turn her relationship with Cortez had taken. Did he always seduce women with the speed and undeniable expertise he'd shown her? How long had the others lasted in his bed before he tired of them?

"How often do you entertain?" she asked, pretending to gaze out to the ocean, not really seeing it. She wasn't sure if she was trying to sound interested, interest*ing*, or if she just wanted a distraction from her thoughts. Maybe what she really wanted was insight into how regularly he brought others to this dazzling bachelor-pad paradise.

Not that she should care.

"It's not a place I think to invite people."

She faced him, taking in his cryptic smile. "Uh-huh?" she murmured, disbelieving. She waved her glass around the sitting room. "This *crème de la bachelor pad* goes untapped? I'm so sure."

He raised a brow at her sarcasm. "I keep the bachelor pad at the other end of the island." His tone was teasing.

"I just bet you do. And it's probably magnificent. The Taj Mahal pales in comparison? Meanwhile you bring me to this dump." In a haughty tone, she added, "I'm afraid I must insist on gold flecks in my bath water and diamonds for breakfast."

Amusement lit his features. "I can see I've already spoiled you."

She nodded happily. "I'm afraid you might be right. Now where is the pile of gems we're meant to sleep atop? I think I'd like to show my *appreciation*." She smiled coyly.

His grin turned carnal. "One pile of gems coming up."

Taking her glass from her, he set it aside and then hefted her over his shoulder barbarian-style. She squealed with laughter as he bound up the stairs to the master bedroom. After lightly tossing her on an impossibly soft mattress, he crawled over her, his gaze intent. When they kissed, his lips were a perfect mix of give and take, his tongue delving to follow the path of her lower lip before retreating and then repeating the process, just enough to tease and make her crave more.

His solid frame cocooned her in deliciously hard muscles. Her fingers flew to the top-most button of his shirt, working it free before moving on to the next. As if he were as impatient as her, he simply shrugged the fabric off and tossed it aside.

Almost reverently, she ran her hands along the planes and dips of his chest, his shoulders, and muscled arms, marveling at the dichotomy of silk over perfectly sculpted stone.

"Your body is unbelievable," she gasped between kisses.

"Ditto," he growled. His head dipped to run his lips along her jaw, down past her collarbone and over the tops of her breasts, straining against the fabric of her dress. His hands scooped around to her back and grappled with her zipper. Fearing he might forego the zipper and rip the fabric clean off her like he had before, she shimmied it halfway down her body, leaving her torso naked to his gaze. He groaned at the sight and then leaned down to trap one of her nipples between his hot lips.

She cried out, raking her fingers through his hair, though it was difficult with her arms half restrained by her dress.

His attention moved to her other breast, languidly swirling his tongue around the sensitive peak. "Oh, God!" Her spine arched. She struggled to squirm the rest of the way out of her dress. Deciphering her need, he gripped the fabric and yanked it down her hips. She didn't think she'd heard anything rip, but then, at this point, she didn't really care. She was left in only her panties while he was still fully dressed. It was titillating, being so vulnerable and exposed. She might have been embarrassed if he wasn't taking her in like she was the most beautiful thing he'd ever beheld.

Kneeling over her, he let out a low, husky sound that could have had several meanings. Something along the line of: *fuck me/all mine/ gorgeous!* Whatever the translation was, that sound poured a hot steaming aphrodisiac directly into her brain, making her feel drunk on lust. Her cheeks flushed, heart hammered, body ached. Why wasn't he fucking her already?

Gripping her by the ankle, he pulled her body to the edge of the mattress, tore off her panties, and dropped to his knees between her thighs, giving her one long mind-numbing lap of his tongue. He groaned; she moaned. Then he pulled back to watch her as his exquisite fingers played her like a flute.

Arching into his touch, she let out another soft moan.

"Is this where you need me?" His voice sounded so rough, on the verge of losing control.

"Yes!"

He increased his pace, circling her swollen bud with his wicked thumb. Rendered nothing more than a pile of sensation, she mindlessly undulated her hips to his rocking finger. Sharp pressure began to build, build, reaching incomprehensible heights, gathering tightly in her loins, readying for—

She cried out as pleasure overwhelmed her, arching her back and causing her breaths to come in short, fast spurts. Her erratic heart pounded against the inner wall of her chest.

Just as she was about to come back to Earth, he delved one thick finger inside, finding a point that made her scream. "Cortez!" A second finger joined the first, extending her pleasure. Her body trembled, on the verge of release once more.

"That's it," he murmured darkly. "Come for me." His roughened voice unrecognizable, and so damn sexy it sent her over the edge. Ecstasy quaked through her, making her shake. Then the heat of his mouth descended on her.

"*Uhn!* Oh, God. Don't stop!"

Soon she was once more tripping toward orgasm. She screamed as he sucked hard on her tender flesh. Maddening. When his hot tongue penetrated her core, he forced another scream from somewhere deep inside her.

Head thrashing, body writhing, fingers laced through his hair, her hips shamelessly sought even more friction.

So good. Can't take it. Too much. Need more.

"Ahh!" Another scream tore out of her as she experienced the most forceful climax yet. This one stole her vision and had her clawing at his shoulders. The ruthless waves of pleasure seemed never ending, and all the while he continued his relentless licking and sucking. He intended to drive her insane from an ecstasy overdose.

When the sensation became too much to bear, she pushed at his head, but he coiled his arms around her thighs and nuzzled her with a growl that skittered through her body. Savage rapture seized her, pushed ferocious shrieks from her lungs as her body shook wildly. Finally she shattered into a trillion tiny pieces of glory and divine bliss that surely would never fit back together in the same fashion again.

After one last pass of his merciless tongue, he released her with a devilish smirk.

She struggled through her ragged breaths. "Not that I'm complaining," she panted, "but I was supposed to be showing *my* appreciation."

He stood to his full glorious height. His torso was a work of art, brawny arms, washboard abs, sculpted waist, lickable goodie trail that disappeared below the waist of his pants. He unbuckled his belt, then undid the button of his slacks. His movements fired a fresh explosion of lust through her. She scrambled to her knees, wetting her lips. His smoldering gaze was drawn to her mouth.

Leaving the zipper up, he spread his arms out in challenge. "Be my guest."

She shuffled across the mattress on her knees, and slowly drew down the zipper, meeting his gaze with an I'm-about-to-rock-your-world, twinkle in her eyes. Pushing the fabric over his hips, the heavy belt thudded to the floor. Hard, rigid cock freed, she lovingly ran her hands along its length. His jaw tightened, gaze intense. He seemed to be keeping himself very still for her. As though any sudden movements would rile the beast within.

She shivered, wanting him riled.

Holding his gaze, she eased close and licked the bulbous tip. His expression tightened, but his husky groan urged her on.

"You want me to make you come like this?" she purred.

Adam's apple bobbing, he replied with a curt nod. She smiled up at him and then drew him between her lips to the root.

He let out a ripe oath, his hips jutting forward. She took him to the back of her throat and played with him there.

"*Uhn!*" His powerful legs shook, just like he'd made her whole body shake. Inwardly, she smirked, loving the power of driving him to the brink.

Through ragged breaths he muttered, "How many men have you undone with this masterful mouth of yours?"

Huh? Why was he thinking about her with other men? She loved giving pleasure like this, the power of it. Unfortunately, her other lovers were more into taking than giving, making her grow weary of the act altogether. It was no fun when it felt like a chore. It wasn't like that with Cortez. He gave as good as he got. Better even. She was going to have to step up her game.

To take his mind off his wayward thoughts, she sucked him harder; he let out a long groan and fisted her hair. She pumped him with her fist as she used her mouth on him. His every grunt and groan fed her own pleasure, making her grow slick and swollen. She moaned, imagining him driving into her the way he was sliding along her tongue.

His body stilled, and he pried her off of him.

"What's wrong?" she asked, wanting her mouth back in place.

"You want me inside you." It wasn't a question. "You're shaking with need." Not giving her time to respond, he tossed her to her back, taking in the sight of her slicked sex. "Sucking me turned you on," he marveled, like it was a foreign notion. "Tell me you need me."

"Don't tease me, Cortez. You know I do." She ran her hands over her breasts, teasing *him*.

Excitement lit his eyes. "Keep acting like this and I might be tempted to give you whatever you want."

Her brows drew together at his loaded words, but then he climbed over her, his glorious body scrambling her thoughts. She welcomed him between the cradle of her thighs. And then with one harsh thrust, his powerful body invaded.

Wondrous friction! Delicious pleasure. She wanted more. He obliged. Driving in and out, harder, faster, deeper than she ever thought possible, burying his thick cock to the hilt and vaulting her into a near-permanent state of nirvana. His pace was wild, wayward, nearly ferocious. She loved every second of it. Went a little wild herself, scratching her nails down his back before sinking them into his well-toned ass.

When her release came, she shattered all over again. As she screamed for him, her core squeezed his shaft while the rest of her body writhed under his toiling body.

Suddenly he went bowstring-taut and bellowed. Heat coated her center. One last thrust, one last cry of ecstasy from them both. He collapsed over her. She luxuriated in his weight, his sweat-dampened skin. For a brief moment she mused that he hadn't bitten her. Then he rolled onto his back, pulling her across his chest. She melted into him, her lids growing heavy. Before she fell asleep, she thought, *a week with this man would never be enough*.

CHAPTER 21

As slumber fluttered away, consciousness breezed in. Warmth permeated Naia's cheek. She was snuggled against a deliciously hard body. For the first time since they'd been together, Cortez was in bed with her when she awoke, their combined body heat cocooning her, his masculine scent drugging. She inhaled deeply for more of his spicy fragrance, resisting the urge to rub her face along his skin like a feline to catnip.

He slept soundly, lying on his back. She debated staying where she was, or slipping away to make sure she looked presentable...maybe sneak back under the covers before he noticed her absence.

But when she shifted to move off the bed, he turned on his side and hooked her around the waist, tugging her into the warm curve of his body. Then he resumed his light snoring. Guess she was staying put. She couldn't bring herself to mind when it felt so damn good in his arms. It made her feel cherished.

The word was like crashing into an icy dunk tank.

Her eyes flashed open and she mentally shook herself.

She realized she was letting this little fling get into her head. Her growing attachment was distracting her from her assignment. At the end of the week, he'd move on to his next conquest, and then another lucky female would be warming his bed.

The thought was crushing.

She shouldn't be entertaining this fantasy anyway—imagining a future with him. It was a ludicrous idea that would only hurt her in the end.

Today she would need to start drilling him for information.

He stirred, burying his nose in the crook of her neck and inhaling deeply just as she had done to him. He let out a groggy, masculine groan, his breath skating along her skin. As if she'd already been conditioned, her body responded to that sound, heating and dampening and softening all at once, and she didn't resist when he wordlessly pulled her underneath him. There was no better way to start the morning.

"I have a surprise for you." Cortez stepped out onto the pool deck where she lounged in her olive-green bathing suit. Again he wore nothing but board shorts, that magnificently sculpted chest on display. She took the sight in with a greedy gaze. Just seeing him like this made her shiver, though it was well above eighty degrees.

"I'm going to overdose on surprises," she informed him. This morning, after they'd made love in bed, and then again in the shower, he'd presented her with a simple box, inside, a pair of sparkling diamond earrings, stating, "I believe the lady demanded diamonds for breakfast." She wore them now.

He really was going to spoil her—then she would

return to her drab apartment and underwhelming life, left with only fond memories of the man who had totally consumed her life for a wondrous, if short, time. She rejected that dismal future, stubbornly kicking it out of mind. *Enjoy it while it lasts* was her new motto.

"You don't have to keep pulling out all the stops. Consider me thoroughly impressed."

Roguish grin. "You think I'm doing all this for *you*?"

She shaded her eyes from the sun to see him better, intrigued by the remark.

"I like it when your eyes light up every time I show you something you've never seen before. It's turning into a rather addictive hobby of mine."

A hobby? Like collecting stamps? If she wasn't careful, he might just collect her heart.

"Perhaps it is my turn to surprise you," she said, giving him a look that needed no translation.

"Everything you say and do is a surprise. Perhaps I'm growing addicted to that as well."

She gulped at the intensity in his gaze. She couldn't decipher the emotion behind it. Then his words registered. *She* surprised *him*? More than others? Why was that? Because he really *could* read minds as Cole had suggested? Only maybe not hers? She mentally scoffed. The whole notion was absurd.

Still, she mused over what it would be like to know what everyone around her was thinking. It would be great! She'd know who to trust. Who not to trust. What people really thought of her. If men liked her for her mind or merely her body.

She glanced up at Cortez, and fought a smirk. *Definitely my body.* Especially if he couldn't even read her mind. Or maybe that's what made her interesting. Maybe it gave her mystery. Made her a challenge. Not that she'd given him much of one.

Suddenly she couldn't stop hypothesising.

An image of Boomer rubbing his paunch in the dressing room entryway slipped through her mind. She cringed. That was one man whose thoughts she could do without. In fact, that went for all the men who came to The Pit. They could keep their undoubtedly disgusting, grubby thoughts to themselves.

If mindreading was in the realm of possibilities, was it feasible to block the thoughts of a crowd and focus on only one person? Or would they all flood in like an unmanageable deluge?

Perhaps reading minds wouldn't be so great.

Moot point, she told herself. Because no one could read minds.

Ignorant to her musings, Cortez held his hand out to her. "Come."

Teasingly, she feigned a scandalized expression. "Right here? Cortez, you are a naughty boy."

He flashed a grin. "Someone's mind is in the gutter. Or is it that you didn't get enough this morning?"

Never get enough. He was making her insatiable. One thing was certain: if he *could* read her mind, they'd never have made it out of the bedroom. Looking at him there with his glorious rippling muscles begging for her touch was turning her on by degrees.

Her desire made her bold. She yanked down the elastic of his shorts, and freed his impressive cock, triumphant that he was already hard as granite for her. "Looks like maybe *you* didn't get enough either."

His gaze was intense, anticipating her next move.

He didn't have to wait long. She gripped his base and drew him into the heat of her mouth.

He hissed in a breath, the muscles of his legs

bunching.

He was full and smooth against her tongue. The perfect dichotomy of silk over steel. Taking her time, she traced the thick length with her tongue, following the small pulsing veins. When she sucked him deep, he let out a rough sound, almost a growl. He gazed down at her, reverent, lust-drugged. She pulled back to circle the tip with her tongue and then sucked him to the root.

Body shaking, he twined his fist in her hair, groaning. "Mmm, you wicked woman. I really want to enjoy this, but *Unh*. You're too goddamn good at that. You'll make me come if you keep that up." She grinned around his girth and then continued her ruthless assault. "Do you want that?"

In answer, she sucked him deeper than she had before.

Back bowing, he bellowed to the sky. His hips matched the rhythm of her mouth, their pace growing more frantic by the second. Then she reached up to tug lightly on his testicles and he lost it. A harsh sound ripped from his chest. His hips stilled. Hot seed shot forth, making its way down her throat. She swallowed him with a soft moan.

Without warning, he gripped her nape and pulled her away from him. His other hand wrapped his cock, and he gave several hard pumps. His seed lashed her breasts in hot spurts. The sensation was oddly arousing, causing her to moan and squirm for her own release.

His chest heaved from the strength of his orgasm. "You need to come, sweets?"

"Yes," she whimpered.

Joining her on the lounge chair, his big hand breached the hem of her bathing suit bottoms and invaded her slick folds. He marveled for a moment at her dampness before caressing her clitoris till she was panting and moaning.

"Is this what you need, luv?"

"Yes! Please don't stop!"

"If only I could keep you here forever."

She looked away, wishing he wouldn't say such impossible, delightful, frightening things. Not while she was falling apart in his arms. When she faced him again he caught her lips in a searing kiss. Their tongues clashed as he stroked her toward a blissful release. So close. Almost.... Her body began to shudder from the intensity of her burgeoning orgasm. She broke away from the kiss on a cry, her body preparing for blast off. Then, with a final stroke, she threw her head back on a scream. He kept her there for a moment in that mindless state, drawing out her orgasm.

As pleasure slowly subsided, she gazed up at his smugly satisfied expression. "I like your surprises," he said.

"I just bet you do." They were like a couple of damn bunnies! And she loved it!

Thirty minutes after she'd changed into hiking gear—*his* surprise consisted of a little off-road trip up the mountain...while her gaze was concealed behind a blindfold!—the jeep came to a halt. She fumbled for the door handle. "Can I take this off now?" Though she could still smell the ocean, there was now also a strong tropical scent that spoke of lush, jungle-esque surroundings.

The drive had been short, if bumpy. Every time they hit a groove or scaled a sharp incline, she'd been jostled in her seat, having to cling to him for stability. From his low chuckles, she suspected he'd enjoyed that.

"No peeking," he scolded. The driver-side door opened, then closed, leaving her alone in the cab. Seconds later, her door opened, and he helped her out, guiding her away. Gravel crunched under her boots. Another, larger-sounding door squeaked open. More walking. She easily determined they were inside a structure of some kind. The air was different, almost musty, as if the place had been closed up for a long period of time. A set of stairs came next. She cautiously climbed them, feeling her way along a banister while Cortez kept a protective hand on the small of her back. Another door opened, letting in a flood of warm light that she felt on her skin. They were outside again. On a balcony?

He removed the blindfold. She had to blink several times, her eyes adjusting to the sudden brightness. Then all she could do was slack-jaw-gape.

They stood on a platform at the summit of the mountain, above the tree line on a flat-top roof, allowing for an unfettered three-sixty view of endless glittering ocean, cloudless blue sky, and the jungle below. She spun in circles, wanting to take it all in at once. "My god, this is...this is..." there were no words except, "Incredible!" And even that was tame.

She glanced over the edge. They weren't even that high off the ground, but with the mild slope of the landscape, the illusion was that they were miles above everything. "This would make a great stage," she blurted. "All I'd need is a mic and an audience. Have you ever thought about putting on a show here? It would be a great venue." She turned to Cortez with a confident grin. "You wouldn't believe how I can rock a crowd."

His lips hardened into a thin line. She didn't understand the muscle bulging in his jaw. Guess he didn't like that idea. Sure, he didn't work with women he slept with, but she still held onto the hope that he would change his mind once this little escapade of theirs ended—and she was sure that it would. Cortez wasn't the settling down type. That was plain to see—except he didn't seem the slightest bit interested in hearing her sing. Not even for fun.

"This is my sanctuary," he said, expression still tight. "It's where I come to get away from people."

She shrugged, and let it drop. Then, almost to himself, added, "I've never wanted to share it with anyone else before."

"Why not?" As beautiful as this place was, hoarding it seemed like such a waste. Keeping something like this to herself, only coming here alone, would make her feel so...well, lonely. She scanned the dazzling horizon from left to right, following the chiseled line where liquid cobalt met the ice-blue sky. It was almost impossible to comprehend the vast expanse of never-ending water. The dark and unfathomable depths hidden below the glittering ocean. How even now someone could be on the opposite side of that horizon, gazing back and contemplating their own tiny existence.

His eyes were on the sea as well, his gaze distant. He waited so long to speak, she wasn't sure he would. "I value my solitude."

"An island unto yourself," she quipped.

His lips twitched. "Something like that."

Again, she thought, *how lonely*. Although she didn't always like the people around her, she generally loved being around people. Give her a crowd and a decent beat and she could dance all night, laugh, and talk. Socializing was a balm to her inner siren. It energized her. Not near as much as singing did. It certainly wouldn't sustain her. But it was like having a cupboard full of food, knowing if you got hungry, all you needed was to grab a snack and you're good to go.

"The rooftop back at your club, that's a sanctuary for you as well, isn't it?"

"Of a sort."

"Why would a guy like you need so many places to hide?"

"Not hide. More like recharge."

"You need to be alone for that?" Could they be any more opposite in that regard?

He nodded. "Sometimes I need things to be quiet."

"And I'm...quiet?" He'd said as much on the yacht.

He slanted her a wry grin. "In a way."

Curiosity prowled her molecules. Could he mean in a way that mind readers would find interesting? Or maybe challenging? Was he trying to dig into her thoughts even now? Trying to crack her like a puzzle? She nearly laughed at her own absurdity. She was letting a silly rumor make her paranoid. And yet, she wasn't totally sure it was a silly rumor.

Deciding to run a test, she conjured the most idiotic thought she could manifest and directed it right at him: a blue-feathered goat in a pink tutu doing pirouettes while clutching a lit cigar between a set of oversized teeth, flatulating yellow puffs of smoke.

She studied his expression intently, his lips especially, waiting for that telltale twitch.

He didn't bat an eyelash. He calmly gazed back out to the sea as if the only thing running through his mind was how great the view was.

Banishing the cartoonish image, she tried again, sending him a vision of the two of them getting hot and heavy right here on this platform with the soft breeze flowing over their sweaty naked skin and the sounds of the waves mingling with their roars of pleasure.

If he could read her thoughts, he didn't take the

bait.

If he could read my thoughts, she reminded herself, *he'd know I was a deceitful spy.* And he would have done something about it.

Although, maybe he had done something about it. Just being here kept her from snooping. Was that the plan? Keep her busy till…. Till what? She couldn't construct a logical theory that didn't delve into a sinister plot. Would he use her and then leave her stranded at the end of the week? Steal away in the night while she was in a post-coitus coma?

All this beauty around her? The splendor? This gorgeous man who seemingly wanted her? Was it all too good to be true? Was she being played?

Was this paranoia or intuition speaking?

She'd allowed herself to become completely alone with a man she didn't really know. Didn't know if she should trust. Her safety depended entirely on his mood and temperament. How the hell had she even gotten herself into such a sketchy situation? Nobody even knew where she was. Sure, she'd told Cole she was on an island, but figuring out which one would be next to impossible. At least in a timeframe that mattered.

Normally she was a very cautious person—especially after the last man she'd been involved with.

If Cortez truly wanted to punish her for attempting to infiltrate his business, he could easily depart this island without her, trapping her—

"I'm enjoying this immensely," Cortez broke into her paranoiac thoughts. His grin was soft. Easygoing. It almost encouraged her to relax, until his next words frayed her nerves all over again. "I may just keep you here indefinitely."

Some part of her realized his statement wasn't meant to be threatening, not meant to be taken literally, but that didn't keep icy terror from crawling up her spine and stabbing poisonous fear into the base of her brain.

Chained to an island like her ancestors? How long might she last? Would she eventually die, withering to nothing?

The acutely disturbing awareness of isolation smothered her in a dark pall of nauseating dread.

As if she was somehow mystically connected to the island, she knew without a doubt they were the only people here—the only people for miles. This level of solitude went against her very nature. No boats on the horizon. No signs of life on this tiny patch of land besides a scattering of little critters scurrying for food.

She could already feel her voice itching for release, the siren within clawing at her insides, panicking. What would happen if Cortez caught her singing her lungs out in the middle of the night like a wolf compelled to howl at the moon? Would he know what she was then?

It was either her increased heart rate or something in her expression that drew his curiosity. "Are you alright?"

"Just dizzying...being so high up." She tried for a gamely smile, but feared it came across more as a grimace.

He studied her for a moment, then offered his arm as though she might need it to keep from falling over. Was she swaying slightly? "Shall we return then? I'm keen to get you back into that bathing suit anyway."

CHAPTER 22

Turned out the cure for a paranoia-induced panic attack was a drop-dead gorgeous vampire chasing you around a beach like a randy teenager.

They had spent so much time playing and splashing around in the surf, she was practically waterlogged, her mood improved tenfold. She could officially check *make love in the ocean* off her fuck-it list. When she'd informed Cortez of that, he'd bellowed with laughter. There was something in the way he reacted to her that made her wonder if he was unused to finding amusement in the company of others.

Maybe because he could read minds?

She was back to speculating.

Did knowing what people were going to say beforehand dampen the effect of jokes? Punchlines would be seen a mile away. Is that why he laughed so readily for her? Because to him everything she said was a mystery uncovered.

In any case, she liked that she could make Cortez laugh.

Earlier, she had asked him what other women thought of his island.

Seemingly perturbed, he'd said, "That's what? The third or fourth time you've brought up other women? Do you just want to come out and ask me if I'm a player?"

"Oh, I don't have to ask."

He cast her an arch look.

"I've had my share of lovers, but *no one* has ever seduced me as quickly as you. You made my panties drop like they were made of cement!"

At that, he belly laughed till he was holding a stitch in his side.

But now she had a more serious conversation planned.

After returning to the house, they'd had dinner on a balcony that overlooked the ocean. Well, *she'd* had dinner; he sipped bourbon, eyeing her with something like suspicion. He might not read minds, but he showed an ever-developing aptitude for reading her. Earlier on the roof, he'd sensed her unease and had worked to lighten her mood. Now she was jittery, plotting the best way to broach her *interrogation*.

Spending time with Cortez had only heightened her curiosity about him. Was Dante right in his assumptions? That although Cortez was a successful business owner, he leaned more toward criminal pursuits? It didn't seem likely. She might not know a lot about the enigmatic vampire, but he didn't come across as the type to get involved in forced prostitution. Or drugs, for that matter. But she'd misjudged the opposite sex before, and it had nearly cost her everything.

Throughout dinner, she'd studied his every move as if there was a hidden confession in the angle of his jaw when he drank, or in the tilt of his head as he glanced her way.

The sun had long since set, and speckled moonlight bounced off the ever churning ocean. Once she'd finished eating, they'd settled on a set of lounge chairs by the pool.

"You've been pensive all evening," he said, propping a hand behind his head. "Care to tell me what's on your mind?" His body went still at his own words, and his lips curled into a marveling smirk.

Now each time he did something like that, she filed it away in her bank of evidence that was quickly piling up.

Down on the beach, she'd asked him how he determined who to hire at the club, curious how she could get on that short list. Again that jaw muscle had ticked, as though he didn't care for this topic, but he'd answered, "It's all about attitude. Even if they haven't worked a day in their lives, anyone can learn anything given the right attitude. I'd prefer to invest in someone eager to improve themselves than someone with experience who's complacent and jaded."

"How do you figure out if they're complacent or jaded?" It was the most loaded question she'd asked him thus far.

"It's not something people can hide from me." Then he'd cocked his head at her. "Well, most people."

She'd added that to the pile, then transitioned her little intake of breath into a nonchalant sigh. "How so?"

Suddenly wary, he changed the subject, directing her instead to thoughts of dinner and what type of wine she'd like this evening and oh yeah, there was something he'd wanted to show her back up at the house.

On the lounge chair, she turned on her side to face him. "I was just thinking about that new drug that's been circulating around town." Boom. Right to the point. No more beating around the bush. There really wasn't a good way to broach this subject so she'd dispensed with tact.

He blinked. "Why would you be thinking about that?"

"I heard it was causing a lot of deaths. Someone I know lost a good friend a little while back. I was just curious. You don't allow drugs like that in your club do you?"

He gave a noncommittal shrug and gazed up at the stars. "I'm not the moral police."

"But it's killing people. Don't you care?"

His head swiveled around. "It's not my job to save people from their own stupidity. Ninety-nine percent of the time that's an exercise in futility. People are going to do what they want. Even knowing it's no good for them. Besides, it's difficult to keep that stuff out of a party atmosphere. I'd say a good third of the people who enter the club are holding, another third are looking to buy. However, I don't condone trafficking in my club. Those who get caught are bounced. Repeat offenders are banned."

She sighed. That was a relief...unless he banned them to get rid of the competition.

Trying for an easy tone, she continued. "And then there's that rumor about a group of individuals forcing women into prostitution. Some say vampire compulsion might be involved."

His expression turned fierce. "Who is saying these things?"

"Just people," she hedged.

He eyed her for a long moment. "Is that why you jumped to such a drastic conclusion the other day?"

She flushed. "It's not hard to believe some vamps might take advantage of their natural abilities. You know, compel a girl to think she was *happy* about that gangbang she *participated* in the night before."

He shot upright, anger roiling in his eyes. "Has someone hurt you?"

Her hands popped up, palms facing him in a calming gesture. "NO! I was speaking metaphorically!"

His body instantly relaxed, yet tension remained around his jaw. Resting his arms on his knees, he let out a heavy breath. "Your concerns are valid, but we have laws against such behavior."

"You do?" She knew nothing of vampire law.

He nodded. "In the past, before The Revelation, keeping vampires in check was largely left to clan leaders and makers—"

"Makers?"

"Those with the ability to sire new vampires," he explained. "Naturally depraved makers unfailingly breed depravity. Eventually those ruthless clans became a threat to our way of life and war broke out, nearly exposing our entire race before we were ready. To cull the poison and keep the peace, the VEA was established. You know what that is, right?"

"The Vampire Enforcement Agency."

"Correct. Our laws are absolute, with harsh consequences. Rarely is there a slap on the wrist for an offender. It offers great incentive to toe the line."

"Are you saying vampires don't commit crimes?"

He shook his head. "That would be something, wouldn't it? Unfortunately, there are always those who test the boundaries, convince themselves they're too smart to get caught, or just plain don't care. However, our transgressions aren't quite the same as yours. For humans, murder is the greatest sin. Ours is the abuse of power."

"Abusing power is *worse* than murder?"

"It is when the abuse of power could cause many

deaths as a result. Murder for the greater good is some-what common in my world. Because we live so long, it is considered admirable for a sire to exterminate his own *bad eggs*, as it were. Especially now with peace between vampires and humans so tentative. Left un-checked, those bad eggs could potentially sire entire clans that lack basic morals. And that wouldn't be good for anyone. More so, as the sire and head of my own clan, I could potentially be held responsible for any crime committed by a member of my clan. Need-less to say, I thoroughly vet anyone I plan to bring into the fold." He sipped his drink and glanced up at the stars.

A worrisome thought popped into her head. "Are you vetting me?"

Bourbon sprayed from his lips followed by a half coughing fit, half belly laugh.

A confounding mix of relief and hurt assaulted her.

When his cutting mirth finally died down, he noticed her frown. "I'm sorry," he said, still slightly chuckling. "I didn't mean to laugh. It's just that this is the first time I've been unable to anticipate what someone will say at any given moment. You can't be-lieve how refreshing that is. And no, I have no desire to turn any more vampires at present."

She tried to keep her eyes from popping out of their sockets. He was accustomed to predicting what people will say? She filed that information away, pre-tending he hadn't inexplicably yet thoroughly offend-ed her by his abject rejection of the notion of her as a vampire. Not that she wanted that. At all.

CHAPTER 23

Naia rolled over and found herself embraced by a strong set of arms.

"Good morning," he muttered drowsily, pulling her closer.

"Morning." She snuggled against his chest, taking in his sexy, addictive scent.

"You slept quite a long time, no? Did you drink too much last night?"

"I don't think so. Why? What time is it?"

"Well past lunch. You looked so peaceful, I didn't want to disturb you."

Past lunch? So why did she still feel exhausted? Her muscles ached as if preparing to battle a flu. The last time she'd felt like this...

"Did you know you sing softly in your sleep?"

She bolted upright. "You heard me singing!?"

Letting her go, he folded his arms behind his head. "Don't be self-conscious. Your voice is actually pleasant." She resented the surprise in his tone, like he hadn't expected her claims about her voice to be true. He'd have known that if he'd let her audition. "I'm not self-conscious." She was horrified! "I didn't do anything else, did I?"

"Like what?"

"Sleepwalk, or anything?"

"No. Is that a common occurrence?"

"Not common, no." At least not when her siren half was well fed.

After a late breakfast, she told Cortez she wanted to explore the island a little on her own, still needing to calm her nerves but not wanting him to notice how freaked she was by her midnight-singing.

Still, he seemed to gauge her curiously. "I should check in at the club, anyway. Have fun."

With that, she scurried down to the beach, pacing like a caged animal. The waves taunted her, boxed her in, the ocean her jailer. The sun ruthlessly beat down on her fevered skin.

How was she already this far along? Sleep-singing meant the siren was growing desperate. Why? She sang just a few days ago at The Pit. It was too soon to be losing it like this. Being on an isolated island was probably just stressing out her siren side.

There was nothing for miles and miles and miles.

Nothing.

This was crazy. She had to get out of here. Just like Cortez, she could eat food, but it didn't provide what she truly needed. Though her belly was full, she felt as empty and dry as an ancient clay jug. She might as well be standing in the middle of a barren desert.

Panic surged.

He'd heard her singing! It would only get worse. How would she explain sleepwalking out into the night to bellow her song at the sky like a freak? He'd figure out what she was.

In their own way, they both fed off the life force of others. Would he understand her nature? Would he understand what she needed?

Would he give her a job at his club then?

She recalled the last man she had trusted with her secret. James had been just as charming and attractive as Cortez.

She'd thought she'd been in love with him. She'd been a fool.

She recalled sitting on a park bench one morning, openly discussing her lineage with him. How had she ever felt comfortable enough to spill her secrets? At first James had laughed, patronizing her, but not believing her story. Then, arrogantly, she had shown him. Singing out to a passerby, she'd snared a stocky man, causing him to go doe-eyed, frozen to the spot like a pup gazing at its new master.

It had just been a light enthrallment, nothing like what she was capable.

When James had recovered from his shock, he'd strolled over to the man, and promptly robbed him of his wallet. Naia had been too stunned to protest, her jaw locked open, even as James had yanked her off the bench and tugged her away. Later she had railed at him; he'd just wanted her to do it again. His true nature? A crook.

She'd broken up with him that same day, but had failed to predict the depth of his immorality. That night James had returned for her, crawling through her bedroom window while she'd slept—wearing sound-dampening ear phones!

She'd fought and clawed for her life that night. Could still recall the feeling of dried blood under her nails...

The terrible memory swarmed her, compounding her building dread. Her lungs seemed to shrink ten sizes. Hand over her racing heart, she fell on shaky knees, gasping for breath.

A full-fledged panic attack.

Breathe.

It will pass.

Just breathe.

Movement on one of the upper balconies drew her attention.

Cortez stood there, gazing her way.

She couldn't make out his expression, but he seemed to be leaning over the edge, looking directly at her. Suddenly he stepped off the ledge, dropping three stories in seconds. Though his form disappeared behind the thick forest that cluttered the base of his home, she had no doubt he'd landed on his feet without a hitch.

Inhuman! her mind screamed.

Had a vampire been the one to attack her that night, she would not have escaped. He'd have overpowered her in seconds. Imagining having to fight off Cortez, picturing that same ruthless intent on his beautiful features seemed so wrong, it made her want to vomit. Could he be so heartless in business? Wanting to use the gift of her voice against people? To dupe and pilfer? According to his own laws, that would be a cardinal sin.

Still, why should she risk it? There was no reason to trust him. She barely knew him. And in less than a week, they would go their separate ways.

With steel in her bones, she reaffirmed her vow never to tell another soul about what she was. Safer that way.

Cortez emerged from behind the foliage moments later, beating a path toward her, concern etched in his features. "Are you ill?" She didn't know whether it was the memory of the attack or the preternatural display of him diving from such a great height without a scratch on him, but when he reached for her, she flinched.

He pulled his hand back, his brows shooting up.

She scrambled to her feet and brushed sand off her knees, striving for a light tone and a little laugh that she hoped didn't sound fake. "Did you just clear a three-story fall to ask how I'm doing?"

Studying her far too closely, he nodded slowly. "It looked like you fell. And you've seemed distressed all morning."

Understatement.

She cleared her throat. "No, no. I'm fine."

He didn't appear to believe her. When he reached to take her hand again, adrenaline was still fresh in her body, and she shuddered at his touch. He immediately dropped her hand, appearing confused...and maybe a little hurt?

She needed to say something so he didn't get the wrong idea. "I've never been away so long. I suppose I'm a little homesick. And worried about Cole." *And in need of a crowd.* "Without me, he finds trouble like water flows downhill."

"Are you saying you want to go back?"

She shrugged. "Would you mind?"

"Why didn't you say something sooner?"

"Honestly, I felt a little guilty."

"Guilty?"

"What it must have cost to get us out here. I was afraid you'd think I was ungrateful." She shrugged. "Or maybe I was afraid you wouldn't care what I wanted."

His brows knit. "You would be with a man you believe doesn't care about your feelings?"

She blinked, surprised by the sudden hollowness in his tone. "That's not what I meant."

"What do you mean then?"

"It's just that you went through all the trouble to get us here, not to mention all the gifts and clothes.

I just didn't feel right about asking you to take me home so soon."

"So you would stay somewhere you didn't really want to be?"

"It's not that I don't want to be here."

He ignored that. "Are you only sleeping with me so that you don't seem ungrateful?"

Her mouth dropped at the question. His expression was...well, she wasn't sure if he was upset, or angry. There was a growing flame behind his eyes that warned her this conversation was going off the rails.

"Of course not."

His gaze narrowed a touch. "I don't know whether or not to believe you."

She crossed her arms, suddenly a little angry herself. "Of course you can believe me."

"You've shown me on several occasions that you are uncomfortable. You must have been feeling this way for a while." When she didn't respond, something cold slammed down over his features. It gave her heart a kick. He glanced down as if he could hear the sudden rise in her pulse, and his withering expression turned glacial.

"I don't abide lying, even in the form of omission." Then he turned his back on her and began walking toward the house. "You won't have to suffer my presence much longer. I'll have the crew here by nightfall. We'll be to the mainland by morning."

CHAPTER 24

She followed his rigid form inside. "I didn't mean to upset you, Cortez."

He gave a bitter laugh. "I'm not upset."

"You don't look happy."

"You've provided me with yet another new experience. I never imagined anyone would feel *obligated* to stay here with me." He actually looked thunderstruck. "Most would lie, cheat, and steal to be the object of my affection."

"That's not it at all. I love it here, with you. I'm just going a little...stir crazy, I suppose. I'm not used to being so far from home. Or civilization. I kind of need to be around people. Around a crowd." She stopped before she revealed too much more.

"Oh, *and* I'm boring you?" He chuckled softly, as though laughing at himself. His temper wasn't mollified.

"That's not it at all. I just feel so isolated."

"Are you afraid of me?"

She shook her head. "Cortez, no."

As if her words were a challenge, he crossed to her with inhuman speed, looming over her, his voice booming, "DO NOT LIE TO ME."

She stumbled back, nearly losing her footing, but she managed to keep her balance while her lungs seized in terror. He watched her as if he were gauging her every reaction. Counting her every harried heartbeat.

Catching her breath, she planted her feet. "Anyone would be afraid when you behave like that!"

He backed away as if her response wasn't what he'd expected. "'Course. Forgive me. Just getting a measure?"

"Of what."

"The difference between truth and lie."

"And what have you deduced? That you can successfully frighten me? Well congratulations. A vampire scared a human. Bravo."

He stared at her, still cool and aloof. "Merely that your body was telling me the truth just now. Something I suspect your mouth doesn't always do."

She swallowed, her heart beating fast for an entirely different reason now.

His eyes narrowed on her.

"My body told you I got startled. That's all."

"That's all you think I learned just then?"

She tried to look uninterested.

"You were startled, yes, but you weren't sweating. Not like you are now after I suggested you don't always offer me the truth. Your eyes didn't dart as if trying to hide something, like they did just now.

"I'm not hiding anything."

"Did you know there's a subtle, almost unavoidable rise in the voice when a lie is told? At least for humans. Difficult to perceive when you're not listening for it."

Something in her stomach squirmed uncomfortably. "Fine. I'm a little afraid of you. Are you happy?

I'm a human alone on an island with a vampire. Is it really that much of a surprise? I have no idea how long you were planning to keep me here, and no indication that I had the option to leave. You sent the boat away and it freaked me out."

He seemed to digest that for a moment. "That makes sense. I wish you would have said something. I don't want you to feel uncomfortable."

"Okay."

When she thought the argument was at an end, he moved on to another topic. "What's all this talk of needing to be around people and crowds? Most people can't wait to get away from the city. It seems like you're still angling to perform at my club?"

"I..." she couldn't exactly deny it. Not with his lie detector senses on high alert. She merely shrugged.

"Is that why you tried to force yourself to stay with me?" He shook his head. "I wish I could say I'm surprised."

She sighed, frustrated. "Obviously I would love a job, but that's not why—"

"What other reason could there be? You want something from me. Like all the rest. You drop hints at every opportunity. On the boat, the beach, in bed. Suggesting I let you use my sanctuary as your own personal stage so you can indulge your ridiculous fantasies of fame."

"Ridiculous?" Now he was out of line.

"Even after I told you I don't mix business and pleasure. Ever. Do you really imagine I don't follow my own rules? Or is it that you think you're the exception?" He gave her a *honey please* look and she felt the sting deep in her chest.

"First off, if I *did* have fantasies of fame, they would be far from ridiculous, and far grander than a two-bit vampire-run club in Riverstone. I sing like I made a deal with the goddamned devil, not that you'd ever bothered to give me a chance to prove it before you slithered your way into my panties—"

"Slithered?"

"—taking the option away from me. Second, *one* little fling and I'm forever banned from Ever Nights as if I've been tainted? That hardly seems fair. Banned from a job that could save...." she trailed off, reluctant to admit how deep in the hole she and Cole were.

He held out his arms. "No. Please, continue. Save you from what? Am I to be held responsible for everyone in your situation then?"

"What do you mean *my* situation?"

"Do you have any idea how many wannabe starlets I encounter? Who proposition me in hopes of getting something out of it? And I stick to my rules because I'm sick of it. Not to mention most of them have petty minds to go along with their worthless dreams." He eyed her as if trying to decide whether she fit into that category.

Through gritted teeth, she muttered, "I am not a wannabe."

"They all say that, sweetheart."

"Or petty."

He went quiet.

She crossed to him and stabbed her finger in his chest. "Or worthless!"

He blinked, losing a bit of his fire. "I didn't mean that you are."

"And you know *nothing* of my dreams," she hissed.

"I know that for someone who entertains as well as you claim to, I'd expect you to be able to afford better than a one room flat in the ghetto."

Dick! "Oh, sure, I could afford a better place if I was willing to shake my ass right out of my clothes like some of the other women in town."

He crossed his arms and snorted. "Isn't that what you did for me last night?"

Rendered speechless by the most potent, purified rage that had ever poisoned her blood, she could only stare at him, aghast.

Dropping his arms, he turned sheepish and scrapped his hand down the back of his neck. "Look, I—"

"You know what? Don't worry about it. Working for you is looking less and less appealing by the second. In fact, doing *anything* with you is looking less and less appealing."

He held his hands out to her in a placating manner. "Naia—"

She cut him off with a sharp look. "Save it. We're done here."

Hurt and outraged, she stormed out of the room and down the hallway, past the kitchen where he'd made her dinner and beyond the bedroom where he'd made her scream his name again and again, not stopping till she found herself sequestered on a balcony on the eastern wing of the house, as far from Cortez as the building would allow. There, she fumed and watched the sky dance for her watery eyes as it darkened with the setting sun, clouds rolling in, bringing with them distant flashes of lightning, all the while trying desperately to convince herself that her soul wasn't flayed raw and ripped to shreds by the shards of her breaking heart.

CHAPTER 25

Naia sat disquietly on the yacht's uppermost deck, watching the island fade to a shadowy smudge against the blackened horizon. The storm had passed them quickly, and now the sky was nearly clear, just a few white puffs obstructing the stars. Sparks of moonlight glinted off the aggressive waves created by the boat's momentum. Had Cortez ordered full speed ahead? Was he that eager to be done with her?

Though she'd been itching for extraction, a part of her would forever miss her all too brief carefree yet consuming fling with her mystifying vampire.

Her emotions were still reeling over their argument? How had things soured so quickly?

They hadn't spoken since their fight. He'd barely even glanced her way when they'd boarded. She didn't even know what she'd done to set him off. Not that it mattered now. Their time together was over.

Still, she couldn't keep from running back through his words. He definitely seemed to sense she was lying to him, and that seemed to be a trigger point for him. Something had made him very suspicious of her, though Naia got the impression he thought she was taking him for a ride. *Like the others*, he'd accused. Someone had hurt him deeply.

She recalled Kenzi mentioning women using Cortez for callous reasons. Going with the assumption he could read minds, he'd know it, too. How awful.

Grudgingly, she had to admit his suspicions of her weren't entirely wrong. Though he didn't know her deception was so much more abominable. What an incompetent spy she'd turned out to be. Dante would not be pleased. Especially since the one thing she'd managed to glean was, recent behavior notwithstanding, Cortez seemed to be honorable...for a vampire. Not at all the type to traffic dangerous drugs or force women into compromising positions. In fact, he'd been furious to learn something like that might be happening in his town. The more she'd gotten to know him, the less likely it seemed Cortez would ever engage in activity so abhorrent.

Would Dante accept her conclusion? His hated competitor cleared of wrongdoing?

Movement to her right drew her attention. Cortez was striding up the stairs. Her heart immediately revved. Was he here to argue with her some more?

In one hand, he held a glass of amber liquor. In the other, a glass of wine.

A peace offering?

His gaze was pensive as he held the wineglass out to her. She glared up at him and crossed her arms, but when his expression turned remorseful, she caved and accepted it.

He gave a tight smile and crossed to sit on the bench across from her. He was silent for several moments, as if gathering his thoughts.

Unwilling to be the first to speak, and afraid to look too interested in what he might have to say, she faced the ocean. Waves played tricks with the moonlight against the water, tossing it around like a ball.

"I may have spoken harshly earlier," Cortez suddenly muttered.

She blinked and glanced back at him.

When she didn't respond, he prompted softly, "Well?"

"Well what?" she replied.

"You must have something to say?"

"What do you expect me to say?" Was he angling for an apology from *her*? Well, he could just hold his breath—

"You must tell me how badly I've hurt you."

That drew her up short, and she lost all her steam. She studied his deep frown and hunched shoulders. He truly looked repentant. She took in a breath and let it out slowly. "You were intentionally and unnecessarily hurtful. You were cruel."

He flinched, then gave a curt nod. "I should not have spoken that way to you. I was...I overreacted."

"I'd like to know why you reacted like that," she said softly. "And don't take this as me finagling for a job, because that's something I'm no longer interested in, this is just curiosity, but what could be so wrong with the idea of me working at Ever Nights? It's the best, safest club in town. Everyone wants a job there. When whatever this is between us"—she gestured between the two of them—"is over anyway, so what would it matter? You have to realize what an amazing opportunity that would have been for someone *in my position*." She tried not to sound sour there at the end, but failed.

That muscle ticked in his jaw.

"Look at you," she said. "Even now you're seething just by my hypothesizing."

He let out a wearied sigh, scrubbing his hand

down his face. "It has been my experience that the women I date...care more for what I can do for them than they actually do for me."

She was preparing for another heated argument, but at his gutted words, and his crumbled expression, her lips parted.

As if realizing how much his expression revealed, he rearranged his features into a cool mask. "You cannot imagine the difficulty, knowing that they would just as soon jump into bed with any of my clan were it to benefit them. Knowing how indifferent they truly were and the finesse with which they tried to hide it."

"*Knowing?*" she picked the word out instantly. Was this a confession? Had Cole been right? "How could you possibly know how they truly felt?"

He shrugged, blasé, but all emotion suddenly drained from his face, leaving behind a stony representation. That was *his* way of lying, she suddenly realized. "These things are easy enough to figure out, if you know what to look for."

She supposed so, but her suspicions about his mystical abilities were now off the charts. "Why did you bring me here, Cortez? I know it's not because you were afraid I'd go from your bed straight to one of your buddies?"

"And how do you know that?"

"Because that would be a really dumb assumption to make, considering you didn't even know me. Not to mention insulting."

His lips twitched. "I've only ever gone to the island alone."

Her brows shot up at that, and she didn't even mind that he was changing the subject. Curiosity about this enigmatic man once more dug at her.

"I wanted to see how it felt to have another with me, to share the experience."

She wasn't sure, but she thought she heard a deep longing in his voice. She felt herself softening toward him even more. "Well, how was it?"

He cocked his head to the side, pondering the question. "Quite enjoyable."

If he'd wanted to bring someone to his island, why hadn't he before? He must have had hundreds of opportunities. Surely not *all* the women he'd dated were users...unless he had a type. Perhaps he felt drawn to certain kind of women, just like some women repeated a pattern of abusive relationships. Perhaps, with Cortez, it was the inherent boldness of females of ambition that drew him back into the cycle. Hadn't she been bold when she'd first walked into Ever Nights? Hadn't she technically been intending to use him? And he'd jumped her like a goddamned thoroughbred.

After a short silence, she said, "Well, it sounds like you're used to dating morons. Present company excluded."

His lips quirked, and he met her gaze. "I suppose you could look at it that way, but it's not just women. Unfortunately, it is the case that most people who get close to me are looking to take advantage of me in some way. A loan, a lay...a *job*." He sighed. "It's tiresome."

She didn't know what to say, so she remained silent.

"Years ago, after so many relationships had gone sour, I vowed never to be with anyone who worked for me. Keeps things simpler. Still, I'm often viewed as little more than a coffer."

She couldn't imagine anyone looking at him and seeing just a pocket to be picked. Sure he was well off in a world that was drowning in poverty, but he was so much more than his holdings. He was funny, intelligent, kind—most of the time—and generous, at least he had been with her. Not to mention he was drop-dead gorgeous and a hurricane in the sack. And yet, was she really any better than the other women from his past? If he only knew what she'd been assigned to do... She went a little pale. He'd toss her over the edge of this boat and leave her to drown.

He noted the subtle change in her mood. "Are you cold."

She sipped her wine. Her hand shook a little. "I'm fine."

"I could have blankets brought up."

"That's sweet of you, but really, I'm okay." They sat for a moment in silence, a current of air playing between them. "So I'm curious," she said finally. "What made you so sure these women you dated only wanted you for your money, or for whatever?"

His lips twisted into a bitter smile. In a low, almost inaudible voice, he said, "It is my burden to know these things."

There was such pain in his words, her heart hurt for him, and she nearly lunged across the deck to throw a comforting arm around him, but she wasn't sure he'd want that, so she stayed where she was.

"Except with you," he mused, almost to himself. "With you I'm completely in the dark. You could be the woman of my dreams, or the embodiment of my self-destruction."

She swallowed an unusually hard lump of wine. "What do you mean?"

For a moment, he looked as though he regretted the cryptic admission, setting his drink aside. "Merely that I don't know where I stand with you after tonight." In a lighter tone, he added, "Have I coaxed your forgiveness yet?"

Is that what he was going for? Was there hope for

their relationship yet? Although, he sounded a little evasive.

She crossed her arms and gave him her profile. "I don't recall hearing an actual apology."

From the corner of her eye, she caught the wolfish curl to his lips. "I am sorry, Naia. Truly." He all but purred her name, making her shiver. With one arm, he pushed off the bench and crossed to sit next to her, curling a finger under her chin to bring her head around to face him. "Am I forgiven?"

She lowered her eyes and pressed her lips together, her own clandestine motives eating at her. She had already decided to cease her undercover act, but what if somehow later on he discovered why she'd been sent to him. It would ruin everything. "I'll forgive you on one condition."

He hesitated. "And what might that be?"

"If I do something that upsets you in the future, you'll forgive me too, okay?" She swallowed against the sudden tightness in her throat as a guilty troll marched up her spine. Even if she was pretty sure now that there was some truth to this mindreading business, it was clear her thoughts were safe. Cortez couldn't know her words were loaded.

His brows drew together, and a frown weighed down the corners of his lips. At length, he said, "Fair enough."

She unconsciously averted her gaze.

"Is there something I should know?" he asked in a slightly flattened tone.

With effort, she assumed a coy expression. "Only that I have one more condition, and it involves you doing that thing you did to me the other day with your tongue."

His grin returned slowly, devilish.

CHAPTER 26

Perfectly sated and deliciously drowsy, Naia walked her fingers up Cortez's magnificent chest, who rested on his back with his eyes closed, her head pillowed comfortably by his thick shoulder. They were in the master cabin, basking in the afterglow of their lovemaking. When she trailed the pads of her fingers back down his chest and over his dazzling abs, his muscles contracted for her, dancing to her touch.

His lips curled up at the corners. In a roughened tone, he said, "I like the way you touch me."

"That's good because I like to touch you."

He caught her hand and brought it to his mouth, placing a soft kiss on the heel of her palm. Her pulse quickened, both from the display of affection and the unintentional reminder that he hadn't fed at all over the last few days, at least not that she knew of, and definitely not from her. Had he been abstaining because she'd balked at first and he didn't want to frighten her? Now that they were back aboard the yacht, would he go back to Emily instead?

She closed her eyes, startled by the sudden pain at the thought.

She opened them again when he settled her palm over his heart and tightened his arm around her. The wayward thought slipped away. Nothing could spoil her good mood right now. Makeup sex with Cortez had been out—of—this—world awesome. She was still floating somewhere between earth and heaven, her body and soul still dancing on a wave of bliss.

She wasn't sure how long they lay like that. Minutes? Hours? She could stay in his arms for days.

After a while, her bone-deep curiosity of this enigmatic, fascinating man riled her curiosity. She wanted to know more about him. Everything. And not because of some seedy mission.

"When were you changed?" she asked lightly.

He didn't respond for a long moment, making her wonder if the question was taboo. Then his words came slow and cautious. "It was before The Revelation."

She gasped, "The Revelation was one hundred years ago!" The fateful day vampires had revealed themselves to the world. "Wait, how long before The Revelation?"

He grinned up at the ceiling. "Why? So you can call me ancient or father time or some other moniker meant to tease me about my age?"

"I would never tease an old man."

His chest rumbled on a husky laugh. She loved that sound and pressed her ear to his chest to experience the full body of it.

"Do you even remember being human?" she asked.

He nodded. "I was the son of a prominent politician. He was grooming me to follow in his footsteps. I'd planned to make some real positive changes in the community."

"I hear a *but* coming."

"Well, naturally all my agendas had humans in mind...that is, until I was changed."

"Why did you decide to become a vampire?"

He let out a breath. "I wasn't given a choice."

"What?" She lifted her head to take in his expression. "You were changed against your will? I thought that was illegal or something."

He seemed passive. "Not illegal. Just frowned upon. Nowadays the injured party has more rights than in my time. Should they decide, they could press charges against the one who sired them, though that is an extremely rare occurrence. Back in my day, the VEA was in its infancy, and new laws were still being established."

"Why would someone change you without your permission?"

"The powers that be in the vampire world were gearing up for The Revelation, even then. Over the course of several years leading up to it, many humans in positions of authority or who were in the public eye were turned to help ease the transition."

And yet there had still been decades of fear-fueled war. Much of the strife continued to this day. "So you were turned for vampire public relations?"

He chuckled at that. "In a manner of speaking."

"That's awful." Whoever his sire was, she wanted to strangle him. "Did you ever get back at the guy who turned you?"

His lips twitched wryly. "He would say so."

She arched a curious brow, but when he left it at that, she got the impression he had no intention of elaborating, and it felt oddly intrusive to pry. "So then you went from human politician to vampire PR agent. I hope they paid you well."

"The transition was not as simple as that. The Revelation came, and so did the fighting. I was drafted instead."

Her jaw dropped. "So you were changed against your will and then forced to become a soldier *for* the person who turned you?" Now she wanted to kill his sire. "What was it like to fight against what used to be your own kind?"

"As you can imagine, it was strange. I was young enough to still *feel* human, yet new enough to be swept up by bloodlust. War only amplified that in young vampires. I don't like to recall those days."

She wouldn't either so she changed the subject. "And now, years later, you're a successful nightclub owner with the world at his fingertips."

"That's the short version."

"Why did you decide to open Ever Nights?"

He turned on his side to face her. "You're full of questions tonight."

She shrugged. "Just curious about you."

"I think it's your turn to tell me something."

Uh oh. This could get tricky. "Okay. What do you want to know?"

"I know you have a brother. Do you have any other siblings?"

She shook her head. "It's just the two of us."

"And your parents?"

"I never knew my father. And my mother, well, she went missing about ten years ago."

"Missing?"

"She just went to work one night and didn't come home. Vanished without a trace. No witnesses. Nothing." Naia swallowed the painful lump that always appeared in her throat when she thought of her mother. One day she was there, the next gone. One day you're sitting there with the normal, safe life you've always known, not realizing the urgency with which you should be cherishing every second of every minute of every day, taking for granted that tomorrow will always come, and you have time to say the things you didn't realize needed saying...you have time.

But then suddenly you don't.

Cortez reached up to cup her cheek, feathering his thumb over her lips. "I'm sorry. That must have been very difficult."

She forced a thin smile. "It's been me and Cole against the world ever since."

His strong arm cinched tighter around her. "You have a good brother."

"What makes you think that?"

"He's protective of you."

"As I am of him. We've always had each other's backs."

"He thinks I'm taking advantage of you."

She blinked up at him. "And how would you know that?"

He gave another of those cagey grins. "Big sis going off with a strange vampire? It's an obvious inference, no?"

She propped herself up on her elbow. "How did you figure I'm older? Most people assume the opposite because he's so much taller than I am." *Explain that, mind reader.*

"He must have mentioned it over the phone... when he was threatening me," he gave a sexy lopsided grin, almost a smirk, as though he found Cole's threats adorable.

She found them embarrassing. "Did he really threaten you? What did he say?"

"Something to the effect of if anything were to happen to you, he'd rip off my head and defecate down my throat."

She ducked her head. "No he didn't."

"Then there was something about objects being

shoved in very uncomfortable places. It was all very inventive."

She laughed, her burning face hidden against his chest.

His tone turned serious. "I want you to know I would never hurt you. Not for any reason."

Her head shot up, shocked by the sudden declaration.

He only smiled. "In case you were worried about that."

"I'm not," she said, her tone a bit higher than she wanted. She wondered if he'd repeat the sentiment if he knew why she'd really come into his life?

"Sometimes humans pretend not to fear us," he continued. "But even for the bravest it's nearly impossible not to on some level. There's an undeniable primal awareness, if you'll forgive the crass analogy, of prey to predator."

She took that in for a minute, and her earlier assumption seemed more plausible. "Is that why you haven't fed from me? Because you don't want to frighten me?"

"Partly. When you agreed, there was hesitation in your voice. I couldn't tell if your offer was genuine and you were just nervous or if you felt *obligated*." He sighed. "Some of the women I've been with thought it was something they'd have to do to stay with me, though they hadn't wanted to. I never forced them. It doesn't have to be an intimate experience."

"What about the ones that *pretended* they wanted to, but really didn't?"

"Usually I can tell what a woman wants from me, and what she doesn't," he said with the confidence of a man who really, really could.

It is my burden to know these things.

"Except with me?"

He gave a crooked smile. "Except with you."

"Why is that?"

His gaze turned wry. "I wish I knew. You are like an exotic creature to me. A mystery. You excite me, entice me, and frustrate me all at once."

"Frustrate?"

He nodded. "I've heard your heart speed from time to time, with no discernable reason. Like on the beach. It was almost akin to approaching a wild animal, one ready to bolt at the first provocation. I can only deduce a part of you fears me. It's either on a level you don't even recognize, or you don't wish to admit it." His tone was even, matter-of-fact, but she sensed the idea bothered him more than he was letting on.

She sat up and faced him fully, legs tucked under her.

He folded his hands behind his head and held her gaze.

"My anxiety wasn't caused by you." Though she had briefly equated him with the monster James, she felt a little guilty about it now because Cortez had never given her any reason to think of him that way. She wouldn't dare spill *all* her secrets, but she could at least put his mind at ease on this. "The island was a dream. You were a dream. I had a wonderful time, I swear."

"But...?"

She offered a bit of veiled honesty. "But the longer I stayed, and this is going to sound weird, but the longer I stayed the more claustrophobic I felt. Like being trapped with no way out."

His lips pursed. "You felt trapped?" Again it seemed her words hurt.

"Not by you. By, oh, I don't know if I can explain correctly. I've never been away from society for so long. Never been so far from people and—"

"Your beloved crowds," he interjected, but in a teasing, what-am-I-going-to-do-with-you sort of way.

"I suppose, kind of, yeah."

He glanced back up at the ceiling. "In all my time working with performers—of *all* kinds—I've never understood the clutching need for the spotlight."

"It's not the spotlight I need," she said, then regretted the outburst.

"Oh? Then what is it?" His tone was soft, filled with a genuine curiosity, but she worried this line of questioning would lead her down a rabbit hole. She couldn't explain what she truly needed.

"Uh-uh," she shook her head, evading. "Your turn. You never answered my question. Why did you decide to open a club like Ever Nights?"

He let out a slight huff as though miffed by the turn around. "After I left my sire to start my own clan, I needed to find us a home. The war was winding down, fighting was sparse, yet chaos was rampant nearly everywhere I went. Some towns had been leveled, others wiped from the map completely. Riverstone seemed like the perfect location to stake a claim. It hadn't been decimated, no one was fighting, but some rebuilding was needed. There were already a few businesses established, a couple clubs and casinos, so I decided Ever Nights would be a hotel. A safe place for vampires and humans alike to rest their heads."

"You didn't intend to create the best nightclub on the east coast?"

He shook his head. "It simply evolved into that over time."

"How?"

"A few club owners were treating their employees poorly. It became necessary for me to...intervene. I ran the worst of them out of town and came to an *understanding* with the rest. After that, the unemployment rate was through the roof, so I came up with an idea for a club/hotel combination to provide more jobs. I knocked down some walls and refurbished the first floor. I turned part of the space into a dance club and hired Kenzi to coordinate that side of the business. As it turned out, the entertainment industry proved incredibly lucrative, so I repurposed the entire second floor, then the third where I allocated space for a casino, and here we are."

"So in a way, you've gone full circle."

"How's that?"

She smiled down at him. "You got yourself into a position to make some positive changes in your community."

He was silent for a moment, then gifted her with a brilliant smile. "I suppose you're right."

CHAPTER 27

Though still unnerving as hell, the helicopter ride back to Riverstone was somewhat less harrowing the second time around. She knew what to expect and was even able to find some enjoyment in the high-flying experience. But, she noticed, as she marveled at the view, Cortez was watching *her* instead of the scenery. At first it made her feel self-conscious, but then she observed how he relished her reactions. When she'd pointed out the sun's dazzling reflection off the lakes and rivers, gold on glass, he'd commented, "Beautiful," though his eyes were on her face. Later, she'd gasped as they'd flown through a patch of low-hanging clouds. She'd been amazed by the sense that, were she not barred by the thick windows, she could reach out and touch them. His grin had only widened at her exuberance.

Back on the boat, he'd been just as delighted with her excitement, when an adorable school of dolphins began following them, bounding and splashing through the waves like living torpedoes. Arching out of the water as if to say hello. She had been utterly enamored, squealing with delight every time one of their sleek bodies caught air. Cortez had seemed bored with the show. He'd only had eyes for her, a self-satisfied curve to his lips, acting as though he'd scheduled the display purely for her amusement. "Ah, right on time," he'd said, glancing at his watch and then shooting her a teasing smile.

She considered his intense interest in her reactions to what had to be pretty mundane activities for one such as he.

Vampire's lives were measured in decades rather than years. Cortez surely must have seen it all, as they say. It was entirely possible he was jaded by this point in his life. Bored. Was she providing a vicarious experience for him? Showing him the world through fresh eyes? Was he finding renewed joy in old pleasures that had long since gone stale? Is that why he'd taken her to his private island? To his coveted sanctuary? Because he'd grown bored even with his personal paradise? He'd sworn to have never brought another there. So why had he dispensed with convention and shared such a wondrous place with her?

Something Dante had said resurfaced as if her subconscious had been holding on to it until this very moment. She'd asked him why he'd decided she, of all people, should spy on Cortez. Cryptically, he'd replied that she was *unique*. That Cortez would be drawn to her, though Dante hadn't elaborated as to why exactly he felt that way.

Was Dante psychic? Or did he just somehow know Cortez's type? Which would be a surprise since his own employees had been boggled by his attention to her.

Three times Cortez had invited her into his private spaces, places that were off limits to others, apparently: his hotel suite, the roof of Ever Nights, and his private island. Man, he had a lot of private spaces.

What would make such a successful man like Cortez feel the need to isolate himself so much? Going from outgoing club owner to wealthy shut-in didn't compute in Naia's mind.

Did it have something to do with his alleged mindreading? He valued his solitude. Was that because on a daily basis he was hammered by everyone's internal jabber?

Curiosity needled her, but she was too afraid to breach these topics with Cortez. The more he opened up to her, the more she felt guilty over her secret investigation. The more she wanted to confess. But if she did, would it only confirm his worst fears? That she was exactly like the other women he'd dated. A liar, a user, a disappointment?

She feared he'd hate her for it. And it would undoubtedly expedite their separation. Or worse. Would he retaliate? What would a man like Cortez do to someone who went after him or his people? She didn't have to ask to know he was fiercely loyal and protective of his people.

The helicopter began to descend, interrupting the frightening thought.

Did he really need to know she'd been sent to betray him when she'd already decided in her heart that she never could? As it was, their week was nearly up. What would happen to her then? Would he send her on her way with a *hey-kid-it's-been-fun* pat on the shoulder? Would he think of her from time to time?

Her stomach twisted, and sorrow seeped into her bones. It snagged in her chest and pulled at her heart. She gulped, knowing what that little twang of anguish meant.

The coming separation was going to affect her more than she should have allowed.

Even over the loud *thwamp* of the helicopter's

blades Cortez somehow detected a change in her mood. Maybe a subtle shift in her expression, her breathing, or perhaps her heart rate when she'd imagined leaving him.

He squeezed her hand, his gaze curious. Then he smiled with a comforting reassurance, and she realized he thought her anxiety was inspired by their declining altitude. She leaned into him, he hugged her close, and she mentally cursed.

Somehow Cortez had burrowed into her heart, carving out a little home for himself there. And when he was done with her, a part of her would be left hollow and empty and lonelier than ever. The dreaded time was coming. There was no doubt about it. She just didn't know when.

At least she'd have Cole to lean on, she reminded herself. He always knew what to say to lift her up. He'd grouse, "He let you go? What an idiot!" And she'd be inclined to agree. If she wasn't worth more than a week, then Cortez wasn't worth her tears. She would make that her mantra.

Thinking of Cole reminded her of their monetary problems. What were they going to do about the twins? The seven grand Dante promised? Well, she had nothing for him to hold over his rival's head. Moreover, she wasn't planning to continue her *investigation*. Even if she did continue, she was too close to him now to be partial. If she happened to discover something illegal going on, she'd only bring it to Cortez's attention so that he might deal with it internally.

She wouldn't confess that little tidbit to Dante, however. Though she would need to tell him something. He must be wondering why she hadn't checked in yet. After she informs him she can't continue this spying game, would he still pay her? She seriously doubted it. She wasn't about to count on it either.

Which meant she had to proceed as though that seven grand was permanently off the table.

Back to plan B.

She leaned her head on Cortez's shoulder and sighed. So much for opting to stay in Riverstone. Now their only option was to run, or else wind up on the sharp, pointy end of the twin's wrath. At least they had nearly another week before those two came looking for payment. Plenty of time to rack up miles between them. To disappear and start again in a new town. Where would they go this time? She grew tired just thinking about it.

Shortly after the helicopter landed, she was ushered into another stretch SUV. The siren in her squirmed almost violently within her, growing desperate with the sense of more humans nearby, but she clamped it down and held it together.

Cortez started making calls from the confines of the back seat, checking in with his club's manager on duty. While he was occupied, she discreetly texted Cole: Initiating Plan B. Time to hit the road. Make sure you're packed and ready to go. She paused, debating. Then added: We leave tomorrow.

Pathetic, she thought, pocketing her phone. Though she should be making plans for their future, she was going to stay one more night with Cortez, use up as much time with him as she could...because she had it bad. The thought of leaving him scorched a hot fissure through her chest. She knew it was a risk to stay, but she just couldn't let it end. Not yet. One more kiss to tide her over. Just one last perfect night. It wouldn't be enough, but it would have to do.

This week with him had been her happiest in a long, long time. She'd forgotten what it meant to simply relax. To feel secure. Safe. To have the bearing of responsibility striped from her shoulders after struggling under its weight for what felt like forever. This week had been a dream, just as she'd told Cortez. A sheer fantasy in the flesh. But dreams didn't last. Nothing did.

Once she and Cole left, it would be back to scrounging for jobs and hustling for cash. Non-stop work to rebuild their lives somewhere far away, during which she'd do what she must: conceal her breaking heart from Cole till she was ready to let him see her pain. She didn't want him in any way feeling guilty about uprooting her. Her heart would have to wait to shatter completely. She'd replace the ruined append-age with fortified steel if she had to. She'd walk away from her home with her head held high and a smile on her face, strained as it might be.

Cortez hung up his phone and wrapped his arm around her and kissed the top of her head as if it were the most natural thing to do. He pulled her closer, and for a heartbreaking second she let the fantasy wash over her, let herself believe everything would work out, that they'd find a way to pay the twins, and that maybe, just maybe, Cortez might want to keep her.

CHAPTER 28

In his suite, Cortez informed her he had some business to take care of and would have to leave her for a bit. She was fine with that. There were things she needed to take care of anyway.

Before he left, he took her lips in a scorching kiss and then whispered in her ear that he had a surprise planned for her later.

She laughed and teased, "Well, it's about time you stepped up your game."

He replied with a heart-wrenching grin. "I haven't even started."

Her heart leapt at his words as her mind tried to work the statement with a key that didn't fit. She couldn't let herself read too much into it. It would only hurt her more in the end. Tonight was all they had.

Unless....

Could she confide in him? Could she trust him with everything? Her darkest secrets his to accept or exploit? Could she swallow her pride and ask him for help with the Twins? It was a lot to ask for. Exactly the type of thing a *user* would do. She couldn't be like that. She couldn't stand it if he saw her that way.

But what if...what if she could stay with him?

She planned to set aside some time to give it all some serious thought, but right now she desperately needed to feed her siren. She had threadbare control as it was. Without Cortez here to distract her with his glorious body and seductive words, she was ready to snap.

After a quick shower, she changed into one of her Kenzi-shopping-spree outfits and then retrieved the dress meant for Goldie as a replacement for the one she—*ahem*, Cortez—had ruined.

In the elevator, she checked her phone. Cole hadn't replied to her text yet.

The lobby was peppered with people lounging on sofas, waiting for a particular show to start in one of the sections of the club. Others lined up at the front desk, checking in for the night. A large-bellied man with a rutty face and two giggling women in evening gowns entered the elevator she'd just vacated. She'd have wished the trio a good night if she wasn't trying so hard not to burst out in song and suck away their energetic life-forces. It was early yet, and this crowd wasn't big enough to fulfill her needs. She'd only over-do it and potentially drive them insane....

Then she'd be trapped in a room with wild-eyed patrons drawn to the source of their madness. Cortez would certainly wonder what she was then...if she survived the melee.

She needed to hurry. Dante's place should be pretty packed by the time she arrived, and would be more conducive to her needs. Before speaking with Dante, she'd take the stage and re-fill her energy, get her fix without taking too much from any one person.

Outside Ever Nights, the sky was dimming to

that rich evening blue that heralded the night. Her skin itched in the dry air. Goosebumps fanned out over her arms. She rubbed them, trying to shake away a sudden, inexplicable feeling of dread. Something was off. She felt odd.

I've waited too long. Any second now I'll lose control.

She hurried off in the direction of The Pit, her heels clacking with each step. The walk seemed a thousand miles long, and her resolve was tested a couple times; once when she passed a homeless man, tempting her to break her silence, then again when she crossed paths with a horde of teens loitering in a park. Both times she'd clenched her teeth and held her breath, fighting past her macabre urges.

It had never been such a relief to see that cracked, gravelly asphalt and flashing broken sign that read DAN E'S IT.

Naia hurried past Fred, the bouncer. He gave a curt nod, and then said something into his radio.

Inside, her mouth dropped. She'd never seen the place so stuffed with people—standing room only. A little unexpected, but oh so perfect. She overheard a conversation about ticket prices and missed opportunities. Someone else mentioned Ever Nights. Was there a coveted event happening there tonight? Whenever Ever Nights put on a huge show, The Pit got some of the spillover.

On stage, one of the exotic dancers who's name Naia couldn't remember, Shannon or Sharon maybe, was in the middle of a striptease. Off to the side, the mic used to announce each act was waiting as if just for her. She didn't even plan to ask, she'd just run up there and do her thing when Shannon/Sharon finished up.

Unfortunately, she never got her chance.

A big, meaty hand gripped Naia by the arm and yanked her back. She stumbled at the unexpected momentum and swiveled her head to see that it was Dante, dragging her to his office. Inside, he shut the door, and then roughly plopped her into the chair across from his desk.

"What did you find out?" His raspy tone was half demanding, half threatening. Dark eyes bore into hers, and she audibly swallowed. Had he always been this menacing?

"I-I haven't found anything."

Both brows lifted nearly to his hairline before drawing together above his narrowing eyes. He placed both his hands on her armrests and then leaned in, too close for comfort. "You haven't found *anything*?" The words were almost a snarl, too aggressive to be a question. "Have you even been looking?"

"I did…a little." He sneered at that, but before he could say anything more, she rushed out, "You were right. He was interested in me. He, uh, took me away from the club for a few days. I could hardly say no. We just got back today."

Dante took that in for a moment, then, eyes flashing, he smiled in a way that made her shiver, his fangs on full display. To her relief, he backed off and took the seat behind his desk. "He found you irresistible, did he?"

For the moment. She nodded

He laughed. "So predictable." His hard gaze settled on her again. "If you have nothing for me, then why are you here?"

"I was hoping to work a shift tonight."

He leaned back and steepled his fingers. "You're here to waitress for me?"

"To sing," she corrected. "I need some money, you see, and I need to keep my vocal cords strong.

Cortez likes having me around, but he won't give me a job. I still have bills to pay and—"

"Darling girl. Why didn't you just say so?" He reached in a drawer and retrieved a wad of cash. Several hundreds landed on the table in front of her.

She gazed at the bills as though they were a nest of snakes ready to strike. A sour sensation churned in her stomach.

"Not enough?" He licked his fingers and counted out more bills.

"It's not that. I...I don't think I can keep spying on Cortez."

Dante went still mid-count, staring at her as though he hadn't heard her correctly. Or maybe he expected her to retract the statement under his threatening glare.

"The money is generous...but it's just not worth the risk. I'm not cut out for spying on people. And I can't stand the lies. I don't want to do it anymore. I can't. It's not right. Besides, I don't believe there's anything for me to find, anyway. I mean, I think his business dealings are pretty clean."

"Nonsense. There's definitely something for you to find. You just need to look, you silly girl." Another flash of his fangs had her pulse revving.

He stood and scooped up the cash, sidestepped the desk, and pulled her to her feet by the arm. He led her back through the throng of people, her siren gnawing at her insides, and ushered her out the front door where the night crushed in around her.

He shoved the cash into her palm. "You have a job to do, and you *will* do it, won't you?"

"I..."

"This isn't a request." His fierce expression was reminiscent of her nightmare, only this was no dream. A primordial urgency took over, *an undeniable primal awareness of prey to predator.* Except this wasn't some primitive trick of the mind. This was bonafide instinct screaming to be heard. Her sense of self-preservation forced a slow nod. She realized if she didn't do as he asked, he might actually hurt her.

"Good girl. Start with the basement, where the vampires feed." He whirled her around by the shoulders and sent her on her way, patting her on the ass for good measure.

Woodenly, she took one step in front of the other, absently clutching the cash to her chest. As the sudden sense of danger tweaked her nerves, the siren in her went mercifully quiet. Thank God, because she had so much more to worry about now.

CHAPTER 29

On the way back to Ever Nights, she dialed Cole, but he didn't answer, so she left him a message, imploring him not to go into work tonight. "I'll see you in the morning," she said. "Then we'll book it."

She'd use tonight to say goodbye to Cortez—

She skittered to a stop as she turned the corner to Ever Nights.

The club was lit up like a Christmas tree. Spotlights danced in the sky and there was a line around the block to get in. Her vocal cords jumped in her throat at the sight of all those people. Ryder and another vampire she hadn't seen were guarding the door and arguing with people that they were at capacity. Ryder looked surprised when he spotted her crossing the car-filled parking lot.

"What are you doing out here?" he asked, glancing around as though looking for a threat. Little did he know *she* was the threat. "You should be inside."

The crowd groused as he escorted her through the doors.

"Shut it!" the other vampire snapped at them. The complaints dimmed.

Ryder ushered her past the lobby, through a short corridor, and into a large open room with high ceilings. The crowd here was thick as well, chortling with excitement. So many people. So much energy. *All for me.*

She bit her tongue to keep from belting out her song. The loud music blasting through heavy speakers would make it impossible for anyone but those closest to hear her at all. It wasn't the right time. Heart thumping, her throat constricted, smothering her vocal cords. Her gaze darted around the room for an answer to her dilemma.

Still holding onto her, she and Ryder had to push past bodies until finally they reached a private VIP table on a dais.

"Wait here!" He had to yell to be heard. "I'll let Cortez know where you are." He vanished into the throng.

People swayed and danced nearby. Her vocal cords whimpered in their cage. Her body quivered, breaths shadowing. She swiped away a fine mist of sweat on her forehead. The thumping in her chest out-drummed the pulsating subwoofers near the stage. She had to stay in control. Only a very few close by people would be snared if she—

The stage!

People were shoved up against it on the opposite side of the room. Complete with instruments and several microphones, it was like a beacon of light in darkness.

No time to think, she hurled herself into the crowd, fighting toward that promised land.

Almost there. Just a little farther.

Bodies keep getting in her way. She must have used violence, because a few people screeched as she passed. One guy called out, "Hey!" as though offended by her macabre need to get to that mic.

Finally, at the edge of the stage, she hefted herself up, scrambled to the mic, and ripped it from its stand.

Blissful screeching feedback hushed the crowd. Thousands of eyes turned on her. Her heart thundered; not from fear, but from anticipation.

Under the hot lights, she caught the sight of Cortez barreling through the door, his eyes darting furiously, his expression strange. Then their gazes locked. At first he seemed surprised to see her on stage, a curious tilt to his brow. His attention bounced to the mic in her hand then back to her face and that surprise turned to anger.

Thinking the show was on, someone landed a spotlight on her. She squinted at the sudden sting, now only able to see the front row. Dozens of people gazed up at her expectantly.

She brought the mic to her lips, and loosed her voice, a soft hymn at first that so easily fell into sync with the rhythmic beat of the bass bumping through the room. Her entire body relaxed as her snare stretched out. So many people in such close quarters meant that she was feeding almost instantly.

She gave her voice room to grow into a confident treble before exploding into a thunderous chime that cut through the air and bled into the farthest walls, the words coming as naturally as the sound was beautiful. She often made up lyrics, letting the moment take her. Now was one of those times.

As her eyes adjusted to the blaring light, she found the hazy form of Cortez slicing through the crowd toward her. He stopped several feet from the front row, glaring up at her. He wasn't happy about her stunt. She'd have to deal with that later. Now all that mattered was the exuberant energy flowing into her, rejuvenating her. It was like candy on Halloween. Presents at Christmas. Cake on Birthdays.

She closed her eyes and smiled as a rhythmic hook exploded from her lungs and she held fast to a single cord. It playfully soared and dove and glided around the room, whipping like a feather in the wind yet landing like a sharpened blade. A hush fell over the crowd.

Her eyelids cracked open when her tone turned soulful, sorrowful. She zeroed in on Cortez, meeting his gaze once more. His expression was now inscrutable.

Somehow this song had turned into something personal. Something gut-wrenching and filled with melancholy. An ode to love and loss and regret.

This song was her heart on a plate.

His expression remained blank.

Fully recharged, she slowed it down, her voice tapering off till her humming tone weaved through the beat, as darkly ambiguous as desire itself. Aria complete, she let the mic fall to her side.

The crowd roared with applause.

She blinked, as though roused from a trance. Cortez was gone. She searched for him. He was stage left, waiting for her, a deep frown cutting into his lips. She took a couple quick bows and replaced the mic before stepping off stage.

"Come with me." His tone was tinged in ice. He gripped her by the arm, much in the same way Dante had, and dragged her after him.

"Look," she started, her legs working to keep up. His grip on her was alarmingly tight. "I'm sorry I did that. It won't happen again, I swear."

He snorted derisively. "Least of your problems."

"Huh?" She hardly noticed where he was taking her till they ended up in something that resembled a conference room with a long rectangular table surrounded by black leather chairs. A flat screen TV was built into the wall. Ryder, Donovan, and several others bordered the room...all glaring at her.

She understood that Cortez didn't like the idea of her performing in his club, but this reaction was a bit much.

"Sit," Cortez ordered, whipping her toward a chair.

Stunned, she sank down, wildly glancing around. "W-What's going on?" Seven vampires sneered at her, their arms crossed. Even Ryder looked pissed, his earlier smile a ghost in her memory. He gazed at her now like he didn't even know who she was. Could that one little performance really have ticked everyone off to this degree?

"It was just a song, guys. I won't do it again." If she wasn't so freaked out right now, she would have applauded her steady tone. She glanced up at Cortez, pleading with her eyes. "Was it really so wrong, what I did?"

Anger twitched his jaw, his stone-cold expression growing even more chilly. He snatched a remote off the table and pressed a button. A still photograph flashed on the screen. The image was shot outside Dante's Pit, taken earlier this evening...at the exact moment when Dante had shoved that cash into her palm. Another photo replaced the first, showing his hand on her ass as she started away, a sickeningly satisfied smile on his face.

Nausea slammed into her stomach. "Y-you had me followed again?"

"Donovan noticed you leaving in quite a hurry...alone. Thought I might want you protected, so he trailed you at a distance. He was shocked to find you'd walked to Dante's Pit, even more so when, minutes after entering, you emerged with the man himself looking all too pleased with himself. Tell me, did he pay you for the sex or for the information you gave him? Or was it just a bonus for screwing me?"

"I-I didn't—"

Cortez stabbed another button on the remote.

Grainy surveillance footage popped up: It was an above shot of her frantically snooping through Cortez's office.

Nausea turned nuclear. Dizzying and sickly, she pleaded, "Cortez, I..."

He punched both his fists down on the table so hard it splintered straight to the middle. She jumped at the loud crack. A matching fisher lashed her heart. "I don't have to read your mind to see the guilt on your face." He stood, his glare sharp. "The ONE person in half a millennia who could lie to me!"

The one person? Was he saying what she thought? Could he truly read minds? It seemed so, but not hers, apparently. The pain in his expression sliced her open.

"I didn't," she began desperately. "I mean, I can explain." She reached for him but he recoiled from her. Another lash to her heart. She pulled her hand back.

"Save it for Dante." He faced the door, and took the knob in a white-knuckle grip, giving her his profile. "If I see you around my club again, you won't like the consequences."

Panic set in. She jumped to her feet. "Won't you even listen to me?" Tears spilled down her cheeks. He was out the door before she finished speaking. It slammed closed behind him.

She caught a sob with her palms and squeezed her eyes shut in an attempt to keep the pain inside.

It didn't work.

Agony didn't cover what she was feeling. In less than five minutes, her heart had been ripped from her chest and shoved in a blender with two ball bearings and a switchblade. She was shredded.

Ryder stepped forward. "Come on. I'll walk you out." His manner was brusque, but there was a hint of pity in his tone. Standing upright was almost painful when all she wanted was to curl into a ball and die.

As she walked, Ryder had to adjust her trajectory several times as they headed for the lobby because she wasn't watching where she was going. The world was a wet blur.

Live music now blared from the room where she'd seized the stage only minutes ago. It took her muddled mind a second to recognize the eclectic voice. She gasped, peeking in to see the famous singer, Kenny Raymond, playing one of her favorite songs to a roaring crowd.

Hand on her heart, she stumbled back, fresh tears stinging her eyes. She recalled Cortez in her room gazing appreciatively at her Kenny Raymond poster.

This was the surprise he'd had planned for her? The sweetest thing anyone had ever done.

She couldn't breathe.

Her chest was caving in.

It took several heartbeats to realize Ryder was holding her upright. People were staring at her strangely. Oh right, because she was openly sobbing and shaking like a paint mixer.

"Come on girl. Get it together. You only knew him for a week. It's not like there were marriage bells in your future."

She suddenly wanted to scratch Ryder's eyes out on principle. But, grudgingly she admitted he was right. She was devastated over the shortest relationship in history. A relationship that would have come to an end anyway, even if Cortez hadn't learned of her treachery. She was leaving town in less than twenty-four hours. She had Cole to think about. She couldn't let her kindhearted brother see her like this. He'd want to march on over here and kick Cortez's ass. And Cortez would not humor him like he had over the phone.

She could hold herself together for a couple of days till they were settled elsewhere. Plenty of time to crumble into pieces later, in private.

Her phone chimed. Finally, a text from Cole. She wiped her face and retrieved the device. He'd sent her a picture? She opened the attachment. The image was of Cole sitting on a chair. He appeared upset? Wait, no, he looked afraid....

Why were his hands behind his back like that? It didn't look comfortable. Who had taken this picture?

A second text popped up: Do as I say, Naia. There was another attachment as well. Thumbing it open, her brain went fuzzy, not registering the bloodied, blob-face thing in the image, a human figure...sitting in the same chair Cole had occupied....

Knees crashing into the tiled floor, she screamed.

CHAPTER 30

Someone handed her some ice water. Unclasping one arm from around her tightly drawn in knees, she accepted the glass. Her hand shook so badly some of the liquid sloshed out and ran down her arm.

Cole was being tortured...if he was even still alive.

Back in the meeting room, the vampires seemed to be arguing amongst themselves. She wasn't listening, was using all her faculties to banish that image of Cole's ruined face from her memory.

Why was Dante doing this to Cole? She'd quickly determined it was he who had sent those texts from Cole's phone, even as her fit of hysteria had drawn the attention of nearly everyone in the club, including Cortez.

Thinking she was just making a scene, he'd whisked her back here to rail at her some more. The only response she'd been able to make was a hoarsely muttered, "*He's hurting him.*" The words were a constant beat in her head.

After Cortez had been shown the pictures, he'd gone quiet, letting his clan openly debate what they should do about Dante's *latest ploy*. Apparently this wasn't the first time Dante had come at them.

Like a king at council, a stoic Cortez leveled his attention on whoever was talking at the moment, and occasionally on those who remained quiet like him, deep in thought. Reading their minds?

She struggled to focus on the conversation.

"...the last fucking straw." A vampire in a leather jacket said, punching his fist into his open palm. "Does he think we won't retaliate?"

"He might be hoping for that," someone else countered, sounding calmer than the others. She recognized him as one of the guys from the first night when she and Cortez had played pool. He was staring at her now. Thoughtful. Cortez was glaring at him.

"What the hell did he hope this heinous slag would find, anyway?" Another guy whose name she didn't know snapped, earning himself an even harsher glare from Cortez.

"Exactly," yet another agreed. "He knows how we do business, for fuck's sake. He knows there's never been anything illegal going on here. She was probably meant to plant something. Frame us."

Unconsciously, she shook her head, but said nothing. That was something Dante had hinted at. But she would never have done something like that. Not that they would believe her—

Her chair jerked around, spinning her body with it. She gasped as someone got in her face. The vampire who'd called her a slag glared down at her, invading her space. "What say you, girl? What were you and that fucker plotting?"

She cringed away from his emerging fangs, an obvious tell-me-or-else kind of threat.

"Dane." The sound of the man's name on Cortez's lips was a solid warning. Dane backed away.

Naia glanced at Cortez, surprised by that small show of defense, but he wasn't looking at her. In fact, he hadn't looked at her once since she'd returned to this room.

"Pose your questions, Lex." Cortez said coldly.

The calm vampire, Lex, stepped forward and took a seat across from her. "First, let's give her a chance to explain herself."

Several of them rolled their eyes, but made no other protest. Instead, like it had been coordinated, they all sat as though expecting a long drawn-out overture in the name of her innocence. Cortez was the only one that remained standing, leaning against the wall with his arms stapled over his chest.

"First, promise me you'll help me get my brother back," she said.

Her words were for Cortez, but the angry vampire, Dane, replied instead. "You're lucky we haven't killed you yet, darlin'. That's the best offer you're going to get till you start talking."

Cortez, the embodiment of indifference, did not admonish him this time.

Knife to chest.

Dropping her eyes to the table, she admitted, "Dante hired me to spy on the club. He was going to pay me seven grand."

Someone whistled.

"I was supposed to get a job here," she added.

Cortez snorted, an ah-it-all-makes-sense-now kind of sound.

Great. Now he assumed her lobbying for a job had been all about Dante's plan. Nothing to be done about it now. She had to focus on helping Cole. Nothing else mattered. "Then I was supposed to inform him of any illicit activity that might be going on, either by Cortez or by his employees. He never actually told me to plant evidence, and I never would have, but…"

"But what?" Lex encouraged.

"He did make it clear that I *should* find something. At first I thought he meant he was sure there was something to find. After tonight, I suspect he meant he'd made sure there was something to find."

The group shared uneasy glances.

"Explain," Cortez ordered from his place against the wall.

"I went there tonight to tell him I didn't want to spy for him anymore—"

Several of them made noises of disbelief.

"—but he wasn't having it. He gave me that cash hoping to appease me, and when I still refused, he basically threatened me. At some point, he must have gotten ahold of Cole's phone. Might have been holding Cole even before I went there tonight, as collateral. I had sent my brother a text earlier, telling him to pack and get ready to leave town."

Cortez's arms dropped, and he finally looked at her, but he said nothing, his expression a mix of anger and surprise.

She went on. "But he never responded. Now I figure Dante must have read that text. He might have even listened to the phone message I left just after he'd rushed me out of his club tonight, warning Cole not to go into work. Dante would realize I had no intention of following orders, and that's why he…that's why Cole is suffering now." She leaned forward, placing her palms together. "Please. *Please* help me get him out of there."

Cortez remained silent, but his stoic mask had cracked slightly. Her hope rested in the crease between his brows.

Lex continued the interrogation. "You said you think Dante made sure there was something to find.

What gave you that impression?"

She shrugged, growing tired and sick with worry. "When I told him I didn't believe anything illegal was going on here, he suggested I look in the basement... where the vampire's feed."

Nearly everyone leaned back in their chairs.

Lex glanced at the others. "Who's on duty down there?"

"Marco," Leather Jacket replied. "He wanted my shift tonight. Was pretty insistent, actually."

"He took my shift yesterday," Ryder admitted.

One of the others cleared his throat. "Mine the day before."

Cortez shoved away from the wall. "I haven't seen Marco for weeks. I wonder if he's been avoiding me. How about we go see what old Marco is up to?" He didn't wait for the others to stand before tearing through the door.

As his cohorts followed, she saw her chance to get out of dodge. Cortez clearly wasn't concerned for her brother's wellbeing. Maybe she could find Dante and reason with him herself.

When she stepped out into the hall, she nearly ran into Lex.

He took her by the arm in a firm yet surprisingly gentle grip. "Sorry, love. You'll have to come with us."

"I have to get to my brother," she protested, trying to shrug him off. "*Dante's hurting him.*"

His expression softened. "Cortez already sent a team to extract Cole."

She stilled. "He did?"

Lex nodded. "If he's being held at Dante's, we'll get him out of there."

Sniffling, tears billowing, she blubbered, "Thank you."

When she thought of a basement, dim lighting and cracked, concrete walls was typically what came to mind, not the plush and elegant atmosphere that she found herself in. And it wasn't exactly a basement, though they were on a lower level. However, it wasn't the lowest level in the building.

Perfectly placed bulbs lovingly highlighted the golden-brown hews in the carpet and walls meant to cultivate a gracefully sophisticated ambience. Hellenistic statues were tastefully scattered through the space, a variety of marble sconces decorated the walls, and small water fountains and potted plants provided a fresh outdoorsy feel. This place was meant to look and feel like paradise. Except, under the deliberate floral scents, there was a distinct metallic fragrance. Coppery.

She got the sense that there was more to this place that went unseen. It almost seemed like an entirely different building, a separate hotel for dark dealings.

They entered a lobby of sorts, a big round room that split off into three hallways that were lined with doors. Bloodletting rooms, she assumed. To the right, there was a seating area where small groups of vampires and humans were ignoring them, busy bargaining for feeding rights and maybe just a little bit more. To the left was an unmanned front-desk.

Marco was suspiciously absent.

"Check the logs," Cortez ordered. "I want to know every transaction that has transpired over the last two weeks. Hell, over the last month. Anything that went down when Marco was on duty."

Ryder slipped behind the desk and started typing on a computer console. A log of vampire liaisons?

Fists clenched, Cortez stomped down one of the corridors. Some of the others took that as a cue to do the same, spreading out like hounds on the hunt. Lex stayed behind, presumably to watch her, though he was making a valiant effort to be cordial to the traitor.

He gestured to an available set of armchairs near the corner. "Would you like to have a seat?" He said it like she had an option. She let him guide her to the chair. He took the one beside her.

"Being nice to me right now makes me wonder if I'm about to be assassinated for my role in all this."

He gave a small grin. "I promise you, no one here is going to hurt you. Cortez is angry, but...just give him some time to cool off."

"Is that why he was glaring at you earlier? Because you were thinking he just needed to *cool off*?" She couldn't keep the suspicion out of her voice.

He seemed to be mulling over his response as though he wanted to get it just right. "I'm sure you've deduced Cortez has some hang-ups, probably regarding his female companions."

She nodded, suddenly very interested in what he had to say.

"Over the years, his...abilities...have amplified his inherent mistrust. Who doesn't think shady thoughts every now and again? Nearly impossible to control one's mind all the time, wouldn't you agree?"

Her mouth dropped but she swiftly closed it and nodded once more.

"To an extent, he understands that, but relationships have been...difficult for him. When I learned of your special resistance to him, I thought you would be good for him. I still think that."

She thought he might say more, but he just leaned back into his seat.

She was dying to ask a thousand and one questions, but only one thing mattered. "When can I know if my brother is safe?"

"You'll know the moment I do, I promise."

She allowed herself to believe him.

"I'm not seeing anything unusual here," Ryder called from behind the desk area. "Just business as usual."

"Any strange shipments or packages?" Lex asked.

More typing. "Nothing noted. You really think Marco is going against the boss? He's not dumb enough to...." A crease formed between his brows.

Lex stood. "What is it?"

Naia pushed to her feet as well, feeling the sudden tension rolling off Ryder.

"Rooms three-oh-five through three-oh-nine were scheduled for renovations last week, but the order has been delayed." He punched another sequence of keys. "And for some reason there are active keycards on file for rooms three-oh-eight and three-oh-nine."

CHAPTER 31

Rooms three-oh-eight and three-oh-nine were actually on the next floor down. Check on the whole more-than-meets-the-eye thing. Once Ryder had grabbed an extra set of keycards, he'd looked to see how many of the rooms on that floor had been booked. Answer? Zero.

Suspicious? Damn right.

In the elevator, Ryder called Cortez with an update. "They're on their way," he told Lex.

Naia's gut twisted and churned, bubbling with an innate terror, a fear of the unknown. What would they find in those rooms? What would Dante deem sufficient enough to take down an empire? What if this was some kind of trap meant for Cortez alone? Or was she being led like cattle to the slaughter? A trick to get her down here without fuss or fight?

A deserted floor? No one to hear her scream?

No one here is going to hurt you, Lex had said. There had only been two people in the room when he made that statement. That left a lot of other people to do the harming.

"Calm yourself," Lex muttered, placing a palm

on her shoulder.

"What, can you read minds too?"

"Your heart is fluttering like a butterfly. If I didn't think you'd run off and get yourself killed, I would have left you in the lobby."

Okay, maybe they weren't going to kill her. Why reassure your murder victim when there was already nowhere to run?

A ding sounded and the elevator doors slid open. The entire floor was darker than dark. The word pitch could be applied.

"I'll be happy to head back up to the lobby now," she said, edging to the back of the brilliantly lit elevator.

"We got you, girl." Ryder disappeared into the darkness. He must have found a switch, because the place was suddenly as bright as the floor above had been; same golden-brown hues and similar motif, only the place was deserted. Ominously silent.

Lex put his palm on the small of her back, stepping with her out of the elevator. She followed behind Ryder who took a right down a corridor lined with identical brown doors that broke up the jasmine colored walls. She tallied off the room numbers in her head as they passed. *Three-oh-four...three-oh-six... three-oh—*

Ryder slowed. "You smell that?"

"Blood," Lex replied. His hands clamped on her shoulders, swiveling her so her back was against the wall. "Stay here."

Her pulse went into hyper-drive. When a vampire looked worried it was damn-well time to worry.

Ryder didn't bother knocking on room three-oh-eight. He swiped the keycard and rushed the room like he was busting in on an armed brigade. She waited, her heart blasting painfully against her ribs.

"Jesus Christ." The solemn curse shot back at them through the opened door.

Lex joined him inside and then huffed a curse of his own.

With no gunfire and no sound of a struggle, the compelling force of curiosity commanded her through the entryway.

Blood was everywhere, the floor, the walls, the ceiling, the lamps. It was a gruesome artist's delight.

Her gaze was drawn to the bed, and she let out a choking sob. The body was so mutilated it was nearly unrecognizable...but those boots. She knew those boots. Goldie never let anyone borrow those boots. Not even *her*.

Mindless, Naia rushed toward her friend, shaking her and crying for her to wake up.

In the next instant, she blinked at her hands, covered in blood. The red stuff was down the front of her shirt as well. One of the vampires was pulling her off of Goldie's lifeless body. It was Ryder, telling her to calm down, that he still sensed a heartbeat. Naia's gasps were little slices of pain in her chest. Her lungs were a furnace of pain.

Suddenly Cortez was there. He swiftly assessed the situation and then took her from Ryder.

Sobbing, she curled into his chest and tried to catch her breath.

"It's okay," he cooed, holding her to his chest. "Shhh." Even as agonized sounds erupted from her that she couldn't seem to control, she was grateful for this small offer of comfort, even though he'd wanted nothing more to do with her.

Someone called from the bathroom to their right. "There's another one in here!" The voice belonged to Dane. When had he arrived? Oh, God. Did he say there was another one?

She blinked slowly, the world swimming.

Cortez was holding her steady by the shoulders now, mouthing that everything was going to be all right. Or maybe he was saying it out loud. Her ears were a rush of white rapids and a harsh rhythmic banging that could only be her heartbeat. Her vision blurred. *My hands are covered in blood.*

"I know," he replied like she had spoken. Had she?

"Goldie's blood." She heard her voice crack. "They killed her."

"Lex is helping her," Cortez said. "She might survive."

She glanced toward the horrifically bloody lump in boots. Lex was hunched over it. Feeding her his blood? As panic stormed her, Cortez seemed to be checking her for injury.

"This one's gone," Dane called again from the bathroom.

Fresh terror stabbed her brain. "Cole?"

"It's another female," Dane replied.

Relief weakened her knees.

Cortez propped her against the wall. "I need to go investigate. Will you be alright if I leave you?"

Woodenly, she nodded and forced her stark eyes to blink.

She must looked freaked out, because he didn't look convinced. "Do you want to wait in the hallway?"

She shook her head. "I'll be okay here." She wanted to stay nearby in case Goldie woke up. She didn't know how fast vampire blood healed, but Goldie shouldn't awaken to strange faces after...whatever horror she'd been through.

Cortez nodded and then went into the bathroom where he, Dane, and a couple others all talked in hushed tones. Naia leaned her back against the wall, working on evening her breath. Lex was talking to Goldie, encouraging her to fight. Had he started CPR?

Shakily, Naia wiped her forehead with her sleeve, managing to smear more of Goldie's blood on her skin.

The room rolled. Bile churned.

She blinked a long blink, then dragged her heavy lids back open.

Everything became like a dream. Warped in a way that said she might just pass out from shock. She fought against the temptation. Lex rhythmically pumped Goldie's red-stained chest. Blood dripped down the headboard.

From the corner of her eye, Naia noticed a door to the adjoining room was cracked open.

"Three-oh-nine." She whispered absently, dizzy.

She blinked. Lex was working Goldie's chest. The others were still in the bathroom. No one had heard her. Maybe she hadn't spoken aloud.

An uneasy feeling skittered over her spine. Her subconscious suspected what her waking mind wasn't quite comprehending. That darkness beckoned.

Abandoning CPR, Lex's wrist was back at Goldie's mouth. Were his efforts working? Naia couldn't tell.

She blinked. Her legs took control. She swayed on her way across the room.

Planting her palms on the adjoining door, she pushed it open—

She blinked.

And lost her ever-loving mind.

CHAPTER 32

"Who's that mommy?" Naia inched closer to the bassinet. A tiny thing lay within, squirming and making annoying sounds.

"That's your baby brother. You're a big sister now. Do you know what that means?"

She shook her head. The child caught the movement and then smiled up at her. That smile was a force of nature. It instantly captured her heart.

"It means you need to help him get big and strong like you. You need to protect him and keep him safe."

"What's his name?"

"Cole. Do you like it?"

She nodded. "I'm going to be the best big sister."

"You leave him alone!" Naia punched the little girl bullying Cole square in the face.

The hit knocked the girl back, and she fell on her ass. "Ow! I was going to give it back."

Cole looked on, now smug where before his face had been wet with tears. His big sister had come to his defense. The little girl, taller than him by a foot, had been holding his favorite action figure out of his reach.

Naia snatched the action figure out of the girl's grasp and handed it to Cole. "Come on, Cole. Let's go play somewhere else."

"A witch used to live there," Davie said, pointing to the condemned four-square home as they all loitered behind a large shrub. With its chipped paint, busted windows shimmering in the moonlight, and overgrown yard, Naia could almost believe it. Almost. She wasn't that gullible. But in lieu of a witch, there could be squatters. Worse, it could be a drug den filled with crack heads.

Flanked by his minions Jamie and Warren, Davie turned to Cole. "You want to be in our club, you got to stay the whole night in there."

The only indication that Cole was scared shitless was the tightness in his jaw. Only Naia knew his tell.

To Naia, Davie's club was nothing more than a bunch of teenage boys pretending to be tough. She would have told them to screw off, but Cole was younger than they were, and he desperately wanted to be their friend. He'd asked for this initiation.

"Come on, Cole," she said. "We'll do it together."

"We don't allow girls in our club," Davie reminded her.

"Who cares," she shot back. "I just want to see the witch. Maybe I can learn a thing or two."

With Cole now looking a little less intimidated, he shrugged to his potential friends as if to say, "Girls, what can you do?" but she knew he was grateful for the company. Then, side by side, they marched for the witches den.

"What if it's haunted in there?" Cole asked her

when they were far enough away not to be heard. "Mallory said it's haunted."

She whispered back, "Then I'll use my voice and make those ghosts haunt Davie for the rest of his life."

"You can't do that," Cole said, but he smiled.

Naia hid her own trepidation as she and Cole pushed open the creaky front door and faced their fears together.

Oh god, they're everywhere! Men stumbled through the streets, drawn for some reason to her. Why was she in the middle of the street singing at the top of her lungs like a mad woman? Harsh wind whipped the hem of her nightgown around her legs as she gazed into the confused faces of the men closing in.

One of them reached for her. "So pretty."

Naia reared back and then raced inside her home, slamming the door closed behind her. The noise woke Cole, who'd been sleeping on the top bunk they both shared in the living room.

Sitting up, he rubbed his eyes. "What's going on?"

"There are men outside. I think they're going to try to break in." She woke her mother next, who ushered them out the back, leaving everything behind.

As they slinked through the neighborhood, Cole kept checking over his shoulder, his expression worried.

"Don't worry," she told him solemnly. "I won't let anyone get you."

He'd grabbed her hand. "I won't let anyone get you either."

Someone's in my room!

Naia awoke to the sound of someone crawling

through her window. The night was missing the moon, but she managed to spot a shadowed silhouette creeping toward her. She recognized the breadth of those shoulders.

James wasn't going to take no for an answer. He wanted to control her and make her do terrible things to innocent people.

She gathered a scream in her chest, but before she could let it out, he was on her, covering her mouth with a cloth that smelled awful. Dizziness swam in her head. She scratched and clawed at him, but he wouldn't let up. He was too strong.

Suddenly his heavy weight was ripped off her. She coughed and wheezed for fresh air. When some of the dizziness abated she could hear wet slapping sounds coming from a darker corner of her room. She lurched for the light switch.

Cole was crouched over James, bashing his meaty fist into the man's face. Blood splayed across the wall. Already James was unconscious, sound-blocking head-phones dangling around his neck. Still Cole didn't stop. She'd never seen him more enraged.

"Cole," she said, placing a soft hand on his muscled shoulder. He was growing so strong. Mother would have been proud.

He glanced up at her for a moment, looked back down at James, and then landed one final jaw-breaking punch.

Her little brother was a big badass.

Nothing could get him....

....Nothing could get him....

CHAPTER 33

Cole's name was a banshee's cry on her lips.

Half-maddened, she lurched for Cole, tied to the same chair from those pictures, hunched forward.

She lifted his bloodied face between her hands. His neck felt weird, like there were no bones inside. "Cole!" she choked. "Please, no, Cole. Wake up. Wake up. Please, wake up."

Swamped by tears, she couldn't tell who was tugging her from the lifeless body of her sweet, tough-as-nails, broken, bleeding brother. She couldn't understand why they were taking her away from him. He needed her! Gasping for air, she punched and kicked and fought to get back to Cole's side, but whoever held her was too strong. Her lungs seemed to be shrinking with each panicked breath. She couldn't think past her desperation to help her brother.

Was Cole even breathing? She tried to pose the question, but she was sobbing so badly the words were unintelligible. Her voice was ragged and raw, her mind clutched by terror. She tried again, and again as she was drawn farther away, through the door.

Suddenly the room was a nest of chaos. People were yelling. No, wait, Cortez was yelling for someone to take her. He handed her off and then ordered everyone else to his side. At whoever held her now, he jerked his chin toward the hall. He was banishing her?

"No! Let me go!"

Cortez and the others filed into three-oh-nine. The door shut behind them while she was dragged into the hallway. She flailed and screamed, killing her voice with each roar of Cole's name, but her struggles did nothing but trigger fatigue. Cole's face had been a reddened mass of swollen flesh.

This is all my fault!

When she was hauled into the elevator and the doors closed, her captor finally released her. She tipped over onto all fours and heaved up her lunch mixed with bile. Large booted feet stepped back, giving her elbowroom.

Finished heaving, she rasped, "Take me back. He needs me. I need to be there."

Ryder, who she now hated with all her being, knelt down next to her. "Let them do what they can for him. If there's any way to bring him back, Cortez will do it."

The world stopped. She glanced up at Ryder. "What do you mean bring him...? Back from the dead!?"

He pursed his lips, the pity in his eyes the only answer she received.

Her mind crashed.

CHAPTER 34

She was like a zombie, doing whatever Ryder said without much thought or care. He'd taken her to Cortez's suite, and pointed her to the shower, softly instructing her to clean up. She did, ignoring the rivulets of red flowing down her body and swirling at her feet.

He'd given her clothes to change into. She'd put them on, not paying attention to their make or color.

In the living area, he'd handed her a glass of whiskey and told her to drink. She did, not feeling the bite that usually accompanied hard liquor. When she finished the glass, he offered her more. She'd accepted, sucking the liquid back as silent tears trailed down her cheeks. When she'd curled up on the couch, he'd covered her with a blanket and told her to let it out.

She did.

She wasn't sure how long she'd cried, or how her body was even still able to produce tears, just that it felt like hours had passed. Dawn was yawning toward the horizon, but it was dark yet, the sky reluctant to let go of night. She and Ryder had been silent for a long while. They'd received no word about Cole or

Goldie.

Was that a bad sign? Or was no news good news?

From her place on the couch, she asked in a scratchy voice, "Why did you bring me to Cortez's room?" There had to be other rooms available for her to wait in.

Ryder glanced up. "Because he wanted me to."

Burrowing deeper into the cushions, she sniffed. "Why would you think that?" Cortez hadn't said anything of the kind. He'd merely jerked his chin for someone to remove her from the vicinity. "For all you know he could have meant for you to escort me out of the building. He might be upset to find me here."

Ryder opened his mouth to respond, but the door burst open, cutting him off.

Someone stomped into the room. By the subtle change in Ryder's posture, it had to be his leader, Cortez.

Naia cringed, sinking deeper into her hovel of blankets, the couch hiding her from where Cortez seemed to have stopped. She was afraid to peek over the couch, afraid to see his expression—it would surely tell her if Cole was dead. For a few more glorious seconds, she could pretend everything would be fine, and she'd have Cole back in no time, everything set to rights.

"The VEA will arrive shortly," Cortez announced, pacing. "They received an anonymous tip. Dante really went all out with this one. A bludgeoning, a draining, and an overdose. It's a tri-fucking-fecta of death."

A choking sound interrupted him. Naia's hands flew to her mouth, a great sob breaking free.

"Shit," he muttered. "I thought you'd be in the bedroom." He skirted the couch and then knelt in front of her. He was more disheveled than she had ever seen him, dark stains cradling his eyes, clothes wet with blood. Too much blood.

She gasped. "Is that Cole's blood?"

He hesitated. "Partly. But he's alive. I was able to save him."

The assurance didn't sink in at first, her heart still trying to bounce back from its devastating fall. Then she saw the truth of it in his eyes and another sob ripped out of her, this one the product of pure happiness and joy. "He's alive?" her voice was hoarse.

"Yes. Everything is going to be fine." Had his eyes darted evasively?

Cole was alive!

She threw her arms around his neck and cried, "Thank you. Oh, God, thank you so much." So grateful was she that she didn't even care about the still-wet blood from his clothes squishing between them.

He didn't seem to mind either. He held her like that for a moment, petting her hair until she realized he might not want her so close. Was probably just being kind in light of the seriously fucked up circumstances.

Though it was the last thing she wanted, she pulled away, sniffing. "Can I see him?"

He snatched her unfinished whiskey off the coffee table and swallowed the contents down in one gulp. After a moment of heavy silence, he said, "He was beaten pretty badly. I-uh had to do something extreme to save his life."

"What does that mean?"

He took a second to refill the glass. She expected this one to disappear the same as the first, but then he handed it to her. Foreboding stole her breath. She sat up and reluctantly accepted the whiskey.

Cortez cleared his throat. "I had to change

him."

"I don't understand. What do you mean change..." The Whiskey slipped from her grasp, landing with a dull thud on the carpet, the contents arching out before conquering the expensive fibers. Her gut twisted painfully as understanding crushed into her skull from every angle, and she was suddenly gasping for air. Her heart tore open, flayed and shredded with the industrial strength of a hydraulic pulverizer. Her sweet, normal, human brother was no more. Changed forever into something...unnatural. *Like me.*

Cortez turned anxious, reading her reaction.

New vampires were notoriously volatile and blood thirsty, often mindless with their need for blood. If it was anything like what she went through as a siren—and she had no doubt that it would be a thousand times worse—everyday would be a struggle. He would never be the same.

"He'll be a freak?" She hadn't meant to allow her fears to whisper through her lips.

Cortez's expression went blank, almost cold. "He would have died had I not changed him."

She dropped her head into her hands. Of course she was grateful, and she tried to convey that through her sobs, each time the sound growing more and more muffled. Cole would live, but the cost was so great. Changed against his will, just like Cortez. Neither had asked for this, but the decision was made and would affect them all forever.

This is all my fault. If only she hadn't taken Dante's job. If only she and Cole had left one day earlier! Damnit! They should have left town weeks ago. It had been selfish of her to stay, not wanting to start over again...and then not wanting to leave Cortez. Because of her, Cole had nearly died. Had suffered unimaginably. Now he was going to be a vampire.

When she finally reined in her sorrow enough that she was able to breathe without gasping, the full ramifications of that settled over her.

"He's part of your clan now." Her voice came out hollow. "He can never leave here."

Cortez didn't respond, which was answer enough.

Her eyes burned, tired and swollen. A headache sparked behind her skull. She glanced at her hands surprised to see red all over them. There was more on her shirt and neck from when she had hugged Cortez.

Blood all over me.

She just stared at her hands.

Cortez, still kneeling in front of her, hooked her chin with his finger to bring her head up. "Jesus, you're beat. How are you even still awake?"

"I need another shower," she grumbled, pushing to a stand. Her head spun a little, and her balance wavered.

Cortez scooped her up in his arms, cradling her. "Ryder, leave us."

Ryder bowed and then slipped out the door.

Dizziness surfed her brain, making her a little loopy. She snorted. "Did he seriously just bow to you?" She laughed then, and even she heard the thread of hysteria. "All hail the king? Is that what my brother has to look forward to now? A life of feeding off the life-force of others and following orders?" At least *she* had her freedom? Could Cole even be happy here? All other choices stolen from him. *Because of me.*

"Be as prickly as you want. I'm not taking the bait."

She wasn't trying to be prickly. She was just running on whiskey and exhaustion and self-loathing, which was making her lash out.

Cortez carried her into the bathroom and set her down on her feet. He waited a moment, as though making sure she wasn't about to fall over, then engaged the shower. When the temperature was right, he shrugged out of his shirt.

"What are you doing?" she asked in a deadened tone.

He jerked his belt loose and snapped his pants button open. "Getting in the shower." His trousers hit the floor.

Then he reached for the hem of her soiled shirt.

The scornful, hate-filled look he'd given her in that meeting room, before all hell had broken loose, popped into her mind. She slapped his hands away. "I'm not getting in there with you." He'd accused her of sleeping with Dante and then warned her never to return to his club. And now, after everything else that had happened, he wanted to get naked with her?

Her headache flared, momentarily stealing her vision. Equilibrium shot to hell, she reached out for something to steady her, coming in contact with Cortez as he propped her against his hard body, one arm hooked her waist.

"You're sure as hell not showering alone. You can barely stand up. I won't have you slipping and cracking your head open. There's been enough tragedy today."

Because of me. Fresh tears filled her eyes.

"It's going to be difficult enough being Cole's sire without letting his beloved sister bite the dust in a needless accident."

Cortez was already a master of a large clan. So what exactly would he find difficult about adding another member? Was it because he hadn't wanted to change Cole? *I have no desire to turn any more vampires.* Or was he referring to Cole's connection to *her*? The traitor that had caused all of this?

Her bottom lip quivered. "I can undress myself."

Cortez sighed and let go of her, backing away. Once fully undressed, she padded toward the stall. Just as she stepped one foot in, Cortez took her hand, helping her with her balance. She tried not to read anything into it. He was right. She was too over-wrought for her own safety. She could easily crack her skull on the tile. Cole was going to need her support in the coming weeks. She couldn't give him that if she was gone.

Washcloth in hand, Cortez followed her under the spray and proceeded to wash the blood off her hands. To her tired mind, his actions almost seemed tender, and for a minute she let herself revel in it, imagining he still cared for her like he had before.

By the time Cortez finished washing the both of them, she had to fight to keep her eyelids open. He quickly toweled her dry and then lifted her back into his arms. Her eyes did close then, and she was out before he settled her under a warm set of covers. She didn't register him crawling in beside her, wrapping his arm around her and pulling her close, or the kiss he placed oh-so-softly on her shoulder.

CHAPTER 35

A nearby rustling roused her from what felt like the dead. The sensation of being naked underneath soft covers registered next. And though she was snugly bundled, there was a slight chill to her flesh, as though the temperature within her cocoon had recently dropped.

After rubbing her eyes, she blearily glanced around, surprised to find she was in Cortez's room. In his bed.

Alone.

Well, not quite.

She spotted Cortez across the room, standing in front of a mirror as he knotted a dark tie at his collar. His crisp suit was tailored to his glorious form, sleek and powerful. His hair was styled in its usual deliberately mussed fashion, perfect for running her nails through—a privilege she'd never get to experience again.

He met her gaze in the mirror.

"The VEA is here," he said in a brusque tone, deftly fashioning the last loop and tightening the knot close to his Adam's apple.

"Oh," she said, suddenly feeling awkward. She didn't know where she stood with him. Did he still want her out of his club, never to return? She barely even remembered their time in the shower. Just that he'd been very clinical about cleaning the blood off the both of them. She should have taken advantage of the moment. Committed every inch of his glorious body to memory. It was very likely the last time she'd be in such close, intimate proximity.

Actually, she was surprised to be in his room. In his bed, no less.

He must have been equally exhausted not to bother setting her up in an unoccupied room somewhere else in the hotel. She had no idea what changing a person into a vampire entailed, but those dark circles under his eyes were an indication. Had he slept at all? She barely felt as though she had.

"They're on their way up to interview you," he added.

She jerked upright and then clutched the covers to her neck. "To interview me?" Heavy tendrils of her hair spilled over her shoulders. She ran her fingers through it, realizing it was still damp. Outside, the early morning sun had just cleared the horizon.

He tossed a pair of men's sweatpants and a T-shirt at her. She clumsily caught the bundle against her chest.

"Get dressed. Quickly."

She considered the outfit. "You want me to look like a slob while you get to look like that?"

"You've just been traumatized. No one expects you to be in an evening gown. And I'm the leader of my clan," he continued. "Right now, I have to look it."

A knock sounded from the entryway. Here already?

"Get dressed," he ordered.

She bristled, but crawled her way into the oversized shirt.

Before he disappeared into the living room, he said in a hushed tone, "Do not reveal that your brother and Goldie live. No matter what. Understand?"

"Um, okay. Why?"

"No time to explain. As far as anyone is concerned, they died. Got it?"

She nodded, but her gut twisted. Why would he want to conceal that information? "Who was the second woman? The one who didn't make it?"

His expression softened. "She was identified as Tiffany Felcot, an employee at—"

"Dante's Pit," she finished for him. Poor Tiffany. Why would Dante drag *her* into this too?

Cortez left to greet whoever was at the door. In the next instant, she heard him curse. "What is he doing here?"

A voice she didn't recognize answered, "He's been accused, and is, in turn, accusing you of the crimes committed here."

The fuck? On her way to the door, she half ran, half hopped as she shoved one foot into the sweats, then the other.

Dante's cool tone caused an all-stop. "I've longed to be invited back to Ever Nights. Pity it's under such deplorable circumstances."

He's here? The shit-bag that had nearly murdered her brother was here. Just feet away. Her palms itched for a weapon.

"You haven't been invited," Cortez fired back.

"Where is the female?" The unfamiliar voice demanded.

"Naia," Cortez called. "Come out here, please."

"Ah," Dante said. "Here comes the little spy

now."

Huh? Now she was confused. Was Dante admitting to hiring her?

In a stern tone, Cortez said. "She has been through a trauma."

She peeked out the door where three vampires stood: Cortez, Dante, and one she didn't recognize. The VEA agent Cortez spoke of?

He was taller than Cortez by about six inches. His hair was dark, cut short, and framed his hard-chiseled features. Though he wore a suit, she got the impression he would feel more comfortable in fatigues with an M16 in one hand and a Glock in the other.

Wringing her fingers, she stepped closer.

Dante's eyes flashed. "Yes, this is the one Cortez hired to infiltrate my club."

"He what now?" Clearly she'd heard wrong. "You're trying to say *Cortez* was the one who wanted me to spy? On you? Whatever for?"

"He's been trying to close me down for years. To run me out of town. I suppose he figured on using you to plant evidence that he could later use as blackmail against me." He faced Cortez. "But you've taken it too far, old man."

"Dante," Cortez coldly countered. "How many times have I told you, your scheming and deceit will be your downfall. You are a slave to your hate and anger and selfishness."

Thinly veiled rage coated Dante's expression. "You are the selfish one! Perhaps if you hadn't banished me from the clan in the first place, you wouldn't have brought us to this low point. You have your own anger and hate to blame."

Cortez sighed. "I never hated you. I merely saw through you. And it took me far too long to do that."

Naia's eyes volleyed between the two as they argued like.... Realization sparked. She gaped at Cortez. "You're his sire?"

Cortez clenched his fists. "The worst decision I ever made. And the last vampire I ever changed." His gaze darted to her and back so fast she almost didn't catch it. Last vampire...till today.

She reminded herself she was supposed to believe her brother was dead. Was supposed to be distraught. Not a difficulty. Not only was she red-eyed from exhaustion, slightly dizzy too, and was probably still in shock from the night's events, but a life *had* been lost...because of this bastard.

She openly glared at Dante. "You're trying to frame your own sire?" Even she knew that was a major no-no in the vampire world. For whatever reason, makers were sacred among their kind—not all vamps had the ability to turn a human.

"What's this?" the VEA agent replied, a strangely amused curl to one side of his mouth. "Is this karma I see unfolding before my eyes?"

Cortez gritted his teeth. "At least when *I* absconded, I had the decency and respect to put several states between us, Trent."

Naia's brain stutter-stepped. "You can't be serious. He's *your* sire?" This was the ass-hat who changed Cortez against his will? That's why she sensed subzero temperatures between them.

She recalled wanting to hurt this man on Cortez's behalf, but judging by the size of him, she'd need a bulldozer and C-4 explosives to do it. The man was a Viking in a suit.

Before he could cover it, she registered Dante's shocked expression. Was this news to him too? Had something like worry just crossed his features? The VEA agent was his grand-sire.

Perhaps this turn of events was a notch in their

favor—

Trent confirmed the association with a grudging nod. "And before Cortez deserted his birth clan, he stole something precious from me. Something priceless and irretrievable."

Perhaps not.

Dante relaxed, smugness returning to his features.

Great. *Two* vampires with a grudge against Cortez; one with real power to do something about it.

"Okay, so this is an unhappy family reunion," said Naia, then faced Trent, her shoulders back. "What can I do to clear Cortez and get this asshole thrown into vampire prison, or jail, or wherever it is you put murdering lying bastards?"

Trent considered her for a moment, a disconcerting curl returning to his lips. "Merely tell me your side of the story."

Easy enough. She began when Dante offered her the seven grand to try and get a job at Ever Nights. How he suggested all the terrible things Cortez was up to in order to encourage her participation.

Dante shook his head. "I have evidence to the contrary."

"Oh?" Trent said.

Dante turned to Naia. "Did you forget you came to me last night to confess your crimes and admit what Cortez was up to? You said you couldn't stand the lies anymore." He retrieved his phone from his pocket and tapped the screen. Her voice jumped from the tiny speakers. *"The money is generous...but it's just not worth the risk. I'm not cut out for spying on people. And I can't stand the lies. I don't want to do it anymore. I can't. It's not right. Besides, I don't believe there's anything for me to find, anyway."*

"That wasn't a confession!" she cried. "That was

me telling you that I couldn't continue to spy on Cortez."

"I'm not sure why you're backtracking now." Dante's expression softened. "If he's threatened you, you can tell us. We can protect you from him."

"That's an oddly short recording," Cortez observed. "Only a few sentences captured at the exact right moment. I wonder how the rest of that conversation went."

"He practically threatened me," Naia declared. "And then tried to bribe me with money, not that it was going to change my mind."

Dante cleared his throat. "I gave you that money so you could afford to go into hiding with your brother. Alas, you had come to me too late, as it would seem." His lips formed an I'm-so-sorry tilt that she wanted to smack right off his face.

"You kidnapped my brother! Had him tortured! Explain that!"

"I think you're confused," Dante replied, actually looking as though he pitied her. "I'm sorry for your loss, but I was nowhere near Ever Nights when those poor people were killed."

Her jaw snapped shut. She looked to Cortez for the assist. His lips were pressed in a hard line. Why wasn't he saying anything?

She turned back to Dante. "You sent me a picture of my brother beaten and bloody and then warned me to do what you asked." That terrible moment was locked in a dark cell in her mind, beating the walls with an urgency that wouldn't cease till she laid eyes on Cole. Until she saw that he was alive and well. That wasn't going to happen unless Dante was dealt with here and now.

"Did I? From a phone that had been given to your brother by none other than Cortez? Taken and sent from this very location? The device found in the boy's pants pocket? If that were the case, I'd have had to physically be here at some point. Besides, I have witnesses who will vouch for my whereabouts all night, and all last week if need be."

Again she looked at Cortez for help. Jaw clenched, he remained silent.

She understood then. It had to have been Marco who'd taken and sent the picture, and the text, and probably did the beating as well. She recalled something Cortez had said to her on his island: *I could be held responsible for any crime committed by a member of my clan.* Dante was setting Cortez up, and using their own vampiric laws to take him down. For some reason, Marco had done Dante's dirty work, leaving Dante to establish an alibi. But why?

Dante gave a shrug, as though he were at a loss. "It only makes sense that Cortez discovered you wanted out of his little charade, might have even discovered you'd come to me to confess and grew enraged. He then threatened you and killed your brother. We can only assume he's holding something else over your head now. Your own life perhaps." He held out his hand as if she would go to him. "It would be a shame if something terrible were to happen to you."

Was that a threat? She sidled closer to Cortez, and Dante dropped his hand with a smirk.

Finally Cortez spoke. "I'm curious how you got Marco to betray me, but I suspect we'll never know. He's mysteriously vanished. Did you have him killed?"

"I should be asking you that."

"In any case, something tells me not even his body will turn up."

Dante shrugged. "Only you would know."

"You must realize this will end badly for you."

"If the evidence is anything to go by, seems to me it will end badly for you. Sire or not, agent Lockhart here is an enforcer, and he'll have to do his job."

Trent finally spoke up. "The man is right, Cortez. You know the law. You know what I have to do."

Cortez sighed and gestured toward Naia. "Be my guest."

"W-what's going on?"

Trent stepped forward. "No need to worry. I have the ability to reverse the compulsion of any vampire I have sired. If Cortez has compelled you to lie, we'll know shortly."

Her chin hiked a notch. "He wouldn't." Would he? She'd know if she'd been compelled. Wouldn't she? Doubt crept in as she glanced at Cortez. He caught her uncertain gaze, and a muscle ticked in his jaw.

"Look at me, Naia." Trent's tone turned soothing, hypnotic. "Is all that you've said tonight the truth?"

"Yes." She nodded. Was she being compelled even now? How was one to know? She didn't *feel* any different.

"Who is the one responsible for the bloodbath downstairs?"

His verbiage brought the memory rushing back at once—Goldie drained and dying. Cole beaten and bloodied—and she flinched. "It was Dante. He's the one behind all of this."

Trent blinked, his eyes widening infinitesimally. They narrowed in the next instant. Why? Did he not like her answer? "Bend over and touch your toes."

She canted her head. "Huh? Why?"

His lips parted in an O and then spread in a slow, menacing grin. Not at all a happy one. "She's a *lurela*."

Cortez went slack jawed, his arms dropping to

his sides. Dante appeared...smug?

"What does that mean?" she asked.

"It means no vampire, not even I, can compel you. You're immune."

Immune to compulsion? She hadn't realized there was such a thing. Nor that they had a name for it. She instantly comprehended two important facts. One: by Cortez's response, he hadn't even known, which meant he'd never attempted to compel her. Gold star for Cortez. Two: Dante had known all along which meant he *had* tried—she must not have behaved as he'd expected, giving her away. Was that the day the seeds of his plan had been planted?

"Interesting," Dante drew out the word as if he'd had no clue. "So we can never know if she's lying."

"So it would seem," Trent concurred.

"I have to give you credit, Dante." Cortez said. "You really thought this one through."

"You can stop trying to insinuate I had anything to do with this. You've been caught, *sire*. It's time for you to accept your punishment." He glanced at Trent as if commanding him to get on with it.

Naia's pulse jumped. Surely they wouldn't pass judgment with so little to go on.

"You've made your case," Cortez said to Dante. "It's my turn. I postulate this was nothing more than a scheme to get back at me for disavowing you."

Dante shook his head. "I hold no animosity toward you."

"If that were true, I wonder why you started a business that mirrored mine only a handful of miles away? Essentially becoming my direct competitor."

"You don't mess with a winning formula."

"Only you aren't winning, are you? You're going into debt. Your company is failing."

Dante pursed his lips.

"For some reason, you blame that on me."

"Because you'll do anything to keep me down," Dante snapped.

Cortez slashed his head back and forth. "Until last night, I couldn't have been less concerned with you or your little *Pit*."

"You lie. You poach my customers every chance you get."

As though speaking to a child, Cortez replied, "I run a club that people enjoy. Nothing more."

Naia blurted, "Yeah, it's not his fault that your club sucks, Dante."

Dante's gaze slashed toward her, his lips twisted into a snarl, fangs displayed.

Eyes flashing, fangs gleaming, Cortez stepped in front of her, his features more menacing than ever.

Hands seated in his pockets, Trent took center stage. "Let's keep it civilized, gentlemen. Cortez, why do you believe Dante would want to frame you?"

Cortez eased his stance, but stayed close. "Our animosity goes way back."

Trent hummed in a you-don't-say kind of way. Naia studied his cold gaze and rigid features. He held himself in a way that put her on edge. Like at any moment he was prepared to produce an automatic weapon and mow them all down. Plus there seemed to be an arctic chilliness between him and Cortez. What had Trent meant about Karma?

Cortez continued. "When I discovered Dante was starting to read minds like me, I paid him more attention."

"You tried to keep me from using my ability," Dante spat.

Trent barely glanced at Dante, his scrutiny was all for Cortez, his stony expression indecipherable. A new kind of nervous energy skittered through Naia.

Had the VEA agent already passed judgment?

Cortez faced Dante. "I tried to help you *control* it. It took me years to learn how to avoid accidentally pulling private thoughts from someone's mind. Though I still struggle with that from time to time, I had hoped to teach you how to self-govern. But you refused to listen. You were more interested in exploiting your gift. You saw it as a power to be used to your benefit, no matter the cost." He sighed, appearing saddened and disappointed. "You became power hungry. Cruel. When I could no longer condone your actions, I had every right to end you. Instead, I let you live, and simply disavowed you."

"You kicked me out! Of my own home. You took everything from me."

"I was wrong," Cortez said on a heavy sigh. Naia could hardly believe her ears. Even Dante looked taken aback. Then Cortez lifted a chilly gaze. "I should have killed you that day."

Dante's lips peeled back into a sneer. "Perhaps you should have." Then he seemed to remember himself. He let his shoulders drop and affected a casual stance. "Maybe I became cruel *after* you exiled me, but you turned out homicidal, didn't you? Tell me again. How many dead bodies did they find in your basement?"

Cortez clasped his hands behind his back. "Your anger toward me wasn't really because I'd disavowed you. You were planning to leave anyway. But not until you dug a secret out of my head. And that's what all this is really about."

"Oh?" Dante was completely shuttered now, but there was a nasty glint in his eyes, as though he thought any minute now Trent was going to arrest Cortez for mass-murder and he could dance a jig in the privacy of his new club. Naia wasn't positive that wasn't exactly what was about to go down.

"What you wanted was the secret to creating a vampire," Cortez muttered.

There was a frozen moment.

Trent crossed his arms and cocked his head at Cortez. Still, there was something in his gaze that she couldn't interpret, but it didn't bode well.

Cortez noticed too, but went on, speaking directly to Dante. "You might be able to block me from reading your mind now, but you couldn't back then. Not like you thought you could. You wanted to start your own clan.... Although, that isn't exactly correct, is it? You wanted to birth your own *minions*. Slaves to do your bidding. I almost confronted you the night I gleaned that from your thoughts, but I more than anyone know thoughts can be random, fleeting, even at times unwanted. So, to verify my suspicions, I fed you incorrect information to see what you'd do and so that I might judge your actions. And what did you do?"

Dante's jaw winched tight, his glare dangerous.

Undaunted, Cortez answered for him. "Not but a few hours later, you tried to turn your most loyal human.... Well, I wouldn't call him a friend since you considered him more of a pet."

"You tricked me," Dante accused, fists clenching.

"When you discovered you'd been duped, you were furious and vowed revenge upon me and all that I love. And so here we are, in the midst of a devious plot—even for you—to take me down. If you succeed this day in proving my guilt, not that you will, Trent would have no choice but to execute me, and possibly the rest of my clan as well, leaving Ever Nights free for the taking. Do you see yourself sitting in my chair, Dante? Ruling my empire?"

Fury cracked through Dante's mask. "I couldn't

care less about this place. And I don't need to prove your guilt. The evidence speaks for itself." He glanced at Trent who made no reply, a stoic observer waiting to pass judgment. Or so it would seem.

Cortez inhaled a wearied breath and let it out slowly. "I wish I had seen sooner what a hollow person you are. You've no qualms about trying to have three innocent people killed, and plotting to pin their deaths on me. And I'm sad to say you might have actually succeeded."

A triumphant micro-grin lifted Dante's features and sparked delight in his eyes, but it was clear he was trying to hide it from Trent. Not that it mattered when Trent only seemed interested in glaring at Cortez like he'd insulted the man's mama.

That's when Cortez dropped the bomb. "Except you didn't count on two of your victims surviving."

Dante frowned, his eyes shifting from Cortez to Naia. She couldn't contain the barest of grins. *Surprise, fucker.*

Finally Trent's attention strolled over to Dante, one scrutinizing brow raised.

"Goldie's statement has already been recorded," Cortez informed Dante. "According to her, you compelled her to come here so that Marco could drain her dry. Sick fuck that you are made her remain completely aware of her own actions. Like I said, cruel. Once Cole wakes up, I have no doubt his account will be similar."

Naia's throat tightened and air inflow restricted. Once he wakes up? Her eyes must have bugged, or maybe she'd made a small choking sound, because Cortez placed his palm on her shoulder.

Dante balked. "See how uneasy she is at his touch, agent Lockart? If he's not using compulsion, then he's somehow coerced these poor people to lie for him." Even as he spoke, he subtly inched toward the door.

Trent decided to finally enter the conversation. "Another interesting fact that you may not know, Dante: as I can reverse the compulsion of my sired vampires, estranged or otherwise, I too can reverse the compulsion of any vampire they themselves have sired."

Dante swallowed, taking another, guilty step back.

"I've spoken with your employees already. You've been a very naughty boy."

Dante lunged for the door.

With blinding speed and a snarl that sent a shiver of terror down Naia's spine, Trent caught the bastard around the neck, lifting him several feet off the ground.

Red-faced, Dante struggled uselessly against Trent's hold, fly to the spider. "You mudder fugger," he pushed through his compressed windpipe. Trent only squeezed harder.

"Not here," Cortez growled, looking a little savage himself. "She's seen enough horrors."

Trent's fearsome gaze snapped to Naia. The veil of civility was sliced away by the sight of his razor-sharp fangs and murderous expression, a beast preparing to make his kill. The sudden painful leaping in her chest was a primordial reaction. Prey to predator. She tried to slow the racing of her pulse, but it was like trying to halt a stampede with the power of one's palm. They could both hear her heart revving out of control...and it was exciting them.

Like an animal, Trent cocked his head at her, keeping Dante's toiling body aloft as though he were a doll of fluff batting at a granite statue.

"Neither of them can read your mind," Trent

muttered, his tone no longer cool and reasonable, but roughened and barely human. "Why is that?"

"I-I don't know."

He smiled, but it was more frightening than friendly. He didn't believe her, but seemed to understand she wouldn't admit to anything unless she was forced to. "I've ignored protocol as a favor to Cortez. You are both indebted to me this day. I will require a favor of you in the future. You will not deny me."

That didn't sound good.

Trent's intense gaze swept to Cortez. "Agreed?"

Cortez stared at his sire for a long while before answering. "Agreed."

CHAPTER 36

"What exactly did you just agree to?" she asked after Trent left with a doomed Dante still grappling for freedom. She'd taken one last look at her former boss and promptly flipped him off. He snarled, but trapped in the cage of Trent's mighty hold, he could do nothing about it.

Now she sat in Cortez's kitchen, trying to choke down a plate of eggs and toast he'd ordered up for her. Her stomach was still in knots. The first couple bites landed in her gut like lead.

"A favor to be redeemed at a time of Trent's choosing. He'll likely call on me first. I'll try to negotiate you out of any obligation then." Cortez leaned against the kitchen counter, arms folded over his chest. He was back to his distant facade, seeming to be contemplating something. Perhaps how to start the conversation they desperately needed to have?

Though the sun was now well above the horizon, rain clouds were moving in fast, blotting out the daylight. A burgeoning storm was softly growling and snapping as if readying to strike.

Cortez pushed away from the counter and

turned for the door. "I have to check on some things. When you've finished with breakfast, come meet me in the lobby."

She pushed her plate away and jumped up. "I can't eat any more."

He glanced back. "You barely touched it."

She shrugged. "Surprisingly I'm not feeling too hungry."

He opened his mouth to say something, then closed it. "Come on then."

The first time they'd been in an elevator together, there had been a kind of electric energy, an excitement that had skittered between them. This time? Dead air fell like a pall. He stared straight ahead; she glanced at her shoes.

"Can I see Cole?" she asked partly to break the silence, partly because she was desperate to verify he was truly alive. She knew Cortez wouldn't lie to her, but being told and seeing are two very different things.

"Not yet. He isn't through the change yet." He glanced down at her. "The transition is...difficult."

She tried not to let her mind run wild, but it was like corralling a buttered mudpuppy. Difficult as in painful? Difficult as in exhausting? Difficult as in the certainty of Cole's survival was tenuous? "What about Goldie?" she asked to block those thoughts.

"She too is still recovering."

"You said Cole has yet to wake up. Is that...normal?"

"In this case, yes. I expect he'll awaken in a couple of days."

The elevator doors slid open. They stepped out into the lobby and...

As though it were a basilisk lying in wait, she skittered to a stop at seeing the stack of luggage by the front entrance.

"I've had your things packed up," Cortez said. "Donovan will take you home."

Her throat closed up, and a bolt cut through her heart. He was sending her away. Was still ending things between them. Even after everything. Why? Because he couldn't see his way past her betrayal? She hadn't known him when she'd made that bargain. She hadn't cared for him like she did now. Surely he understood that.

Or would stubbornness and hurt pride rule?

Was he planning to make her stay away forever? To keep her from Cole?

She planted her feet. "If you think I'm leaving before I see Cole, you're crazy."

He faced her, brows drawn up. "I'm not banishing you, Naia. As soon as Cole wakes up, you'll be notified. I'll even send a car, if you like."

"How magnanimous."

"There's no need to make this difficult."

"Isn't there? As you said, I've just been through a trauma. I was used by a madman for a vengeful purpose, threatened and terrorized. I saw my best friend and brother brutalized. I thought they were dead, and I still haven't seen either of them to confirm otherwise. And now I'm getting thrown out on my ass?" The full weight of her situation railroaded her, and her stomach twisted.

"I'm not throwing you out on your ass—"

"Not to mention the Boyle twins will still want their money. Guess who they'll come after when they can't find Cole?" She threw her arms out to the side.

"You don't have to worry—"

"On top of all that, you're breaking up with me for a teeny-weeny little thing like taking a job to infiltrate and spy on you and your clan, which, when said out loud, sounds worse than it really is, I admit. I mean, come on. I didn't even accomplish any serious spying, and really, what choice did I have? The twins don't take *Sorry, I'm broke* as an excuse, and did you just say I don't have to worry about it?"

"I did. I've settled your brother's debt." He sounded so much more calm and collected than she did. Which was irritating. "I also sent them a message that you and your brother are now under my protection."

"You did?"

"Cole is now one of my clan and, by extension, so are you. You're welcome to come visit him whenever you like. Once he's awakened, that is."

But she was still expected to leave the premises.

He walked her out to the sedan that was waiting by the curb. Pellets of rain had begun to fall, the sky darkening like the closing of a curtain. As if her insides weren't crumbling, he and Donovan began packing up her luggage. Stuff she'd never asked for, never needed. She'd give it all back, every damn scrap of fabric, every damn bauble, every damn wedge, pump, or peep-toed shoe, if Cortez would only look at her the way he had on his island.

When he opened the sedan's back door for her, two rogue tears trickled down her cheeks, and her chest heaved for air. "You said you'd forgive me."

He appeared confused at first, then seemed to recall their conversation on the boat.

"Don't cry," he muttered, looking remorseful. Or was he just pitying her? How many women had he sent packing after seducing their hearts?

As if to confirm that, his expression turned neutral.

Humiliated by her show of emotion, she crawled into the car and hid her face behind the curtain of her hair, soft tears coming faster. He didn't close the door. Instead, he knelt down, setting one knee in the dirty gutter. She blinked, confused, and looked at him. Really looked. His lips were turned down in a way that made her wonder if this was just as hard for him as it was for her. But if so, then why send her away?

His controlled expression cracked, and he suddenly appeared so very tired. "Please don't cry," he repeated, wiping a tear away from her damp cheek. "It guts me."

"I don't want to go." *I want to stay with you*, she didn't say.

He bowed his head. "I know."

"So then why must I?"

"A lot has happened." He hesitated. "Too much."

Meaning she'd betrayed him too badly for him to forgive her?

He paused again as though to choose his words. "If you stay, there will be consequences. Things I... things you and I might not be ready for."

She sniffed. "What? What things?"

He shook his head and stood. "We need some time apart. I need to clear my head. So do you. I'll call you when Cole wakes up."

With that, he closed the car door. Through blurry eyes, she watched Cortez walk away from her and vanish into his club.

He hadn't glanced back. Not once.

CHAPTER 37

Four days! Four grueling, agonizing, nail-biting days.

So far that's how long she'd been waited for news about Cole. Four days of carpet fretting, hair-pulling worry. Well, *three* if you didn't count the day Donovan had dropped her off. Mental and physical exhaustion had dragged her straight to bed where she'd sprawled unconscious for twenty-four hours straight.

Unconsciousness was bliss. Wakefulness, gruesome. Especially when she wasn't only anxious to finally, *finally* see her brother, but apparently she was experiencing Cortez withdrawals.

He needs time away from me.

She hadn't received so much as a text updating her on Cole's condition....

Or one asking how she was doing.

When her tummy rumbled, she popped some cheap instant noodles in the microwave, then leaned back against her warped linoleum counter to watch the number tick down.

She'd gone from seeing him every day, smelling

his clean, woodsy scent as she slept, touching his luscious body at her leisure, to not even having the simple luxury of hearing his deep baritone voice. It was like sensory deprivation torture.

Before there was joy, music, vibrancy. Now there was muted silence, a lonely apartment, and the act of pretending she was fine. Going through the motions. Eating when she needed to eat. Bathing when she needed to bathe. The rest of her time dedicated to sleep. Or at least attempting to. Even when exhaustion rode her, she would tango with the covers, both trying to ignore and soothe her aching heart, not only due to the absence of the man who had burrowed a nook straight to its center, but she and Cole had never been apart for more than a few hours, twenty-four at the most if they both worked a double.

She tried to recall the last time she'd spoken to him. Was it over the phone on the island? Hadn't he told her then about Tiffany missing her shift? Was that when Marco had started his gruesome task? While Naia had been having the time of her life, living it up with the most gorgeous, glorious, sexiest beast of a man she had ever encountered. Giving him access under her skin, deep in her bones, way past the mysterious place where the soul lived. That was where Cortez had claimed his niche, marked his spot, and would forever haunt her. Leaving her fractured and not quite whole, but like some sort of puzzle that was missing its corner.

She'd never been so alone.

Nights were the worst.

Last night, the true pain of her loss had hit her square in the chest, waking her with a gasp that had been swallowed up by the darkness of her empty room. Before waking sense had returned, she'd frantically checked her torso, making sure her ribs hadn't been ruthlessly cracked open.

Of course they hadn't. She was intact, but only from the outside. The insides were a jumble of marbles and fine-spun glass.

She was done lying to herself. It only prolonged her suffering to hold any form of hope that she and Cortez could return to their former joyous state. The lack of a phone call told her that at least. He probably wanted to break things off with her completely, sever the ties, were it not for Cole.

So instead of ripping off the band aid and admitting that straight-out, he'd sent her away. *Don't cry. It guts me.* At the time, those words had sparked a fuse of hope within her, but it had since burned out. He just didn't want the guilt of witnessing her devastation.

The only bright point over the last few days had been when Goldie had stopped by. Newly released from *Hotel de Vampire*, as she'd dubbed it—and how after everything she could make jokes was beyond Naia—she'd appeared almost good as new but for a few visible contusions around the face and neck.

When Naia had answered the door and saw who it was, she had leapt on her friend as though they'd been parted for years, hugging her so hard Goldie had lightly complained about bruised ribs, though she'd held onto Naia just as tightly. When they did let go, Goldie had produced a bottle of wine from her tote and declared, "It's half past girl's night! Time to get twisted!"

Glasses filled, they'd curled up on the couch where Cole used to sleep, she cruelly reminded herself. Self-flagellation was now a favorite pastime it would seem. She'd never again walk in on him, limbs sprawled, full-on drool face, snoring the roof off the place. He'd likely be staying at Ever Nights for the foreseeable future. Learning to be a vampire.

Recently turned, how dependent would he be on blood? Where would he get it? Who would he drink from? She couldn't even picture her little baby brother with fangs. Ugh, or sucking on necks.

She shuddered.

Goldie had distracted her from these thoughts with a gruesome retelling of her ordeal, though the diversion wasn't exactly favorable. It had happened precisely as Cortez had described, with Dante compelling her to meet Marco behind Ever Nights. By the time she'd found him, Marco's hands had already been bloody.

From pummeling Cole?

From there, Goldie and Marco rode a service elevator to the basement. Tiffany was already there in room three-oh-eight, drugged out of her mind, shivering, yet drenched in her own sweat. Goldie recalled Marco muttering something like *soon now*, then proceeded to beat and drain her dry.

Because Dante kept her aware of everything around her, she remembered every blow, had known she was about to die. Naia couldn't even imagine the horror of that. Thankfully Goldie'd had the good sense to go limp and play dead, which might very well have saved her life—Marco, apparently, had wanted to take things slow—but noises from the floor's lobby had alerted him to the presence of others. He'd fled, leaving Goldie on the brink of death, but with help on the way.

Too bad they hadn't arrived sooner. During the time it had taken Marco to abuse and nearly drain Goldie, and for Naia, Lex, and Ryder to get there, the drugs had claimed Tiffany's life.

The microwave dinged. Naia retrieved her

dinner and sat at her tiny kitchen table, waiting for the noodles to cool.

It had seemed almost cathartic for Goldie to unburden herself, so Naia had dutifully listened, though it revived every terrible moment for her as well. The violence. The blood. The carnage. The sheer panic that had flooded her. The total and complete helplessness.... The warmth of Cortez holding her so close, so protectively, while she'd lost her shit.

Thinking back, she was pretty sure he had held her as she'd slept as well. But no, that couldn't be right.

A faint memory surfaced of him pulling her into the warm curve of his body...tenderly kissing her shoulder.

That couldn't have happened. She had to be remembering incorrectly, her wounded heart wishing for the impossible.

She recalled the way he'd looked at her after discovering her motive behind seeking him out. Like she was a stranger. An enemy. Yet another person who'd sought to use him.

The image was replaced by the way he'd regarded her on his island. Like she was treasured.

She'd felt treasured.

That feeling was gone now. Siphoned away through the hole in her heart left by Cortez. A wide, dark cavern where she wanted to curl up and grow roots.

She had fallen for him completely; he wanted her out of his life.

So then why had he saved Cole?

She knotted some stringy noodles around her fork and popped them into her mouth, the flavor conspicuously absent. Compared to Victor's salmon, this was dog chow.

She swallowed the bite and forced herself to eat more, her thoughts drifting back to Cortez.

He'd had no plans to sire any more vampires. He hadn't even vetted Cole. After Dante, Cortez was understandably cautious and extremely selective about who he brought into his clan. Turning a mortal was serious business under *any* circumstances.

Not to mention, in all respects, Cole had essentially been dead—it was becoming easier for that morbid thought to bypass the pain center in her brain. With Tiffany's death, the damage Dante intended had been done. Either Cortez would be held responsible, or not. Transforming Cole, thereby saving his life, wouldn't have changed that. And now Cortez had a new, if not unwanted, certainly unintended, member of his clan. A responsibility she couldn't begin to fathom. There'd been no obligation to save him by such extreme measures unless....

Had he done it expressly for her? Because he didn't want her to suffer the loss of her beloved brother and only family? The ultimate gift? She hardly dared to hope at his motivation. By doing what he'd done, he pretty much guaranteed she'd be in his life for as long as Cole was, whether he wanted that or not. And he didn't.

Right?

If you stay, there will be consequences. Things you and I might not be ready for.

At first she'd assumed *consequences* meant punishment for her role in Dante's plan. Now she wasn't sure. He'd included himself in that dictum. Meaning there would be consequences for him as well? And what *things* had he been talking about?

Her phone chimed. She glanced at the caller ID.

Her heart did a flying trapeze flip.

"Hello," she blurted eagerly.

"Good evening, Naia." His supple voice liquefied her insides, warming them like chocolate over flame. Then, registering the strain in his tone, she tightened back up.

She got straight to the point. "How's Cole doing?"

"Good. He's awake now. You can come see him, if you like."

Abandoning her dinner, she bolted to her room on the hunt for her shoes. "Yes. Okay. I'll leave now." She spotted the soul of one tennis shoe peeking out from under the bed. She went to all fours and scanned for the other.

"I'll send a car."

There it was way underneath. She must have kicked it there at some point. "A car? Okay. I'll be ready," she uttered, reaching her arm into the tight space, the excitement making her impatient.

"I'll see you shortly."

She froze, ass in the air, fingertips straining. "*You'll* see me?" But he had already hung up. She hadn't expected for Cortez to stick around when she visited Cole long enough to even say boo. She'd pictured him in isolation, up in his lonely tower of solitude, waiting to reclaim his territory the minute she left again.

That still might be the case. Maybe his last words were just something one said instead of goodbye. *See you soon. Talk to you soon. See you later.*

But just in case....

She found her reflection in the bathroom mirror. When had she showered last? Had she even brushed hair since returning home? The nest on her head was practically growing a personality. And she looked pale and weary. The picture of grief.

Frantically she tore off her clothes and jumped in the shower, scrubbing her hair and skin like she was staving off Ebola. She'd be damned if he saw the evidence of how thoroughly their breakup affected her.

Wrapped in a towel, she padded to her closet and tore through her wardrobe. Stained, faded, wrinkled, frayed.

Unacceptable.

Her eyes darted to the pile of luggage she had yet to unpack. She'd left it in the corner where Donovan had dropped it. She unzipped the biggest one. Inside one of the garment bags was an elegant looking dress with an above-the-knee hem and a deep V neckline. Perfect.

She slipped the dress on and inspected the fit. It hugged her hips and waist and provided a flirty swing to the flowy skirt whenever she moved. Yet her cleavage was the star.

After finger combing her hair—it would dry in a wavy fashion—she attacked the other suitcases till she found some sex-kitten shoes to match, a black strappy pair that wrapped her feet in loving bondage.

Twisting for her reflection, she wondered if it screamed of desperation, but before she could decide on another outfit, the doorbell rang. Anticipating her eagerness to see Cole, Cortez had sent the car before calling her.

Donovan stood on the porch. When he saw her, he did a double take. A slow smirk twisted his features.

She suddenly grew self-conscious and glanced down at herself. "Overkill?"

He chuckled and said simply, "This ought to be good. Let's go."

CHAPTER 38

The sight of Ever Nights was dazzling with its soft outside lighting and neon OPEN sign.

Donovan pulled up to the front entrance. When she stepped onto the sidewalk something in her relaxed, a tightness unfurrowing. Like Ever Nights had become *her* sanctuary.

Only it wasn't.

She had to reign in those thoughts. Hope for the best, but prepare for the worst. Whoever had said that had to have either been very insightful or had experienced some pretty shitty days. Her *worst* would be if Cortez treated her as if she were just another person, no different than any other in this club. A short term visitor that didn't really belong. No. That wouldn't be the worst. The worst would be if he treated her as a nuisance.

She lifted her chin. She was here for Cole. She'd support him despite how she felt about Cortez. Or how he felt about her.

There was a bouncer tonight. Dane. He silently opened the door for her. She thanked him though his expression was hard, dangerous, with an edge of disdain. She supposed they all hated her now.

Inside was business as usual, music tapering from

several doorways connected to the lobby and hallway.

Kenzi was there, chatting with the desk clerk, a woman Naia had never seen before. When Kenzi's gaze casually slipped her way, she straightened in surprise, then rushed toward her. "Naia. My god. I heard about what happened." Kenzi threw her arms around Naia, her forward momentum knocking them both off balance. When they recovered, Kenzi set her at arm's length. "Are you okay, honey? I'm going to take you for a spa day. No arguments." As if just processing Naia's appearance, she blurted, "Although you look fabulous. Lady killers around the world, eat your hearts out."

Naia smiled weakly. "Thanks, Kenzi."

"You're here for Cole, aren't you?" She scanned Naia once more and gave her a conspiratorial smile. "And apparently to flaunt what the good lord gave you."

She fought a full body flush. "It's too much, isn't it?"

"Never. Right this way, *mon ami*." Looping their arms together, Kenzi dragged her through the club, into a room that was lit by brilliant, golden hews. Like the sun itself had taken a minute to stop in for a nightcap.

Kenzi pointed. "Just head in that direction. And just between us, it wouldn't hurt to flip your hair as you go."

"Huh?"

Kenzi just winked and waved goodbye, returning to the lobby. Naia looked in the direction she had pointed. All she saw was clubbers laughing, dancing, and drinking, but then suddenly the crowd parted, and she spied Cortez on the opposite side of the room with his back toward her. He was speaking with Ryder. Even from behind, she was stunned by how gorgeous he was. More so than she remembered, if that was even possible. Damn him.

His arms were folded across his front, over a solid chest she remembered tracing with her fingers. Her tongue. The grey suit he wore amplified the powerful breadth of his shoulders. From what she could see of his profile, there was more stubble there than he'd ever permitted before. And he still looked sexy as hell.

He was a colossal dream. Her very own fairytale prince.

Don't be stupid. Fairytales only exist in books.

Attempting to fix things between them would be like crossing the ocean in a canoe, surrounded by sharks. She'd only get hurt in the end.

After taking in a fortifying breath, she swallowed, lifted her chin, and then made her way toward him. A song with a hard beat started up as she crossed the dance floor, raising the energy of the room. A couple guys tried to engage her in dance, but she ignored them, her eyes fixed on her target.

Ryder spotted her first. He blinked, taking her in from top to bottom and then mouthed something that resembled, "*oh shit.*"

Cortez curiously swung around. His arms dropped to his sides as whiskey eyes scanned her slowly up, then down, then back again. Adrenaline whipped through her bloodstream. Was that a shadow of desire stalking behind his eyes?

A second later she wondered if she'd imagined it. As soon as she reached him, he was back to that chilled version of himself that she hated. It was the face of rejection.

Ryder was still gaping, however, so she figured she had to look pretty amazing.

"Hi," she said, for lack of a better greeting.

"Naia," Cortez replied coolly with a slight incline of his head.

Formal reception? Fine. Whatever.

"I'm eager to see my brother," she said, just as stiff.

"Of course. Follow me." He started back through the crowd.

Dejected by their hollow interaction, Naia started to trail after him, but before she did, she caught a furtive thumbs up from Ryder. She cocked an eyebrow at him, but he'd already spun away, heading in the opposite direction.

Her heels clacked almost silently under the layer of loud music as she scurried to catch up to Cortez's long strides. He led her back out into the lobby—Kenzi was still there, with a surreptitious smirk as they passed—then through the hallway where their disastrous meeting had changed everything, and finally through another corridor she had never seen before till they reached an elevator that only seemed to go down.

To the basement? She shivered.

Cortez noticed. "Are you cold?"

"No, just...no, I'm fine."

He eyed her for a moment longer as though intensely wanting to question her. Not being able to read someone's mind would do that to a guy, but he appeared to conquer his curiosity and didn't push.

He retrieved a key from his pocket and inserted it into a keyhole in the elevator's panel before pressing a sequence of buttons. The doors slid closed, and the compartment began its descent. The silence between them was stuffed with everything they refused to say. Naia fidgeted with her hair. The ends were still a little damp. She glanced up at Cortez. He was facing forward. She opened her mouth to say something, then closed it again, coming up empty.

"Don't be alarmed when you see your brother," he broke the silence. "It is imperative that he remain contained for the time being."

That sounded cryptic. The elevator came to a stop, and the doors parted to reveal a large, dim room walled by stone. It took her a moment to realize she was surrounded by several barred cells, like a prison from the wild west.

Cautiously, she stepped out of the elevator. Movement drew her attention to where Cole lay on a cot with his hands tucked behind his head.

Realizing he had visitors, he sat up and then zipped toward the front of his...cage. His speed was unnatural. Inhuman.

He wrapped his fingers around the bars. "Naia?"

"Oh, Cole." She lurched forward, needing to hug those big shoulders and verify he was real, but Cortez locked one arm around her and snatched her back by the waist. The contact was a shock to her system, and suddenly she was caught between a set of conflicting desires: sink against his brawny chest like an addict getting a fix, or start throwing elbows to get to Cole.

"Let me go!"

"I can't do that," he informed her, his tone a low rumble that reverberated through her body. "You can't get within his reach. He's too young. He'd sink his teeth into you and not even realize what he was doing. He's here for his own protection as well as others until he learns to control the hunger."

She noticed Cole's fangs then, bright and gleaming. A kind of garbled, horrified sob slipped out.

Cole turned sheepish. "I really fucked up this time, didn't I sis?"

Her eyes burned as her heart shattered a thousand different ways. "No, Cole. This is my fault. I'm the one that fucked up. I should never have accepted Dante's offer. I knew it was wrong. We should have left town when you wanted to. If we had, none of this would have happened."

Cortez stiffened, still holding her as though fearing any second she'd leap at Cole to embrace him through the bars in a big sister thank-god-you're-alive hug. He was right to restrain her.

"Dante would never have let us go," Cole replied. "His plans started the moment he met you."

Because he knew Cortez would find the woman whose mind he couldn't read irresistible. "So you see? It *is* my fault."

"Don't," Cole hissed. "Don't blame yourself for this. If anything, blame *him*." Cole jerked a narrowed gaze at Cortez. "He's the one who created that monster."

She expected Cortez to sling something back at Cole, but he remained silent. Did he blame himself too? Were they all taking on that weight?

Suddenly Cole's breath changed. His hands tightened around the bars. He shook his head as if trying to clear it, then growled—literally growled—like an animal. "Take her away." His voice had roughened in a way she'd never heard before. "She smells too good." Another hard shake of his head. "I can't.... It's...."

She gasped at his pained expression, her throat thickening. *My being here is hurting him.* Trying to conceal her injured tone, she asked, "Do you...Do you want me to stay away?"

"No," he rushed out, suddenly panicked. "Please. Visit me tomorrow. After I've *fed*." He sneered the last.

Cortez dragged her back into the elevator. Just before the sliding doors stole him from her sight, she choked out, "I'm so sorry, Cole."

CHAPTER 39

Drowning in the dichotomy of both grief and gratitude, Naia turned and threw her arms around Cortez, her breath hitching as she thanked him for saving her brother's life. He seemed startled at first, his body stiff, but then he rigidly returned her embrace.

Cole was alive. Alive! Locked away, sure, but not forever. He just needed to learn to control his cravings, much in the same way she had learned to use her abilities. She'd be here to help him in any way she could. Soon enough he'd be out hustling again.

When the elevator doors opened to the main floor, she realized Cortez had permitted her to hold onto him for the entire ride. She was grateful for that small show of kindness.

He gazed down at her with a strange expression. If she didn't know better, she'd say he appeared almost unsure. Maybe he didn't know how to tell her it was time for her to go back to her apartment.

She offered him an I-can-play-ball smile. She would do anything to stay in Cole's life, even pretend she wasn't gutted whenever she looked at Cortez. "I'll see you around," she said and then started for the exit.

Cortez cleared his throat. "I have something else to show you." With that, he stalked past her, expecting her to follow.

She did.

He led her to his office, the one she had snooped through. She sat across from him and placed her hands in her lap to keep from wringing them. Was he preparing to chew her out again? Did he want to talk about their relationship? Whatever *things* he didn't think they were ready for?

Silently he rummaged through the desk drawer and then pulled out a large navy-blue binder and placed it in front of her. Hesitantly, she flipped it open and gazed down at a calendar...no, wait, it was a schedule sheet. In elegant scrawl, her name was written in a timeslot (eight to eight thirty) under the column designated Whitlock Stage.

She blinked up at Cortez. "You...you're giving me a job?"

"Three days a week, you can come here and sing. I'll pay you a salary. We can talk numbers later."

"Why? Why now?" Why did this feel like a nail in the coffin of their relationship?

"As long as Cole is my charge, you'll be taken care of." He was so business-like, calm, cool, and collected, Naia wanted to spit just to get a different reaction from him.

"That's the only reason?"

He leaned back in his chair. "The vampires I sire are unable to lie to me when I ask them direct enough questions." He paused and raised a brow. "I questioned Cole extensively."

She swallowed painfully. Translation: he knew all her secrets. He knew what she was. Knew that singing wasn't an ego-driven desire, but a necessity of life. Cortez felt obligated to her because of Cole. He might not be happy about it, but he was breaking his own rules to give her what she needed. Was making sure she was taken care of. It was what she'd wanted. So why did she suddenly feel like pelting the schedule at him while telling him to shove it up his ass?

"And what about us?" She kept very still lest she betrayed her emotion.

"I've come to the conclusion that it might be better if we remain...friends."

She lost the air in her lungs. Devastation was a plague in her system that was spreading fast. He wanted to be friends? She had fallen for him completely, and he wanted to be *friends*?

He continued as if he hadn't just stomped on her heart. "You know a relationship with an employee isn't something I'm interested in."

That was an easy fix. "Okay, so then I won't take the job."

"That's ludicrous. Don't be stubborn."

"*I'm* the one being stubborn? You won't even give us a shot."

"Naia," he sighed. "It would never work out in the long run."

"So you're a relationship psychic now?"

"I've been through enough of them to know—"

"Oh pa-lease."

"Pardon?"

"I'd understand if there was no spark between us, or even if it was just mere attraction, you have to feel it. I know it's not just me. We're combustible. Have you ever experienced that with anyone else?"

His expression shuttered and he didn't respond, which was a big fat answer if there ever was one.

"I know *I* haven't. What we had...have is incredible. And I'm not ready to let it go. What are you afraid of?"

He scoffed. "I'm not afraid of anything. We had fun. That's all it was."

That boot twisted.

"You are just another member of my clan now."

Planting both palms on his desk, she stood and leaned forward.

"Tell me you don't want me."

It seemed to take him a moment to realize what she'd said since his gaze had dipped to her cleavage, turning heated. "I don't want you," he muttered, his tone guttural.

She grinned triumphantly.

His brows knit.

"Then I'll take the job." She stood and headed for the door, glancing back over her shoulder where he sat, confounded. "Call me when Cole has fed." Then she left, a plan forming in her mind.

CHAPTER 40

One hundred percent without a doubt Cortez had lied when he said he didn't want her. Blind nuns could have seen through him. He'd tried to project indifference, but every part of him had betrayed his true feelings. A slight flinch, an audible swallow, a clenched fist, the false note in his voice, the pain in his eyes. Oh, he wanted her a great deal, but the idiot was going to deny himself because of some dumb rule he'd placed on himself? It didn't make any sense. There had to be more to it than not wanting to date someone who worked for him. He'd determined she needed to sing, but she could easily get a lesser paying job somewhere else. Hell, she'd sing on a busy street corner for change if it meant they could be together.

She spent most of the next day preparing. Step one, make herself drop-dead gorgeous, even more so than yesterday, all stops pulled out. If he really didn't want her, it shouldn't be a problem for him. Step two, figure out how to seduce a male...or maybe that should be the first step. Seduction had never been her thing. Cortez had been the one to sweep her off her feet, beguile and bewitch her. She just had to do what he did, only in reverse.

She'd unpacked all her new clothes and had taken inventory of her sexiest outfits. Cortez had sent her away with an arsenal to be used against him. She wore a black, gauzy piece with an elegant open scoop back that was aloft by a set of delicate spaghetti strap bows at the shoulders. Pull the strings and the whole thing would come crashing down.

Along with her provisions, she'd also picked up a large bouquet of roses, red, of course, with a risqué note that read: *I wanted to thank you for everything, but since I can't have my mouth around your cock, I went with flowers instead. xoxo—friends forever.*

She felt diabolical.

Her cell rang. Cortez's name flashed on the screen. She waited a couple rings and then answered with a saucy purr in her voice. "Hello?"

There was a brief silence. Had she thrown him? "Cole just fed. Would you like me to send a car?"

"Oh, yes, please."

Another short silence. "Donovan will be there shortly."

Hanging up, she snickered.

When she met Donovan at the door, he eyed her outfit, her makeup and the vase stuffed with flowers. His lips twitched. "You ready for round one?"

"I'm going for the knockout." With any luck, Cortez was going to be blindsided. On the ride over, however, doubt crept in. "Donovan?" she asked just as they pulled up to the front entrance.

"Mm?"

"I could be about to make a huge fool of myself, so I'm asking you honestly. Should I just let him go?"

Donovan met her gaze in the mirror. "Are you kidding? After last night, I put a grand on you for the win."

"You did not." She laughed, but then his eyes turned serious, and she decided he was telling the truth. "You're gambling on our relationship?"

He nodded proudly. "Best entertainment we've had in a while. And when he sees you in that dress, you'll have him by the short and curlies."

Another laugh burst out of her, the kind that ran amuck and took one's breath with it. After a minute, she sobered. "So, you're okay if I get back together with him? You don't hate me?"

"For what? Trying to get us all annually flogged by Dante and the VEA?"

She cringed.

"Nah. You were duped, same as us. I don't like that it had to go down the way it did, but if you work the boss like I think you're going to, then maybe things worked out the way they were supposed to."

"And if I don't?"

"I've seen the way he is with you...and how he is without you." Donovan glanced up at Ever Nights. "He's better with you. Whether Cortez wants to admit it or not, you two have something very rare. You don't just give that up without a fight."

She nodded, mentally donning her boxing gloves. "Got any tips for me?"

A sly grin spread across his face. "He had a new camera installed yesterday. Aimed at the Whitlock Stage."

So he could watch her perform? "Doesn't want me my ass," she muttered under her breath and then stepped out of the car.

CHAPTER 41

Donovan followed her inside, presumably for ringside seats. The lobby was unusually full. Ryder was there chatting with Kenzi, both trying to act inconspicuous as they slid glances her way. They were ready for a show. Briefly she wondered how many of them had made bets on her and Cortez.

She spotted the man in question, and her mind stutter stepped. Glorious, gorgeous male in his tailored suit with his tussled hair and lips that—

Focus!

He was glaring at his employees—reading their thoughts?—and hadn't noticed her entrance. No doubt he knew all about the bets.

Then his gaze snapped to her and something like a jolt shot through him. His mouth parted, eyes widening.

And the crowd cheers!

He scraped a hand down his face and then affected a neutral manner. "Naia," he greeted coolly.

"Cortez," she mocked his tone, letting a smile play along the corners of her lips as she crossed the room. "I got these for you," she handed over the bou-quiet.

His brows shot skyward. "I don't think anyone has ever given me flowers before."

"It's a first for me, too. Read the note." She folded her hands behind her back and innocently swayed.

He rolled his eyes as though this was a chore and then plucked the note off its plastic holder. She watched his eyes scroll over the card.

A strangled gust of air wheezed out of him.

She grinned and leaned in a bit closer, lowering her voice to a smoky whisper. "You can always exchange the flowers for the other option."

He was a wire ready to snap. That was where she wanted him, racked with raw, carnal desire just like she'd been as she'd written those rousing words.

Gazing up at him from under her lashes, she added, "In fact, I can't stop thinking about it."

Sweet tension stole through him. He glanced at her lips with an intensity she felt in her bones. She was pretty sure Donovan was about to win his bet, because it looked as though Cortez was about to kiss her. She let her head fall back slightly.

Then a vein popped on his forehead, and he crushed the note in his fist. "Ryder will take you to see Cole today." He stalked away. Her heat sank. He'd bolted like he'd just discovered she was a bomb ready to detonate. To Ryder, he called over his shoulder, "Make sure she doesn't get close to the bars."

With that he was gone, and she was left wondering if she'd been wrong about the whole situation. Maybe he really didn't want her.

A sharp pang darted her heart.

Ryder stepped up beside her. "Okay. What the hell did that note say?"

She pursed her lips, blushing in response.

"That good, huh?"

"How was that even remotely good?" she said, dejected. Clearly Cortez hated it.

He pointed in the direction Cortez had escaped. "That's a man ready to blow."

Blow a gasket, maybe. She sighed. "So who did you bet on?"

At first Ryder was stunned by her comment, then he smirked. "Money's on you, babe."

Cole did seem better today, or, at least, he wasn't gripping the bars like he was thinking about tearing through them on his way to her throat. *Way to go, baby bro. Progress.*

However, when she took a step just a bit too close for Ryder's comfort, Ryder stayed her by the elbow—very different than Cortez. Ryder's was the grip of a body guard; Cortez's had been that of a lover. Had he even realized it?

"How are you feeling?" she asked Cole.

Cole leaned one shoulder against the bars. "Weird. But...not bad. Different. And also not."

"What's it like?"

He took a moment to think. "Intense. I can hear better. Like crazy good. I can hear you breathing. The sound of clothes swishing when someone walks...your heart beating."

As if to torture him, her heart did a nervous dance. "Sorry."

"For what? Being alive? It's not like you can help it."

There's my good-humored Cole, still in there. "Not just for that."

"I'm just grateful I was the one targeted and not you. And don't give me that look. It was not your fault. By the way, I can smell you too. That perfume is awful."

She bristled. "It cost me a pretty penny. And you're one to talk. Don't they let you shower in there, or should I consider that your permanent stench?"

"Hey, I smell manly." He dipped his head to check his pits. Then they both laughed.

When their humor eased, she sniffed herself wrists where she had applied her perfume and asked seriously, "Is my perfume really bad?"

Cole shook his head. "It's just a bit strong for my new nose." Then he pried. "You trying to impress someone or something?"

"Three guesses who," she grumbled. "And you'll only need one."

He whistled. "You really know how to pick 'em."

"Don't I though? Speaking of, you told him about me."

"Yeah. The thing about having a vampire daddy, you can't say no to him unless he lets you."

"So does he know about..." she glanced back at Ryder. "I don't suppose we could get some privacy?"

He shot her an are-you-fucking-kidding-me look.

"Didn't think so." Still, no reason to reveal her deepest sin to everyone if she could help it.

She faced Cole. "Does he know about James?"

Cole nodded solemnly. "He knows everything."

She tried not to let panic overwhelm her, but her heart began to hammer behind her ribcage. Was that why he was rejecting her now? Because of her crime?

Cole's fangs appeared, and he took on a wild look. "Naia," he warned, and she realized it was because her pulse was teasing him.

"Sorry, sorry!"

"Who's James?" Ryder asked.

"Don't be a nosey-nelly," she scolded.

He gave her a pitying look. "He your baby daddy?"

She rolled her eyes. "Knock it off."

"Secret lover?"

"Ugh. Enough."

"You kill the guy?"

She choked on her rebuttal and her spine shot ramrod straight.

"No shit?"

"I...I...of course not!" *Oh, real convincing.*

"So what'd he do?" Ryder asked, no sign of judgment in his tone.

Cole answered. "He tried to kidnap her in the middle of the night, so I pulled him off her and knocked him out. Next thing I know, Naia's bashing his brains in with the ass end of a solid brass lamp." He sounded proud.

"It was the adrenaline," Naia defended pathetically.

Ryder appraised her with new interest. "Nice. I knew there was a reason I liked you."

Exasperated, Naia shook her head. "Jeez, you two are way too much alike."

"Buds for life." Ryder tapped his fist against his chest and then held it out at Cole. Cole mimicked the move like they'd done it before.

She teased, "Oh my god, you guys are soooo lame." And she suddenly liked Ryder a whole lot more.

Ryder put his arm around her shoulder and pulled her into his side. "And now you're stuck with us."

A warm feeling wrapped her heart, and she couldn't stop a pleased grin. "Just for that, I'm going to kick your ass at pool later."

"You're on."

She stayed and chatted with Cole for another minute before returning to the elevator with Ryder.

When they were alone, she told him, "I never thanked you for taking care of me that night."

He smiled down at her. "Guess you just did. Ready to sing?"

She nodded, battling a sudden wave of nerves as they made their way to the Whitlock Stage within one of the medium-sized rooms.

Ryder stood off to the side as she claimed the mic. The crowd was rather small compared to the night of the concert. People sipped drinks and idly conversed, disinterested in her, for the most part. She didn't care. There was only one purpose for tonight's performance.

She glanced around.

Ah, there it was, the camera on the back wall, trained on her. She hid a smirk. The music began. The beat was sultry, just as she'd requested. The lights dimmed, and a spotlight hit her. Her gaze remained on the camera as her body began to move to the music. Mic raised, her voice sashayed forth, smoky and sexy, instantly demanding the room's attention. None of them mattered. She wasn't even sending out her snare yet. This show was meant for one.

The beat rolled over her hips, and she began to move. It was like waking from a deep sleep, stretching and praising the sun. Her voice shimmied and danced in the air, slow and sensual to start, hinting at something larger than life. She hovered there in that tense space of anticipation and excitement.

The crowd was with her, having stopped their conversations to watch her. But she didn't care about them. Was Cortez watching her now? Did he like what he saw? The thought was more arousing than anything she had experienced on stage, and she let it shine through her eyes, straight into that camera. With a clang of the drums and a snap of her body, she let her voice fly. The core of her desire for him poured out in a flame of bright need. Her hips succumbed to a smooth undulation that crested through the rest of her body.

The energy in the room shifted with her. It moved and swayed under her command. The audience begged for direction, and she was their conductor. Her voice shifted slightly, turning breathy, wanton. She pictured Cortez staring at his screen and wondered if he was even half as turned on as she was. The thought of his hands on her, loving her the way only he can, tightened every part of her body, kindling a heat that had her thrumming from the inside out.

Just as the song climaxed, she practically did too, only it was hollow and empty because Cortez wasn't there, and perhaps she was singing to a camera that wasn't even filming.

Her voice died down then, and she brought the song to a close, coming back into her body.

The sound of someone in the crowd climaxing startled her. The crowd was going at it like a group of wild, horny monkeys, kissing, touching, and fondling their closest neighbor.

"Oops," she said, breathless.

A slack-jawed Ryder gaped at her hungry disbelief. "Girl, if you didn't belong to my sire, I might be tempted—"

A murderous tone barked from the entryway. "Ryder!"

He came.

Naia hummed with anticipation.

Ryder went stiff. "Boss, hey, I didn't see you

there."

He looked wild, and hungry, and super pissed. Vaguely she realized this was a—if not *the*—pivotal moment in their relationship. After this, they'd either give their relationship an honest shot, or let the spark die forever.

She hurried off the stage to cross toward him. His furious gaze followed her. She wasn't daunted. He might be angry, but it was only because he was so turned on. She was sure of it.

"Is there something you need, Cortez?" she said sweetly.

His nostrils flared. With a snarl, he gripped her by the elbow and dragged her from the room. He was all coiled muscle and determination as he led her into an empty room. The door slammed behind them. It didn't bode well that he'd taken her to the very meeting room where their relationship had been shattered by a video and a few pictures.

She hated this meeting room.

With his body, he crushed her against the door and then took her mouth in a rough kiss that set fire to her spine and lit her nerves. Burying her fingers in his hair, she deepened the kiss.

Their tongues did battle around harsh gasps, the pressure cutting off her lungs. It was as if he were trying to punish her with his brutal, carnal, bruising kiss. Bring it on. She answered his challenge by sucking his lower lip between her teeth and lightly nipping him. A rough sound rumbled out of him, and his body trapped her harder against the wall.

He yanked aside the shoulder strap of her dress and attacked the tender flesh there with urgent, wet kisses. Liquid heat flooded her body. "Cortez, oh God."

"That was a dangerous stunt," he muttered between searing kisses.

"So worth it," she panted, unbuttoning his coat and pushing it over his shoulders. The fabric flopped to the ground.

"You plan to torture me at every turn." Her other shoulder strap vanished so he could lavish attention on that side.

She went for his belt. "I plan to make you mine again."

He fisted the hem of her skirt with both hands and yanked the fabric up over her hips. "What if I was never yours?"

There went her thong, now useless scraps. "Yes you were. And I was yours. That hasn't changed."

His zipper sounded, and his pants dropped. Less than a second later, they came together in an explosion of heat and fire and madness, his hips thrusting while hers rolled. Then there was no more talking, just bliss and gasps and cries.

As if he felt he should remind her, he grunted, "I don't date people who work for me." Even as his rhythm turned frantic.

"You do now, so get used to it." She kissed him, hard, brutal, hands locked in his hair, heels spurring his hips. Then she pulled back with a final lick of his lips and met his gaze, saying with her eyes everything she couldn't with words.

His body bucked hard. "We are not dating."

"Then maybe you should stop fucking my brains out."

His thrusts took on a brutal, mind blowing, tempo. She threw her head back on a moan, melting into the carnal pleasure and sensation and friction. Never wanting it to stop. Her nails dug into his back as his cock slammed home again and again, drawing screams from her with every blissful thrust.

"I love you," she blurted.

His hips pounded harder, his body straining. "Fuck me," he grated, looking pained. Then he buried his face in the crook of her neck. Fangs pierced flesh. She blasted off, screaming into the ceiling. White-hot ecstasy splintered her every nerve. Almost too much to handle, yet could never be enough.

On the verge of his release, his muscles stiffened, and he roared along with her. Together they rode the pleasure till their bodies turned boneless and their brains succumbed to a dizzy stupor. His forehead came to rest against hers, both of them panting, shattering. Or maybe it was just her who felt as though she had to pick up all her pieces.

When she met his gaze, she was stunned by his naked vulnerability. "You have to think about what you're asking of me."

He sounded so defeated. It was confusing.

"You're asking for everything," he said.

Did he still think she was like the others? "I'm just asking for you. I don't care about the rest."

He backed away, going for his clothes. Cool air attacked the places he'd been touching her. "You don't understand. This isn't a decision that can be made lightly." He stabbed one leg into his pants, then the other. As he buttoned up, she shimmied her skirt back into place.

Adrenaline was seeping away, making her feel sluggish. "Why can't we just be like we were? What's the big deal? We were having fun. I know I screwed up, taking that job and all, but I didn't know you then. I didn't realize what you'd become to me. And, to be fair, I was kind of stuck between a rock and the Boyle twins."

"It's not that." He retrieved his sports coat next, draping it over his arm.

"Then what is it?"

His gaze flooded with an intensity that suddenly gave her chills. "I don't want to just date you. I want to make you mine."

She canted her head, not understanding.

He spoke as if putting a nail in a coffin. "If I made you mine, the arrangement would be permanent."

CHAPTER 42

Blood bond.

That's what Cortez had called it.

The sedan's engine rumbled softly down the road with Donovan silent behind the wheel. From the back seat she rolled the word around in her head, glancing aimlessly out the window.

After sitting her down, Cortez had explained a blood bond was basically the equivalent of a vampire marriage, only, unlike human matrimony, divorce was not an option, which was why he'd asserted once again the need to take a step back. Ruminate. Come to their senses. He'd once more hinted about separation, time to think, as if they had both caught an illness, and distance was the cure. As if a couple of days would reverse the fact that she'd fallen head over heels in love with him.

Already she feared no other man would do. Still, to commit to forever? After knowing him so short a time? He was right. It was crazy. Maybe love was an affliction that could be remedied with time.

They were halfway to a bond already. Cortez had taken her blood, finally. And by god what those wicked sexy fangs had done to her. Addiction thy name is Cortez.

To complete the bond, all she'd have to do was drink his blood too. Then, bam, *dunzo*. She wasn't normally squeamish, but yikes.

You have to think about what you're asking of me, he'd said.

Cortez had been right to be cautious. Forever was a lot to ask. Talk about commitment. No wonder he'd wanted to distance himself. When a vampire was contemplating marriage, things had to be serious. Especially after she'd heard the second part of his explanation: if they went through with it, he'd only be able to derive sustenance from her blood from then on. Pressure much?

Since she was human, she'd have no such restriction. She'd still need to eat human food and sing, per usual. However, by drinking from him every so often, her life would be extended, not forever, but she'd age much more slowly. Then there was the more permanent option: change her.

What would that do to her siren? Could she abide drinking blood for the rest of her unnatural life?

It was all too much to take in, and she didn't know how she felt about any of it. Which was why she was currently on her way back to her place. She needed time to think.

Donovan stopped the car in front of her apartment.

Mumbling her goodbyes, she shouldered the door open and stepped into the night. It was cool out this evening. A storm was rolling in. Clouds overhead rumbled with the threat of thunder.

She fumbled for her keys, stabbed the metal into the dime-store lock with chipped faux gold plating, and then spent the next few seconds jimmying the thing into the exact right position before it twisted with a resounding click, and her door swung open.

She waved at Donovan who had gallantly waited for her to get inside before driving off. Then she meandered into the living room and sank onto the couch. Her options were this: Bond with Cortez and risk everything, or remain cordial friends and nothing more.

"Why are those the only two options?" she had asked him. "Why can't we just keep dating and see where things go?"

"Because I want you more than reason allows," he'd said, sounding ardent yet overtaxed. She'd told him she loved him and it had thrown him for a loop. "Trust me when I say a vampire my age understands eternity. Never in a million years did I believe I'd offer myself up for a blood bond. Then you go and walk out of my dreams and I'm fucked." He'd stabbed his hands through his hair and began pacing. "You have me on my knees here. Even when I thought you'd betrayed me and my clan, I wanted you. You're either dangerous to me or you're...everything."

She'd gone speechless.

"I can't fall any farther—" He'd cut himself off, verbally stumbling for a moment. He paced, scraped a hand down his face, then gave her his back as though it were easier to communicate that way. "I can't maintain intimacy with you. Not if I'm going to lose you in the end. You might change your mind about us. Maybe not in a year, but in five? fifty? A thousand?"

Her mind hit a wall, unable to compute. A thousand years or more with Cortez? She couldn't even contemplate forever.

"You're dangerous to me because I already want to cut my heart out at the thought of losing you."

Emotion thickened in her throat. "Who's to say you wouldn't tire of me?"

He shook his head. "With consequences so great, my kind does not give in to matters such as this without one-hundred percent certainty." He paused. "When a vampire falls, he falls all the way or not at all." He met her gaze. "I've fallen hard."

Her heart had done a drum solo behind her rib cage because she'd wanted to tell him how much she loved him and wanted him, but she was also scared. What if she was only experiencing infatuation? What if he was too? Could they make such a permanent decision after so little time together? What if her heart was lying to her?

Noting her apprehension, his shoulders had sagged. "Like I said. You need to think on this. You need to be sure. If there's even a smidgen of doubt, you should ask yourself: could that doubt turn to regret over time? Regret to resentment? Resentment to hate? I've seen it happen."

On her couch, she dropped her head in her hands.

She couldn't imagine ever resenting him, let alone hating him. It was like an alien concept that didn't mesh with her DNA. He'd saved her brother, and for that, she owed him everything, yet she hadn't been able to answer. Her mind had been scrambled. He'd laid a lot out there. More than she had expected. Basically said he wanted her for eternity...yet he'd also been reluctant to confess these things, like she was forcing it out of him. A sign of his own doubt?

Had he tried to let her go because he feared he didn't love her enough?

The thought was a stabbing pain in her chest.

I've fallen hard, he'd said

Well, so have I, she thought.

She wanted to be with him now. Hated that she wasn't. She wanted to be there for Cole, too. In case he needed someone to talk to about the overwhelming urges she was all too familiar with. Although, now he had plenty of other clan members to draw support from, didn't he? They were bound to protect him. He didn't really need her any more.

But I still need him.

Her thoughts drifted back to Cortez, about their time together. Their relationship had been explosive from the start. Like freefalling off a cliff and landing into bliss. Aside from Cole, she had never felt so comfortable with a man. So at ease.

And the sex.

Gods themselves don't have sex that good. She could spend an eternity just exploring his body.

She'd dreamed of the fairy tale. Was it staring her in the face? *I want you more than reason allows.*

Who was she kidding with all this dithering? She'd wanted to tell him yes back at his place. He thought she needed to think it over. Whether for a year, a hundred years, or a thousand, she'd love him. She felt it like an etching in her DNA.

She crossed to her room, dressed in a long t-shirt, and slipped under the covers. Tomorrow she would give him her answer, and then they could start their lives together.

CHAPTER 43

In the morning, the sound of heavy rainfall beating the earth outside stirred her from her slumber, but it was the sharp bite of instinct that snapped her fully awake.

Strange eyes stared down at her. Menacing eyes.

Adrenaline went off like a shot in her bloodstream. She kicked back to her headboard.

The strange man took several steps back and lifted the gun in his right hand. She froze, eyeing that barrel with a laser focus, as if by doing so she could mentally keep it from firing.

After a frightened moment, her gaze traveled back to the man. Recognition crushed over her like a monstrous avalanche. The hunter from the mountain.

"What do you want?" she asked weakly.

The hunter gave her a tooth-decayed grin. "I've been looking all over for you."

"Why? Leave me alone." That barrel was still trained on her, square between the eyes. "I have very powerful friends. They'd kill you if you do anything to me."

"They'll never find you," he replied ominously, a maddened shine to his bloodshot eyes. She saw the shadow of her doom in those eyes.

She forced herself to remain outwardly calm, though her blood rushed like the running of the bulls, tearing its way through her veins. "Please. Put the gun down. You don't want to do this."

He glanced at the weapon in his hand. A crease formed between his brows as though he'd momentarily forgotten he had it. His finger eased off the trigger. "Yes. Too soon for this. We haven't had our fun yet."

A sick feeling turned in her stomach.

He jerked the tip of his gun toward her door. "Get moving." In the living room, he pointed to a stool next to the breakfast bar. "Sit."

Mind racing, she eased onto the stool. *What do I do?* She focused on the gun. If only she could safely get that weapon away from him? *Could I attack?* His finger was dangerously close to that trigger.

Cortez might never know what happened to her—if this man was to be believed.

He began rummaging through her fridge one-handed, intermittently peeking back at her to make sure she stayed where she was. If he turned his back again, could she make it around this counter and slam his head in the door? And avoid getting shot in the process? She didn't have high odds. The probability of knocking him out was slim as well.

Before she could muster the courage, he pulled out a wrapped plate of old cooked chicken that must have been in there for two weeks at least. He didn't seem to mind, tearing away the plastic, curling one meaty fist around an icy hunk of meat, and shoving it in his mouth. He pushed the plate toward her, mouthing around the bite. "Want some?"

She shook her head.

He shrugged and yanked the plate back.

Absently, he muttered. "All them damn vampires around you all the time. Couldn't get close. Finally got my hands on the rounds that could take them fuckers out." He glanced over at the front entrance. Next to it, a rifle rested against the wall. "Turns out I just needed to be patient." He shoved another hunk of cold meat into his mouth, chewing loudly.

Her eyes darted nervously, seeking some kind of weapon. Nothing was near. "You've been enthralled. You can fight this."

"Enthralled?" Confusion spread over his features.

"Yes. Because you heard me singing that night. I'm a siren. I didn't mean to enthrall you. But you see, it was an accident. You can fight it. You don't have to do anything you'll regret. Just let me go."

His gaze narrowed. "Was I enthralled with all the others, too?"

Mallet blow to the gut. "W-What others?"

"The other girls Billy and I took up the mountain. The six before you. It was nice when they screamed. Was I enthralled then?"

Oh god. "I-I—"

The gun swung her way again. "Perhaps this ends with you, then. It's your fault I'm this way. And those damn bitches."

Her pulse palpitated. *Keep him talking.* "Billy? Is that the man you killed? Was he your friend?"

Slow nod. "Our tastes ran the same." He seemed to lose interest in the conversation. "Get up. We have a long hike ahead of us."

No, no, no! Can't go with him.

Her cell phone rang.

She jumped; he stiffened.

They stared at each other for a tense moment as

the ringer blared once, twice, three times.

"If I don't answer, someone will come looking for me," she told him with unquestionable confidence, though she was unsure if that was true. Would Cortez send Donovan to see if she was alright or just call back later. He had no reason to suspect the danger she was in.

The hunter eyed her suspiciously for a second, then said, "Whoever it is, get rid of them. Warn them in any way and I'll shoot you now, and kill them later."

Shakily, she answered. "Hello?"

At her uneasy voice, the hunter's eyes split into threatening slits. He walked around the counter and placed the barrel against her temple, then leaned close to listen in, his rancid breath wafting over her.

"Naia?" Cortez said. "Cole has fed. Would you like to come see him? Afterward we can...uh...can we talk some more?"

The hunter slowly shook his head. She thought of his threat with the rounds that could take out vampires. She'd heard of such things. Ammo like that was illegal, but could still be acquired, given the right connections.

"I can't right now," she said.

"Oh? Why's that?"

The warning in the hunter's eyes turned deadly.

"Goldie's here. She's still a little freaked out and wants to chat."

"Goldie is there? I could have sworn I just saw her around here somewhere."

The finger on that trigger grew tight. "She just arrived. I'll stop by a little later, okay?" Then she had a flash of brilliance. "I'll bring some of that *butterscotch* Cole likes."

Please remember.

"I doubt he'll be interested in sweets for at least a year. Say hi to Goldie for me. Call me when you're ready and I'll send Donovan over to pick you up."

Her heart sank. "Yeah, okay." *I may never see you again.* "Cortez, I...I love you."

There was silence on the other end as she watched the hunter's eyes go from mild madness to off the rails pissed. That barrel dug painfully into her scalp, thrusting her head to the side. She closed her eyes and held her breath.

"I love you too, Naia. See you later." The line went dead.

The hunter took the phone and then smashed it on the countertop. The sudden ferocity seized her lungs, and she shook violently. A stray tear dove from her lower lid. She wasn't sure if that salty drop had manifested out of fear or because that was the first, and probably the last, time she'd hear Cortez tell her he loved her.

The hunter waved his gun through the air, his voice booming. "Get up. Let's go." Not taking his eyes off her, he retrieved his rifle.

"Where are we going?"

"Move," he barked. "Out the back."

"I don't have shoes on."

Don't give a shit, his eyes said.

With her in the lead, she opened the sliding glass door. Over the years, she'd learned to avoid the little metal sliver in the frame that often snagged her clothes and skin. Now she aimed right for it. As she stepped through the threshold, she reached up and sliced her finger on it. Blood welled. She surreptitiously flicked splatters of red on the ground.

The gun nudged her in the back, but the hunter didn't seem to notice what she was doing, only that she had hesitated.

She stepped out onto the porch and then past the covered terrace. Raindrops clung to her hair like glossy beads, poking damp spots in her shoulders and stabbing her bare legs with icy pinpricks. When he guided her toward the forest, she suddenly knew where he was taking her. Up the mountain. To his camp site...where six others had likely never returned.

Driven by instinct, she faked a stumble to plant more blood at the entrance to the pathway.

The rain came down harder.

Damn.

It might wash away the scent of her blood.

For good measure, she feigned a stumble and ripped her mother's necklace from her neck, and planted it just under the umbrella of a shrub with a smear of her blood. She'd leave a trail as best she could. If for no other reason that Cortez would find her remains so that neither he nor Cole would be tormented with never knowing what had become of her. Wondering for the rest of their days. Poor Cole would blame himself, like he had with their mother.

"Get up," the hunter snapped, gripping her by the arm and yanking her to her feet. He shoved her forward with a warning. "I'm on to that stumbling bit you females like to do. Do it again and you'll be hiking with a gunshot wound."

"It's raining, and the path is slippery."

He shoved her hard again, and this time she really did lose her footing. She crashed down on her shoulder, cutting the skin on a jutting rock. More blood poured into the tiny rivulets made by the rain. *Way to help a girl out, buddy.*

"Maybe I'll make you crawl all the way there."

She stood and started walking, ignoring his threat. As she went, she pretended to hold her wound as though it pained her, which it did. Stuffed with gravel, it hurt like hell, but her true intention was to transfer blood to her fingers and then wipe it on the undersides of leaves that she passed where the rain couldn't quickly eliminate them.

Cortez might have deciphered her code, figuring she was in danger, but then again, he might not have. He hadn't sounded concerned on the other end of the line. Actually, he'd seemed almost upbeat. Because he thought they were going to talk some more? Her heart wanted to break.

Time elapsed as she trekked through the rain with an armed madman behind her who got a kick out of her now very real struggle not to slip and fall. He probably thought it was out of fear of his threat, when in fact she was bleeding quite well from her shoulder and didn't need any more gashes. Her blood now ran freely down her arm to her fingers where she could flick it all over the forest like a grisly Jackson Pollock.

Never thought I'd be grateful to be sliced open.

Her thoughts shifted wildly between survival strategies (none making the cut), scenarios of her upcoming death (all bad), and how devastated Cole and Cortez were going to be if the hunter was allowed to go through with whatever sick thing he had planned (they'd be wracked with grief).

Part of her, the part that clung to the naive belief that everything happened for a reason and that things would always work out in the end, wanted to believe Cortez was on his way to save her even now. The other part of her, the prudent, shrewd bitch that maintained life sucks and then you die, understood she was on her own. If she was going to survive, she was going to have to fight for her life. But the hunter was armed, and she wasn't. Even if he wasn't, he had a few hundred pounds on her. He was plump, but she could tell it was a solid type of plump. One hit from him, and she'd be down for the count. She'd have to catch him off guard.

"Almost there now," the hunter said, mostly to himself.

Have to stall.

The rain was now a twofold attack, it both came at her from the sky in large wet, frigid drops, and ran at her feet in ever-growing streams that wanted to pull her legs out from under her. The mud was softening, coating her up to the ankles. The bottoms of her feet were torn up from the unforgiving gravel, but they were so numb, she could barely feel them.

Thinking fast, she let her leg twist in an awkward position, and then dropped to the ground, feigning a sprained ankle. "Ow! Can we stop for a minute? I hurt myself."

"Tough shit. No stopping."

Shuffling to a nearby tree, she used it to pull herself up and then leaned on it, grabbing her ankle, pretending to be in excruciating pain. She surreptitiously glanced back at him. He was on an incline, but too far away for a quick attack. If he were closer, she could try for a flat-footed kick to his chest, knocking him off balance, maybe he'd fall back and crack his skull on a rock. But right now, he'd see it coming.

"I said no stopping."

"It hurts really bad."

He angled the gun at her.

"Okay, okay."

She continued up the hill with a fake limp. "So, if you and Billy both brought girls up here together, why did you kill him?"

"He used the girls up too fast and was a greedy fuck. He wanted you for himself. I wasn't about to share. I saw you first."

She feigned outrage. "The guy didn't respect the sanctity of dibs? Well then, he had it coming, I guess."

The hunter threw his head back and roared with laughter.

Now's my chance.

She twirled around, braced herself, and kicked out with her heel. She caught him in the throat. Wide-eyed and choking, he grabbed his throat and fell backward exactly as she'd envisioned, but so much force went into her kick that she lost her footing as well and went tumbling after him. Together they slid down the mud-slicked path. Fiery pain scored her right leg and straight up the side of her back. She grappled for purchase, but found none and barreled into him when he came to a crashing halt. Flat on his back, he gasped for air, red-faced and madder than ever. For a moment, he struggled like a toppled turtle.

Without thinking, she lunged for the gun in his loosened grip. His hold on it tightened like stone. Though he sputtered and sucked in air, he was still stronger than her. The gun was ripped away and the butt smashed against her temple.

Nauseous dizziness swam in her head. The world spun, taking her balance with it. She fell to the ground, blinking rapidly in a desperate attempt to stay conscious. Her vision dimmed, returned, blurred, and dimmed again. Mini explosions of light stabbed her eyes whenever she opened them.

Have to get up, she thought, but couldn't remember why. *Why am I so cold?* She absently reached out, feeling a wet gritty substance. *Where am I?*

A pair of deep resonating baritones alerted her to people around her. She attempted to lift her head, finding it impossible.

"...back! Stay back," someone said. "I can take

your heads off with this."

Confusion danced with nausea. Who was that speaking?

"We're not leaving here without her," another voice said, this one familiar. She held a great affection for the owner of that voice. What was his name? A snapshot of his beautiful face flashed in her mind. Her eyes squinted open, desperate to see him, but he looked...strange. So pale and fraught with worry. His palms were up in the air, though his body seemed taut as if ready to lunge.

Her gaze traveled to a set of men flanking him a few yards back, then to the large man standing over her, pointing a dark black stick at the three. No, a rifle. Aimed at Cortez!

And then it happened.

The hunter fired.

Cortez fell back.

The piercing scream that tore from her lungs warped the air in explosive ripples. Raindrops pitched in all directions, creating a bubble around them.

The hunter dropped his gun to cover his ears, his eyes bulging as her strident bellow blasted his eardrums. Face twisting in agony, he fell to his knees, and with painful-looking effort strained his neck her way.

She reveled in the terror hunched behind his horrified gaze, the same kind of terror he'd inflicted on so many others. And like so many others, he begged for mercy, but mercy was a mirage at the edge of a desert. She was both unwilling and incapable of granting his wish as revenge grew into a beast she could no longer control.

The caustic sound emanating from her was something dark and twisted, a splintered mutation of righteous anger, a death note, grating and riotous and bloodthirsty. For the first time in her life, the siren in her clamored to take a life.

And she obeyed, giving her voice the freedom to do as it will.

The hunter's skin grew jaundice and taut, his cheeks hollowing, lower lids drooping grotesquely. His eyeballs rolled back in this head. Blood dripped from his nose and the corners of his mouth. The pigment in his stringy hair disintegrated, the strands becoming brittle and white.

A fierce tremor rolled through him, seizing his muscles and snapping his bones. Finally his arms dropped to his sides, his face slackened, and like a felled tree, he flopped forward, lifeless, his front sinking into the mud.

Her grisly song died out then, and she too sank down, her cheek resting in the grainy muck. Raindrops resumed pelting her, mixing with her tears. Bile churned in her gut as darkness encroached, her vision murky.

Movement blurred in front of her, and a face appeared. Not the one she wanted to see. Donovan's voice echoed as though from the end of a tunnel. "You'll be okay. Naia? Stay with me." In the next instant, she fell into oblivion.

CHAPTER 44

Consciousness crashed into Naia like fifty-pound cymbals. She snapped upright and quickly oriented herself. She was in her room, tucked neatly under her covers. How did she get here?

Throwing the covers off, she checked her limbs for the cuts and bruises she'd amassed, but she had none. Her shoulder was completely healed. Her legs were baby smooth. Someone had dressed her in a clean nightgown. She rubbed her skull where there should be a massive lump where she'd been pistol-whipped. There wasn't even a tinge of pain. The only evidence of her violent scuffle was the dirt caked under her nails from when she had clawed and fought for her life.

Her throat should be burning from how hard she'd sung. Had she truly sung a man to his death? Was that even possible? Was she a two-time killer? She mentally dug around in her self-evaluation bin, seeking a shred of guilt, finding not even a kernel. That fucker had shot Cortez—

Oh, god! Cortez!

Leaping out of bed, she raced for the living room. She skidded to a halt when she spotted Cortez sitting on the couch. Ryder was next to him and Donovan was across the room, leaning against the wall with his arms crossed. Their heads shot up at her entrance, worry etched in their features.

She let out a sound of pure relief and then burst across the room, landing in his lap and throwing her arms around his neck.

He winced at her hold and she immediately pulled back. "Are you hurt?" He'd changed into one of Cole's old sweaters. A spot of blood had already seeped through the fabric near his shoulder. She shifted to get off his lap, but he stayed her at the waist.

"The bastard had gotten his hands on some illegal ammo. I'll heal, though it's taking longer than normal."

"How long was I out?"

"A couple hours."

Yet I'm completely healed? "Is the hunter...is he really dead?"

Cortez nodded solemnly, warily, and she knew the answer to her next question.

"I...I killed him?"

Ryder interjected with his typical enthusiasm. "You've got a scary set of lungs on you, girl. I thought my brain was going to explode."

She gasped. "You were affected too?"

"Dropped us all like stones," Donovan said. "Never thought a sound could be worse than torture."

Vampires had never before been affected by her abilities. "I hurt all three of you?"

"Seven," Ryder said.

Her eyes bugged.

Cortez lightly squeezed her hips. It was oddly comforting and despite herself, she relaxed. "After we talked on the phone, I summoned all the available members of my clan, and we set out to bring you home."

The word home fluttered through her like a cool drink on a hot day. "You remembered the code Cole and I use."

He nodded. "I nearly panicked when you said it, but your voice was strained. I figured someone might be listening in if I let on I knew something was up. I wasn't sure of the level of danger you were in, so I thought it best to come in full force. Then I scented your blood and I thought I was too late." He closed his eyes momentarily as though the memory pained him. "But it was only traces, and we were able to follow it like a trail."

She smiled, preening.

He noted the triumph in her expression. "That was your plan?"

"Yes. I cut myself before he forced me out of the apartment, but I feared the rain would wash it away too quickly."

"Luck was on our side tonight. The hunter only saw the three of us, but we had him surrounded. Dane was getting in position to take him out when he fired on me. Then you went all banshee." She flushed, but he only grinned at her with pride and cupped her cheek. "My beautiful banshee. Remind me not to bring out your vengeful side."

She rolled her eyes. "Are the others alright?" she glanced around as if they'd appear on command.

"I sent them up to his campsite. As we caught up to you, I read his thoughts and learned he's been holding another woman up there. They've gone to help her."

Naia slumped forward, resting her forehead on his good shoulder. "That poor woman."

"If she's still alive, we'll do what we can to help

her."

Considering what that woman had probably endured, Naia didn't think a dose of vampire blood was going to be enough. "That reminds me." She sat back. "Did you feed me your blood?"

He eyed her for a moment before slowly shaking his head.

"Then how am I completely healed?" In turn, she glanced at Ryder and Donovan.

Ryder put his hands up. "Don't look at me."

"Nope." Donovan shook his head.

"Whatever you did to the hunter healed you simultaneously," Cortez informed her. "There wasn't a scratch on you."

She contemplated that a moment. Sucking the life-force from him had made her whole again. She didn't know how to feel about that, and honestly didn't want to think about it right now. Plus she had more important things on her mind.

She faced Cortez. "So we're not bonded yet?"

He hesitated. "Not yet. No."

"When can we make that happen?"

He smiled, letting all his relief and desire and love shine through his eyes. "As soon as these two assholes leave us alone."

"You think they're giving us a hint?" Donovan asked Ryder.

"It's more like a big flashing sign that says FUCK OFF," Ryder replied.

Naia laughed, then said to Cortez. "Take me home first."

"As you wish," he replied, still grinning like he'd won some kind of lottery, and impossibly, she fell even deeper in love with him.

CHAPTER 45

At Ever Nights, Cortez suggested she visit Cole. "He's been worried."

She groaned. "You told him?"

"I made sure he was kept informed. He knows you're safe now, but he wants to see for himself. Ryder will escort you."

"Okay, but...why not you?"

"I have something to take care of. I'll see you shortly."

She couldn't help the tinge of disappointment. She figured he wouldn't be able to wait to sweep her up to his suite to get this whole bonding business over with.

As if sensing her reluctance to part ways, he drew her in for a quick, yet searing kiss that had butterfly wings skimming her insides. His eyes said that was just a prelude. Then he turned to leave, and she followed Ryder.

When she entered the room lined with cells, Cole jumped off his cot and rushed the bars. "Are you alright?"

She gave him a smile. "I'm okay."

When his body slumped like he'd been riding a wave of tension, she wanted to put her arms around him and hold on forever.

On the same page, he said, "I wish I could hug you right now."

"Me too." She paused. "So how are the cravings going?"

He scraped a hand down the back of his neck. "It's like you're suddenly a drug addict, but you can't quit taking it because you need it to live. Let's just say it's a good thing I'm in here. But hey, if I have to be caged, at least it's gilded. Got a TV, and all the blood I can drink. Ryder even brought me a game console. I can already beat his ass at Battle Max Extreme."

"He beat me *once*," Ryder qualified, indignant. "And I want a rematch."

Cole spread his arms out. "Bring it on, bitch."

"I've got time to wipe the floor with you. Fire it up," Ryder challenged, growing lively.

Naia sighed, said her goodbyes, and then returned to the main floor alone. Kenzi was there when she entered the lobby, and suddenly Naia was swept up in a painfully tight embrace.

"My God, are you alright? I heard what happened. Is there anything I can do?"

"Thanks, I'm fine. Do you know where Cortez is?"

"I saw him go into one of the conference rooms a little while ago."

She didn't need to ask which one. "Thanks. We'll talk later, okay?"

"Yeah. Okay."

She hurried through the club and found Cortez sitting at the table alone. His fingers were steeple over his tightened lips. Instantly she hated the look on his face. "You're having second thoughts already?"

He let out a heavy sigh and leaned back. "Naia, there's still a lot to consider before you agree to this. I'm afraid you're jumping in with both feet because you just had a near-death experience. You might not be in your rational mind, and I might be taking advantage of that fact."

She shook her head. "I had already decided last night what I wanted, and I haven't changed my mind. Today's events have only solidified my decision."

"That's exactly my point. You decided because you were nearly about to die. That's why you told me you loved me over the phone, I could hear it in your voice. You thought it would be the last time you ever could."

"You're not hearing me. And in case you've forgotten, I told you I loved you before that. I'm not confused."

He hesitated as if he couldn't quite bring himself to believe. "True, you told me you loved me before that, but then you learned about the blood bond. I'll never forget your stricken expression after I told you everything. It freaked you out."

"Yeah, it was a lot to take in. And you were right. I did need to think it through. Which I have. Why are you doing this? I'm not going to change my mind."

He met her gaze, and she saw all the fear and vulnerability and hope he'd been concealing till now. He was a man who was used to being sure about his every decision, planning for every outcome. Only now he didn't know which way was up, and they were both on a ledge about to dive off.

She crossed to him and placed her hands on either side of his face, forcing him to look up at her. "What I went through today was significant and traumatizing and terrible, and, well, you're right, it did affect my decision. It chased away all my doubt. *All of it*. When I believed I was going to die, I thought of only two people in the world and how much I loved them and would miss them and wished only the best for their future with or without me. The two men I love most in the world and always will. I love you, you big stupid dummy. You're my family now, and there's nothing you can do about it, so get used to it."

At length, his lips twitched, but then that stubborn frown returned, and she knew he was about to piece together another weak protest.

"Come with me." She grabbed his hand and tugged him out of the chair.

"Where are we going?" he asked, offering no resistance, which told her more than he probably realized.

"I've got an idea that will settle this matter once and for all." Leading him through the lobby, past the main room, she stopped in the pool hall. "I'll play you for it. I win, you take me upstairs and make wicked love to me before I make you mine forever. You win, we forget the whole thing." She waved her hand airily as if that wouldn't shatter her to her core.

She turned to face him and raised her chin. Several people in the corner overheard her speech, their mouths agape. She didn't care.

"Shall I break?" Cortez asked, ignoring their audience. He moved with swift intent, racking the balls and selecting a cue stick.

Would he really try to beat her? Was she playing a losing hand? She chewed her lip, breath stunted.

He glanced over his shoulder at her, meeting her gaze. The cue stick slammed forward. The cue ball shot straight into a corner pocket.

He straightened to his full height, looking into her eyes, and set the cue stick on the felt. "I guess I win."

She was about to correct him, but then he was suddenly in front of her, arms hooking her waist, lips kissing her with a passion that scrambled her brain in the best possible way.

When he released her, she blinked up at him in a daze. Then he did something so outrageous, for a split second, she thought she was dreaming. But no. He really was kneeling in front of her, balanced on one knee. And that was a ring sized box he was pulling out of his pocket.

All the air seeped from her lungs as he opened it. Inside rested a ring with a massive, glittering diamond surrounded by a spiral of smaller sapphires. She cursed her sudden tears for momentarily obstructing her view of the glorious, glorious thing.

"If I truly get to have you," Cortez said, "then I want to make you mine in every way possible. Will you marry me?"

"God yes! Gimme-gimme!" She bounced with anticipation, trying to hold her hand steady so that Cortez could slip it on her finger. A perfect fit.

He stood and swept her up in his arms, their lips crushing together with pure joy. She barely registered the clapping and cheering from the small audience.

She broke the kiss to whisper in his ear, "If you don't take me someplace where I can have you naked right now, we're going to put on a different kind of show for your guests."

"Noted."

CHAPTER 46

They'd practically traumatized a young couple in the elevator with their rabid kissing before realizing they weren't alone and took measures to keep their groping to a minimum. Somehow they'd made it to his suite without tearing each other's clothes off.

When she entered, she saw what he'd had to take care of before. Aside from fetching the ring, he'd had a fully stocked dessert cart sent up. She turned to him with mischievous eyes. "Someone was pretty confident he was getting laid tonight."

"You see dessert and think of sex? What a dirty mind you have." He stalked toward her as she slowly backed her way to the cart.

"So you weren't thinking about licking sugary goodness off every inch of my body?" She plucked the chocolate syrup off the cart and dangled it loosely in the air.

"I never said my mind wasn't dirty."

He snatched the syrup from her and then grabbed several other items. "You. Bed. Naked. Now."

Eager feet guided her to his bed, both of them attacking her clothes as they went, leaving a trail of fabric behind them.

"Lie back," he ordered. Eagerly, she did. He began to drizzle chocolate over her breasts and down her stomach, leaving a chilly path that made her nipples pucker. Next he spritzed her with whipped cream, making her squirm for his tongue in all those naughty places before crossing to pick up a small container.

"Really?" she said, raising a brow. "Sprinkles?"

"What? I'm making the perfect dessert." He rolled his eyes. "Fine, no sprinkles." He tossed the package behind him, then crawled onto the mattress. "We're going to have to work on your patience, Wife."

Oh, she liked the sound of that word in his husky tone.

"I'm going to start with my favorite part." He dipped his head and began to devour her. She moaned, her mind clearing of everything but the wonderful friction of his tongue on her body. Pleasure mounted as he assaulted her swollen flesh over and over, relentlessly, till she was panting and groaning and moaning. Her fingers fisted his hair as her body writhed beneath him. He laved her till she thought she might go mad from an overload of bliss, his mouth sliding back and forth over her like he couldn't get enough.

It wasn't until he forced the deliciously sharp spike of ecstasy up her spine that he moved on to follow the trail of chocolate he'd made along her torso. His wicked tongue scored a white-hot path over her stomach where he planted a soft kiss before moving higher. He caught a sugary nipple between his lips and sucked.

When he lightly nipped her, she yelped, then moaned long and hard when he did it again. Kneading and sucking and nipping, he nearly made her come a second time. If he kept this up, she'd be spent before they got to the big finale, and she wasn't about to let him have all the fun.

Gaze filled with desire, she pushed against his chest. He obeyed her silent directive, laying back on the bed and giving over control. She drizzled a bit of chocolate over his beautiful cock, licking her lips at the sight. A rough sound escaped him that was part pained, part impatience. She leaned close to tease him with her tongue, forcing another rumble from somewhere deep within him. If she weren't so eager to taste him, she might be tempted to torture him for him a bit. Instead, she sucked him deep. Every muscle in his body contracted and he groaned for her.

When she drew him in all the way to the root, he blurted a fervent curse. "You'll not unman me on our *first* wedding night." Even as his hips thrusted for more.

With a tantalizing suction, she slowly drew back, circling the tip with her tongue before she release him completely. "First? How many wedding nights do we get to have?"

"As many as you want." He pulled her over him, her knees straddling his hips, and kissed her hard and demanding, sugar mixing with their unique flavors. "Need you now," he growled, gripping her hips and aiming her over his shaft. He slammed her down atop him; they both cried out at the blissful contact. Hips rocking, she began to move, seeking more. More friction, more him, deeper, harder, faster. Hands on her, he encouraged the increasingly wild tempo. As she rode him, pressure mounted till sparks of pleasure exploded within her, and she threw her head back and roared.

Suddenly she was under him, his hips pistoning her into a state of wild passion, extending her orgasm to the point where madness met genius. "Yes! Oh,

God, yes! You feel so good!" Her nails scored down his back.

"You're mine," he grunted. "Never get enough."

As he moved in and out of her, hard and fast and without abandon, she screamed her pleasure for him, telling him between breaths how much she adored him, needed him, wanted him forever.

Not stopping his fevered pace, he knotted his fingers in her hair and angled her face so that she was looking directly at him. "Are you ready?"

"Yes," she said without hesitation. He planted his fangs in her neck and she screamed with unhinged ecstasy, his thrusts never slowing. As he drew from her neck, he groaned. She felt the vibrations like a second assault on her nerves, and screamed once more as the most explosive orgasm of her life blasted through her.

Extracting his fangs, he pulled back and brought his hand up to sink one clean, white fang into the pad of his thumb. A red dot beaded there, beautiful and glistening and calling to her. This was it. This would unite them forever. She licked her lips in anticipation and he groaned once more as if that were the sexiest thing she'd done all night.

Holding his gaze, she took his hand with hers and brought it closer to her lips. His gaze widened, his hips rocking into her.

She sucked his thumb into her mouth.

He let out a strangled, almost agonized sound. "Fuck. You are the sexiest fucking thing I have ever seen."

With her tongue curling around his thumb, one final climax claimed them both, and they cried out. Together they rode that wild, unbridled wave of pleasure, moving and licking and sucking and kissing each other till they had exhausted every last wave of ecstasy.

Panting, floating back down to Earth, she ran her hands along his back as he turned boneless atop her. His weight was a blissful sensation for a moment. Then he rolled to the side and drew her across his chest. "You are mine, now and forever."

She smiled. "Finally."

CHAPTER 47

Naia waved at Kenzi and a woman named Justine who were sitting at a booth in the employee lounge with two other employees whose names she'd yet to commit to memory, partaking of the breakfast buffet. Several others perched nearby nodded at her as she passed. The shock at her relationship with Cortez was diminishing, though a few people still gazed at her with keen curiosity, like she held a map to a secret treasure.

And she secretly felt like she did.

One day soon she'd memorize everyone's names. There were a lot of employees to meet yet. Cortez was planning a party later in the week to announce their engagement, but it seemed most had already figured it out. The giant diamond on her finger probably had a lot to do with that.

After filling a plate with food, she joined Kenzi, who immediately demanded, "Let me see it."

Naia stuck her left hand out, preening.

Kenzi sighed. "It's gorgeous. Are those sapphires? Awww. For your stage name?"

She nodded. "He had it made days ago."

Already preparing his proposal. The sillyhead had only been vacillating because he feared she wasn't ready for such a commitment.

This morning he gave her the best engagement gift ever: her mother's necklace. He'd found it and had the chain fixed. While she was sleeping, he'd surprised her by trailing the pendent along her arm to tickle her awake, and then had kissed her soundly. Sweetest man ever.

"So jealous," Kenzi chirped.

After finishing her meal, Naia headed down to hang out with Cole for a little bit. He had games, TV, and Internet access, but she could tell he was still going stir-crazy. She'd procured a deck of cards. He always loved beating her at Texas hold 'em, rummy, poker, and, well, any game really, which he did nine times out of ten, but she didn't mind. The boy needed a win.

She still wasn't allowed to be alone with him even though five-inch steel bars separated them and, reportedly, he was gaining ground on his cravings. But when hunger hit, he was at its mercy, so Ryder joined her.

In the elevator, she inquired about the rescued woman.

"Poor girl had been up there for weeks," Ryder said. "Was nearly catatonic when they found her, until they tried to give her blood to heal her wounds. Dane said she fought like a wild cat. Now she's calm, but won't speak, won't eat, hasn't left her room, and freaks if anything male comes too close."

"She's here?"

He nodded. "Boss set her up in one of the subterranean rooms. You know, with no high-up windows or balconies. She's on suicide watch."

"You think it would be okay if I visit her after

this?"

"I think that's a good idea."

Immediately Cole perked up when they arrived. They set up a poker table next to his cell. "What's the game, sis?"

"Loser's choice," she mocked, setting the deck in the middle of the table where he could reach.

"Then shouldn't it be *your* call?" he fired back.

Indignant, she scooped the deck back up, shuffled, then started to deal. "Rummy," she announced, her competitive side emerging. It was, after all, the game she most often emerged victorious.

Ryder sat to her right, closest to the bars, in no danger if Cole decided to fang out.

As Naia dealt, she exaggerated the movement whenever she placed Cole's cards so that he might see the ring. She'd been adamant that no one tell him before she did, but he didn't seem to be paying much attention to the glistening spot on her hand. When she retracted her hand for the last time, he snatched up his cards and began to organize them.

Pursing her lips, she did the same, holding the cards in such a way that the back of her hand was pointed in his direction.

"Ha! You're going down," he said, focused solely on his cards.

Ryder's lips quirked, but he said nothing as he flipped through his own set of cards.

To her detriment, this went on for the first quarter of the game as she discarded and picked up cards in an unnecessarily dramatic way. Cole remained oblivious, and she was seriously beginning to worry that his eyesight had been compromised. Either that or he was just incredibly obtuse.

Ryder, increasingly amused, was having trouble keeping his chuckles silent.

Finally Naia loudly cleared her throat for Cole's attention and overtly fluttered her fingers in front of her face.

"Is there something wrong with your throat? Why are you doing that with your hand?"

She scowled. "Hello. Could you be any more dense?"

Blankly he stared at her.

"The *ring*, you dummy."

He shook his head in confusion, gazing at the diamond for a moment. Then he swallowed, the color draining from his face. "What is that?"

"It's a wedding ring. I'm getting married."

He blinked, growing even paler.

"Well, technically I'm already married and engaged to be married again. We're going to hold the official ceremony after you get out of here so you can be the best man. Or maybe you should be my bridesmaid," she teased, suddenly nervous by his reaction. "I've always wanted to put you in a dress. It's a shame you weren't born a girl. A girl wouldn't have sat here for half an hour oblivious to the giant diamond ring on my finger."

"To who?"

"Pardon?"

"Married to who?"

"To whom," she corrected, discarding a five of hearts and then picking up a fresh card from the deck.

"Naia."

"Cortez, duh. Who else?"

He was silent for a moment. "I...I didn't realize it was so serious. This is...I haven't even had time to put him through all the tests."

"He'd pass them all. Trust me."

"How do I know he'll be good to you?"

"He's the best."

"But how do I know that? How do I know if he's good enough?"

She gave him a fond smile. "I love you too."

"If he hurts you, I'm going to have to kick his ass—"

"You're not going to have to—"

"—which is going to be difficult, considering he's my sire and all, and I basically have to obey him."

"Cole—"

"And here I am, stuck in here while some vulture swoops in on my sister, completely unchecked..."

Naia sighed and let him go on like this as she plotted her pending victory. With him distracted she might just win this hand. Alas, a couple discards later and he laid out his win, ending his tirade with, "Have you thought this through? I mean really thought it through?"

"I have."

He snatched the deck and shuffled like he was murdering those cards with a flutter of angry, slapping sounds. He switched the game to poker, his favorite. "And you love him?"

"More than anything." At his scalded look, she added, "Other than you, of course." She glanced at her crappy hand. Not even a pair to stand on.

"Shit," he sighed. "Then I guess... congratulations? Yeah. Congratulations."

She laughed at his sullen expression. "It's not the end of the world. I'm still your sister. That'll never change, even if you have turned into a freak."

He grinned. "Look at that, I'm just like you now."

She stuck her tongue out at him. They all handed in a couple cards hoping for better replacements. Yay, she managed to get two pairs. "By the way, as a wedding present I asked him to run the Boyle twins out of town, but if you prefer, I can..." With a sound in the back of her throat she ran her forefinger across her neck.

Cole laughed. "Kill a bad guy and suddenly you think you're an assassin." He laid his hand down. "Three of a kind."

Ryder dropped down a full house. "Sorry, son. Maybe next time."

Naia folded her paltry hand in defeat.

Cole scooped up the cards to deal again. "At least have him break a few of their fingers for me."

"I'll relay the request." She pretended to crack her knuckles. "Now both of you get ready to take a nice big bite of loser pie."

CHAPTER 48

Loser pie is bitter, she thought sardonically, not really bothered that she'd only won one hand out of the lot. When she left, Cole and Ryder were still at it, seemingly equally matched and neither willing to call it quits till a clear winner had been named...or hell freezes over.

She headed toward the room where the hunter's other victim was staying, where, after entering, she discovered, of all people, Dane was the one watching over her. Just to the right of the doorway, he stood fiercely rigid, jaw tight and arms crossed. His inherent imposing and intimidating visage hinted at violent tendencies. Hardly comforting on a good day.

The poor girl was curled on the bed with her back against the headboard, knees shoved up to her chin, and arms wrapped around her legs. Light-brown hair tangled around her face, shading her stark eyes. Naia guessed she was in her late twenties, maybe early thirties. She appeared to be staring at nothing, eyes slightly downcast, but Naia got the sense she had Dane in her peripheral.

He couldn't be helping matters with his tough

bouncer's stance and biker's build. If Naia wasn't his sire's bride, she wouldn't feel safe alone with him either.

To his credit, he stood as far from the woman as the room allowed, though he could try to loosen up a bit.

She crossed toward the girl slowly, like one might approach a wounded animal so as not to alarm her. The girl's mile-long stare didn't waver, even when Naia sat down on the edge of the mattress.

"Hi," she said softly.

No response. There was an angry ring of abrasions around the girl's wrists like she'd been cuffed or tied up. Naia's heart twisted with the need to kill the bastard all over again. Ryder said she'd fought like a wildcat when they'd tried to heal her. Looks like this small female had won that battle, to her own detriment. On closer inspection, there were some marks on her neck as well.

"My name is Naia," she said, not sure if the stone-faced girl was even listening. "I know you've probably been told this already, but I want you to know you're safe now. We're here to help you. So if there's anything you need, just let us know, okay?"

Again, there was no response, like the girl had just checked out.

"That man that took you," Naia tried again. "He tried to take me too, but I killed him. He can never hurt you again. Not ever."

It was like talking to a statue. The trauma this girl had endured must have been horrendous. Hopefully all she needed was time to process. The outward physical damage would eventually heal, erasing the evidence of her ordeal to the naked eye, but mental damage was a fracture to one's very soul, longer lasting and more difficult to mend.

Naia sighed and rose to leave when delicate fingers clamped around her wrist. She gazed down at the woman's surprisingly strong hold then met her dark-rimmed eyes. Though no words passed between them in that moment, Naia observed a shadow of something behind the woman's olive-toned irises, a fusion of gratitude and relief.

Naia placed her hand over hers and employed a reassuring smile. "You see that guy over there?" She indicated Dane with a tick of her head. The woman didn't look, but imposed a tighter grip on Naia's arm. A signal that she was excruciatingly aware of the big bad-looking vampire.

"His name is Dane. He's a really nice guy," Naia said.

Dane raised a brow at that. The single experience she'd had with him was of him screaming in her face, venomously accusing her of plotting against Cortez. BFFs they might never be, but Cortez trusted him to keep this girl safe, and she trusted Cortez.

"He's a teddy bear, really," she chirped.

Da fuck? His expression said.

Over the top? Maybe. But if it helped to abate some of the white knuckling going on....? "He's here for your protection. That's all. And if I hadn't killed that hunter, Dane here would have taken his head off."

At the mention of her attacker, the girl's arm returned to hug her legs and her chin dipped to her knees, but her eyes quickly darted toward Dane. He inclined his head once, still poised like a soldier ready to be deployed. Hardly encouraging, though a little tension did appear to seep from the girl's extremities.

Naia examined the bags under her eyes. "You should try to get some sleep. I can come back and visit you later if you like." She wasn't expecting a response, but then there was the most minute nod. "Okay then. Maybe when I return you'll actually talk to me, huh?"

No response.

Before leaving, she took the back of her hand and smacked Dane playfully on the arm. He glanced down at her like she was nuts.

"Try to loosen up, would you? This military thing you have going on here isn't helping." Her voice was low enough not to be heard across the room.

"I was charged with one task: keep the human alive." He gestured toward the girl. *The human is alive.*

She shrugged. "Well okay. Do what you want. Just curious, though. Has she relaxed at all since you've been here?"

He didn't respond, which was answer enough.

"I just get the feeling she's going to be around for a while, at least if it were up to me, and, well, she might end up associating her trauma with your ugly mien, soldier boy. You probably don't care about that, though, do you?"

"Nope," he said, the picture of insensitivity. Yet, an instant later, his arms dropped to his sides. Then he scowled and crossed them again.

"It was you that found her, right?" she asked. Everyone already knew what had gone down up at that campground. This place was a den of gossip-mongers.

Dane had found her bound and gagged in the hunter's tent, in a near catatonic state. He'd cut her free, carried her out, handed her off, and then proceeded to rage all over the hunter's meager dwelling, rendering the campsite a litter of tattered debris.

When Naia had heard that, Dane had risen a bit in her esteem. She reached out and placed her palm on his rigid arm. "Thank you." Then she left, leaving Dane looking slightly off balance, and went off in search of Cortez, feeling like she was going through withdrawals. All she wanted was to curl up in his arms and just be for as long as the world allowed. No worries or fears to cloud the moment. Merely the two of them, loving each other.

She had no idea what the future held for her and Cole, but for the first time in her life, uncertainty was muted. Cole was stronger than ever. He didn't only have her, but an entire clan of badasses who'd have his back if he got into trouble, which he undoubtedly would. She had the love of the most amazing man she had ever known, who could conquer the world with one hand and tend her so gently with the other. A man who had smashed and ripped his way into the bow of her heart with all the grace of a fire-breathing kraken...

...A man who she couldn't find.

She'd searched the main floor, passing spirited club goers dancing to industrial music, peeked into the quiet meeting rooms, checked around the many stages where shows were in full swing, and then stopped in the employee lounge before planning to head up to their suite.

Kenzi caught her first. "He asked me to give this to you." She handed over a note written in Cortez's element script: *Meet me on the roof.*

After thanking Kenzi, she wasted no time, following the path Cortez had shown her their first night together. The night everything had changed. The night reality had flipped over on her and turned into something too beautiful to comprehend.

The stairwell that lead to the roof was deceptively dark, so when she opened the door, a rush of warm daylight pelted her. She shielded her eyes, giving them a moment to adjust.

His back was to her as he stared out over the ledge at the pacific gleaming in the distance. He turned to her and smiled brightly, making her heart melt into her bones and her body tingle. *Love this man.*

The anguish of their distance forced them both forward, meeting halfway. In an impassioned embrace, their lips came into contact with hungry urgency as if they'd been parted for weeks rather than just a few hours. She sighed against his savory lips and relaxed against him.

"I missed you," she said when they broke away.

"And I you," he replied, almost confounded. "I've never missed anyone before. Not like this. It was tormenting not having you here those few days."

Understatement. "Now you have me for always."

"Be warned, my greed for you is insatiable."

"I'm up for the challenge." She twirled out of his grip and glanced back at him coyly. Then she added in a faux dramatic voice. "But you should know I killed my last boyfriend."

He grinned at her wolfishly and followed her to one of the lounge chairs. "As I understand it, the man needed killing."

As she relaxed back, he pulled her close till they were comfortably snuggled together, gazing at the blue sky painted with white cloudy wisps.

After a while, he asked. "What are you thinking?"

"How happy I am. But sometimes I worry this is all just a dream."

"Oh? Because I'm too good to be true?" he teased.

She playfully bopped him on the chest.

He chuckled. "If it's a dream, it's one I hope to never wake from because being without you would be a nightmare."

She kissed his cheek, "That's more like it. So we're in agreement. Let's never wake up."

He grunted. "Sounds like a plan. I'm eager to get this wedding over with so that I can have you all to myself again."

"Where do you want to honeymoon?"

"Our island, of course. Would you like that?"

Just the two of them, alone, drowning in each other? Now that he knew what she was, her previous worries were moot. He'd make sure she was taken care of in every way that mattered. "I'd love that."

"And I love you. Now and forever."

Hungry for more? Check out all of
Kiersten's books on her webiste:
www.kierstenfay.com

Here are just a few...

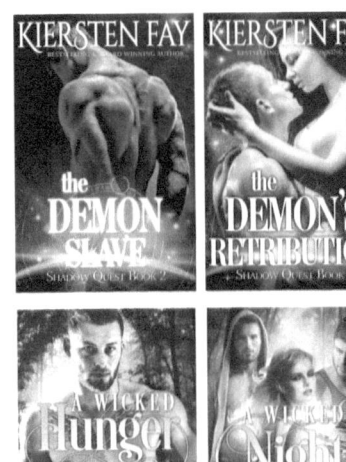